Chris Bohjalian is the critically acclaimed author of 11 novels, including *Midwives* which was an Oprah Book Club Selection, and his most recent *New York Times* bestseller, *The Double Bind*, published by Pocket Books. His work has been translated into 18 languages and published in 21 countries. He lives with his wife and daughter in Vermont. Visit www.chrisbohjalian.com

Praise for *Skeletons at the Feast*

'Few writers can manipulate a plot with Bohjalian's grace and power' *New York Times*

'A tragic but hugely uplifting tale of love, loss and friendship, bringing together people who would be enemies during a time of unspeakable adversity. It is often gruesome and graphic, but never gratuitous. Bohjalian has created a stunning, eminently readable piece of work. He clearly understands humanity and has the enviable ability to commit this to the page' *Gay Times*

Praise for *The Double Bind*

'It's the sort of book you want to read in one sitting, and it packs a twist at the end that leaves you speechless' Jodi Picoult

'A mystery anchored in sorrow, a harrowing and even haunting tale of literary influence, delusion, intervention. Chris Bohjalian has done it again' Gregory Maguire, author of *Wicked*

Skeletons
AT THE
Feast

CHRIS
BOHJALIAN

POCKET
BOOKS

LONDON • SYDNEY • NEW YORK • TORONTO

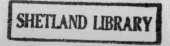

First published in the United States by Shaye Areheart Books, 2008
An imprint of the Crown Publishing Group, a division of Random House, Inc.
First published in Great Britain by Simon & Schuster UK Ltd, 2008
This edition published by Pocket Books UK, 2009
An imprint of Simon & Schuster UK Ltd
A CBS COMPANY

1 3 5 7 9 10 8 6 4 2

Simon & Schuster UK Ltd
1st Floor
222 Gray's Inn Road
London WC1X 8HB

Simon & Schuster Australia
Sydney

www.simonsays.co.uk

A CIP catalogue record for this book is available
from the British Library.

ISBN 978-1-84739-340-1

This book is a work of fiction. Though some of the characters
and scenes were inspired in part by the personal diary of Eva Henatsch,
the names, characters, places and incidents are either a product of the author's
imagination or are used fictitiously. Any resemblance to actual people
living or dead, events or locales, is entirely coincidental.

Design by Lynne Amft
Reading Group Guide © Shaye Areheart Books, 2008
An imprint of the Crown Publishing Group, a division of Random House, Inc.

Printed by CPI Cox & Wyman, Reading, Berkshire RG1 8EX

For Stephen Kiernan,
Adam Turteltaub,
and
Dana Yeaton

And for Victoria, who reads every word

The past is never dead.
It's not even past.

WILLIAM FAULKNER

SKELETONS AT THE FEAST

PROLOGUE

January 1945

THE GIRL—A YOUNG WOMAN, REALLY, EIGHTEEN, HAIR
the color of corn silk—had been hearing the murmur of artillery
fire for two days now. Everyone had. A rare and peculiar winter
thunderstorm in the far distance. Little more. The sconces in the
living room hadn't twitched, the chandelier in the ballroom (a
modest ballroom, but a ballroom nonetheless) barely had trembled. The horses, while she was harnessing them and helping to
load the wagons—short trips with bags full of oats (because, after
all, so much would depend on the horses) and longer ones with
some of the clothes and the silver and the jewelry they were going
to take with them—had looked up. But the animals hadn't expressed particular interest. If, Anna surmised, they had thought of
anything they had thought of the cold: It was one of those frigid
weeks when the days would alternate between whiteout-like
snowstorms and periods so still that the smoke from the chimneys
would rise up into a slate gray sky in lines that were perfectly
straight.

These shells, however, the ones that were falling this afternoon, were great concussive blasts that had the people and the
horses—a seemingly endless caravan of strangers that clogged
the road and crushed the snow and ice along the sides, and had

come almost to a complete stall now before the river—fretting
and fidgeting in place. At each explosion the animals whinnied
and the babies, hungry and chilled despite the blankets and furs in
which they were swaddled, cried out. If they managed to free one
of their little hands, the blue fist would lash out, a small, spring-
loaded paddle. Clearly, however, the artillery had leapfrogged
over them. Passed them. Hours earlier it had been many kilometers to the east. Now it was ahead of them to the west. Some of the
shells were falling so nearby that they heard the screech—a
strange foreign animal, something that might exist in a tree in
Africa or South America, the girl thought—before the reverber-
ant burst left them crouching, anxious, in their places in line. At
first she presumed the Russians were trying to hit them, this long
line of families trying desperately to flee to the west, to take out
the carts and the wagons and the walkers piecemeal, but then she
understood their real intent: It was the river itself. They were trying to smash the buttress-thick ice that coated this stretch of the
Vistula from shore to shore like a skating rink and was serving as
a bridge, because the nearest stone and cement overpass was
twenty-five kilometers to the north. Along the shore she saw soldiers and Volkssturm teenagers—boys who were easily two and
three years younger than her twin brother and her—funneling
the refugees across what they believed was the safest part of the
ice, but she had the sense that any moment now people were
going to start leaving the queue and fanning out into the woods,
where they would cross the river wherever they could.

Or, at least, believed that they could. The girl had heard stories of wagons and families disappearing yesterday and the day
before through the ice to the north and the south. She wasn't sure
if they were true, but so much of the last month had been a study
in how things she had once thought were inconceivable were actually happening. They'd all heard what had occurred three
months earlier in Nemmersdorf. The Russians had captured the
East Prussian village in October and held it for five days. When

their own soldiers recaptured the small town, almost all of the civilians were dead. She had heard tales of girls her age (and younger) nailed naked to the sides of barns and farm carts, their arms spread wide as if they were being crucified but their legs splayed open so that even in death the men could violate them. There were the stories of small children flattened into the main roads of the village by the treads of tanks. Of live babies held by their ankles and swung like scythes into stone walls while their mothers were forced to watch, their children's own blood and brains splattered like so much butcher's waste onto their over-coats. Of the French prisoners of war—some people claimed as many as forty of them—who had been executed by the Russians for reasons that no one could fathom.

And then there were the stories of what her own people had done. BBC propaganda, maybe. But probably not. She knew people who knew people. Her older brother, whom she hadn't seen now since October, told her of an SS officer he had met who—suppos-edly—had served inside Treblinka in 1943. When her twin, Hel-mut, was on a hike with his Jungvolk friends last summer, the last they would take before the drills grew serious, he told her there were rumors (implausible and offensive, in his opinion) that some of the less committed boys would share when they thought no one was listening. Rumors of what really went on in some of the camps. And, of course, there was what their English POWs had claimed was occurring, stories that Helmut would dispute as half-truths and cant spread by the Allies to further demonize the Ger-mans. It got to the point where he threatened to tell his father on them if they uttered so much as one more syllable.

She tensed when she heard the high-pitched whistle of another shell, and saw her mother once again pull little Theo, the youngest of her children, against her. Then there was the blast. Ahead of her there was shouting, screaming. She couldn't tell whether the ex-plosive had landed on the road or the river, whether people were wounded or merely panicked. More panicked, actually. Because certainly numbness had not completely subsumed the animal panic that coursed just below the skin and behind the bloodshot eyes of this long and plodding throng of parents and children and very old people. Only as Anna watched the nearest soldiers and Volkssturm recruits trying to prevent the line from spreading north and south into the woods—here is that panic, she thought, we are like desperate beetles scurrying from a giant's boots—did she understand. The bomb had created a great spider's web of cracks in the ice.

For a moment her father and Helmut conferred, the two of them murmuring softly into each other's ears. Their army uniforms were still crisp. Then each of them walked to the front of a wagon—they were traveling with two—and her brother ordered her to come help him with the horses. After all, he muttered, they were more her horses than his. She thought he was being needlessly bossy, but she also knew that she didn't dare question him now. It seemed that their family, too, was going to leave the caravan and trek into the woods, and he was going to run ahead and find a spot along the river that looked suitable for a crossing.

Beside her, beneath the blanket in the wagon filled with oats, their sole remaining POW cleared his throat.

THE PRISONER, a twenty-year-old Scotsman named Callum Finella—a name that initially had made both Anna and her younger brother giggle, but struck her now as infinitely more lyric than the suddenly wolfish-sounding names of most of the males in her family—had been with them since September. He was one of seven British POWs who had been sent to the Emmerich family estate from the prison camp just outside of Thorn to help with the harvest. When the other six men—older by four and five and six years than Callum, but still he had called them his mates—had been returned to the stalag in mid-October, the family had used their party clout and simply kept Finella since their Polish servants had fled or been put to work in the coal mines in

Silesia, the oldest of their three boys was fighting somewhere far to the south on the outskirts of Budapest, the middle one had been pressed into service in the Volkssturm, and Theo, at ten, was barely beyond short pants.

Now Anna removed her glove and snaked her hand between two of the burlap sacks, searching for Callum's fingers. She found one of his thumbs and the fleshy pad of his palm just beside it and thought, much to her surprise, of his penis. The sudden way it would grow in her hand, a dangerous but irresistible animal wholly independent of him. Then he whispered her name. At least it sounded to Anna like a whisper. But, perhaps, it was actually more like a stage whisper. Beckoned by her hand, his head emerged from beneath the bags of feed like a chick from a shell, his sunset red hair only partly smothered by one of Helmut's knit caps. From atop the driver's box her mother glared at them both. Anna didn't believe that her mother could possibly think that anyone other than their own family could either hear or see the young soldier—not with the clamor all around them from this distraught and pathetic parade of refugees; rather, she guessed, Mutti simply didn't want to be reminded of the reality that they had the (his term for himself, not theirs) lad with them. When the war had been far to the east and the west in the autumn, Callum had been a harmless, albeit brawny and tall, exotic animal: He knew how to play the accordion that her father's brother, Uncle Felix, had left behind when he'd been transferred—to everyone's relief—to the western front. And he hadn't even fired a shot before he'd been captured. He and Helmut were never going to be friends, but Anna was confident that her mother appreciated the time the Scot spent entertaining her and her little brother (though, of course, Mutti hadn't an inkling of either the details or the depth of the way he had entertained her one and only daughter). Quickly Callum retreated back beneath the grain and Anna withdrew her hand, moving forward to help her father steer the horses into the copse of pine to their right. As she was grasping the reins, she heard once more the shriek of a Russian shell. She looked deep into the creature's eyes, hoping to keep the animal calm when it exploded.

THIS TIME THE shell landed beside them. One moment she was gazing into the face of a velvety bay stallion she had named after a castle—Balga, a fortress that was nearly seven hundred years old—and the next she was on the ground, awash in snow and pine boughs and small frozen clods of dirt. She looked up and saw Helmut was talking to her, saying something—perhaps even yelling—but she couldn't hear a thing. It was as if he were mouthing the words. He was standing over her, then squatting beside her, staring at her with those hazel eyes and girlishly long eyelashes that sometimes she couldn't believe he had gotten instead of her. Her father and Callum were kneeling, too. They were sitting her up, each holding an arm and appraising her, dusting the debris off her cape. Slowly her hearing returned, and the first sound she was aware of was the wailing of women not more than fifteen or twenty meters behind them, their cries for help. Someone swearing at the Soviets. Apparently, a shell had exploded just behind them, too.

She opened her mouth to tell Helmut and Callum and her father that she was fine, she wasn't hurt—at least she didn't believe that she was—but suddenly the simple act of speaking seemed like too much work. Something was pinching her stomach, and she realized it was the earrings and the necklace she had bandaged against her flesh when she had been unable to fit another piece of jewelry into the secret pouch she had sewn into her skirt. She saw there was a trail of blood now on one of the sleeves and shoulders of her father's usually immaculate uniform coat—the stain was shaped, she thought, like monkshood—and she reached out her arm to him. He seemed to notice the wet blotch for the first time and remarked casually, "It's not mine." His head jerked reflexively toward the line behind them and so she turned. Men were pushing an overturned cart into the snowbank beside the road, trying either to move it out of the way or to reach whoever was underneath it, or both.

Finally she uttered a word, a two-syllable question: "Mutti?"

"Mother is fine. Theo is fine. We're all fine," Helmut told her.

"Callum? Are you—"

"I said we're all fine," Helmut hissed. Then to the Scotsman he ordered, "You. Back beneath the feed."

She glanced at the wagon that had been upended by the explosion and understood now why someone was howling: There in the snow were a man's unattached legs, the limbs still in their wool trousers, and a steaming, Medusa-like nest of tendon and muscle emerging from the pants where there should have been an abdomen or a waist.

Her father chastened her brother for being short with her and for snarling at Callum. She looked around now for Mutti and Theo and saw that her mother had pulled Theo ever deeper against her chest, shielding his face from the debacle just behind them. Then, with the awkward jerks of a marionette—Mutti was shaking, this woman who in 1939 had single-handedly buried the Luftwaffe pilot whose plane had been shot down by the Poles and would crash in their hunting park, was actually trembling—she turned her eyes to the sky. There was another plane. A Russian plane now, because that was about all that filled the skies these days. It was approaching from the south, perhaps paralleling the path the Vistula had carved through this section of the country. Some of the trekkers stood frozen in their spots in the queue, but others scurried, despite the knee-deep snow, like frightened mice into the comparative safety of the forest. But the plane, for whatever the reason, didn't bother to strafe them. Neither did it drop a single bomb on the ice. It simply continued on its course toward the north.

An elegant old woman beside a sled with four large suitcases balanced upon it pulled her hands from a fur muff and shook her fist at the sky. She said something dismissive about Göring. Wanted to know where the German planes were.

Slowly Anna climbed to her feet and smiled for her mother and young Theo.

"I'm okay, Mutti," she said. "Really. Just a little shaken."

And then, no longer hushed by the burlap bags of oats beneath which he had been hiding for hours, came the voice that spoke a German that was lighthearted, enthusiastic, and still, on occasion, inept. "It takes more than a little bomb to slow Anna Emmerich," Callum said. Despite the characteristic irreverence in his tone, however, his smile was forced and his eyes were wide ovals of dread.

WHERE TWO YEARS before there had been a yellow Star of David, there was now a small Nuremberg eagle made of bronze. The star, by law, had been sewn onto his overcoat with the stitches so tight that a pencil point couldn't be pressed between them. The police or some Brownshirt bully would check. This eagle, dangling from his uniform beside an Iron Cross, was merely attached with a pin. He stood now on the east bank of the Vistula with his hand on the grip of his pistol, though the gun was still holstered and the safety was on, wondering if it all wouldn't be easier if he were just decapitated by a fragment from one of the Soviet shells that clearly were inching closer. Just get it over with. Unfortunately, by even the most liberal definition this wasn't a bombardment: He had endured Red Army bombardments, and this was nothing like them. But these civilian Prussians in the lines before him now? These once proud Aryans and anti-Semites who had literally leapt for joy when Hitler's tanks had rolled into Poland in 1939 and made them Germans once more? They seemed to think it was the end of the world. Oh, please. It was as if they had never seen a limb—a leg, an arm, a fist—fly through the air like a falcon.

The irony of the exodus approaching the river wasn't lost on him. On his own, he had read, he had studied. The difference between this flight and the others? These souls were fleeing a retribution they had asked for. They had brought these shells down upon themselves.

Now, of course, he was on this nightmarish sinking ship with them, though if he had to wager he would bet he would figure a way off. Find yet one more lifeboat. He was, apparently, unkillable. But how much would it really help him to become a Jew again now? It wasn't as if the Russians had such great love for his people either. The Lithuanians were stringing the Jews up back in '41 while the Nazis were still en route; the Ukrainians and the Latvians had been all too happy to handle the heavy lifting when it came to machine-gunning the Jews in the early days. They had practically volunteered for the opportunity!

No, he should have started to work his way west months ago, as soon as it was clear that the western Allies had no intention of being pushed back into the English Channel.

"Manfred?"

In the midst of the turmoil and the noise, for a moment Uri had forgotten that he had renamed himself Manfred. It was the most Teutonic alias he had been able to come up with when he'd realized what was expected of him as reservist Henrik Schreiner with Police Battalion 101, and so in the chaos of the retreat from Łuków he had commandeered this uniform from a Wehrmacht soldier who had been shot cleanly in the back of the head. Before that, since jumping off the train almost two years ago now, he had been Hartmut, Adler, Jurgen, and Franz. Sometimes he had found the dead soldier's name in the papers in the uniform pocket. Other times, there hadn't been any papers at all and he'd come up with a moniker such as Manfred (which, he'd realized in hindsight, was both Teutonic *and* the name of the doctrinaire Nazi pedant who'd lived in the town house beside his family back in Schweinfurt, before they had been forced to move).

He turned now to the one-armed captain beside him, a fellow roughly three or four years older than he was. Twenty-nine or thirty, Uri guessed. The officer had served in Poland and France and North Africa and Italy and Russia, a virtual travelogue of Nazi victories and defeats, with little more than the scratches and bruises that are inevitable with a life in the field. But no serious wounds. Then in October, while home on leave in Dortmund, his left arm was crushed when he was helping his grandmother down the stairs of her home during an air raid, and the house had sustained a direct hit. His grandmother had died pretty near instantly, he'd told Uri, but he'd thought his arm might have a chance. It hadn't. The good news to losing the wing? It meant that he had been relegated, for the moment anyway, to this sort of police action many kilometers behind the front.

Though, the captain had rued, those kilometers had collapsed exponentially since the Russians had begun this most recent offensive.

Uri wondered if years from now, if somehow they both survived, he and this captain might actually be friends. The fellow was unflappable, a trait Uri respected, and he seemed to see the misery that was marking the end of their world as more Chaplinesque than Wagnerian—which, most days, Uri did, too. But then he decided a postwar friendship was unlikely. Not because this Captain Hanke was anti-Semitic, though Uri supposed on some level he was. Rather, he had the sense that the two of them had been too lucky for too long, and it was absolutely inconceivable that they would both be alive when this steamroller was done lumbering over them. And if he, Uri, was indestructible, then the odds could not be especially good for this poor fellow beside him.

"The engineers are coming to destroy the ice now," the captain was saying. Then he motioned toward the teenage boys in their Jungvolk uniforms who were helping to keep order. "Send the children across the Vistula."

Uri nodded and approached the oldest of the group, one of

the few who actually wasn't dwarfed by the rifle in his arms. "Son," he said, "take your squad to safety on the other side of the river. They're going to blow up the ice."

The boy saluted, and Uri had to restrain the reflexive urge to shake his head in bemusement.

"And then, sir?" the boy asked. He had almost periwinkle blue eyes and a movie star's aquiline nose. Perfect skin. Fifteen or sixteen years old now, Uri surmised. He could have modeled for those idiotic propaganda posters that so disturbed his mother and father when they were alive—he didn't know for a fact they were dead, but he had to presume that they were—and as early as the Olympics in '36 had made them scared for their son and their daughter.

"Wait for orders."

The boy seemed to want to say something more, and so Uri told him, "Go, go. The captain and I will handle the people here." *We'll probably be run over*, he thought, crushed in the last-ditch stampede that would occur the moment the engineers appeared with their satchels.

But still the boy stood there, his lips slightly parted. Little puffs of smoke with each exhalation.

"Yes?"

"My family, sir. They're in the line. Back there."

He nodded. He was fairly confident that he knew what the boy was driving at, but he wanted to be sure. "You want to join them?" he asked. A lesser boy, he knew, or most of the middle-aged Nazis he had dealt with lately, would have been hinting about some scheme to get his family across the Vistula before it became nothing more than a river of ice shavings and splinters. But not this one.

"May I, sir?"

"Yes. But do yourself—and them—a favor. Find another place to cross. Under no circumstances stop moving west."

Above them they heard the shriek of another approaching

Soviet shell, and—as was frequently the case—it reminded Uri of the sound of a train whistle.

AND URI SINGER knew the sound of train whistles well. He had heard them often as a boy, when he and his parents and his little sister would travel from Schweinfurt to Dresden to visit his aunt and uncle, or to the Alps to go hiking. But it was only in March of 1943, when he was finally deported and spent nearly three days in a cattle car, that he began to appreciate (and loathe) the subtle differences in ululation. He'd been at work at the ball-bearing factory, wondering in a vague sort of way how he and his family would be degraded next, when the SA came for him. He was twenty-four years old, and his life could not have been more different from the one he had anticipated a decade earlier. At fourteen, even in the first months after Hitler had come to power, he had still assumed he would start and finish at the university, and he would be a journalist by now. Perhaps he might even be writing a book. He ended up getting to spend a single year at the college before it was closed to the Jews.

It was midmorning when the SA had arrived at the factory. The two thugs in their greatcoats told him he would meet his parents and his sister at the train station. He didn't. He never saw them again, though God knew he had tried to find his sister. Nor had he ever been back to Schweinfurt. He had heard that first the RAF and then the Americans had started pummeling the city four months after he was taken away, and most of the place now was rubble.

Except, of course, for the factory where he had worked. It was damaged, people said, but still operating. That, he guessed, was pretty typical. The apartments and town houses and butcher shops that had been laid waste were rarely rebuilt, but the Nazis would try to find the resources to repair the factories. And so the war effort went on. Even the killing in the concentration camps.

And the evacuations from the concentration camps. The Russians, last he'd heard, were approaching Auschwitz. And while there were rumors that most of the prisoners were being walked to the west, he understood that some were being wedged back into the boxcars. Imagine: While the enemies of the (and he heard these two words mordantly in his mind) *Greater Reich* were at the Rhine and the Vistula, someone somehow was still finding the rolling stock to expend upon the plan to exterminate the Jews. Rather than move troops or tanks or boxcars full of *panzerfausts*, they were moving the Jews. Just so they could kill them in Germany instead of Poland.

Maybe, he concluded, it was because they didn't have any troops or tanks or *panzerfausts* left to move. They only had Jews.

He watched this frightened but enthusiastic boy run back to his family and considered for a moment if the teen would be naive enough to try to stop a Soviet tank with that rifle of his. Probably. He shook his head: They didn't have a *panzerfaust* to give him.

Uri wondered, as he did often, whether he would be alive now if he hadn't jumped from that train nearly two years ago. Initially he'd presumed he would have died at Auschwitz, because even his youth and his strength would have bought him only so much time. But as he'd survived one normally fatal indignity after another in and out of the Wehrmacht, he'd begun to question this. It was as if he were being spared, his negligible soul cradled time after time by providence. For all he knew, if he'd stayed on that train going east two years ago, he'd be on another one right now going west.

No. Not likely. He'd have died. No one lived nearly two years at Auschwitz. It was why he'd hurled himself along with the slop bucket out the cattle car door that unusually balmy night when the opportunity had presented itself. He had, inevitably, just heard another of those stultifying train whistle blasts.

By 1943, the vast majority of the Schweinfurt Jews were gone, and Uri and his parents and their few remaining friends had a pretty good idea about what was going on at the concentration camps. At least the ones in the east. In his opinion, anyone with eyes in Schweinfurt, Jew or Catholic or Lutheran, had to have figured it out. How could they not have had serious suspicions about the deportations? One afternoon he'd passed the train station and seen the Jews who were being transported that month. They had been rounded up from a different part of the city and so he hadn't known anyone who had been taken that particular day. He'd only wound up near the station because a friend from the factory lived in the neighborhood, and this buddy had an antenna he could attach to their pathetic Volksempfänger radio ("All Nazi, All the Time," his father would joke cryptically) that would allow them, when the weather was right, to receive the BBC. Still, he was wearing his star and so he didn't dare get too close: He could just imagine himself being accidentally herded onto the train by some Nazi moron, even though he clearly hadn't packed a suitcase and had brought none of his clothing or his valuables with him.

But even from the distance he saw something that caused him to stand perfectly still for a long moment, watching, as the cacophonic sounds of the city around him seemed to vanish. He could hear himself breathing, but nothing more. The Jews were being herded into the first three cars—far too many for each one, it was clear; dozens and dozens were going to be forced to stand—and their luggage was being loaded onto the fourth car. A freight car. And then, as Uri watched, that fourth car was uncoupled, and the first three pulled away. The luggage, he saw, wasn't going with them. Luggage, he realized, never went with them.

When his hearing returned he ran as fast as he could back to the ball-bearing factory. It would be three days before he would have the courage to venture once more to his friend's neighborhood for the special antenna.

Over the following months, more and more of the city's Jews were deported, including Uri's acquaintance who had helped him with the radio, and every evening he and his sister and his parents would crowd around the Volksempfänger in their cramped and dingy apartment—a single room in a shabby hotel that had been converted to Jewish housing—and wait for the four tones that signaled the start of a BBC broadcast. When the broadcast was in German, everyone listened; when it was in English, either Uri or his father would translate it, invariably missing some of the subtleties but usually understanding its gist.

Before the war, the family had lived in an elegant, three-bedroom town house with a yard that looked out upon the gazebo in the city's small park. Now? A dark room in a ramshackle hotel with a squalid bathroom at the end of the corridor that they shared with at least two dozen other evicted Jews crammed onto their floor. And they only had that because his father was a decorated veteran of the earlier world war, and now both he and his father were, more or less, slave labor in a factory the Nazis deemed critical to the war effort. Prior to that, his father had owned a not-insubstantial trucking company. Seven vehicles and twelve employees. The fascists had just drooled when they had forced him to sell it to them for next to nothing. No longer did anyone try to face this stoically or philosophically, to murmur how one didn't blame the ocean for tidal waves. Because, in fact, it wasn't a random act of nature behind this nightmare; it was their neighbors.

Slowly his parents' health began to fail. Somehow his father soldiered on at the factory, but both of his parents were weakened by their steadily diminished rations and the cold and the daily struggle to make do in their squalor. Their Shabbat dinner at sunset on Friday night—already shrunken because of curfews and the reality that as Jews they had almost no food to eat—grew even more intimate, because Uri's aunt and his uncle and his cousins were taken away. And then his grandmother. And, soon, another aunt who never had married. When this last woman—a nurse until the fact she was Jewish had cost her her job, a woman who even as a teenager had been an angel of mercy to wounded soldiers in the previous world war—was deported to the east, his own mother took him and his sister aside and with completely un-characteristic melodrama told them that they had to live through this nightmare. No matter what, they had to survive. Someone had to let the world know what was going on. What the Nazis were doing.

When they came for him at the factory, he actually asked if he had time to run home to pack a suitcase, even though he knew it would never go with him to the camp. His escort, those two heavyset men from the SA with eyebrows that reminded him of cater-pillars and oddly similar wattles of flesh dangling under their chins, told him that his mother had packed one for him. Two, as a matter of fact. Uri had considered informing them that he only owned a single valise, but knew there wasn't a point. He tried to find his family at the station but they didn't seem to be there. Someone told him one train already had left for the east, and in all likelihood they were on it. Still, he searched for them in the mob, moving as best as he could among the throng and twice being struck in the back by different guards when inadvertently he had strayed too near to one of the exits.

Most of the time, the Nazis weren't even bothering with pas-senger cars by then, and so he was herded into an unheated cattle car that still had giant twinelike balls of straw in the corners and along one of the long walls. Though he recognized a half-dozen people in the car with him, it was mostly a surreal and kaleido-scopic pastiche of shapes and faces he might see on any given day on the street or in the park: surreal because the people were crowded—though not, as he would hear often occurred, packed so tightly that the victims could neither sit nor move, and some would actually asphyxiate—and were constantly fidgeting and shuffling as they struggled to get comfortable, and so one mo-ment he would spy a pretty young woman named Rivka in a spot across the car, and in the next he would see standing there a very old woman named Sarah; kaleidoscopic because in the variegated light from the slats high on the walls, light that changed as the day wore on and the train chugged its way (dear God, no) east, their eyes and lips and kerchiefs seemed constantly to be changing color. They were, he guessed, the very last Jews left in Schweinfurt: the labor, the technical help—Jews with some rare expertise—and their elderly parents and children.

He asked virtually everyone in the car whether his parents or his sister might be somewhere on the train and he might be reunited with them at their destination, but no one could say. Everyone agreed that there had been plenty of couples roughly his parents' age and a great many girls who looked fourteen at the station—even some who, roughly, matched his description of Rebekah. Still, he hadn't seen any of them there and it didn't appear that anyone else had, either. At least not for sure. And Rebekah was a hard girl to miss. She was tall for her age, womanly, and—partly because they were practically being starved to death and partly because the Singers were naturally slender—thin. She had gorgeous, creosote black hair that reflected the sun like glass. If she were anywhere on this train, the men, at least, would have noticed.

It was evident to Uri after the first day that they were not going to be released from the cars until they arrived at the camp. Periodically the train stopped and a pair of soldiers would slide open the doors to see if anyone inside had died (no one did, at least that first day, not even any of the older people), and to allow one of the passengers to empty the buckets of excrement over the side. The soldiers certainly had no plans to do it. There wasn't room to lie down in the car, but Uri could sit if he curled his knees against his chest—though this, too, posed a certain hazard: It meant that his nose was close to the level of the arses and the pant legs of the people around him, and his own face and hair would brush up against the pee that had sopped into their wool trousers and the crap that had turned their underwear into unsalvageable diapers. Some of the people who had been brought to the train directly from their homes had a little food with them, and some

were kind enough to share their crusts of pumpernickel or rye.
But that was gone within hours. From then on, everyone grew
more hungry and thirsty and frightened. And the smell from the
buckets and, yes, from the people around him—the oldest people
around him, he realized, were unable to squat to use the contain-
ers; others were simply too modest—grew unbearable. It wasn't
merely the stench of sweat and fear, the acrid smell of the urine,
or the feces that filled the pails, the pants, and the corners of the
cattle car. It was the vomit. Increasingly, the stink alone was
making people sick, and that was creating a vicious, malodorous
circle.

During the second day, when the threshold of his own gag reflex had become downright heroic and he had grown inured to the
touch of someone else's shit-soddened fabric, he would encourage
the old people and the children to lean against him. Or sit against
him. Or use his shoulders as a pillow or his knees as a hassock.
And they did. No one, not even the children, had the energy to
sing, but he would tell anyone who was interested stories about . .
. anything. He would make up anecdotes about the ball-bearing
factory, he would recall whatever he could about his aunt's service
on the western front a quarter of a century earlier. Or his father's.
There was an older fellow in the car who, it would turn out, had
served in the same stretch of trenches as Uri's father, though the
two men had never met. Sometimes people listened to Uri and he
thought it might have helped a little bit. But he also knew he was
merely throwing a glass of water on a house fire.

By the third day, he and some of the others were sure they
were going to Auschwitz. Much to Uri's astonishment, there
were actually grown-ups in the car who hadn't heard of the
place. Oh, they knew of the concentration camps and the deportations. But they honestly believed—had, almost inconceivably,
managed to reassure themselves—that this was all about resettlement. Not extermination.

It was this, he decided later, the fact that there were Jews—

Jews, for God's sake!—who didn't believe what was happening that finally propelled him with his bucket of shit through the opened cattle car doors. It wasn't the reality that a wonderful old man who had consoled his wife with the sighs and murmurs of an angel had expired beside him, it wasn't the death of one of the car's two babies—he honestly missed the infant's howls because it meant the little one had died—and it wasn't even his own fear about what awaited him at the train's eventual destination. It was, in essence, what his mother had said: Someone had to survive this inferno and, indeed, it might as well be him.

And so when the train was starting to move once more (and, yes, there was that whistle), as a soldier was jogging beside the car and sliding the door shut—just as this middle-aged corporal of the Reich was using his own gimpy legs to jump back onto the train—Uri acted as if he were merely tossing one more pail of waste into the woods and weeds that lined the tracks. But this time he allowed his body to follow his arms. He landed on his side, drenching his shirt and his face in diarrheic muck, and rolled into the brush. He heard the guard screaming at him, the train accelerating. Almost simultaneously he was aware of the crackle of gunfire and felt something stinging his arm. But he knew they weren't about to stop the train for one shit-covered Jew, and the guard wasn't about to remain behind and miss the trip east. And so he kept pinwheeling, spinning like a rolling pin amid shrubs and high grass and spring weeds and then, much to his relief, among actual trees. There he stood and he started to run, and he didn't stop until the sound of the train (and its infernal whistle) had receded far into the distance.

He had no idea where he was, but he was nowhere near a railway station or a town and that was probably a pretty good sign. He leaned against what he thought, in the dusk, was an oak tree, and looked at his arm. His shirtsleeve was sliced open and his upper arm was bleeding, but the bullet had just grazed him. It was actually his right hip that hurt like hell. And his knees. Clearly he had banged up his hip and his knees when he'd fallen. Well, he thought, that's what you get when you dive from a rolling, accelerating train.

But, initially, he was still very glad that he had.

It was only after he had caught his breath and begun to concentrate on the sounds of the odd and unfamiliar animals he heard all around him—owls and bats and somewhere not terribly far away, a wolf—that he began to fear that he just might have deserted his family. Rebekah. Yes, she was tall and pretty, but she was only fourteen. And perhaps because there had been a child, another girl, born between him and his sister who had died within days of her birth, he and his parents had always doted on Rebekah to the point that she was really rather helpless. And what if she was on that train, in one of the other cars? His parents, too? The thought left him a little sickened, and he wasn't sure now what he would do next. He was, he realized, worse than a stranger in a strange land. He was a Jew in the east. And so the very first thing he did was to rip his star from his shirt. He'd figure out the rest—clothes, a name, a ration card for food—after he'd gotten some sleep.

AS THE EMMERICH FAMILY was preparing to leave the estate—Kaminheim was their name for their home, because the house had so many fireplaces, some of them the height and width of a pony—much to Anna's astonishment, Mutti was actually dusting. And, with the cook—the lone servant who remained—mopping the floor. And then beating throw rugs outside on the terrace in the icy January air. Apparently she believed that someday they might return, and then they would whisk the crisp white sheets off the couches and chairs—a magician's reveal—and their life would resume as if they had only been away on a holiday.

Anna presumed that her mother had been disabused of this notion by now, as they trekked through the snow in the woods and away from the caravan of refugees, trying to catch up to Helmut.

But perhaps not. This was a woman, after all, who had always maintained a completely illogic faith in her führer and a naive ability to compartmentalize what she deemed his good and his bad attributes. Back in 1940, Anna recalled, the very summer when Jewish friends of her parents from Danzig would appear, homeless, on their door-step, Mutti had insisted on hanging in the parlor the signed, framed photo she owned of Hitler. They had taken the Jewish family in without a moment's hesitation, and Mutti had seen no inconsistency in celebrating the führer and offering shelter to her friends. Even now, after Soviet shells had pummeled her brother's estate a mere twenty-five kilometers farther east, she could still sound like a star-struck little girl when she talked of Hitler's blue eyes, or the entire afternoon she had spent on the Schlossplatz in 1940 because the man was staying at the Hotel Bellevue and she was hoping to steal a glance of him. She hadn't been alone. There had been very big crowds that day—including Mutti and her sister-in-law and some other women from the corner of Poland that, thanks to Hitler, recently had been returned to Germany—and they hadn't been disappointed. They had gotten to stand within yards of their leader when he had walked from the hotel to the Café Weber; they had, as one, thanked him for reuniting them with their country.

This was why Mutti still seemed to expect a miracle from her führer. The estate, Kaminheim, on which she had grown up as a little girl had always been a part of Germany and she had viewed herself as a German. Then, in 1919, it was on land ceded to Poland and she was supposed to become a Pole. All the Germans there were. Or they could relocate. But her family wasn't about to leave Kaminheim. There was no place else for them to go, nothing else for them to do. They grew sugar beets. It was what they did. And so, with the signing of a treaty in a palace outside of Paris, she went from being the daughter of Prussian farming gentry to a disliked little foreigner. A minority. An alien. A part of a discredited nobility. Initially, like most Prussians, Mutti's parents—Anna's grandparents—had thought this Hitler character was decidedly low-rent. There were rumors that he'd once been a paperhanger, that he'd painted bad still lifes and tried to sell them on the street. The man might not even have been completely sane. But then he got people working again and he built those highways. Gave Germans back their pride. And then, best of all, he gave them back Prussia. All of Prussia. Not just a kidney-shaped patch of earth surrounding Danzig, separated from the rest of Germany by a vast tract of Poland. Sadly, Mutti's parents died before the reunification in 1939. For most of the war, Mutti had lamented that her mother and father hadn't lived to see the return of their precious Kaminheim to Germany; now, however, Anna wondered if Mutti wasn't relieved on some level that neither had they been forced to witness their treasured land occupied by what her mother considered the savages from the east.

Finally, between the explosions and the pathetic cries of a little boy calling out not for food but for a lost dog named after food ("I want Spaetzle, Mommy! Please, please, we can't go on without Spaetzle!"), over the sound of the birdsong—still, somehow, there were birds—she heard Helmut yelling their names and high-stepping his way toward them through the snow. It sounded as if he had found another spot on the river where the ice seemed thick enough for their horses and wagons.

"Are there other people there?" their father asked him.

"Yes, but not many. Not yet."

He said the spot was no more than fifteen minutes farther. There was a steep hill just ahead and it might be difficult for the horses to pull the wagons through some drifts of thigh-deep snow, but assuming they could make the knoll, it was no more than fifty or sixty meters from there to the edge of the river.

BENEATH THE OATS, Callum listened carefully. His right arm and leg had, once more, gone to sleep. Unfortunately, it was hard to breathe if he tried to lie on his back or his stomach. In a moment, he guessed, he would roll over and spend a few seconds gasping for air so he could allow a semblance of circulation to return to those limbs. He was a big man—powerfully built, with shoulders that flattened out like a mesa and a back that was as straight and solid as granite quarry walls—and in his opinion he was, pure and simple, too large for these quarters.

He and Anna were hoping that once they were west of the Vistula, periodically he would be allowed to walk beside the wagons. Her father had said he thought this was extremely unlikely. Though he was dressed in her older brother's winter clothes instead of his ragged British paratrooper's uniform—Werner wasn't nearly as muscular as Callum, but he was almost as tall, and Mutti had been able to doctor some pants and a jacket—if he was seen by anyone in authority he might be hanged on the spot as a German deserter.

Unless, of course, he opened his mouth first.

Then he would simply be shot on the spot as an escaped POW.

Still, he couldn't spend forever curled like a hermit crab beneath their food and the horses' feed in this wagon. And while Anna's father had surmised that he would have to remain in the cart until they reached either Mutti's cousin in Stettin or, eventually, the British and American lines somewhere far to the west, her mother was firmly convinced that he would be up and about within days. Why? Any day now, she said, certainly inside of two or three weeks, they would all be allies together: the Brits and the Yanks and the Germans. The civilized nations of the world would band together to repel the Russians. Prevent them from barbarizing all of Europe. It was, she had said, inevitable.

Callum wasn't quite so sure. In point of fact, he thought Mutti was absolutely loopy. A sweet lady with fortitude and courage. But also, alas, bloody bonkers.

Nevertheless, ever since he had jumped from an airplane

seven months ago now—almost eight, if he was going to be precise—his entire life had been bonkers. The whole world, it seemed, had gone mad. And, of course, jumping from an airplane—and jumping in the dark while people below you were firing machine guns into the night sky—was hardly an indication that the world was especially sane to begin with.

The drop, at least his portion, had been a disaster almost from the moment he had first hurled himself from the plane. First there had been all that gunfire from the hedgerows and the woods. He hadn't been hit, but he had heard the agonized screams of the men drifting—sometimes minus an arm or a leg or towing their entrails like kite tails—to the earth all around him. And then, instead of landing in a meadow just east of the Orne, he had landed in quicksand. At least it had struck him as quicksand in the dark. In reality it was a mere swamp, but clutching a rifle and weighed down by his harness, the risers, and the pack with his reserve chute, it might just as well have been quicksand. And, again, the cries, though this time they were punctuated by the choking hacks of men who were drowning as they pleaded for help. Yes, indeed, they were drowning in a few feet of water and a little Norman muck. He was on his side, disoriented in the bog, but he found if he arched his back and his neck he could keep his nose above the water and slime. Finally he was able to right himself and half-crawl, half-dog-paddle his way out of the marsh.

When he was free, when he was actually emerging onto turf that was solid, the world around him was abruptly lit as if it were noon: A troop plane had exploded, hit by a shell as it approached his corner of the drop zone. It slammed like a comet—blue and yellow flames streaming behind it, its descent marked by a screech far louder than any noise he had ever heard in his life— into the ground within a stone's throw of where he was standing, dumbstruck. Instantly it set fire to the understory and the brush all around him. Inside his pack were ammunition and a land mine, and so he actually ran back into the swamp, the only ground he could see now that wasn't ablaze.

There he helped a trooper named Bingham and a radioman named Lane save themselves from drowning, literally grabbing Bingham by his harness as if he were a big dog he had by the collar and raising him up and out of the slime. There they watched the flames in the plane and the woods burn themselves out. And the fires really didn't last all that long, despite whatever fuel the aircraft had left in its tanks, because the air was moist and the ground was a bog. When they staggered from the marsh onto dry land, a half-dozen wet and scared and lost paratroopers, it was still dark. But not for long. Almost the moment their boots touched ground that didn't squash beneath their feet for the first time in hours, the world once more went bright as midday, and the men squinted as one and shielded their eyes against searchlights. The Germans took them prisoner rather than machine-gunning them dead on the spot because they didn't know if this was the actual invasion or a mere feint, and they wanted to interrogate the Brits.

Callum was thus taken into custody without ever firing a single shot at a German. This would only endear him further to Mutti and her lone daughter, though it also led Helmut and even Theo to think a little less of him than they already did.

Nevertheless, he had become yet one more pet in the Emmerichs' extensive menagerie. And their anticipated goodwill offering when they reached the British or American lines. And, though neither Mutti nor Rolf—her husband—nor their sons had a clue, Anna Emmerich's lover.

THE HORSES DID make it up the small knoll with the thigh-deep drifts of snow, despite the weight in the wagons, and they made it with relative ease. But Anna had never had any doubts. Helmut was right, they *were* more her horses than anyone's, and she knew what they were capable of. Balga especially, the animal that she rode most often. Balga was a massive, powerful stallion that wanted only to run. He had been chafing all morning at the very idea that these humans expected him to walk at their pace, even as—along with a second horse—he pulled a cart full of feed.

All of the horses were named after castles. Not just Balga. The others? Labiau, Ragnit, and Waldau. Though it had been the child Helmut who had been obsessed with the knights of East Prussia, Anna as well had appreciated the medieval romance of the stories that surrounded the citadels. And the first of the horses that she suggested be christened with the name of a castle, Balga, was regal and proud and seemed to lack completely the skittishness that marked so many of the estate's other horses. Altogether they had twelve, but only these four were coming with them on the trek west.

Now it was their turn to join the queue crossing the ice on the river. Still, Anna understood the river wouldn't keep the Russians at bay for long. Already they had a bridgehead at Kulm.

There were explosions echoing to their south and—farther away—to the north, but at the moment no shells were falling here. Gingerly she stepped onto the ice, found her footing, and then she started to lead Balga and Waldau onto the glassy plane with her. The horses were actually better off than she was because yesterday the Emmerichs' farrier had drilled ice nails into the bottom of their shoes. Helmut was behind the family on the ridge, scanning the far side of the river with his binoculars. As far as she could tell, all that was over there were the lucky refugees who had preceded them, but her father and brother feared the front was so fluid that it was possible they might cross a stretch of river where the Russians already were encamped.

Her mother and Theo had climbed off the wagon and were walking beside her, because her parents wanted everyone in the family off the carts in the event one plunged through the ice. That had happened, they knew, to other trekkers. One moment the wagons were atop the ice, and the next—after a groan and a snap—the horses and people were drowning in the frigid current of the Vistula. Only Callum was still in a cart, and Anna wasn't sure how seriously devastated anyone other than she would be if he drowned. Certainly Helmut wouldn't care, and he didn't even know how she and Callum had been spending their secret, private moments together since the winter had started to set in.

Helmut placed his field glasses back into their case and started across the ice, leading Labiau and Ragnit and the wagon they were pulling. Her father marched beside Mutti, taking her hand as they walked, occasionally whispering something into her ear, but Anna and Theo and Helmut remained silent, listening largely to the breathing of the horses and the periodic curses and whimpers from the trekkers around them who had discovered this section of river about the same time that her brother had. There were no Volkssturm or Wehrmacht soldiers here to prevent more than a family or two from starting across the river at a time, and slowly the refugees were fanning out: Instead of a single line, it was fast becoming a wave, and Anna worried that the ice would go and they would all flop into the frigid water at once.

But that didn't happen. It was all, in a way, stunningly anticlimactic. One moment they were on the eastern bank, and now, ten minutes later, they were on the west. Apparently, the road to Schwetz, the nearest village, was no more than two or three kilometers distant, and most of the trek there would be across flat meadows and fields. No more woods, at least not today, or inching forward in the midst of an endless line of equally pathetic— no, far more pathetic—refugees. She felt an almost debilitating surge of relief, an outpouring of exhaustion that made her long to sit where she was in the snow, because they were on the far shore and they were alive. And, despite the rumble of gunfire in the distance, they were safe. At least for the moment. Her father and Helmut had gotten them across the Vistula, and now they would bring them safely from this frontier of the Reich to the cocoon of its interior. She wanted, she realized, to do more than sit: She wanted to lie down, and she didn't care whether it was in her bed or the autumn-scented fields of Kaminheim or here in the cold and the ice on the western (*Western*. Had there ever been a more lovely word?) bank of the Vistula and daydream. But she saw that her father and her mother were approaching her. Helmut was approaching her. Theo looked up apprehensively.

"Anna," her father was saying, pulling her from the lovely, enervating stupor into which she was descending. He placed his hands squarely on her shoulders. "My Anna."

"Yes, Father?"

He reached over with one arm and seemed about to pull both Theo and her against him. Into him. Then he remembered the blood, a frozen swath of burgundy-colored ice crystals that clung to his wool sleeve like honey, and instead simply rested his fingers on the scarf that swaddled her neck.

"My children," he murmured. "Here is where you must be as strong as your mother. As strong as Helmut and Werner."

"We have been strong, haven't we?" Theo asked. The boy wanted desperately to be as respected as his two older—in his mind, venerated—brothers. He wanted to be a soldier, too. To be needed. To not be a burden, a child who had to be watched over and managed.

Their father nodded at Theo, but he didn't smile. And instantly Anna understood. She glanced over at Helmut, the instinctive, yearning reflex of a twin for a twin. Her brother wouldn't look at her. Or he couldn't. He folded his arms against his chest and gazed at the caravan of wagons and wheelbarrows and carts that was inching its way over the ice. When she turned toward her mother, Mutti looked away. Her lips were thin and flat, and she had that stoic, gritty gaze she got whenever she did something that took enormous resolve: when she had buried the Luftwaffe pilot; when she had learned that her oldest son, Werner, had been wounded and she had had to share the news with the rest of the children; and when, only yesterday, she had been draping the chalk-white sheets on the divan and the chairs in the parlor.

And so Anna was only half-listening when her father told Theo and her that he and Helmut were leaving them here. They were returning east across the Vistula. Something about a counterattack on the Russians' bridgehead at Kulm. The need to defend Germany. Theo burrowed his face in his father's uniform jacket, oblivious of the cold and the wet and the frozen blood, his head bobbing either because he was trying hard not to cry or because he was trying to nod obediently or, perhaps, both.

And then Helmut was beside her, or—she realized after a moment—beside the wagon with Callum. Because it was to Callum he wanted to speak.

"You," he barked at the oats. "Take care of my mother and Anna and Theo. No surrendering this time. Do you hear?"

With a grunt Callum pushed his head and his arms free, a turtlehead emerging from its shell. "You know, I can't do a whole hell of a lot in here, Helmut," he said.

"No, but—" her brother started to snarl at the Scot, but before he could say more their father was silencing him. Reminding him that it was in no one's interest for Callum to make his presence known until they had reached the British or American lines—or until they were overtaken by the Brits or the Americans. He reassured both Helmut and Callum that the rest of the Emmerichs were more than strong enough—physically, emotionally—to get to the west on their own.

And then Callum was back beneath the feed and Helmut was checking his pistol and her father was saying something more to her. "I know it is an awful responsibility I am giving you, Anna. Awful. But you know the horses. And I know you can do this. Just keep moving. You are never to look back or turn back until we are all together again as a family. Do you understand?"

She had the sense that Helmut was too young and brash to

understand for certain that he was going to die if he left them now to join in the fight against the Russians. But he probably suspected how badly the odds were stacked against him. He wasn't stupid. And, clearly, their father knew. She could tell by the way he was gently saying good-bye to Mutti, and the way he was lying—her father, lying!—about their return to Kaminheim. Joking now about the scavenger hunt they would have when they started to dig up the silver and crystal and china they had buried in their hunting park. Anna knew the truth: After a month in the deep freeze of January, the soil had become solid as granite. They had buried nothing. She and her father had simply thrown up their arms and left the serving trays and decanters and whole place settings upright in the snow like tombstones in a cemetery. If servants from the neighboring estates hadn't stolen the pieces by now, the Russians had. Or would any moment.

His message when he told her not to look back until they were together again as a family? Never look back, period. She wanted to throw herself against him just the way Theo had, beg him to come with them. Tell him how little sense it made to get killed by the Russians at this point in the war. But, clearly, he understood there wasn't a point. Everyone except Mutti seemed to realize it was over. Even Helmut: He had talked with the British POWs in the autumn. With Callum when he was home in the winter. Until yesterday, he had been the one who was putting the markers in the map in the parlor that showed the locations, as far as they could tell, of the different armies and the boundaries of the Reich.

Yet despite what they knew, now her father was going to join a bunch of other old men and boys and counterattack the Russian bridgehead at Kulm.

He took off one of his gloves and stroked the side of her cheek, his fingers coarse, but still gentle and warm. His eyes were milky in the cold and he—a man who she knew loved her but was never going to verbalize such a notion—actually pulled her into him, and so he had both her and Theo wrapped in his arms. They stayed that way for a long, quiet moment, and then he pushed them away. He embraced Mutti once more, as Helmut awkwardly, almost tentatively, hugged their brother and her. Then, without another word, he took Helmut and the two of them started back across the Vistula, this time moving against the long procession of sleighs and wagons traveling west.

She told her mother that they should probably continue if they wanted to reach Klinger by nightfall, but Mutti said that she wanted to be sure that her husband and her son made it safely across the ice. And so they waited and watched. Thus they saw the men, one in so many ways still a boy, reach the east bank and start back into the woods. And then, seconds later, they heard the screech of shells—not a single one this time, this was no solo diving raptor—approaching and instinctively they curled themselves against the carts, but they continued to stare to the east. Instantly, in a series of blasts that reduced the ice on the river to slivers and sent shards and spray raining down upon them like hail—shards and spray, the grips and leather sides of valises, wood splinters from crates, wheels from wagons and the runners from sleighs, the flesh of horses and people, hooves and feet (bare somehow, as if their boots had been blown off them by the blasts)—the natural bridge was gone. Where seconds before there had been perhaps a dozen families working their way gingerly across the ice, now there was only the once more violently churning waters of the Vistula, the brief, choking screams of the living as they disappeared beneath the current, and the more prolonged wails of the German families on the eastern shore, still alive. Anna couldn't tell if they were despairing over what they had just witnessed, or because they knew what awaited them now that they had failed to escape the Russians.

Beside her, without saying a single word, her mother and

Theo started leading Labiau and Ragnit west across the snowy meadow. And so Anna looped the reins of the other two animals around her wrists, stroked Balga once along his forehead and poll, and followed.

PART I

Autumn 1944

Chapter One

USUALLY, IT WAS ONLY WHEN ONE OF THE LOCAL SOLDIERS
was home on leave that Anna and her girlfriends ever saw the
sorts of young men with whom, in different times, they might
have danced. And, as the war had dragged on, the pool of mar-
riage prospects—in Anna's mind, often enough that meant
merely her older brother Werner's acquaintances—dried up completely. The soldiers were either missing or disfigured or dead.

But then came the POWs. Seven of them, sent from the prison
camp to help with the harvest.

And a week after the POWs arrived at Kaminheim, when the
corn was almost completely harvested and everyone was about
to begin to gather the sugar beets and the apples, there came
four naval officers in search of a plow. They were planning to
mark a groove through the estate that would be the start of an
antitank trench. When it was complete, the trench would span
the length of the district, bisecting some farms, skirting the
edges of others. Meanwhile, different officers were visiting
neighboring estates as well, and the Emmerichs were told that at
some point in the coming month hundreds of foreigners and old
men would follow them, and descend on the estate to actually
construct the trench.

And while the very idea of an antitank trench was alarming, the presence of all those handsome young men—the Germans, the Brits, and that one very young Scot—made it a burden Anna was willing to shoulder. This was true, at least in part, because she didn't honestly believe the fighting would ever come this far west. It couldn't. Even the naval officers said this was a mere precaution. And so she would flirt with the Brits during the day in the fields, where she would work, too, and dance with the naval officers in the evenings in the manor house's small but elegant ballroom. Mutti would play the piano, joined after that first night by Callum Finella on Uncle Felix's accordion, while her father—though distracted by the news from the east—would look on benignly. Sometimes Theo would put his toy cavalrymen away and watch as well, appalled in the manner of any ten-year-old boy that these brave and accomplished soldiers wanted to waste their time with the likes of his sister and her friends. He followed the men around like a puppy.

Helmut did, too. But Helmut actually would work with the officers as long as their father allowed him away from the harvest, helping them to find their way around the endless acres of Kaminheim, and thus mark out the optimum design and placement of the trench. Then, after dinner, he would dance with Anna's friends—girls who, previously, he had insisted were too puerile to be interesting. Seeing them now through the eyes of the navy men, however, he was suddenly discovering their charms.

Certainly Anna worried about her older brother, Werner, who had already been wounded once in this war and was fighting somewhere to the south. But she had rarely spent any time with men as interesting as this eclectic group who had descended upon their farm that autumn. She and Helmut had learned to speak English in school, though she had taken her studies far more seriously than her brother, which meant that she alone in the assemblage could speak easily to everybody—the POWs during the day and the naval officers at night—and appreciate how erudite and experienced everyone was. At least, she thought, in comparison to her. She was, on occasion, left almost dizzy as she swiveled among conversations and translated asides and remarks. And the longer stories? She felt like a star-struck child. When she was in grade school she had met English families the winter her family had gone skiing in Switzerland, but by 1944 she remembered little more than a very large man in a very poor bear costume, and the way she and the English children together had endured his clownish shenanigans because all of the parents had thought the fellow was wildly entertaining. But since the war had begun, she hadn't been west of Berlin. In the early years, they had still taken summer holidays on the beaches of the Baltic or ventured to Danzig for concerts, but lately even those trips had ceased completely. Two of their POWs, however, had seen the pyramids; another had been to America; and Callum—the youngest of the group, the tallest of the group, and the only one from Scotland—had been born in India, where his father had been a colonial official, and had traveled extensively throughout Bengali and Burma and Madras as a little boy.

Even the German naval officers were more interesting than any of the country boys—or men—she had met in her district. They, too, had seen places in Europe and Africa she'd only read about in books.

Initially, she had worried that there might be unpleasant sparks when the Germans and the Brits crossed paths, especially on the first morning when the naval officers would be marking out a segment of the antitank trench in the very same beet fields where the POWs were working. But the two groups of men had largely ignored each other.

It was the next day, when she was working alongside the prisoners in the apple orchard, that one of the POWs—that exuberant young giant named Callum—segued from the usual flirtatious banter to which she had grown accustomed and had come to expect from him, to guarded innuendos about Adolf

Hitler and then (even more problematic, in some ways) to questions about the work camps.

"You're such a nice girl, Anna, and so sharp," he said, as the two of them stood together beside a particularly wiry tree, resting for a moment midmorning. There was a military policeman who must have been somebody's grandfather standing guard a hundred meters away, but he was so old he probably wouldn't have heard a word they were saying if they had been standing directly beside him. "And your family is much more hospitable than necessary—given the circumstances and all." The POWs were sleeping in the bunkhouse that the farmhands had used before they had either run off or been commandeered by the Reich for work in the mines and the munitions factories.

"Thank you," she said simply. She was unsure where this conversation was going, but that opening, that apparent surprise that she was *such a nice girl,* had her slightly wary. She'd been laughing with Callum for days, and the thought crossed her mind that perhaps she had misjudged him. Grown too comfortable—too friendly—with him. With all the POWs.

"So, I was wondering," he continued, his voice nonchalant. "What do you think your Hitler is doing with the Jews?"

"*My* Hitler? You make him sound like one of my horses," she said, aware that she was not answering his question.

"I didn't mean that. I meant . . ."

"What did you mean?"

"I had a mate in Scotland who was Jewish, a chum I played soccer with. We were friends, our parents were friends. He had family somewhere in Germany. And they just disappeared. There was talk of them trying to come to Edinburgh, but they couldn't get out. Eventually, the letters just dried up. Stopped coming. Then, at the stalag this summer, I met two chaps from Wales who had been in intelligence. And they said—"

She cut him off: "At school, they told me not to ask when I inquired. They told me I didn't know what I was talking about."

"But you asked?"

Aware that she couldn't help but sound oversensitive, she answered, "Maybe it would surprise you, but I do have a brain behind my eyes. Yes, I asked."

"It wouldn't surprise me a bit," he said, smiling.

"I asked them where the Jews were going," she continued. "Before the war, my parents had friends in Danzig who were Jewish. That's where my father went to university: Danzig. He grew up on a farm in another part of Prussia, but for a time he considered becoming a lawyer. But he's a very scientific man. And he likes working the earth too much. Anyway, he has never understood the Nazis' obsession with Jews. Never. My mother? It's different for her: She's lived her whole life here. She, too, thinks it's ridiculous, but she has always been a little oblivious of anything that doesn't involve the farm or this corner of the country."

"They're both party members, right?"

She nodded. "My father wouldn't have the contracts he has if he weren't a member of the party. Even I know that."

"Tell me, then: These friends. Your parents' Jewish friends. Where are they now?"

"One, I know, was my father's banker. I don't know his name, but he took very good care of Father and Mutti on their honeymoon. The inflation was so horrible that suddenly they couldn't pay their bills and Father's stocks were worth nothing. Somehow, the banker solved everything for them and they had a perfectly lovely holiday after that."

"What do you think became of him?"

"He and Father lost touch. But I can tell you this: My father wrote letters on his family's behalf to different people. I don't know who or what the letters were supposed to accomplish. But he wrote letters for other friends, too. And for a few weeks in the summer of 1940, my parents had some Jewish friends who lived with us: a younger couple and their baby. A little baby girl. She was adorable. They had lost their apartment in Danzig. I was thirteen and I always wanted to babysit, but the mother wouldn't let the child out of her sight." She could have gone on, but it was a memory she tried not to think about. There had been some talk about hiding the family—and *hiding* was indeed the word her parents had used—but so many people in the village had been aware of the Emmerichs' visitors from Danzig that the couple had refused her mother and father's offer of sanctuary and simply disappeared into the fog one August morning.

"I'm badgering you," he said. "I'm sorry. I didn't mean to. I have a habit of talking too much. You might have noticed."

"You're inquisitive," she said, unable to mask the small tremor she heard in her voice. The truth was, she didn't want to be having this conversation. She knew she wouldn't dare discuss these sorts of things on one of the streets in the village or in a city. One never knew who might be listening or how they might be connected to the party. And, suddenly, she felt an odd spike of defensiveness. "But you tell me: How am I supposed to know where everyone is in the midst of a war?"

"Well," he said evenly. "You can keep track of the Jews because of the stars on their clothes. You've seen them."

"Yes, of course I have. I've seen them in Danzig and I've seen them in Berlin."

"Lately?"

"I haven't been to Berlin lately. Or Danzig."

He used a handkerchief to wipe the perspiration away from his temples. The hair there was a bay that reminded her of Balga, her favorite horse. "The folks who will be coming to build the anti-tank trench," he began, and she could tell that he was choosing his words with great care. "You know, actually digging where those navy blokes are leaving the plow marks? They're the lucky ones."

"They'll be more prisoners like you."

"Maybe. But I think they're going to come instead from those work camps. Not the prison camps. It will take hundreds of people just to dig through your farm. And, besides, it's one thing to put a group of us soldiers to work harvesting apples and corn and sugar beets. Trust me, this is luxurious compared to life in the stalag, and we are all deeply appreciative of your family's kindness. But it's quite another to make us dig antitank trenches. The Red Cross and the folks who penned the Geneva convention wouldn't exactly approve."

"So, the workers will be the criminals from the camps? Communists and Gypsies. Why should that trouble me?"

"And Jews. That's my point, Anna. They're in those camps for no other reason than because they're Jewish."

"What?"

"The Jews have been sent to the camps."

"No," she said. "No. That's not true."

"I'm sorry, Anna. But it is."

"The Jews have just been resettled," she continued, repeating what she had been told at school and at her meetings with other teen girls in the Bund Deutscher Mädel whenever she had asked the question, but until that moment had never said aloud herself. Somehow, verbalizing the idea made it seem ludicrous. She certainly didn't add what so many of her teachers or BDM leaders had added over the years: *They have to be resettled because they are not Aryan. They are inferior in every imaginable way, they are worse than the Russians and the Poles. Most have nothing that resembles an Aryan conscience, and they are interested in nothing but their money and mezuzahs and diamonds. Many are evil; all are conniving.*

"And doesn't even resettlement seem, I don't know, a trifle uncivilized—even if it really is what's occurring?" he went on. "Think of that little family that was with you when you were thirteen. Why do you think there was talk of hiding them? I mean, suppose my government in England just decided to 'resettle' the Catholics—to take away their homes, their animals, their possessions, and then just send them away?"

Another prisoner, the balding mason named Wally, passed by with one of the wicker baskets they used for the apples and gave

Callum a look that Anna recognized instantly as the universal sign to shut up. His head was cocked slightly and his eyes were wide. Callum ignored him and continued, "Those intelligence chaps from Wales. They told us about another camp. One further east in Poland. They had heard rumors—"

"I've heard rumors. We've all heard rumors. I've listened to your propaganda on the radio."

"You listen to the BBC? That's illegal, Anna, you know that," he told her, his voice mocking her good-naturedly.

"Everyone listens. And *you* know that."

Wally dumped his apples in one of the shipping crates in the back of a wagon and started to say something, his mouth opening into an anxiety-ridden O, but then stopped himself and returned to the trees where he was working, shaking his head in bewilderment.

"Besides," she said, angry now, "what am I supposed to do? Am I supposed to go have tea with the führer and advise him on policy?" He paused, seeming to think about this, unsure what to say. She decided to press her advantage. "You would be in serious trouble, you know, if I told anyone what you were saying."

"Indeed I would. I am putting my trust completely at your discretion."

"Why?"

"Because you are very pretty and very smart, and until I was sent here I hadn't spoken to a girl who was either in a very, very long time."

"Spare me," she said, but she couldn't help being flattered. "I've gone just as long without the company of boys. They're all off fighting somewhere."

"Ah, but then your navy men arrived," he said, and she realized he was actually a little jealous of them. He seemed about to say more when Wally returned, this time accompanied by the Yorkshire schoolteacher named Arthur Frost. "Come along,

Callum," Arthur said firmly, "those apples won't pick themselves. No more dillydallying."

Callum nodded agreeably and left, turning back to Anna once to bring his index and middle finger to the tip of his lips. At the time, she thought he was shushing her; later, she would conclude he had in fact blown her a kiss.

THEO MOVED TWO of his toy cavalrymen to the front of his column, and then had them ride to the river that Anna had helped him paint a year ago now on a piece of barn board. The board was at least a meter and a half square and he could carry it by himself—but just barely. Helmut had found it and his father had sanded it flat. In addition to the river, he and Anna had also painted trees and wooden fences on it, and a long trench winding its way down one of the sides, all as if seen from a low-flying airplane. He had wanted to add barbed wire near the trench, but Anna had convinced him that it would reduce the number of conflicts he could reenact by limiting his scenarios to the Great War. The trench, she had suggested, could be a streambed that had dried up in the summer if he wanted to stage a battle from the nineteenth century.

"Or," he had suggested helpfully at the time, "one of the firefights Werner has been in."

"That's right," she had said, but he had been able to tell by the pause and the way her voice had quivered just the tiniest bit that for some reason she was troubled by the idea of him using his lead soldiers to reenact battles along the eastern front. He hadn't really expected at the time that he would, because he had only a pair of toy tanks, and battles these days demanded lots and lots of armor. Moreover, his two tanks were of a different scale than his lead soldiers. They were from another collection and they were barely the height of his fighting men, which meant that he rarely used them.

He did know boys who owned model tanks that would have worked quite well with his men. But they wouldn't have shared their tanks with him and he never played with them. He wanted to, and he would have been happy to join them if they had ever asked—he would have been happy and flattered and more than a little grateful—but they never did. Moreover, he knew they never would. Once he made the mistake of telling some of the boys in school about the scene he and Anna had painted for his soldiers, hinting that they should come to Kaminheim and bring their own model cannons and tanks, but they had laughed at him and suggested that they would sooner have gone and played in Moscow. It wasn't, of course, Kaminheim that kept them away; it was him.

He had set up his playing board this evening after dinner in a corner of the dining room underneath one of the sconces, and these two cavalry officers were reconnoitering the terrain. It was the summer of 1870, and they were deciding whether this might be a good spot to try and force a battle with the French Army of the Rhine.

He heard his father and the naval officer named Oskar in the hallway walking toward Father's office, and he went very still. Oskar had small eyes, a high forehead, and almost no lips, but he was calm and intelligent and Theo knew that his parents respected him. He heard his father pushing the door shut, but it didn't close all the way and he could hear some of what they were saying if he didn't move. They were discussing, as the grown-ups did all the time these days, the Russian front, but it seemed that Oskar was talking as well about the attempt that summer on the life of the führer. A few months earlier, in July, a group of officers had set off a bomb in the führer's headquarters in Prussia. Hitler had survived, but it seemed the conspiracy was extensive. Even now, months later, the SS was still rounding up individuals who were involved. At school and among the Jungvolk, people referred to those officers as traitors and discussed with undisguised glee how cowardly they had been when they were executed for their crime, but Theo had the sense when the subject came up at dinner that his parents believed the plotters had only had Germany's best interests in mind.

It seemed, from what Theo could hear, that Oskar did, too.

"The problem," the officer was telling his father now, "is that we can't win the war. But we can't negotiate a peace now because of what some of Hitler's lackeys have done."

"A negotiated peace was never an option. Churchill and Roosevelt said years ago they would only accept a complete surrender," his father said.

"We are speaking in confidence, true?"

"Of course."

"Have you heard about the camps?"

"I've heard whispers."

"When the Russians find them? Or the Americans and the Brits? There will be hell to pay."

"Tell me: What do you know?"

Suddenly Theo's heart was beating fast in his chest, in part because his father and this officer were discussing the possibility that Germany might actually lose the war, and in part because of whatever it was that Oskar was about to reveal. Before the officer had continued, however, there were great whoops of laughter and the sound of the front door swinging open. He felt a rush of cool air. Two of the other naval officers, Oskar's friends, had come inside, and then he heard Anna and Mutti greeting them and helping them off with their coats. Any moment now they would bring that giant Scotsman in from the bunkhouse and hand him the accordion, and everyone would start dancing. No doubt, one of Anna's friends had arrived with the officers. The two men had probably been off somewhere picking her up.

His father and Oskar emerged from the office, and Oskar greeted his associates. His father noticed him now on the floor and knelt beside him.

"I didn't hear you out here," he said, and he rubbed the top of his head. "Have you been playing long?"

He had the sense that he would worry his father if he told him that he had. And his father had worries enough right now.

"No. I just sat down," he answered.

This seemed to make his father happy. He motioned down at the cavalrymen. "The battle of Mars-la-Tour?" he asked.

"I hadn't decided."

"Oskar reminded me of a book I think you're old enough to read now. It has a wonderful description of Von Bredow's Death Ride and the Prussian cavalry charge. Would you like me to see if I can find you a copy?"

"Yes, thank you."

Over their shoulder one of the officers was boasting that he had brought honey for the schnapps from the village, and Theo heard a female voice he couldn't quite recognize start to giggle. No doubt, it was indeed one of Anna's friends: She had so many. Another night, Theo thought, he might have continued to move his lead soldiers around the board, alone on the dining room floor, but not this evening. He would join the crowd that would gather in the ballroom. Perhaps if he was unobtrusive, the grown-ups would let down their guards and he might learn whatever it was that Oskar had been about to reveal.

ANOTHER DAY, CALLUM told Anna about his uncle's library in Edinburgh. His uncle was a university professor there, and among the books on his shelves were novels by Russians that he was confident would convince her that not everyone born east of Warsaw was a barbarian.

"I don't think that," she said. "My mother might. But I don't."

Still, she was only dimly aware of most of the authors he mentioned. She wondered if their books had been banned in Germany, or whether they simply weren't available in their rural corner of the Reich. The same seemed to be true of movies he had seen, and specific operas and dramas he'd attended. It all made Callum seem almost impossibly erudite for someone so physically imposing and, yes, so young—it was hard to believe he was only twenty— and it caused her to rue, for the first time, all of the things she was being denied.

They also compared the beaches on the Baltic with those along the North Sea, and the castle ruins that dotted their land-scapes. She expressed envy for how civilized the winters sounded in Scotland, and he, in turn, said he thought Scotch farmers would be jealous of the soil in which her family grew sugar beets and corn, and cared for their apple trees.

She found herself wishing she had a fraction of the stories and experiences he had, and worrying that soon he would come to find her boring. All she knew, she realized, were horses. Horses and housework. Her father had taught her to ride—and, in all fairness, to ski and to hike—and her mother had groomed her well to be the wife, someday, of a farmer. A gentleman farmer, certainly. A landowner. An aristocrat, even. But, like her father, a farmer nonetheless.

He was completely unlike her three brothers—even little Theo—whose posture had always been perfect at the dining room table, and who seemed to stand with their ankles together and (in-evitably) their arms folded imperiously across their chests. Could Werner and Helmut ever be anything but stern? She didn't think so. Perhaps there was still hope for Theo, but already he was being trained to be a soldier in carriage if not, in the end, in profession.

And yet their father was no martinet. He laughed and drank beer and had stories of his own he could tell. He would slouch on occasion. Listen with them to the BBC. Tell jokes about the Nazis, despite the reality that both he and his wife were party members. She asked her father that night if he had ever read books by the Russians Callum had mentioned, and he said that he had. Mutti had, too.

Of course, they had grown up in a different era. A different time. The world they knew wasn't decorated solely with red flags and black swastikas, and a person could still read novels written by Russians.

Chapter Two

JUDENJAGD. A JEW HUNT.

Not unlike a fox hunt. You searched for the Jews in the woods, and then you shot them. You shot them if they were mothers hiding alone with their children; you shot them if they were old men oblivious of the roundup in the village and were here in the woods gathering mushrooms. Or, if you didn't have the time or the inclination to view it as sport, you marched them at gunpoint—or with a whip—back to the village. You sat them in the square in the heat of the sun, and you shot the first one who happened to stand up and stretch.

Because, of course, you had ordered them to sit and rising was an act of disobedience.

Sometimes, as they were marched to the square, they would actually call out their farewells to their neighbors. You'd walk them down the street, past the houses with the windows shuttered—the local people always closed their curtains and windows—and you'd hear, *Farewell, Edyta.* Or, *Good-bye, Roza.* Or, *Zofia, look after my cat—please!*

Occasionally, when you were waiting for the last of the Jews to be rounded up, you'd make the ones you had perform—badly, of course—circus stunts. A human pyramid. Walking the clothesline you'd string a few feet off the ground between half-tracks. Basic gymnastics. These little stunts were most fun if you happened to have the rabbi among the lot.

And when the square was completely filled and the Jews were hot and thirsty and weak, then you herded them to a field outside of the town—often at the edge of the very woods where the Judenjagd had commenced. There the men would dig the graves. Sometimes, this talkative, stocky soldier named Joachim continued, taking another long swallow from the bottle of vodka he had commandeered—he was drunk, Uri thought, because no one would tell a person they had done such things if they were sober—you had them strip first so they were stark naked when they started to dig. Then, when the hole was roughly the size of the foundation for a modest house, you would order them to toss their shovels from the pit and lie facedown in the muck.

And they would, they would, Joachim went on, his voice incredulous. They would, they all would, even though they knew they were about to be shot.

And then any of the men who hadn't been ordered to strip and dig would be told to undress and walk into the grave, and they would, too! Occasionally, they'd be told to lie on top of the corpses below them. Facedown. And they walked just like sheep. The women were a little more resistant, especially when they had babes in their arms or toddlers squealing at their shins. They might beg for the lives of their children. But, eventually, they'd go, too.

It wasn't easy work, he said, even though the Jews were never armed. And it was never pleasant. The locals hated the clatter of the machine guns so much that the women would blast the volume on their radios—nothing but static most of the time—so their children wouldn't have to hear the sound of their neighbors being executed. One time, Joachim continued, he had to walk into the pit himself with—dear God—the Ukrainian volunteers (absolute pigs, he said) and shoot the Jews whose bodies were continuing to twitch, and he discovered that he was ankle deep in their blood. There was so much blood, the bodies were actually starting to float.

And so Uri asked him—and he phrased the sentence in a very few words—You did this yourself? They were sitting alone in the kitchen of a house on the outskirts of Łuków on a beautiful autumn evening in September, because their company commander was in the village itself, meeting with their major about the withdrawal that was about to begin from this corner of Poland. Not a retreat, exactly, because they weren't turning and running as fast as they could this time. Ostensibly, they were merely pulling back to a more defensible position.

Still, this fellow soldier named Joachim had grabbed the vodka because he knew—they all knew—that eventually they would run out of more defensible positions and that maniac with the mustache in Berlin would tell them to stand and fight where they were. When Uri had first approached him, he had hoped to discover something more about the Jews shipped east from Schweinfurt because of the man's history with the Einsatzgruppen and the police battalions, and because he, too, was a Bavarian from the neighboring city of Würzburg. Uri had already learned that many of the group had indeed gone to Auschwitz, but some veterans from the First World War and their families had been diverted elsewhere. Some to Theresienstadt in the west, and some to Chełmno in the east. Ostensibly, these other destinations were survivable. At least that was what people said. If his family had gone to Auschwitz, then almost certainly his mother and father were dead. Given the way their health had been deteriorating in their last few months in Schweinfurt, they were probably dead wherever they had gone. But Rebekah? She looked like a fit young woman, and thus was likely to have survived the initial selection at any of these camps. Joachim hadn't known much, but he told Uri that—as far as he knew—at least some of the Jews from Schweinfurt had been sent to work in clothing and munitions factories.

Now Uri repeated his question to this other soldier, unsure whether Joachim hadn't answered him because he was contemplating a response or because he was just so drunk that he hadn't been listening. And so Uri asked again: You did this yourself?

This time Joachim looked him squarely in the eye, and after a beat nodded. And so Uri shot him. He reached for his pistol and blew a hole the size of an orange into the part of Joachim's face where there once had sat a jowly cheek and a champagne cork of a nose, sending the body tilting backward in the chair and onto the floor.

Uri stood, contemplating for a moment whether to bury the body, but then decided there wasn't a reason to bother. The front was unstable and the Polish partisans were taking greater liberties all the time. Other than in Warsaw, where the uprising was being smothered with barbarous ease, the Germans were too busy trying to consolidate their lines and keep the Russians at bay to waste any manpower on the partisans here near the front. And so whenever somebody found this Joachim's body, they were as likely as not to assume it was the work of the partisans. Or the Russians.

Or, perhaps, some reservist named Henrik Schreiner.

Once more Uri would flee, leave this role of Henrik Schreiner behind, and take the name and uniform of some soldier who had just died or whom Uri himself would murder.

Joachim wasn't the first Nazi Uri had killed. Far from it. He wasn't, Uri realized, even the first he had killed in a kitchen.

That distinction belonged to the pair of SS troopers he had met almost a year and a half ago now, within days of the night he had jumped off the train on the way to a death camp.

ANOTHER KITCHEN, another shack. A spring evening, 1943.

Uri was watching the old woman, her back almost parallel to the floorboards in her kitchen, drop the potatoes in the kettle that hung on a rod over the flames in the fireplace. Her mouth was a lipless, toothless maw, and she spoke a dialect that he was relatively sure would have been largely incomprehensible to him even if the woman had done more than mumble or had had any teeth. She reeked of garlic and sweat and what he had come to believe was chicken shit. He presumed that he didn't smell a whole lot better, though he had tried to clean himself up in the small stream he had come across a few kilometers from the railroad tracks. Unfortunately, the water was fetid with oil and gasoline and he had been forced to use one of his socks as a washcloth.

After the potatoes were in the pot, she looked over at him and motioned for him to help himself to one of the limp, rotting stalks of what he thought may once have been celery in a chipped bowl on the table. A film the color of a robin's egg coated the woman's eyes completely, but she insisted she was not totally blind. Still, she was blind enough that she hadn't questioned him, despite his tattered clothing and limp, when he had told her that he was with Organisation Todt and he was researching the area for a railroad spur they were contemplating. She lived alone with a half-dozen chickens in this ramshackle cottage on the outskirts of the village—no electricity or telephone or running water—and he guessed he would be safe here until she ventured into the small hamlet and told someone there was a stranger passing through. He felt a bit, in this regard, like Frankenstein in that moment in the story when the monster is befriended by the blind old man in his house in the woods.

He thought about how he had always liked that part of the book, and how his sister had, too. His family's copy of the novel was tattered and old, because it was one of the stories the Nazi regime had considered decadent. They had banned it, and so Uri's edition had been his father's when he had been a teenaged boy.

He wondered where his family was now. How he could go about finding them. Whether he could go about finding them. Probably not. He realized he had never been so alone in his life, and the sensation was so upsetting—disturbing both because his family was gone and because he felt, on some level, that he had deserted them—that he imagined if he were a child he would just curl up in a ball and wail. He knew he would never have jumped from the train if his parents or Rebekah had been in that cattle car with him.

The woman insisted that she was, like most of her neighbors in the town, a German who had never fully accepted Polish rule for the two decades between the wars. Whether this was true or she was lying to him because she believed he was a Nazi was irrelevant in his mind. No doubt, she was a staunch anti-Semite. But he wouldn't have given a damn if she were the devil himself, because for the first time in four nights he was going to sleep in neither a cattle car nor the woods. Granted, his bed was a rag-filled comforter in a corner of a kitchen that, he speculated, hadn't been mopped in his lifetime. But he was exhausted and, thus, deeply relieved by the prospect of sharing a nook in this cottage with the rats and the spiders and the balls of living dust the size of his fists. He was grateful to this old woman, and if it wouldn't have revealed too much about his life and put himself at risk, he would have thrown himself at her feet and kissed those gnarled toes with mustard-colored talons for nails.

URI AWOKE THE next morning with the sun, and for a moment was unsure where he was. He thought he must have slept oddly for his hip and his knees to be so sore. Then, when he heard the chickens outside the back door, he recalled the woman, the cottage, and the train. Gingerly he stood and looked around for her, wondering if she was outside feeding the birds. She wasn't. Nor did she seem to be planting potatoes in the rows of mounds that marked most of her yard. For dinner last night they had eaten potatoes from last autumn's harvest, eggs, and still more moldering celery. He wasn't sure if this old woman ever ate anything but potatoes and eggs and moldering celery. Still, he had eaten raven-ously. He was glad the woman was blind: His own mother would never have forgiven the ill-mannered barbarity with which he had devoured the meal.

She had an outhouse, primitive he guessed, even by the stan-dards of outhouses, beside the chicken coop, and he was just about to pick his way there through the birds when he heard the voices. Neither, he realized with alarm, was the impenetrable blend of Polish and German and who knew what else that marked the woman's conversation. They were speaking German—his Ger-man. Bavarian German. And, worse, they were male.

He peeked carefully through the remnant of what she had told him was her late husband's nightshirt that served now as a win-dow curtain, and felt the hairs on his neck bristle and a wave of nausea rise up from his abdomen into the back of his throat. There approaching the front door were a pair of soldiers in the black uniforms of the SS. They were young and tall and moving with the assurance of predators in a wood in which they know they are the very top of the food chain. A chicken scuttled across their path, and one of the men kicked it so violently that the bird squawked in pain as it briefly went airborne. Uri fell away from the window, against the wall, realizing that they were about to knock, would hear nothing, and then enter the shack. There was no lock on the door, but he didn't believe it would have mattered if there had been. They would have come in anyway, because the old woman must have ventured into the village this morning while he slept, and either ratted him out on purpose or inadver-tently said something to someone that sounded suspicious. An en-gineer with Organisation Todt? Him? After three days in a cattle car and a night in the woods? Plausible if you're seven years old, maybe.

Now one of them was rapping on the door and calling inside. His voice was crisp, businesslike, brutal. And then he heard the word: *Judenschwein*. They were calling inside for the . . . Jewish

pig. Telling him they knew he was there. They called a second
time. Then the door was sliding open—it couldn't swing precisely because of the way it rubbed against the coarse wooden
boards that served as the floor—and there was absolutely no
place where he could hide, no place where he could run. No train
from which he could jump.

And so, unsure what he really was going to do with it, he
grabbed the poker that was leaning against the fireplace, the only
item he saw with which he might defend himself, and he swung it
like an ax into the first of the two men to come through the door,
not aiming, just twirling, a dervish with a baton, the wrought iron
slamming into the soldier's chest, breaking bones in his rib cage
and knocking the wind from him, as it sent him spiraling back
into his partner. Uri saw the second man, a corporal, reaching for
the handle of the Luger in his holster, but the fellow never had the
time to withdraw it. The next half-minute was a blur in which Uri
would recall what he had done with only the vaguest outlines:
Raising the poker over his head and repeatedly clubbing each of
the soldiers in the skull until he had broken through bone and
begun to mash the steaming gray and white tissue beneath it into
pudding. Using the pointed tip of the instrument to spear the soldier who continued to groan through the abdomen, the metal
poking a hole through his uniform jacket and shirt and impaling
him against one of the floorboards in a geyser of peritoneal fluid
and blood. Kicking—one final repayment for the deaths he had
witnessed in the cattle car and the myriad afflictions and indignities he had endured for about as long as he could remember—
both corpses so violently that they bounced on the wood.

When he was finished he stood back, shaking, on the verge of
hyperventilation. He heard the noise of his rapid, labored breathing, the clucking of the chickens in the yard, and what he thought
for a second was the sound of water dripping. He wondered
briefly if the old woman indeed had a pump somewhere that he
had missed. Then he understood: A thin rivulet the color of claret

was trickling out from beneath the soldier pinned to the floor with the poker and dripping off a warped, sloping timber near the front entrance.

The magnitude of what he had done slowly set in. He had killed someone. He had killed *two* someones. And while he had to presume that they would have killed him first if he'd given them half a chance—or shipped him off to a camp that would have done the dirty work for them—a small part of him couldn't help but wonder about their lives when they weren't wearing those black uniforms and polished black boots. For all he knew, they had wives or girlfriends; they may have had small children waiting for them somewhere beautiful. Dresden, maybe. Or some lovely village on the Rhine. And while it was merely conceivable that he had just killed somebody's husband or lover or father, it was absolutely certain that he had just killed somebody's son. He had just killed *two* somebodies' sons. In addition to snuffing out the lives of these men, he had brought sadness and despair to their mothers. He leaned over the corpses and stared at the mangled remains of their faces, at the pitch of their noses and the clefts in their chins. One had a receding hairline, evident despite the great gaping gouge marks in his skull, which seemed to make him even more human to Uri. The other, his ear dangling by a thin tendril of pinkish flesh to a flap of skin by his jawbone—a leaf, he thought, clinging to a twig in October—had eyebrows so thin they looked girlish.

Imperceptibly, his exhausted gasping had morphed into sobbing, and he fell to his knees and allowed himself to cry.

URI DIDN'T KNOW if the old woman failed to return because she didn't want to be present while he was being arrested or executed, or whether a more prosaic concern had detained her. But it didn't really matter to him. All that counted was that she was still gone and he had cleaned up the cottage as best he could, sopping up the dead soldiers' blood with his own clothing and sweeping their fragments of bone and broken teeth into the hearth. Then he started the hottest fire that he could, hoping to reduce his pants and his shirt and his shoes to ashes, while cremating the pieces of human flesh that he had swept with a broom into the blaze. Meanwhile, he buried the two soldiers in a section of earth where the woman's potato mounds merged with the dirt and feed and excrement of her chickens. One of the soldiers, the one whose uniform had holes in the coat and the shirt, was fully clothed. The other was buried naked.

And when Uri started down the road away from the village, he was wearing the uniform of an SS corporal, and in his breast pocket were the official papers of a soldier roughly his age from Cologne with the alliterative (almost whimsical in Uri's mind) name of Hartmut Hildebrand.

Chapter Three

IN THIS QUADRANT OF THE CAMP THERE WERE ONLY women, all of them young and (once) healthy. The middle-aged women and the old women had been separated out and executed upon arrival. So had the sick. But, Cecile thought, when her mind could focus on anything other than hunger, they—the survivors—all looked like dying old men. Small, stooped, dying old men. Bony old men. Their heads had been shaved and the hair never seemed to grow back. Instead they grew sores that never quite healed. Cecile had worried when she arrived and most of her clothes were taken from her—her angora-trimmed coat, her cashmere sweaters—but it wasn't the loss of a skirt or a blouse that had caused her to panic. It was the confiscation of her purse. Inside it were the pads that she needed because she was menstruating. When she had asked an SS guard what she was supposed to do—standing there naked with two small rivulets of blood trickling down her thighs—the woman had laughed at her, pushed her over the edge of a metal table, and then shoved the handle of her riding crop deep inside her vagina. When she had removed it, she had insisted that another prisoner, a secretary from Troyes with whom Cecile would become friends, lick off the blood.

"Eat, eat," the guard had ordered, "it's the most nutritious food you'll get here."

Since then Cecile had stopped menstruating. Most of the prisoners had. Here she was a twenty-three-year-old woman from a wealthy family in Lyon, and she hadn't had her period in five months. And, obviously, she wasn't pregnant. She hadn't seen her fiancé since he had been taken to a forced-labor unit over a year ago, and now she was being told by the other prisoners that she should give up hope that she would ever see him again. Even if somehow he survived—she told everyone that although he was an accountant, he was strong and in impeccable physical condition—they said that she wouldn't. They said that none of them would.

But she disagreed. After all, she still had good shoes. Very good shoes. It was a small thing, but when life was reduced to conditions this primitive and painful and demeaning, the small things were magnified greatly. Moreover, those shoes were her fiancé's hiking boots, a trace of the man that she loved. Certainly the boots were too big for her, but everyone had warned her to have warm, comfortable shoes at her disposal when they came to take her away. And so she did. She had also brought with her a pair of her crocodile dress flats, largely because she couldn't bear to leave them behind. But, thank God, she had. Thank God, she had brought the boots and the shoes with her. The camp had been running low on the clogs they were distributing to the new prisoners, and so the guards who were processing the trainload from France had told Cecile to keep her boots and then given her crocodile shoes to the prisoner nearest her, that secretary from Troyes.

And so while she was astonished some moments that she had survived this long in these conditions—while she was surprised that anyone had—there were other times when she simply didn't believe that she was going to die here. Death was no abstraction to her: She saw it daily. But her own death? She was young and (once) beautiful, and she had lived a life of such perfect entitlement that her own death was almost completely inconceivable.

A CART WITH DESSERTS. A tart. A torte. A small pot with crème brûlée.

The cart was draped in white linen, and the desserts were surrounding a purple vase overflowing with lilies and edelweiss. The secretary from Troyes was beside it in her mind, reveling in the warmth of a dining room in a restaurant in Paris with her mother and father and sisters, until the wind lashed a piece of broken twig against her eye and she blinked. Instantly the vision was gone, all of it.

Still, she stood where she was as the cold rain continued to soak through her uniform and tattered sweater and fill those bizarre crocodile flats as if they were buckets. Her toes were beyond cold; they had fallen numb. When they were inside, she cherished these shoes, and she understood how much better off she was with them than with those coarse wooden clogs many of the prisoners wore. But not today. Today she was as badly off as everyone else.

Normally they toiled in a clothing factory near the camp, but this afternoon they were working outdoors. The pile of dirt before her was not yet frozen, but it had grown hard, and she decided now that she was too weak to jam the shovel into the mound one more time. She simply couldn't lift it, she could no longer bear to place her foot—so frigid that she felt spikes of pain through the sole of her shoe whenever she pressed it against the rolled shoulder of the spade—on the shovel and force it once more into the earth. Her name was Jeanne, and she feared the only person left in the world whom she trusted, Cecile, was at least fifty or sixty meters farther down the track. Too far to help her. Had she been next to her, Jeanne imagined that Cecile would say something—

find the right words or the right tone—to give her the strength to help dig out these buried railroad ties for another half hour. Or, if there were no words left (at least ones that could possibly matter), to be with her when she expired.

Because, Jeanne concluded, she was going to expire. Right here, right now. With her back to this damaged railway station, a low building with gray stucco walls and a roof—largely collapsed—of blue slate that looked almost like ocean water. She was going to die right beside this angry, quiet, determined prisoner whose name she didn't know and whose teeth were dropping from her mouth as if they were acorns in autumn. It was a certainty. Every moment she wasn't digging was a moment the guards might see her not working. And then they would prod her to dig more, and—when she couldn't—they would shoot her. They shot girls in the fields all the time in the summer and on the way back from the clothing works in the early days of autumn; she'd witnessed at least a dozen and a half die this way. Why not shoot one more here by the station, where last night Allied bombs had buried the track beneath small mountains of earth? Other prisoners would then dig her grave, which couldn't be any more difficult than trying to do the work of a bulldozer to excavate a patch of railway. And Jeanne didn't want to make work any harder for anyone. And so, she thought, let it all end here. Right here. Fine. It had been too much to shoulder for too long.

She was about to open her cold, gnarled fingers—fingers that once were straight and manicured and, in her opinion, one of her best features—and let the shovel slip to the ground, when she felt an arm on her shoulder. She turned and saw Cecile. Somehow her friend had worked her way over to her.

"Dig. They'll bring us back to the camp soon," Cecile murmured, jabbing her own shovel into a looser section of soil. "A few more minutes, that's all. It's almost dark. Just dig. Or look like you're digging."

"I can't," she said, and she began to cry. She dropped the shovel and fell to her knees. Behind her she was aware that Cecile was trying to lift her up, to hoist her off the ground as if she were already a cadaver. The woman's arms were sliding beneath her armpits, the bones in Cecile's fingers blunt rods against her ribs and the bones beneath her shoulders.

"Leave me alone," she sobbed. "Go away! Just leave me here!" But she was, somehow, once more on her feet. Cecile reached down and handed her the shovel.

"Lean on it. Really, just lean on it for a moment. Catch your breath. Then shovel a little bit more. That's all. Then we'll be done. You'll see. Just another few minutes."

Just another few minutes. This was what her life had come down to: A series of small increments to be suffered, brief moments of torture to be endured. A walk across the camp without an SS officer talking to you. Singling you out for . . . something. A day, one more, when the infections in your feet hadn't spread up into your legs. Another morning when you were able to avoid the certain death that marked anyone sick enough or stupid enough to ask to go to the camp hospital. Another few minutes of shoveling.

Yet she was standing again. And holding the shovel. As if the towering mountain of dirt before her were food on a plate and she were the well-fed little girl she'd been twenty years earlier, she used her shovel like a fork and pushed the earth around like a vegetable that didn't interest her.

"I HAD A CAT," Cecile was murmuring in the dark of the barracks. "She had tortoiseshell fur."

"Her name?" asked Jeanne, her voice the insubstantial wisp it became in the night. For a week now, if she tried to speak much above a whisper at the end of the day, she would be reduced to paroxysms of coughing that angered some prisoners and caused others to worry that there was nothing they could do for her.

Either way, Jeanne loathed the way the coughing drew attention to herself.

"Amelie. My fiancé loved her. Carried her around in his arms like a baby."

"Where do you think she is now?"

"I couldn't guess. But she's a survivor. She's alive somewhere."

"In Lyon?"

"I presume."

"My boyfriend used to hate cats."

"What made him change his mind?" Cecile asked.

"He didn't. He died. You know that."

"You know what I mean."

"And you know what I meant. He didn't change his mind. That's all."

Cecile hated the way almost every topic of conversation eventually circled back to grief and death. She had begun with Amelie, her cat, and wound up . . . here. Perhaps this was why almost nobody spoke in the night. What was the point? "Maybe he's alive," she said simply. "You don't know for sure he died."

"I do."

"But how?"

Jeanne sighed so loudly and clearly that for a moment Cecile thought it was the wind. Then: "Because he wasn't like your cat. He wasn't a survivor."

"What did he do?" a new woman nearby asked. Cecile didn't realize anyone else was listening to them.

"He was a jeweler," Jeanne said. "He was much older than me. For a while, he fixed the Nazis' watches. Their ladies' necklaces. He hoped that he could protect us both by being useful."

"How much older was he?"

"He would have been forty-seven this winter."

Cecile smiled, though she knew Jeanne couldn't see her face. "He must have been a friend of your parents. He was, wasn't he?"

"My parents hated the idea I was with him."

"Did he fight in the last war?" this other woman asked Jeanne.

"He did. He was wounded twice. He thought it was pathetic how quickly the boys lost this time. He always felt his generation would have fought much longer."

Cecile thought about this. Her fiancé had fought hard. His whole regiment had fought hard. But one moment the Germans had been on the other side of the river from them, and the next there had been German tanks in their rear and German planes diving upon them and German artillery shells falling among them. What choice had they but to surrender? He had spent nine months in a POW camp before he was repatriated, and allowed, briefly, to resume his accounting practice. Soon after that he had been sent to work in a tire factory, and then—within eighteen months—to the forced-labor unit somewhere in the east. Neither job had demanded his skills as an accountant.

"That was a different war," she said finally, hoping she didn't sound defensive.

"This isn't even a war. It's just a slaughter."

"Soon the Russians will rescue us. They're fighting in Warsaw this very moment, you know."

Jeanne rolled onto her side and groaned. "They're not. That's a rumor. The smoke? The Nazis are just burning the city. Last year they killed the Jews in the ghetto. Now they're killing the Poles."

"Either way, there's fighting. And the Russians will get here."

"Oh, God . . ."

"What?"

"You are always so hopeful. Maybe they'll get here, Cecile. Maybe. But this I know: Unless they get here tomorrow, or maybe the day after that, they won't get here in time for me."

Cecile reached over and ran two fingers in circles over Jeanne's temples.

"That feels good," the woman told her.

"Let me tell you a story," Cecile said, resolved to find a memory she could share that no one, not even Jeanne, would associate with want and sadness and loss.

Chapter Four

MUTTI—IRMGARD WAS HER REAL NAME, BUT EVEN her husband now called her Mutti—was decorating a cake for Helmut with lingonberries while the Polish cook was baking bread. The kitchen was warm from the oven, a great iron box as black as the coal that fueled it. The cook was a woman from the village named Basha who Mutti guessed had been pretty once in a common sort of way but hadn't taken care of herself—she probably didn't get enough exercise or spend enough time outdoors—and thus had grown round and flabby with age. Her eyebrows were as thick and bushy as an old man's, and whiter than daisies. She had been with the Emmerichs almost a year now, arriving each day in the morning and staying until dinner was served.

Helmut, along with all the boys his age in his school, had been drafted into the Volkssturm and would be leaving in two days for training in Bromberg. The students had been told that their group would only be defending their district, but Mutti wasn't sure she believed this. And Helmut himself hoped this wasn't the case: In two months he would be joining the Wehrmacht anyway, hoping for the chance to fight in the sorts of faraway places his older brother, the visiting naval officers, and those English POWs all had seen.

"You know Mr. Emmerich will be next," Basha was saying. "The Volkssturm will want him, too."

"I know," Mutti agreed. The cook wasn't precisely trying to start a fight, she decided, but she was endeavoring to poke at those spots that were the most tender. The Emmerichs already had one son in the army and a second now conscripted into the home guard. The idea that the country would take her husband as well was profoundly dispiriting. Mutti feared that she couldn't run Kaminheim on her own, especially once those workers—hundreds of them, perhaps!—arrived to dig the antitank trench. She had just returned from a shopping trip to Kulm, and even with her ration card it had been impossible to get half the items she needed. She felt that the natural order of things—a husband cares for his wife, and a mother cares for her children—was being upended.

"He fought the Russians twenty-five years ago, right?" Basha was saying.

"Twenty-seven. He rose to captain."

"Then maybe he won't be needed in the Volkssturm."

"No?" she asked, her voice in that single syllable betraying the small kernel of optimism the cook had given her. Perhaps he would be rewarded for his past service by being allowed to remain home. It didn't seem likely: Everyone was supposed to sacrifice for the Fatherland and the war effort, especially now.

"No. They'll give him some men of his own and put him right into the army instead. They'll send him off to face Ivan," Basha continued, referring to the deeply feared Russian army with the oddly pejorative nickname some of the soldiers themselves used.

Mutti looked down at the bowl of frosting on the counter before her so the cook wouldn't see the way she had been taken in by this cruel joke. Dangling such a wondrous hope before her, and then whisking it away. Basha should be ashamed of herself. If Mutti had thought it was even remotely possible to find another cook, she would have fired the woman on the spot.

No, she wouldn't have done that. Mutti knew she was much

fiercer in her mind than she was in reality. Besides, more days than not she actually enjoyed Basha's company, and the woman's relentlessly bleak sense of humor. Lately they had all been feeling the stress as the Russians had driven the army farther toward the borders of the Reich, and maybe they had all grown a little more snappish than usual.

She found three of the candles they used on the Christmas tree every year and placed them among the berries on the top of the cake. The twins' birthday was still months away, but the candles seemed like a cheerful idea to her. And Mutti desperately wanted something to seem cheerful—festive—right now.

"Well, if the army needs Rolf, that's where he'll go," she told Basha, but the idea of her forty-nine-year-old husband being ex-pected to fight the Soviet barbarians terrified her. He could still handle a rifle, but he hadn't shot more than foxes and hares on hunting parties in their park in a quarter century. And the weapons they seemed to use now? So different from that earlier war. So much more effective. So much more lethal. "We are all making sacrifices, aren't we?"

Both women looked up when they saw young Theo listening in the doorway. She thought the boy had taken his flat box with his wooden letters into the den to practice his spelling. This after-noon he was supposed to be working on his words and then, when he was through, with his penmanship. Clearly not. He had over-heard what they had been discussing, and Mutti could see in Basha's eyes that the woman felt a small pang of guilt: It was one thing for her to torment a person she viewed as an entitled Ger-man aristocrat with the notion that her husband was about to be commandeered to fight the Bolsheviks; it was quite another to needlessly frighten a ten-year-old boy.

"Would you like a spoonful of icing?" Mutti asked her son the moment she saw him.

The child stared back at her, but said nothing. He was as shy as his two older brothers and Anna were extroverted, the sort of boy who was picked to play the enemy—the Russian or the American, usually—when the children played their loud, exuberant war games in the school yard. One night, in a moment of weakness before bed, he had let down his guard and confessed to her how most of the time he was just cast aside by the other boys and sent to the corner of the gymnasium or the field they had cordoned off as the POW camp. He would sit there, all alone, while the other children—even the girls as the army nurses with their pretend bandages made from white paper—ran and screamed and played.

"Icing?" she asked again when he remained silent.

Finally he shook his head no, and abruptly turned and dashed from the house. A moment later, through the kitchen window, Mutti saw him racing like a colt on his deceptively long legs— thin and sticklike, even in his wool trousers—along the manicured grass in the yard and then off into the apple orchard where the real POWs were at work.

THEO NO LONGER pretended to be one of Anna's horses when he ran—even when he was very little, he had never imagined he was his own pony, Bogdana, because that animal was too sweet and good-natured to fly across Kaminheim the way the stallions who had been named after castles would—but he did see the stallion Balga in his mind now as he raced away from the house and the kitchen and that witch of a cook. He ran past the elderly guard who more times than not seemed to have his ancient eyes closed, past the English schoolteacher and mason, and past the young men who he guessed hadn't done anything at all before they'd become soldiers. He was vaguely aware they were watching him, their hands full of apples, but he didn't care. He was just running, he was running fast. It was, in his opinion—and in the opinion of his schoolteachers and the women and old men who ran the youth camps where he spent so much of each summer—what he did

best. He wanted to be as far as he could from the idea that his father might be about to be stolen from him, too. His father seemed
to Theo to be the only grown man in the world who didn't seem
to be lecturing him all the time about German honor and German
bravery and German posture (what posture and bravery had to do
with one another was inexplicable to Theo, but apparently they
were related), or didn't find reasons to rap his knuckles with birch
rods. Some days at school he would be so lost in a daydream that
he wouldn't even be aware that his teacher, Fraulein Grolsch, was
standing beside his desk until he would hear the whoosh of the
rod and feel its sting on the bones of his knuckles. Of all the children in the school, there was no one whom Fraulein Grolsch—
the niece of the district's gauleiter and someone who clearly cared
passionately about all that Nazi marching and singing and flag-
waving—seemed to dislike more than him. One day she made him
march around the courtyard for two hours with a Nazi flag on a
shaft so tall and heavy that he could barely lift it. If it fell, she
warned him, she would beat him worse than she had beaten any
child ever. His sin this time? He'd forgotten his pencil box at
home.

Only when he had reached the edge of the orchard did he stop
running and place his hands on his knees, catching his breath. As
he gulped down great puffs of air, he looked up. There he saw two
of the wicker baskets that were used to harvest the apples, and on
the ground beside one was his big sister's navy cardigan sweater.

ANNA LEANED AGAINST one of the trees in the arbored
apple orchard and felt the bark scratch her back through her
blouse. She wondered how angry her parents or Helmut or
Werner would be if they knew that just this moment she had
kissed a Scotsman. She tried to envision the faces of the girls from
her school or her summer camps if she were to tell them. Imagine:
Her first kiss—soft, serious, mouths open and probing—and it

had come from a prisoner of war. One moment they had been harmlessly flirting, as they did often, and the next they were kissing.

"Of all the places you've lived, which is your favorite?" she asked him now. It was not a subject that actually interested her this very second, but she felt she had to say something to fill the quiet that suddenly was enveloping them like a tent.

"Elgin," he said simply.

"And that's in Scotland?"

"It is. Moray Scotland. North. On the ocean. But a very hospitable climate. That's where we lived when we returned from India."

"Are your parents still there?"

He bowed toward her and she thought he was going to kiss her once more, and so she closed her eyes as a lock of his unruly hair fell away from his forehead and she parted her lips. But he didn't kiss her, and—embarrassed and angry—she opened her eyes. He was smiling, his face close to her, one arm straight against the tree behind her.

"You know," he murmured, "I am sure someone could shoot me for kissing you. They wouldn't shoot you, of course. At least I hope they wouldn't. But me? It wouldn't be pretty, Anna."

"Then why did you do it? Has it been that long since you kissed a girl?"

"Well, let's see. There were all those girls while I was being interrogated in France. And then there were the ones the guards brought into the prison camp for us. And, of course, there are just girls everywhere here on your estate. So, not all that long, really."

She ducked beneath his elbow and gave herself some distance from him. She wished he had simply kissed her.

"You didn't tell me: Do your parents still live in . . ."

"Elgin."

"Yes. That place. On the ocean."

"My mother does. My father died."

"How?"

"He drowned."

The violence of his death jolted her, and she wasn't sure what to say. Then, after a moment, she told him honestly, "I'm sorry. I don't know what I'd do if something happened to my father—or to Mutti. Was he near the beach?"

"No. Nowhere near it, actually. Middle of the ocean."

She saw behind him a dark red apple at the end of a spindly branch. It was enfolded by leaves and swaying ever so slightly in the wind. She understood she should leave this line of questioning alone, but she couldn't. And then, perhaps because it was better for her to speak aloud her conjecture than allow it to wallow inside her, she said, "It was a U-boat, wasn't it?"

"It was."

"You must hate us."

"I just kissed you."

"Still. You must . . ."

"I try not to generalize with my hate. Certainly my father never did."

"Your mother?"

"She's another story, a very interesting woman. Very complicated. *She* is quite capable of generalizing hate. As the wife of a colonial administrator, I gather, she started out rather well. But she managed to see slights everywhere. Especially when we were in India. I was just a boy, but even I could tell that she wasn't happy there. Didn't like being an outsider. Couldn't abide the heat. Still, she's resourceful—a bit like your Mutti. These days, she's a very tough war widow. Bitter. But, in all fairness, she is also extremely capable."

"I presume she hates us."

"Well, in her opinion you killed her husband and now you've taken her only son prisoner. So, yes, I'd say she doesn't have particularly generous feelings toward the Germans these days. But if she knew you, Anna, I think she might be slightly more forgiving.

Not a lot, mind you. But you, I think, would at least give her pause."

He leaned toward her again, but this time she kept her eyes open until she saw Callum close his and she felt his lips pressing gently against hers.

THE NAVAL OFFICERS left the Emmerichs' once they had finished gouging the long, painful-looking slices from the skin of the earth at Kaminheim, and Helmut went to the parlor in the manor house that night a little unmoored. Everyone felt that way: Suddenly, the very soil in which the family had grown sugar beets and apples and corn had been upended. And for what purpose? An antitank trench. And as deep as those great, sluicing grooves were, they were mere runnels compared to the chasms the naval officers said would replace them. Imagine, the captain had explained, the difference between a toddler's little dig at the seashore and an actual moat. After all, he'd added ruefully, these would have to stop tanks.

Helmut knew that he wasn't alone in his unease. Everyone felt a little anxious. But he also surmised that he was, justifiably, more anxious than the rest of his family—with the exception, no doubt, of poor Mutti—because he was the one who was leaving the next morning to join a Volkssturm unit in Bromberg. The reality was starting to sink in: He would no longer be a boy in short pants with a Hitler Youth dagger. He was about to become a soldier. And then, assuming he survived the next few months, he would graduate from the Volkssturm to the Wehrmacht. From a mere armband to a full uniform. To real training.

He thought it interesting that his mother had responded to the reality that her second son was now a man by baking him a cake and decorating it with lingonberries and candles—as if he were still a boy. Of course, those lingonberries had been delicious. Nevertheless, he felt as if the seriousness of what loomed before him had been diminished. It was as if Mutti didn't want to accept the fact that he, too, was about to become a soldier.

Alone now, he leaned over the table with the family's maps in the parlor. For over three years he had tracked the progress of the armies in the east, as they had neared Moscow and Leningrad and almost (but not quite) conquered Stalingrad. With toothpicks and colored paper he had made small flags denoting the divisions whose victories he would hear about on the radio, and whose defeats he would glean from rumor and innuendo and the simple fact that (suddenly) they seemed to be fifty or seventy-five kilometers west of where he had understood them to be. Occasionally, the German broadcasters would explain casually that the army was straightening its line or consolidating its front, but Helmut understood that was just a euphemism for withdrawal or outright retreat. It was clear that the Germans were not simply losing—Lord, that had been apparent for at least a year and a half—but that the end was near. The Russians were just east of Warsaw, and that summer there had been some sort of uprising inside the city itself. The Polish Home Army and Communists attempting to retake it block by block, he gathered. And while the rebellion was being successfully quashed—for all he knew, it was over now—the fact remained that the Germans there had their backs to the very same river that he had grown up with: the Vistula. Warsaw was a mere 180 kilometers to the southeast.

Only last year, nineteen months ago, the fighting had been as much as two thousand kilometers to the east. Of course, nineteen months ago they had also been fighting in North Africa. And France was a part of the Reich. As was Italy—the whole boot. Now Paris and Rome were gone, and eventually Warsaw would be, too.

He thought of his brother near Budapest—another of the great cities that would, he imagine, fall into the Allies' hands soon enough. Werner would have great scars on both of his legs for the rest of his life, a result of the burns he had endured when the tank on which he had been riding had been shelled and caught fire. Helmut didn't like the idea of Werner in a prison camp somewhere, but it crossed his mind that it wouldn't be the worst thing to happen to his brother at this point in the war if he was captured. Look at the way his own family was treating the Englishmen the stalag had sent them: They were more like houseguests than POWs. Surely the British or the Americans would treat his brother that kindly. Unfortunately, unless Werner's division was transferred to the Siegfried Line or Holland or Italy, that wasn't likely. If Werner was captured, it would be by the Russians, and that meant a prison camp in Siberia—if he didn't die first on the way there. Besides, it was almost inconceivable that his brother would ever wind up a POW: Werner would die fighting.

Helmut hoped he would die that way, too.

If, of course, he had to die.

In a perfect world, they would somehow find a way to repel the Russians and, just maybe, he himself would do something heroic in a great, final battle. Even though the Russians were on the verge of capturing Warsaw, it still didn't seem quite possible to him that these barbarians eventually would brutalize all of Europe.

From the ballroom on the other side of the house he heard the sound of music: Mutti was playing the piano and the Scotsman was playing the accordion. His uncle's accordion. If the naval officers hadn't left, there would be dancing, and he would have had to polka and waltz with one of Anna's friends: Frieda or Gudrun. Here, at least, was one small consolation to their departure: He thought Anna's friends were juvenile and frivolous—insufficiently committed to the war effort—and he didn't much like them (though lately, he had to admit, he did see the appeal of having a girl as pretty as Gudrun in your arms when you danced, and feeling her beautiful, small hands in yours).

He found it interesting that his father was allowing this

Callum so much latitude. The other POWs had gone back to the bunkhouse for the night, where they belonged. Even their captain, that schoolteacher, didn't seem to want Callum spending so much time in the house. It was, in the schoolteacher's opinion, fraternizing with the enemy.

Well, yes.

Perhaps that was precisely why his father was not simply allowing it, but was actually condoning it. Encouraging it. Maybe he was, in some way, trying to drive a wedge between Callum and his fellow POWs. Create a rift. Give them something to talk about other than, Helmut guessed, escaping.

Or, he wondered, did his parents actually like Callum? Clearly Anna did.

Helmut understood that his family didn't know the party leader well in their district, and had only met the governor once. This was farm country and the area was vast. But he knew that his father had never been impressed with either the party leader or the governor in their few face-to-face encounters. Nor did he approve of the way the district was being managed. Both officials had been brought in from Bavaria, the party leader actually taking control of a farm that previously had been owned by an officer in the Polish army, and running it about as poorly as humanly possible. His father had once called the two of them "real Nazis," and he had meant this as an insult: In his opinion, they were uneducated and vulgar and coarse, and they didn't know how to handle an agrarian landscape at all. They didn't understand farmers at all. It was an insult to the region.

And they certainly wouldn't approve of the way a Scot POW was ingratiating himself into the Emmerich family.

One time, Helmut recalled, almost a year ago now, his teacher had pulled him aside and asked him all sorts of questions about his father. The teacher was an older man who took his party membership very seriously, and thought Rolf Emmerich did not treat his own with sufficient gravity. The teacher couldn't fight anymore, but he sure could march—and demand that his students march. Apparently, he felt that Rolf Emmerich had greeted him on the street with an insincere *Heil Hitler*. Had felt the salute was halfhearted at best, and downright condescending at worst. As if his father thought the very greeting had become a joke. This was what he had told Helmut, anyway. But it was also painfully clear to Helmut that the fellow had heard or overheard a lot more about his father's attitudes toward the party. Toward some of Hitler's lieutenants. Father was usually careful about what he said in public, and the truth was that he was of two minds about National Socialism. Certainly things had gotten better for most Germans. At least at the beginning. And while he wished that Poland and Germany had been able to negotiate a peaceful return of the German lands to the Fatherland instead of having to resort to war, he was as grateful as Mutti that Kaminheim was back where it belonged. But there was also an awful lot about National Socialism that he considered either ripe for ridicule or deeply troubling. The replacement of the old Christmas carols with those ridiculous songs about the solstice and motherhood? Absurd. The fixation on the Jews? Inexplicable at first. Then alarming. It was evident by the teacher's line of questioning that at some point his father had been indiscreet—perhaps made fun of those new song lyrics or the way one of the district's little Hitlers had been screaming at some rally—and the word had gotten back to this teacher. The salute, Helmut guessed, was only the last straw.

For a moment Helmut had paused in thought with the teacher, as they had sat alone in the classroom. It wasn't that he was contemplating actually validating the teacher's concerns or turning his own father in—even though there were moments when he considered his father's ambivalence about their government and their führer disloyal. It seemed to Helmut that the world had always been against Germany: jealous of its people and its culture, and determined to crush both. The country was fighting now for its very survival, and the last thing the führer needed was Rolf Emmerich badmouthing the party or party officials. Still, the primary reason that Helmut had sat there silently for seconds was the sheer unreality of the moment, the idea that here before him was an honest-to-God informant. Someone who ratted people out to the Gestapo. Perhaps there were those who needed ratting out. Shirkers and spies and people who really did want to undermine the regime. But not his father. And so Helmut had taken a breath and composed himself and, with as simple and unrevealing a face as he could assume, told his teacher that his father must have been distracted that day on the street when he saluted, and that his father cared deeply about the government and about the führer. Fearful that he hadn't said enough, he added quickly that they even had their signed photograph of the führer matted with red silk and framed, and it hung on the wall of their parlor. This was the truth. What he would have said if he were going to be scrupulously honest was that it hung there because his father was rarely in the parlor: He was more likely to be in the den or the dining room or the ballroom. Greeting a guest or a business associate in his office. It was Mutti who had cherished that image of Adolf Hitler—his mother had once had the sort of crush on the führer that was not uncommon among her middle-aged female friends—and it was Mutti who savored the light in the parlor. Still, he had said enough. The teacher let him go, and suggested they could speak again if Helmut had anything new to report: If he had heard or seen anything—heard or seen anything about anyone, not merely his father—that the teacher should know about.

As Helmut studied the placement of the flags of the German and Soviet armies on the map and the way the Reich was narrowing in its old age, he took some comfort from the reality that the party leader and the governor—his own teachers, even—clearly had far more pressing issues before them right now than the way the Allied prisoners were being treated at Kaminheim, or whether his father saluted people on the street with ample enthusiasm.

BEFORE BREAKFAST, when the sun had barely risen and the fog was only beginning to burn off the fields, Anna took Theo with her to the horse barn and together they saddled Balga and Theo's small pony, Bogdana. Anna honestly wasn't sure she had been as happy in years as she was in those final days of that harvest, and she felt almost flighty that morning. The two siblings rode past the fields where any moment the men would begin pulling the last of the sugar beets from the soil, past the orchards where Anna would join them in the afternoon, and past the pond where in August she had swum with her friends and her brothers those hot, steaming days when they hadn't been hiking or away at their summer camps. Anna was wearing a white linen shirt that she had ironed before going to bed last night, and the jodhpurs in which she thought she looked prettiest from behind. Never before had she worried about what she was wearing when she and her little brother had gone riding, but never before had there been a man at Kaminheim who had interested her in quite the way Callum had. She hoped she might see him—and, yes, he would see her—when they returned to the barn.

As they were riding through the marsh on the far side of the pond, Theo pulled his pony to a stop and called out to her.

"Yes, Theo?" she said, reining in Balga. The horse was dying to run—she could feel his muscles tensing beneath his satin coat—and Anna had the sense that when they had cleared the marsh she was going to have to let the animal air it out. Theo would be fine for a few minutes on his own.

"What will happen if the Russians get here?"

"The Russians won't get here," she said reflexively. She wasn't sure she believed this, but she could hear the fear in her little brother's voice and felt the need to reassure him.

"But how do you know? How can you be so sure?"

Anna watched the pony, more plump than was probably healthy, snitch at a clump of high grass.

"I guess I don't know. Not for certain. But . . ."

"Tell me."

"Well, it's one thing for them to take back the land we had conquered. It's quite another to take our land from us. Just imagine how fiercely Werner would be fighting if he were defending this country right here."

Theo nodded and seemed to be taking this in. Then: "They might take Father, you know."

For a moment Anna wasn't sure who *they* were. Did Theo mean the Russians? She must have looked puzzled, because Theo continued, "The army. Maybe the Volkssturm, but maybe the Wehrmacht."

"Father? He's already done his duty—and that was a very long time ago. He's . . . old," she said, and as that last word formed on her lips she couldn't help but smile in bemusement. Their father? In the army? He was strong and disciplined and smart, but these days he was a businessman and farmer. He ran the estate. She couldn't see him enduring the sorts of misery that had seemed to dog Werner. She didn't see why he should have to. "Why would you ever think such a thing?" she added.

"Yesterday I heard Mutti and Basha talking."

"About Father leaving for the army?"

"Yes!"

She felt Balga once more straining beneath her and motioned to Theo that they needed to keep moving. When they reached the drier land on the far side of the marsh they began to trot, and over the sound of the horses' hooves she called back to her brother, "I'm sure if they did take him, it would just be for desk work. Right here, maybe. Or in Kulm. But he wouldn't be fighting like Werner."

"Or Helmut soon," Theo muttered.

"Yes."

"But if Father does leave, there will hardly be any grown-up men left here at all. And that means I . . ."

"Go on."

"It means I would have to be the man of the house. And I'm not ready for that. I know I'm not."

"Oh, Theo, sweetie, you don't have to worry about such things!" she told him, working hard to suppress a small smile so he wouldn't think she was laughing at his expense when all she was feeling was affection for him. To her relief, he was still young enough to allow his vulnerabilities and his fears a small voice. All the other males—even the boys Theo's age—were already growing into blustering strongmen. Powerful Aryans who didn't dare admit to anyone that they just might be scared. "Everyone loves you as you are," she went on. "No one expects you suddenly to be older than ten."

"But I could be if I had to be. Don't you think so?"

"Of course I think so."

"I just don't want to if I don't have to."

"No, I agree. Who would? Besides, there will always be the prisoners," she said, only half-serious, hoping to get a small laugh out of Theo.

Instead, however, her brother told her in a voice that was completely earnest, "No, they're leaving the day after tomorrow. I heard Father on the phone yesterday!"

Instantly she pulled her horse to a stop and turned to face the boy. "What?"

"They're being sent back to their prison camp."

"No, that's not possible—"

"Yes, it is possible," he said, his tone growing defensive because she hadn't believed him. "Even . . ."

"Tell me!"

"Even your boyfriend, Callum! I'm telling you, they're all going to be taken away!"

If she hadn't needed both hands on the leather reins, she thought she might have slapped him for that remark about the Scotsman. She'd never hit her brother before, but there was always a first time. "He's not my boyfriend," she said simply, allowing a little sharpness into her tone.

Theo looked away. He didn't believe her, but clearly he had no plans to argue about this. Whether Callum was her boyfriend was the least of his concerns. "They're almost done with the harvest," he went on, an apparently helpful clarification on his part.

"Who was Father talking to?" she asked.

"I don't know."

"The agriculture minister? The commandant of the prison camp?"

"I said, I don't know."

"Well, just because the harvest is finished doesn't mean Father can run Kaminheim with only you and me and Mutti to help him. He certainly can't. And—"

"And Father will be gone, too!" Theo snapped, turning back toward her. "It will just be the three of us! That's what I mean: I'm going to have to be the man of the house!"

She felt herself growing a little exasperated, and offered a litany of the different men from the village—the farrier, the veterinarian, the logger, the mechanic, the handyman, the chimney sweep—who would appear periodically at the estate.

"Have you seen Mr. Schenck lately? Or Mr. Lutz?" Theo asked, referring to the veterinarian and the mechanic.

"No, of course I haven't. We haven't needed them."

"They're gone!"

"What do you mean they're gone?"

"I heard Father! Mr. Schenck is in the army now and Mr. Lutz has been taken to some factory in Germany. They're taking everybody!"

The contentment—the outright happiness—she had been experiencing at the horse barn had evaporated completely, along with the final vestiges of the morning fog, and she spurred Balga forward. Behind her she heard Theo urging on Bogdana. She realized she would have to slow her own horse when they reached the apple orchard so Theo could catch up to her before they returned to the grounds, and this only annoyed her further.

Chapter Five

THE WORKERS FROM ORGANISATION TODT NEVER CAME.
The long, meticulous lines the naval officers had scratched into
the eastern edges of Kaminheim slowly disappeared beneath wind
and sleet and the winter grasses that sprung up even as the days
grew despairingly short and the temperature in the evenings fell
below freezing. There would be no deep crevasses gouged from
the clay, no strategically placed gun emplacements, no firing pits
from which anyone—boys closer in age to Theo than Helmut—
might discharge their *panzerfausts* in desperation at stalled Russian armor.

No one from Todt called or wrote to tell the Emmerichs why,
but as October faded along with the sunlight into November, they
all presumed there simply weren't enough men. Apparently, there
weren't even enough prisoners. The dike that was the Greater
Reich was collapsing in so many spots, there were so many
breaches on so many fronts, that the need to construct an antitank
trench in their corner of the district was all but forgotten. Anna
told Theo that the reason the trench wasn't being built was that it
was no longer necessary: Their armies were stemming the Russian advance far to the east, and he needn't be afraid. It wasn't true,
of course, but it made them both happy when she verbalized the

notion, especially now that news of the slaughter in the recaptured village of Nemmersdorf had reached them.

And that news had reached them in every conceivable way the Ministry of Propaganda could imagine. Though Mutti had tried to shield her children from the stories, the tales of rape and mutilation were on the radio, in the newsreels, and in the press. There were leaflets about the slaughter distributed along with ration cards; there were posters on the walls of the villages and nailed to the trees along the roads. The underlying message always was clear: This—*this unspeakable brutality, this unparalleled violence*—is what awaits our women and children if we don't fight to the death to preserve our precious Fatherland. For weeks, Nemmersdorf was all anyone could talk about.

Meanwhile, the men from the village continued to leave as the weather grew cold. When Father needed the logger to help clear land for firewood because coal was growing more rare than gold, he was told that the fellow was gone, taken away at gunpoint in a truck along with his brothers and son. There was no sweep to prepare the manor house's many chimneys for the winter, and so Werner, home from Budapest in October for three days of leave, found the chains and brushes and spent his few days at Kaminheim climbing over the slate on the peaks and the eaves to clean the chimneys him-self. No one in the town had any idea where the chimney sweep had been taken.

Soon after the naval officers left, most of the prisoners and their aged guard were taken away, too, returned to the stalag where they had spent the summer. The one exception? Callum Finella. Certainly there were martinets in the district, such as Helmut's schoolteacher, who questioned Rolf Emmerich's patriotism or wondered if he was a party member only because it made it easier to run the business that was Kaminheim; but his farm also produced a great deal of food and he was part of a distinguished Aryan family. He had just enough clout that the authorities heard his plea for slave labor—just as, before that, Rolf had heard the pleas of his only daughter for Callum. She insisted that the two of them were friends and nothing more, and he acted as if he believed her. Mutti did, too. And since the needs of his estate matched the wants of his daughter—since, in his experience, there had to be another man on the farm capable of the heavy lifting that was demanded daily on an estate the size of Kaminheim, even in winter—he had argued convincingly that one of the prisoners should remain in his possession. The presence of the individual was going to be especially critical, Rolf realized, once he was pressed into service.

And that date came in the middle of November. Precisely as Basha, their cook, had speculated, Rolf Emmerich, though forty-nine years old, returned to the Wehrmacht. Not the Volkssturm. The army. Initially, his uniform had made his younger son Helmut envious, since Helmut would have to be satisfied with a mere Volkssturm armband until he turned eighteen in December and would graduate into the army, as well.

No one seemed to care that this meant a POW was left alone with two women, a boy, and a part-time cook on the estate outside of Kulm. No one worried for the two women because, after all, this Callum Finella was British—not Russian. And the Emmerichs (and their friends and relatives on the neighboring estates) had no idea why they were even at war with the British.

Might he try to leave the grounds of Kaminheim and escape? It was possible. But why would he? they asked themselves. If he went west he would only be going deeper into Germany and the likelihood that he would be shot as an escaped POW. And if he went east? Dear God, no one went east. All that was east were the Russians.

CALLUM HAD JUST wedged the hay bale against the barn wall and was starting down the stairs from the loft when he heard the boy singing. Theo's voice hadn't begun to change yet, and so it was still a lovely soprano. He was singing a folk song, something about a horse and some clouds, as he was mucking the stalls. For a long moment Callum stood perfectly still on the wooden stairs, listening to the child. He had studied French and German in school and had learned a fair amount more since he'd been taken prisoner—most in the last few months under Anna's tutelage—but he was still not completely sure what the song was about. When he finally moved, the step groaned loudly and Theo heard him and went quiet.

"Don't stop because of me," Callum reassured him, jumping down the last few steps onto the barn floor. Theo wouldn't meet his eyes, and he realized the boy was embarrassed. "You have a wonderful voice."

Now Theo looked up at him, but he was wary. He was in his pony's stall, shoveling methodically.

"You ever sing in a choir?" Callum asked, when the boy remained silent.

At this he shook his head.

"Well, you should. A church choir, maybe."

"We don't go to church anymore," he said evenly. Then he unhooked the stall door and emerged with the cart and his shovel, walking right past Callum as if he were invisible and into the stall for one of the draft horses.

"I rarely sing, but only because I can't," he confessed to Theo. "I wish I could."

The child threw him a bone and nodded, but Callum could tell he was only being polite. And so he was about to leave and get on with his other chores, when Theo surprised him. "I like the old songs," he said. "Not the new ones they make us sing at school or they teach at the Jungvolk meetings. Helmut sings them much better than I do."

"I doubt that."

"He does. Werner, too. They have much bigger voices and can really sing the marching songs. I don't . . ."

"You don't what?"

He shrugged.

"Go ahead, Theo. You can tell me."

"I don't like the marching songs."

"I don't blame you. Seems to me they're just drinking songs anyway. You always want to sing them with a stein in your hand."

"But everyone else likes them."

"I just told you: I don't."

The boy looked at him, but said nothing.

"You know, Theo, you don't need to apologize to the world that you're not Helmut or Werner."

"What do you mean?"

"I mean," he said, realizing that he had just initiated a conversation he hadn't anticipated a moment ago, "that you seem to talk a lot about what you're not. Who you're not." He leaned over the wooden half-wall of the stall, noticed the pyramidal clumps of manure in the straw.

"So?"

"So? Well, you're a good boy in your own right. Take your singing. Maybe your voice isn't as loud as your brothers'. I have no idea. But there isn't a boys' choir in Scotland that couldn't find a use for a voice like yours. You'd be a soloist."

Theo sighed and blew on his hands. "I don't seem to like the things everyone else does."

"I don't either."

"No?"

"No. And it seems to me, no one thinks they like the right things at your age," Callum said, though he guessed he was lying. But he also knew that ten-year-old boys always had the potential to bully the odd duck, and that tendency was undoubtedly exacerbated in this corner of the globe. He had a feeling the master race didn't have a lot of patience for a kid like Theo.

"Werner and Helmut were always popular. Somehow, they always knew their duty and did things correctly. People liked them. Students, teachers."

"Is that what you've been told?"

"It's what I know."

"I'll bet if you asked them, they'd tell you they never felt like they did everything right. Anyone who thinks he does—and this is one of my favorite words of yours—is a *dummkopf*. But that really doesn't matter. You're Theo. That's all that counts. And you don't ever have to apologize for who you are."

The boy seemed to contemplate this. Ran his free hand along the well-muscled shoulder of the enormous horse.

"Besides," he added. "Think of all the things you do better than anyone."

"There isn't anything I do better than anyone," Theo said.

"You are a very fast runner."

"I guess."

"And you ride very well."

"Just ponies."

"Someday it will be horses."

"I hope so."

Outside the barn he heard the wind, and high above them the weather vane swiveled with a shriek. The wind was coming from the north.

"I know so," he told the boy, though he really knew nothing of the sort. "In the meantime, you sing. And don't worry that you're not Helmut or Werner. You're Theo, and that should be good enough for anyone."

He felt a twinge of self-satisfaction after he'd spoken. Perhaps he had buoyed the boy's spirits after all. But then, his head down and his small shoulders hunched in his coat, Theo went to the rear of the stall and silently cleaned up the animal's droppings.

SHE CLOSED HER EYES, her mouth against the side of his neck. His skin was warm against her lips, and the collar from his shirt tickled her just beneath her chin if she moved. And so she didn't move. She remained there, perfectly still, aware only of the metronomic rise and fall of his chest as he breathed, and the sound of the logs that were being consumed by the flames in the fireplace. She was afraid to open her eyes, because the moment—the feel of his hand on her waist, his fingers firm against the flesh of her hip because her blouse had come untucked—was exquisite. She had never before felt a man's hands on the skin near her waist, and she could feel her whole body starting to flush. It was as if she had a high fever, except there was no pain. There was only eagerness (though precisely for what, she could admit to no one, not even to herself) and her sense that this was the start of something wondrous and new.

They were standing now in the bay window in the ballroom that overlooked the edges of the hunting park. Mutti and Theo and Basha were shopping in the village, and the two of them had Kaminheim to themselves. Anna had seen Callum carting the furniture from their terrace into the shed beside the house, and beckoned him inside when the sleet and hail had started falling in earnest. There were many chores that had to be completed regardless of the weather, but bringing the outdoor tables and chairs in for the winter wasn't among them in Anna's opinion. Especially with everyone else away for the afternoon.

Finally she felt him pulling her even closer into him, dancing her body so that they were facing each other. She opened her eyes and looked up, her breasts against his chest, and—without even thinking about what she was doing—she moved her legs so that they were surrounding one of his thighs, pressing her groin through her skirt against the hard muscle there. She thought he was about to kiss her, but instead he brought his lips to her ear and whispered simply, "You know, I dream of you."

She did not know this, but she nodded, savoring the way his breath had given her goose bumps along her arms, and he continued, "I haven't dreamed of Scotland. Not lately. I've dreamed only of you."

...dered telling him that she dreamed of him, too, but ... be a lie and she didn't want to lie to Callum. But she ... of him all the time—while assisting Basha in the ki..., while mucking the horse stalls and feeding the animals, while sewing with her mother or reading with Theo in the evening—and so she confessed this to him. She told him how often she imagined being like this in his arms, the two of them alone, and how frequently she recalled their few, brief kisses in the apple orchard.

"Like this?" he asked, and then he kissed her chastely, a tease, barely parting his lips when he brought them to hers.

"No," she said, emboldened. "Like this." And she stood on her toes in her pumps and separated his lips with her tongue, burrowing and exploring the moistness and warmth inside his mouth.

There was a part of her that understood this was wrong, all wrong. So wrong that she was shaking. Trembling now in his arms as they kissed. But then she decided that her quivering had nothing to do with the reality that Callum was a prisoner and she was violating her family's trust by inviting him into the house now. By making love to him here in the ballroom. It had nothing to do with the reality that he was the enemy. Her trembling had nothing to do with anything, she concluded, but the fact that she was approaching eighteen and she was in the arms of a handsome and interesting man who was twenty.

BOYS, IT SEEMED to Anna, grew up faster than girls. They were sent off to war and vastly more was expected of them. She and Helmut were the same age, and yet he was treated as more of an adult than she was. Apparently this wasn't the case everywhere. She had the distinct sense that women had more responsibilities in the cities—and in other countries, even the Soviet Union. And, of course, there was no place in the world more barbaric than Russia.

"Here, look at this one," her mother was saying to her now as she sat at the edge of her parents' bed, a small mountain of her mother's old clothes rising beside her. Her mother's voice was filled with mirth as she showed her another of her dresses from the 1920s. "I wore it when your father and I went to Berlin. Once I wore it to the opera in Danzig, but I felt completely out of place."

Anna couldn't imagine her mother wearing a dress like this: It was a sheath of silk and it must have barely reached her knees. The straps were thin and the hem was trimmed with sequins and fringe. It was a crimson more lush than the red on the Nazi flag.

"It's very pretty," she told Mutti. "You must have turned everyone's head."

"Well, I certainly turned your grandmother's head. She gave me one of her dubious sniffs when she saw me wearing it. Couldn't believe I would appear in public in such a thing. But it was what many of us wore in those days when we wanted to look like we belonged with the city girls."

They were taking her mother's old clothes from her dressing room closet and deciding which ones could be ripped apart and the fabric refashioned into something more appropriate. They had decided spontaneously that they were sick of their old dresses and would have to sew new ones.

"I don't know if there's enough material here for another dress," she told Mutti, running her fingertips lightly over the frock.

"I agree. Perhaps we can turn it into a skirt for you—minus, of course, those ridiculous sequins," she said. After a brief moment she added, "I have very fond memories of this dress. Your grandmother thought it looked like a slip, but your father certainly liked it. Those were fun days."

"And nights, apparently."

"Anna!" her mother said, feigning embarrassment, but Anna could tell that she was far more delighted by the memories than she was scandalized by her daughter's innuendo.

"I only meant those years must have been a lovely period. Better days than now."

"Yes, they were."

"Were you ever jealous of those city girls?"

"Sometimes. They all seemed so glamorous if you came from a community such as ours."

"If I ever said I wanted to go to Berlin to be, I don't know, a secretary, what would you say?"

"I would say no," Mutti said, but she sat down beside Anna on the bed and turned her attention squarely from the dresses to her daughter. "No sane parent these days would send her child to Berlin—or to any city. Parents who live in the cities are trying to send their children away. Get them as far away from the bombs as they can."

"But after the war? Would you mind if I went to work in a city after the war?"

Mutti seemed to think about this. "I would. Your father would. We would miss you. But whether we would or we could prevent you? That would be something else. Now, you tell me: Why would you want to? This is the first I've heard of such a thing."

"Well, it's the first time I've contemplated such an idea. I'm not sure if, in the end, I ever would want to."

"Is there something particular behind this notion?"

She sighed. "Maybe it was the naval officers. And the POWs. And Callum. They have all seen so much of the world, they have all been to so many places. They all seem so sophisticated compared to me. And it's not merely that I feel sheltered. It's that I feel frivolous."

"Do you think I have led a frivolous life?"

"Not at all. It just seems . . ."

"Go on."

"It just seems there is a very big world beyond Kaminheim."

Mutti looked at her with uncharacteristic intensity, and Anna couldn't decide whether her mother's eyes had grown wide because she was anxious or defensive. "There is, my dear. There is. But let us hope you don't have to see it any sooner than necessary."

"I DON'T FEEL disloyal precisely," Callum was saying to Anna another afternoon, when Mutti and Theo had gone to Uncle Karl's estate twenty-five kilometers to the east and once again left them alone at Kaminheim. They had just thrown another log into the fireplace, and the ice that was pelting the windowpanes seemed very far away. "I feel guilty. Horribly guilty. I am eating as well as you and your family and—"

"You think we are eating well?" she asked him, incredulous. They were on the floor before the fire, and she was leaning against his chest, her body between his legs. She knew they would have to get dressed soon, but she couldn't bear the idea that their time alone was just about over. She felt a little giddy. Mature, too. But still blissfully dizzy. Her hands rested upon his bent, oddly hairless knees, and she imagined for a brief second they were the oarlocks on the small rowboat the family owned for their pond.

"Well, perhaps you don't eat like you did before the war—"

"We don't eat like we did even a year ago."

"But you still eat considerably better than a POW. And so I am eating dramatically better than I would have if your father hadn't finagled a way for me to remain here. Plus, I am sleeping in a bunkhouse, not the barracks of a prison camp—"

"And that will change. Any day now it will get much, much colder, and that bunkhouse was never meant to be used in the winter. Besides, it's absurd for you to sleep out there alone when we have nothing but bedrooms here in the house. I'll talk to Mutti tonight."

"That's not exactly my point. My accommodations are fine."

"But you will move into the house. I'll see to that."

"My point," he said, wrapping her more tightly in his arms, "is that your family may need me, but nothing I've done here has been especially onerous. A little heavy lifting. Cleaning some farm machinery. A bit of carpentry. And so a part of me feels as if I've deserted my mates—that I should be enduring their trials with them."

"You didn't desert them. That would mean you had a choice. You didn't. Father wanted someone here and you were picked."

"Still . . ."

She turned and craned her neck to face him. "I think I should be angry that you're not more grateful," she said playfully. "I doubt most POWs had an afternoon like you just had."

He moved out from behind her. Gazed at her. Pushed her bangs off her forehead, still a little slick with perspiration. "Oh, I doubt any did."

"And so?"

He was, much to her surprise, blushing. When he didn't say anything, she added, "Maybe you'll protect us from the Russians. Maybe that's why you're here."

"The Russians are British allies, my dear. It's one thing for me to replace the spark plugs on a tractor; it would be quite another for me to take up arms against my comrades. There's a word for that, you know: *treason*. And armies, mine included, frown upon it."

"The Russians are not your comrades."

"You know they are."

"The Russians are the comrades of no civilized person. And you are very civilized—even if you do take advantage of German farm girls while their mothers are away for the day." She tried to add a cosmopolitan pout to her voice when she spoke; she hoped she sounded like a flirtatious adult. But then she saw the look of trepidation on Callum's face, and she realized that inadvertently she had hit a nerve: He honestly did feel guilty. He really did have misgivings.

"The Russians are doing horrible things," she continued simply.

"Everyone has been doing horrible things," he corrected her. "We both know your army was not especially charitable toward the women and children in Warsaw when they finished quashing the uprising there this past autumn," he added. Nevertheless, he brought her hands to his lips and kissed them. Then he stood up and, much to her disappointment, looked around for his clothes.

"You're not leaving, are you?" she asked.

"I am. But only with great frustration—and only because I would hate to see your reputation in tatters."

She stood reluctantly and handed him his shirt. She admired his back, the way the muscles swelled near his shoulder blades as he pushed his arm into a sleeve, and how hairless this whole side of his body seemed to be—at least compared to his front. The sheer size of his back and his shoulders reminded her suddenly of Balga, and she tried and failed to suppress a small giggle.

"What? My nakedness makes you chuckle?" he asked, pretending to sound insulted.

"You're not naked anymore. You're wearing a shirt."

She, however, was still completely nude, and was interested in—and intrigued by—how powerful this made her feel. She felt in command and surprised herself by scooting across the floor to him and taking his cock in her hand. He smiled down at her as she started to stroke it, and seemed about to shake his head no, no, they should stop. He should resume getting dressed. She should *start* getting dressed. But she could feel the blood engorging his penis and the organ growing once more against the palm of her hand, and he breathed in deeply and closed his eyes, his head rearing back like—again—her horse.

"Aren't you worried about your mother?" he murmured, the words drifting aimlessly up toward the ceiling.

She leaned her forehead against his thigh and looked at what she was doing, at the way the tip of his penis would appear and disappear, a magic hat in the midst of her fingers. "No," she said, "not at all. At the moment, I'm not worried about a thing."

Chapter Six

BY THE END OF JANUARY, THE FIGHTING WAS SO CLOSE they could hear it, the distant cannonade reminiscent of the soft and airy gurgle the prisoners sometimes heard from the women in the barracks before they died in the night. Almost without exception, those survivors who could still stand found themselves less likely to avert their eyes when they saw the guards. It wasn't that they had suddenly grown bold; it was that watching the transformation of each of the guards was irresistible. No two guards (or officers) seemed to change in precisely the same fashion, but when Cecile thought about it—and she thought about it almost as often as she thought about hunger and what she would do when, finally, she was home and saw her precious Lyon again—she concluded that any day now the Germans were either going to up and flee or they were going to start feeding them. Really feeding them. Caring for them. They would fatten them up so the Russians wouldn't see how severely they had been mistreated. How could they not? Whenever there was no falling snow to muffle the sound, everyone—prisoners and guards alike—could hear the explosions rolling slowly in the direction of the camp. The guards had to save their own hides. There were even rumors that the Red Cross was going to visit, and somewhere nearby there was a train

car filled with cans and cans of tomatoes—one for each prisoner—that were going to be given to them any day now.

Meanwhile, most of the guards seemed less likely to fire a
shot into the back of anyone's skull because the prisoner no
longer could stand, or pour buckets of cold water on someone's
head so they could watch her eyelashes freeze solid. Three days
passed without a single woman being hanged by the camp gate
because her sewing at the clothing works had been deemed sub-
par. There was one guard named Hedda who made a special effort to ask Cecile where she was from, and then told her how
much she liked the French—how she had even visited Paris in
1937. Another guard had seen Jeanne swaying in line one morning, her strength flagging, and secretly given her the sausage
that she had planned on tossing into the pile of scraps they gave
to the camp dogs.

Clearly, the pace of death was slowing. It wasn't just the absence of dangling corpses at the entrance to the camp. A whole
week went by when they were marched back to their barracks
after a day stitching SS uniforms at the factory and saw that the
guards had felt no need to build a bonfire at the edge of the camp
for the corpses. ("At least, they're getting out," a woman named
Rosa had once mumbled to Cecile and Jeanne while they were
standing in line, watching the thick, black smoke from the bonfire, to which Cecile had quietly replied, "I'd rather not leave here
via the wind, thank you very much.")

There was a different spirit in the camp. Not optimism precisely: Everyone was too tired or too hungry or too sick to feel
optimism. But the sense of dread was starting to lift. The other
prisoners stopped ignoring Cecile when she would prattle on about
the future, or envying her formidable resiliency. They realized they
all were alive—hundreds of them, still able to stand and walk and
stitch—and soon the Russians would be here. And the Germans
would be gone. And before they knew it, they would be home.

Not all the guards, of course, were discovering suddenly that they were still capable of feigning kindness, or that it might be time to treat their prisoners like human beings. Trammler and Pusch may not have shot anyone that week, but the two men had allowed the dogs to maul one woman badly; the black joke among the prisoners was that the animals would have killed the girl if there had been any meat left on her bones they could eat. And a female guard named Inga had whipped a prisoner because she had tried to be the last in line for their soup at lunchtime. There was occasionally something solid at the bottom of the great metal pots, something of substance, and so there was always some jockeying to be toward the end of the queue. This time Inga had seen the girl trying to lag behind and disciplined her severely. And so Cecile and the other prisoners did what they could to avoid those guards, wondering if at some point their instinct for self-preservation would kick in and they would come around, too.

Consequently, the prisoners were caught completely off guard when they were lined up in the snow one morning and informed they were going to be relocated. Moved west to another camp, one closer to the heart of the Reich. There their work would continue. The war would continue. Some of the prisoners, including Jeanne, had to stifle small sobs. But almost instantly they started to march—no cattle cars this time, they were going to walk west—most of the prisoners in coarse wooden clogs, few with socks, many with feet that were a moonscape of open lesions and raging abscesses. The fortunate had either a cape or a coat or a blanket. A coarse or ratty old sweater. Some had only their prison shirts. They were going to march, they were told, as long as there was daylight.

As they walked for the last time past the barbed wire and the guard towers, staggering in the direction opposite the clothing works, two jeeps filled with soldiers and wooden crates drove past them into the camp. A rumor was whispered along the line that the crates were filled with explosives, and the satchels with detonators and wires. Hours later they heard explosions that were louder than the distant rumbling they'd been aware of for days, and Cecile told everyone that she wouldn't be surprised if their rickety wooden barracks now were gone, if the piles of smoldering ashes—as well as the blackened but not obliterated bones that lay among the cinders at the perimeter of the camp—were buried beneath the churned-up dirt from the center commons. The idea gave her pause, and she wasn't precisely sure how she felt about this: Though she didn't want such unambiguous testimony to cruelty and barbarism to remain on the planet, she wondered if people would ever believe what she'd seen if there wasn't concrete proof.

Chapter Seven

URI HAD SEEN IT BEFORE AND HE IMAGINED HE WOULD see it again. The woods were starting to move.

The first time he had witnessed such a thing he had squinted, rubbed his eyes, and then stared. He'd worried that something he had eaten in the forest was poisoning him. Weren't there mushrooms out there that could kill you? Give you hallucinations? After all, he was not witnessing boughs and branches swaying in a breeze or being whipped about in great swirling gusts: Here before him were shrubs and trees—small trees, but trees nonetheless—rolling forward, as if they had been uprooted from the earth and were lumbering toward him in a wide, slow wave.

Which, in fact, they were. Because they had been attached to the front and the sides of tanks and assault guns and armored personnel carriers. There were at least a dozen mechanized vehicles altogether that first time, emerging at once from the woods.

This time the foliage was camouflaging a mere pair of battered Tiger tanks, a jeep so crowded that it looked like a clown car from a circus, and a single assault gun. Such was the fate of the once-vaunted Wehrmacht. He heard the Germans were trying to counterattack the Russians at Thorn, but at this point the whole front was collapsing and this small assault group might be off to fight anywhere. If these warriors had seen him a year and a half ago, they would have ignored him completely. After all, he wasn't a part of their brigade. Now, however, they would be likely to recruit him. Manpower was so short and the divisions so maimed that assault groups were being cobbled together from whatever remnants could be found wandering aimlessly (often shell-shocked) in the woods. Signalmen. Medics. Cooks. It no longer mattered. And so Uri fell back into the copse of trees, retreating so quickly that he banged into a branch and a river of snow cascaded behind his collar and inside the back of his uniform coat.

When the group was across the field and beyond him, he continued walking west toward the Vistula. He had a little cheese left in some butcher's paper, moldy but certainly edible, and he decided to finish it off.

HE HAD HEARD there was a recently abandoned concentration camp a few kilometers south of the village, and he considered detouring there. Talking to the residents who lived closest to it. Asking whether any Jews from Schweinfurt or Bavaria had once been imprisoned in the place—and, if so, where they might be now. It was one of the smaller camps, all women, and they worked in a nearby clothing factory. He had been told by another soldier with whom he'd walked briefly that the camp didn't have a crematorium. That was a big distinction he had discovered: If there was no towering smokestack, it probably wasn't one of the death camps. This wasn't an absolute rule, of course, because even now they sometimes just marched the inmates into a field, had them dig ditches, and machine-gunned them en masse.

Unfortunately, the Russians were so close by the time he reached the town that a hobbled old man told him the buildings there already had been dynamited. There were no soldiers to ask about the camp, not even a few local Volkssturm recruits hoping to stall the Soviets with a brief rearguard action. And other than this old man, there didn't seem to be any locals who had stuck around. Not that the locals ever said much. Often they acted like they knew nothing. Still, if he was persistent he could usually learn whether the inmates were marched into the town to work, where most of the prisoners were from, and whether there were women who might be his sister's age. If you asked enough questions, someone always knew something.

In the end, he didn't bother to visit the remains of the camp or the farmhouses near its perimeter. He'd stood outside the barbed wire at other camps and gazed at their decrepit wooden barracks. And this time there wouldn't even be barracks to see. There would be only blackened debris and piles of earth. Likewise, he'd followed stories and rumors before: A train of Jews here. A train of Jews there. A group of women from Bavaria, some of whom might—*might*—have been from Schweinfurt. But it had never led anywhere concrete. His sister had to be dead, and there was no reason to remain this far east. At this point, he should do all that he could to get west.

EXHAUSTED, HE STOPPED at dusk in the ruins of a long-abandoned castle. He wasn't completely sure in the twilight, but he had the sense that the fortress had fallen into disrepair centuries before Nazi or Soviet bombs had demolished it. He didn't detect the acrid stench of gunpowder, and despite the ice and the snow that covered the ramparts like frosting and filled the crenels in the sole remaining turret like mascarpone cream in a parfait glass (a dessert his mother would make him as a child), he could see the dormant tendrils of ivy and the leafless branches of the thin trees that had grown up between the stones.

He climbed the stairs to the tower where he planned to try to sleep for a few hours. He was just starting to kick away the snow there with his boot when below him he saw the children. Three of them. They were bundled up so tightly in blankets and furs that he couldn't tell if they were boys or girls, but he guessed by their height that they were all between the ages of nine and twelve. They were strolling almost leisurely through the arch where once there might have existed a great wooden door with a wrought-iron grate and wrought-iron spikes. Then, behind them, came two adults, both women. The small group had entered the castle from the side opposite him, and thus hadn't yet discovered his footprints. He crouched behind one of the crumbling stones along the wall and watched them, unsure whether he should reveal he was here. There was a good chance one of those women was armed, and in the dusk she might think he was a Russian and shoot him on the spot. That, of course, would be a fitting irony: For almost two years now he had shot Nazis, knifed Nazis, garroted Nazis, and—that very first time—bludgeoned and impaled Nazis with a fireplace poker. Conversely, he had fought Russians with rifles, *panzerfausts*, machine guns, and potato-masher grenades. If there was a God, and at this point he had no reason to believe that there was, Uri thought he would have a lot of explaining to do when he died. A lot of death to account for.

Most of it, however, had been in self-defense. Even when he was part of various attacks and counterattacks on Soviet positions, it had been self-preservation.

And so just imagine, he speculated, if it all turned out to have been for naught because one refugee mother or sister or aunt, protecting her cubs, took a potshot at him in the dusk of some crumbling castle with her late husband's (or brother's) Luger because she thought he was Russian. Or, perhaps, because she recognized his uniform and presumed (not unreasonably, given how he was dressed) that he was a Nazi himself. It was possible. Maybe the men absent now from this family were a part of the Polish resistance—or had been before some SS sadist had executed them—and these women would shoot anything in German attire.

They were clearly going to camp here for the night, and that meant that any moment one of them might cross the inner bailey and ascend the very same steps he had to this tower to see precisely where they were or to stand guard. And the last thing he wanted was to shoot some poor woman simply because he had surprised her and she was about to shoot him, and so he decided he would call down to them. First in German, but then in his pigeon Polish. Before he had opened his mouth, however, just as the three children were trying to cocoon inside one of the casemates that was still standing—trees seemed to be bookending the castle slabs now—he heard the sound of a vehicle and then, after the engine had stopped, laughter. Deep, guttural, back-of-the-throat laughter. There, just outside the castle wall below him, was a Russian jeep with two soldiers.

Had the front disintegrated so totally that the Russians had gotten behind him? Now that would be a disaster, as well: To have survived nearly two years by masquerading as a German soldier—German soldiers, actually—only to be overrun by the rampaging Soviets before he could either return to his original self or find a new guise.

As the soldiers emerged from the jeep, Uri realized that he could see the women and the children on one side of the castle wall, and the Russian soldiers on the other. But the Russians were oblivious of the civilians and the civilians were unaware of the Russians. One of the soldiers, a stout, walleyed sergeant with a rat's nest of red hair, was peeing into the snow, and Uri gave himself license to hope they would be here but a moment and move on. And after that he would figure out how he himself would move on. But then the second soldier, a lanky fellow with deeply pockmarked cheeks and a crooked beak for a nose, motioned toward the castle, and they started walking through the gate and inside the ruins.

Now the women saw them and, exactly as Uri had feared, one pulled a small gun from beneath her cape and fired. Her aim was comically bad and she missed both men completely. Instantly the soldiers were upon her. Both of them. The sergeant tackled her, the air reverberating with his howls of relief and mirth that the shooter was a woman and they had not stumbled upon retreating Wehr-macht or home guard. His partner ripped the gun from her fingers, chuckling when he saw the diminutive size of the pistol that almost had killed them. Together they pulled away the hood of her cloak and discovered that the woman was perhaps thirty, with golden hair and a long and gaunt but not unattractive face. She looked more angry than terrified.

Then the soldiers stood and motioned for the woman to remain there on the ground, while they rounded up her sister or friend and their three . . . girls. Yes, Uri could see now that they were girls. The four other females were lined up against the wall, a grown-up and three youngsters, and when the woman on the ground tried to roll in the snow to see what was happening, the Russian sergeant stepped on her. Barely bothering to look down at her, as if he were popping a rolling balloon at a birthday party with his foot, he smashed his boot flat into her stomach, causing what might have been a shriek of pain to be reduced to an airless gasp.

"Mommy!" the smallest of the three girls cried, and it looked as if she were going to say more but one of the older girls silenced her. Still, it was too late. She had drawn attention to herself and the tall soldier was scrutinizing her carefully. Then he pulled off his glove with his teeth and slid his hand under her coat, reaching down, it seemed, deep into her underwear. He said something to his comrade in a language that was largely foreign to Uri, but he got the gist of it: He'd take this girl first. They were going to begin by raping the girls in front of the women rather than starting with the two adults. The sergeant chuckled at this idea, removed his pistol from his holster, and aimed it down at the woman beneath his boot. She pleaded with him, begged him to take her instead, and he smirked and nodded. Said, Uri thought, that everyone would have a chance.

Quietly Uri pulled his rifle off his shoulder and unclipped the safety. He could take out the Russian standing with his foot atop this mother easily, but the other soldier would be a tougher shot. He was no more than fifty or sixty meters away, and at that distance there was no reason to believe the bullet wouldn't travel right through the fellow and lodge itself deep inside the child: The angle was such that if he aimed for his head, he might shoot the poor girl in the chest. If he aimed for his heart, he might shoot the child in the stomach. Certainly there was a chance that the moment he fired at the first Bolshevik—that one who was now seeming to grind his boot into the woman on the ground—the second would reflexively move away or take cover, and in that instant Uri could blast him, too. But it was equally likely that he might use the child as a shield and fire back at him from behind her.

Already, however, with almost preternatural speed, the Bolshevik had ripped off the poor girl's coat and was tearing open her dress, turning her nearly upside down as he pulled her underpants off her spindly legs so, suddenly, she was stark naked in the cold and the snow. She was screaming, a hairless wild animal with a hillockless chest—all rib cage and pancake-flat areolae, with a pencil dot for a navel—screaming so loudly that the soldier smacked her hard with the back of his hand and her whole body corkscrewed into the ground.

And so Uri gazed at the sergeant through the sight on his Mauser, aimed at a spot on his tunic just about where the fellow's heart would be, and fired. As if the gunshot were the dial that turned down the volume on a radio, the world instantly went quiet except for the echo from the blast. The child stopped howling and the woman stopped pleading, and even the wind seemed abruptly to cease. The sergeant never even turned to see the source of the shot, he simply collapsed into the snow beside the woman. Already, however, Uri was spinning the barrel of his rifle toward the second Russian, who he saw in his sight had his pants at his knees and was fumbling for something—his holster, his penis, Uri couldn't say—and gazing like a frightened animal directly at him. Instinctively Uri calculated the girl would be safer if he fired at the Russian's head, even if it meant a smaller target. This shot wasn't as clean: He took off the soldier's ear and a thin sliver of skull, sending a sizable chunk of hair and scalp splattering against the naked abdomen of the child. Still, he hadn't killed him. It looked like there was a lot of blood, but he barely had slowed him. Fortunately, as the soldier reached for his own gun, he put just enough distance between himself and the girl that this time Uri was able to fire into his stomach. And then, as he fell to his knees, into his chest. And, because Uri was absolutely furious that this bastard had been about to rape a child, into his face one more time.

Only then did Uri stand from his firing position in the tower and work his way down the stone steps to the family. He figured they should get that child dressed and take advantage of the fact they now had a jeep, and drive as far west as they could.

Chapter Eight

IN HIS CRISP, FRESHLY TAILORED UNIFORM AS A Wehrmacht private, Helmut accompanied his father east to Uncle Karl's estate. The drive usually took less than an hour, but today they had to battle against the crush of evacuees who were clogging the roads, and the trip took most of the morning. They weren't completely sure what they would find when they arrived at the home of Mutti's garrulous, indefatigably good-natured older brother, because the day before the phone service that far east had been cut. But when Mutti had called Karl two days earlier, the last time the siblings had spoken, shells had been falling sporadically in the corners of his property and the outbuilding where he stored the tractors in the winter had been damaged. Nonetheless, Karl had been adamant about staying.

As far back as Christmas Day he had told the Emmerichs, "I will greet the Russian commander as one civilized man to another. Maybe their soldiers are peasants, but I've heard their leaders are well educated. Some grew up before the revolution with the sort of reasonable privilege one expects from officers. On occasion, you know, class means more than country. Really, that's often the case. And so I wouldn't be surprised if we have more in common than any of us realizes. Of course, that presumes it ever comes to that and they actually reach this part of the Vistula. But who's to say they will? War is all about tides, and the tide should be with us again soon."

Helmut knew that his father thought Uncle Karl's optimism was completely unwarranted—that the man was dangerously sanguine about the prospects for his house and his farm and his family. His wife had succumbed to cancer two years earlier and his children were grown: His younger son had died in Stalingrad (and still, *still*, Karl harbored the delusion that the Russians and Germans would get along if they came from a certain class) and his older son was a staff officer with a Volksgrenadier division in the west. But his older son's wife lived with him now. Karl's one daughter did, too, returning home after her husband was captured in France, and bringing with her Karl's first grandson, a robust toddler with blond spit curls who was built like a beer keg. Neither Helmut nor his father liked the idea of two young women being left to the mercy of the Russians, but throughout the whole month of January Karl had rebuffed his brother-in-law's entreaties to join the Emmerichs if they went west.

When Helmut and his father reached the gates of the estate, the shelling had momentarily subsided. But there were great potholes in the driveway and the splinters from one of Karl's favorite oaks—as well as pieces of trunk the size of railroad ties—littered the road to the manor house. They finally gave up and parked in the snow a hundred meters from the front entrance.

Karl's daughter, Jutta, greeted them, her son swaying uncertainly beside her, despite the fleshy Doric columns that passed for his legs. Her lips were the pink of cooked fish, and thin as paper. But her eyes were wide and darting around her—out into the yard, up into the sky—and though she was standing still there was a frenzied quality about her that reminded Helmut of the way boars twitched when they were cornered at the end of a long hunt. Jutta was a decade older than Helmut, and once—before she had become a mother, before her husband had been captured, before the Russians had retaken most of Poland—he had thought she was among the most glamorous women he had ever seen outside of Danzig or Berlin. No longer.

She brought them into the den, where Karl was having a glass of schnapps and staring out the mullioned windows toward the east. It was a flat white vista, the snow having long smothered even the foot-high remnants of the corn, with the edge of a silvery birch forest in the distance. Karl was wearing a paisley dressing gown made of silk, his bulbous cheeks were covered with white stubble, and Helmut found himself growing embarrassed for the man. Helmut had never viewed his uncle as especially slothful (though he did feel that Uncle Karl indeed lacked Rolf Emmerich's tireless discipline), but he had never before seen the man in a dressing gown at lunchtime. He had never before seen him drinking at lunchtime. Then he grew more than embarrassed: He grew angry. The idea that he and his father were in their uniforms—that they had risked their lives to come here, that they were using precious hours of leave when they should have been packing their own estate—started to rankle him.

The man pulled the drapes, instantly darkening the room. All of the furniture—the desk, the sofa, the cherry bookshelves that climbed along two of the walls from the floor to the ceiling—was cumbersome and heavy. He offered them both a drink, cavalierly waving the crystal decanter in their direction. Helmut listened as his father politely declined, then watched as Rolf sat down on the arm of the sofa, hooking his thumbs inside his wide black officer's belt. Helmut took this as an indication that he could sit, too. His cousin and her son watched from the doorway, standing. Then the child clicked the heels of his feet together, imitating other soldiers he had seen. Quickly Helmut stood and clicked his heels together in response, and the chubby boy grinned. For a moment he wondered how he could have missed how beautiful this tiny boy's smile was. Then he recognized it: It was the lively smile he remembered from his cousin before her life had started to come apart.

"I'm not going, Rolf," his uncle was saying. "I grew up here and I plan to die here—though not, I assure you, anytime soon. But I stayed back in thirty-nine when our troops crossed the border and everyone said the Poles were going to kill us. You did, too. And it was all a great disturbance, great chaos. And for what? The Poles were fine—"

"The Poles are not the Russians. And things were different in 1939."

Karl poured yet more schnapps into his glass, and finally put the decanter down on the blotter on a corner of his desk. Helmut saw there were three stacked cardboard boxes beside it, and for a moment thought that while his uncle was insisting he was going to stay, he was nonetheless gathering up those items he would take with him in the event he did decide to evacuate. Then, however, he saw the note his uncle had scribbled on the top of the highest of the cartons: Karl was instructing one of the servants who remained to burn it. To burn them all. To, it seems, burn these three boxes along with the other papers that already had been gathered and left in the shed.

"Yes," his uncle said, "things were different. We were younger. But otherwise, war is war and—"

"Things happened in Russia. You know that. For them, this is revenge. Retribution."

"Oh, please, don't talk to me about revenge and retribution. My son died in Stalingrad. If anyone should feel there are scores to be settled, it's me. It's us. It's the Germans, who at the moment are getting hammered on all sides."

"You've talked to Felix," Rolf said, referring to his own brother who had served in Russia before being transferred to the western front. "And I know you've talked to my son. I know what Werner has told you."

"So? This was war. War is never pretty."

"This was beyond war."

"SS brutes and thugs," he said, shaking his head dismissively.

"Neither of my boys—and neither of yours—was responsible. My sons were soldiers, nothing more. No axes to grind. Same with Werner, and young Helmut here. I'm a farmer, Rolf, and so are you—despite that fancy uniform you've put on. The fact is, we grow food, and whether you're a National Socialist or a Bolshevik, you have to eat."

"The Russians are not going to distinguish between the SS and the rest of us. We're all just Germans to them. Don't forget Nemmersdorf."

Karl seemed to contemplate this for a moment, and then motioned for his daughter and grandson to leave the doorway where they'd been listening, waving his hand without the glass as if he were brushing a fly away from his nose. Almost instantly Jutta retreated, taking her son by his fingertips. Briefly the boy resisted her, but Helmut smiled, again clicked the heels of his boots, and the child went, too.

"I am sure ghastly things happened there," he said finally. "Ghastly. But I am also sure that Nemmersdorf was an aberration, and the Russian officers have since reined their men in. Besides, I wouldn't be surprised if our illustrious Ministry of Propaganda hasn't exaggerated things a bit. They do have a tendency to scream when a whisper would suffice."

"We did worse."

"Not my son. And not your brother. My son told me a great deal before he died, and so I understand it was vicious. But, more times than not, we were simply defending—"

"And as for the work camps—"

"You believe those stories? My God, Rolf, we're a civilized people!"

His father rose from the arm of the sofa. "Mutti would like you to come with us," he said, his voice verging on stern. "And even if you refuse, I must insist that we take your grandson and the girls."

"You are referring to my daughter and my daughter-in-law. I

believe the role of father trumps uncle. You are in no position to insist upon anything, Rolf. I'm sorry."

"You're being ridiculous."

"And you're panicking. When it's time to leave, the authorities will tell us."

"No, they won't. That would mean admitting defeat. The Russians will be at your door before anyone official will tell you to go."

"Fine. Then I will greet Commander Ivan with"—and here he pointed at the decanter of schnapps on the desk—"Commander Berentzen, and we'll get along famously. Let's face it: These days, you and I—our families, our world—are nothing more than skeletons at the feast anyway."

Helmut didn't think his uncle was drunk, but he recalled how the man was known for an almost superhuman ability to hold his liquor. He wondered now if his uncle had been drinking all morning.

"Karl—"

"No. There is nothing more to discuss."

When they left, Jutta and the boy were there in the front hallway, and this time Helmut saw real fear in the poor woman's eyes.

ANNA AND HER father stared for a long moment at the silver and crystal and china they had left in the snow in the hunting park, and neither said a word. Both, however, were thinking the same thing: The platters and salvers looked like headstones, and the park now resembled a graveyard. But the ground was rock solid, and they hadn't the time to bury anything properly. They had tried, but it was just impossible.

Now her father put his gloved hand upon her shoulder and murmured, "Don't tell Mutti." He was sweating from his exertions, despite the cold, despite the way their breath rose like steam in the still air. "We'll tell her it's safely hidden."

She nodded. "She thinks we're coming back," Anna said simply.

"And we might, sweetheart. We might."

"But you don't really believe that."

He paused, and in the silence the rumble of the distant artillery seemed to grow closer. Then: "No. But I've been wrong before in my life. And I will be again."

"We're still leaving tomorrow?"

"That's the plan," he said, and then he changed the subject. "We got a long letter from Werner this morning. I haven't read it yet, but Mutti says he sounded good—better, even, than one might expect."

"How . . ."

"Yes?"

"How will he find us if we're not here?"

"Mutti's writing him. We'll find each other."

His answer wasn't at all satisfying, but Anna didn't want to burden him further by pressing the issue. He was, she realized, about to leave his life's work. This farm, the estate. He had grown up on a farm, but for a time had left that world behind when he had contemplated becoming a lawyer. But he had missed it too much, and as a young man had married a country girl and thus wound up a farmer after all. An excellent farmer, it would turn out, as well as an exceptional businessman. He had been a quick study and a hard worker. He had also been profoundly intuitive, always, and now, as if he sensed what she was thinking, he went on, "We'll wire Werner from Stettin. It'll be fine."

"We're going that far?"

"We might have to."

Mutti had a cousin in Stettin. Once they had visited the family, detouring there after an excursion to Berlin, but that had been years ago. In the first months of the war. She had been twelve, and this cousin was older than Mutti and her children had already left home. Anna's principal memories of the visit were the hours she spent entertaining young Theo while the grown-ups reminisced for hours in a light and cheerful room that looked out upon a lake that fed into the Baltic.

Her father took his fingers off her shoulders and clapped his hands together with the sort of exuberance he might have exhibited if he were about to build a snowman with her. It was so sudden that it caught her off guard. Then he picked up the two shovels from the ground, brushed the snow off them, and said—his voice almost mirthful—"You are the world to me, Anna: you and your brothers and Mutti. I hope you have always known that. At this point, you're all that matters. Everything else? Irrelevant. Those plates in the snow? The wineglasses? The carving knives? The Russians can have them, for all I care."

"Grandmother wouldn't want that, of course," she said, trying to sound equally cavalier about all they were losing. Though she hadn't known her grandmother well, the woman's inordinate affection for the family crystal and china was legendary, and a source of running jokes at holiday meals. The woman had been dead for nearly a decade, and still everyone would look warily toward the stairway that led to her long-empty bedroom and sitting room whenever someone accidentally broke a glass or discovered a chip on one of the plates. They half-expected to see her gliding down the steps and into the dining room, her nearly floor-length dark skirts sweeping across the heavy carpets and polished wood.

Her father smiled at her small joke and Anna was pleased. "No, she wouldn't," he agreed. "But your grandmother was not completely unreasonable. Unlike your uncle Karl, she would see that we haven't any choice but to leave. To go west. She would . . ."

"Yes?"

"She would have been a veritable whirlwind of organization and efficiency," he said and then sighed. "I don't know what the next weeks or months hold for us. For any of us. All we can do is our duty. I'm sorry it has come to this. But it has, and there is nothing else to be done. Now, since we can't bury these valuables, please start loading one of the wagons with feed for the horses. I think that should be the next task. Leave room in the other for the suitcases and trunks, and whatever your mother will pull from the pantry."

"How many horses will be coming?"

"Four. Two wagons. Four horses."

"Bogdana won't be one of them, will he?" she asked, referring to Theo's pony. She knew how this would sadden her brother.

Her father shook his head ruefully. "I'm sorry for that, too. I realize how disappointed Theo will be. But I want only the strongest horses we have."

"What about Balga? I know when you think of him, you think only of his speed, but—"

"I know how powerful Balga is. Plan on having him help lead one of the wagons. Also, bring Waldau. Theo likes him, too, doesn't he?"

Anna nodded. Theo wasn't a strong enough rider yet or even physically large enough to manage Waldau outside of their training ring, but he did indeed love that animal. Bringing that horse would be some consolation for the boy.

"Pair him with Balga," her father continued.

"And the other animals?"

He hesitated. Then: "The Russians will be here soon enough. The horses won't go hungry."

"And the car, Father?"

The car—the vehicle that her father and Helmut had driven to Uncle Karl's that morning—was a BMW sedan from 1934. It was big and roomy, and Anna had fond memories of long drives in which she had dozed in the deeply cushioned backseat. It had grown nearly impossible to find replacement parts for the engine as the war had dragged on, however, and there was no longer a spare tire.

"No car. We don't have much petrol left. We used almost the last we had this morning when Helmut and I went to your uncle's." Together they started back toward the house, and the snow felt heavy on her boots. She noted once again how differently her father moved in his army uniform: His strides were longer, his posture more erect. "And I can't imagine petrol will be easy to come by in the coming months," he added. "Whatever Germany has will be needed by the army."

There was one final question pressing upon her, and she wasn't sure how to broach it. Whether she could broach it. But it was a subject that had been troubling her for days: their prisoner. Her Callum. Neither her father nor Mutti had given her any indication at all of their plans for the man. He had been living inside the house for over a month now, but his room was the slim maid's quarters off the kitchen and she had been careful to give her parents no inkling that he was anything more to her than a field hand she found entertaining in the absence of other, more appropriate companions. He had dined with them while her father and Helmut had been gone, but now that they were back to load up the house, once more—with an unspoken understanding of his real position—he had vanquished himself from the dining room.

"Father?"

"Yes, sweetheart."

"There is one thing we haven't talked about," she began tentatively, aware that she could still raise a different topic if she proved unable to ask about the POW.

"The Scotsman," he said.

"How . . ."

"How did I know?"

"Yes."

He shrugged. "This farm works because I do. I'm sure I'm not aware of everything that goes on under my roof," he said, and she glanced at him, but he seemed to be consciously averting his eyes.

"But I do think about the people who live here. My family. My servants. My farmhands. I try to do what's best for them—what, *in my opinion,* is best for them."

Behind them there was a particularly loud blast, but her father seemed almost oblivious of it. He continued, "And that includes the Scotsman. A part of me thought it would be best for everyone if we just left him behind. Allowed the Russians to find him— emancipate him, if you will—and let them send him home to his Scotland. The Russians are, after all, his allies."

"But you're not going to do that," she said, hoping there had been no trace of entreaty in her voice and it had sounded to her father as if she were merely continuing his train of thought.

"No, I'm not," he told her. "I'm not because I don't trust the Russians. And, in truth, I don't trust the Germans. At least all of us. The Russians are slaughtering virtually everyone in their path, and we—SS, SA, Wehrmacht, it no longer matters— wouldn't look much more kindly on a British soldier wandering aimlessly in our midst. But Callum is a good man. And he has value."

"As a worker?"

"As a Brit. We're going west, Anna. Your mother and I agreed last night that to keep you and your little brother safe, we will trek as far west as we have to. And that means that eventually we may reach the British or the Americans at the western edge of the Reich. If we do, it would be helpful to have Callum with us to, well, vouch for us. Speak on our behalf."

She said nothing because she knew her voice would betray the giddiness and the relief she was feeling. She couldn't imagine where she would be in a week, but the idea that Callum would be with her made the future less ominous.

"Go get him," her father said. "Have him help you load the feed."

She nodded carefully, biting her lower lip so it wouldn't transform itself into a smile. It was starting to spit snow once again, and it was possible to imagine that the field guns in the distance were merely the echoes of an approaching storm.

NORMALLY IN THE NIGHT they might have played music or unraveled sweaters to make mittens for the men fighting at the front. Anna and Mutti would knit, and Theo would write the soldiers small notes. It was part of the total war effort, and now that Theo was old enough to be a member of the Hitler Youth, his contribution was the letters. He liked writing the notes, because it meant that he had something to bring when he attended the meetings. And that, in turn, lessened the chance that the boys who led the group would find reasons to pick on him. But he also liked the challenge of finding something to say to a stranger that might make him feel better. Perhaps make him feel a little less frightened. Theo knew he would be scared if he were a soldier. All he had to do was envision his brother Werner's scarred legs to know how dangerous it was out there, or think of the long list of neighbors and cousins and the older brothers— and fathers!—of schoolmates who were dead or missing in action to know how hazardous it was to be a soldier. He didn't honestly know if more people were dying now than two or three years ago, because he wasn't sure how aware he had been of what was occurring when he was seven and eight years old. But you couldn't go into the village, it seemed, without seeing a young man on the street with an empty sleeve where there should have been an arm, or the pants leg of his trousers pinned up as he hobbled along on a pair of crutches. It was awfully clear that he had to be certain that what he wrote to the soldiers was uplifting.

Sometimes, he would begin with the suggestions of the older man who was in charge of their unit. The ideas were bland, but the words nonetheless seemed to give him momentum. *Thank you for protecting us from our enemies*, he would begin. Or *Thank you for serving the Fatherland. Heil Hitler!* But then he would allow himself a little creativity.

> *I hope these mittens keep you warm. My sister knitted them. She's the prettiest girl I know.*

> *I hope these mittens keep you very warm. My sister knitted them. The wool is from an old sweater my brother doesn't need anymore.*

> *I hope these mittens keep you very warm. My sister knitted them. The wool is from an old sweater my brother doesn't need anymore, but only because he's gotten very big in the shoulders from fighting and marching. He was hurt once when he was riding on a tank, but he's fine now. He has scars on his legs, but he can walk and run.*

> *I hope these mittens are the warmest you've ever had. My sister knitted them. The wool is from an old blue sweater my brother doesn't need anymore, but only because he's gotten very big and strong in the shoulders from fighting and marching. He's an excellent soldier. He was hurt once when he was riding on a tank and a Russian fired a shell at it, but he's fine now. Mostly he's fine. He has bad scars on his legs, but he can walk and run and I know he is very proud to serve the Fatherland. He wants to be a farmer when the war is over, like our father. I hope you are safe. Heil Hitler!*

There were always more notes than there were mittens, because it took a lot longer to knit a pair of mittens than it did to write a note—even when you were as conscientious as Theo. As a result, the care packages were supplemented with decks of playing cards and hard candies and whatever trinkets a local family could spare. Almost everything of value was scarce, but the group leader said it was the notes that mattered most—which left Theo even more worried that his letters were painfully inadequate, and thus resolved to spend even more time on each one. It also left him wondering why in the world some young man hunkered down in Italy or behind the Siegfried Line wanted to hear from some boy from the middle of nowhere. Didn't they have families of their own to write them? Their own girlfriends and wives and, in some cases, children?

Evidently not. At least not always.

Still, he had to be careful not to write notes that were too long, because he had a quota he was supposed to bring to each meeting. If he brought too few notes, he would be yelled at. If he wrote notes that were too brief, he would be yelled at. It was a balancing act and—like everything else, it seemed—a source of pressure.

He thought there had once been a time in his life when his days had been fun. Wasn't he smiling in the photographs taken when he was a very small child? But he honestly wasn't sure.

And now tonight, instead of gathering with his family in the ballroom or the parlor, he was alone in his room and he was supposed to be packing—though he wasn't supposed to pack much. Again, the mixed message: Be thorough, but bring as little as you can. And so instead of watching Anna knit or listening to his mother or Callum play music, he was finding his warmest clothes and his favorite books and trying to wedge everything into a suitcase. Not even a trunk. A suitcase. It just didn't seem possible.

Tomorrow they were going to leave, but he hoped it was only for a short while. He wasn't sure how he was going to say good-bye to his pony. When his father had told him that Bogdana wasn't coming, he had had to fight hard not to cry. Same as when he had been mucking the animal's stall later that afternoon. He had felt his eyes welling up, and he'd had to look away from the animal as he worked. Who was going to care for him until they returned? Everybody was leaving. His father had suggested that Basha—

their cook—and her brother would care for the animals, but he had his doubts. He detested Basha. Thought she had never liked the Germans. Her brother, too. The man was a mean-spirited giant with a single eye and an arm that was always twitching, which was probably the reason why he was even still around, rather than working in a coal mine or a factory in Silesia. He certainly couldn't—or wouldn't—help much with the animals. And neither Basha nor her brother was about to stand up to the Russians if they asked for the horses.

He looked now at the books and the shirts and sweaters and underpants he had folded on his bed. At the long pants. No short pants, not on this trip. That, he guessed, was the one consolation to leaving home in the winter. He hated short pants. When he was wearing them, it reminded everyone that he was a boy and his legs were thin. Pathetically thin. So thin that the other children invariably made fun of them—as if they needed one more reason to tease him or hurt his feelings. Still, even without the short pants he had no idea how he could possibly bring everything with him that Mutti had said he must pack. Just no idea at all.

WHEN ANNA HAD FINISHED packing and she knew that her parents and her brothers were in their rooms for the night, she crept silently to the maid's room where Callum slept. The house's front door had been open so often during the day and evening as they had traipsed back and forth to the wagons that the downstairs was frigid, far colder than the bedrooms upstairs—especially her room, which had had a small blaze burning in the fireplace for the last couple of hours. The air was far from arctic, but she found herself pulling her robe tightly around her.

"Is my family trying to freeze you to death?" she asked him, kicking off her slippers and crawling beside him beneath the quilt on the slim bed as quickly as she could. He was still awake, too, since he was expecting her. Normally the room was warmed slightly by the stove in the kitchen, but they had been so busy organizing and packing that evening that Mutti had instructed Basha simply to create a buffet from whatever was left in the icebox. Apparently, there had been nothing worth heating up, and Basha had never lit the stove.

"Don't tell me a little ice on the windows is too much for a Daughter of the Reich," he murmured, teasing her and pulling her against him. He was wearing Werner's woolen long underwear, and even in the dark she could tell that it was far too small for him. She ran her toe along his leg and realized that the ankle of the underwear was stretched tightly around his shin. Reflexively she ran her fingers down his sleeve and discovered that the wrist of the long underwear was at least two inches up his forearm.

"How can you breathe in this outfit?" she asked him.

"Oh, I'm fine. I was actually wearing considerably more layers until a few moments ago."

"Well, if you think you have any chance of convincing me to remove one single article of clothing, you are mistaken."

"You've already taken off your slippers."

"And that's going to be all, I assure you." She curled her hands into small balls and pressed them between their chests. She heard a mouse racing along inside the exterior wall, and couldn't imagine how a creature that tiny could survive in cold this severe.

"Ah, but you're here," he whispered, and she thought about this—how her entire world was starting to collapse, and that she had chosen *here*, this thin mattress, on which to take solace. They didn't even know where they would be sleeping tomorrow night. After a moment she nodded. "Are you warm enough?" she asked him. "I was kidding a minute ago when I mentioned my family. But maybe you should be sleeping upstairs."

"I'm all right. Really, my sweet, I am. But you don't need to stay here. I'm flattered you've come to the icebox to join me, but I think you should savor a few hours of sleep in your bed. Tomorrow will be here before you know it."

She hadn't considered how long she was going to stay. There was no question that she would be in her own room when Mutti would come for her at dawn. But she hadn't decided whether she had come downstairs to hold him briefly and kiss him good night, or whether she might stay longer. Before her father and Helmut had returned, she had come here with some frequency. Now? It was a considerably more risky endeavor.

"Of course, I never slept the night before a jump," he went on. "Even the practice jumps."

"It must be terrifying to jump from a plane. I've never even flown."

"It wasn't the fear of getting killed that kept me awake. After all, on the practice runs there was no one shooting at you. It was the fear of botching the jump in some fashion—in some fashion that would be embarrassing or might complicate the whole affair for your mates. And I worried about how I would respond during the actual fight."

"From what you've told me, you responded just fine," she said, though the truth was that he had told her almost nothing. Like Werner, he shared with her only the most basic, unembellished details—and not particularly many of them, at that. It wasn't that she was the enemy and he had secrets to protect; it was merely that he was a soldier and soldiers, even young ones such as Werner and Callum, didn't seem to want to discuss what they had seen and done. And so all she really knew was that he hadn't shot anyone—at least that's what he had said. And that he had spent most of his time on the ground the night of the jump in a swamp, while the woods around him were on fire because another plane had crashed there. Whenever she envisioned that Allied plane, she thought of the Luftwaffe fighter that had been shot down over Kaminheim, and the dead pilot in the wreckage in the hunting park. Nevertheless, she hoped that someday she would get to see the world from an airplane, and she told him that now.

"It's overrated," he said.

"Really?"

"Well, it is if you're a paratrooper. No windows. Bad seating. Most blokes spend a good part of the ride either vomiting or trying not to vomit. Airsickness and terror: a mighty bad combination."

"Maybe if you had a comfortable seat and a window."

He rose up on his elbow now and looked down at her. She could see his face in the light from the candle on the windowsill, and he was smiling at her. "Maybe," he said, the two syllables oddly wistful. Except that he was smiling.

"Your face doesn't match your words," she said.

"What?"

"You sound sad. But you look happy."

He seemed to think about this, but only briefly. And then, instead of answering her, he bent toward her and kissed her, his lips soft and his tongue tasting slightly of candy cane—probably from one of the very last treats they had remaining from Christmas. His fingers started to inch under her robe and against her nightgown, and then they were grazing her collarbone and her neck. They were oddly, surprisingly warm, and suddenly the layers of flannel separating their bodies seemed a barrier that was at once considerable and frustrating: She loved him and who could say when they would ever get to lie together like this again. She wanted to feel his skin against her skin, the cold be damned, and she wanted to feel him running his fingers over her nipples and holding her breasts in the palms of his hands. She wanted to feel him inside her. And so she sat up and pulled her nightgown over her head, and he followed her lead and climbed from her brother's long underwear. She had planned on leading his fingers to her breasts, but already his hands were there, and she felt a shiver as they started to brush in circles over her nipples. She allowed herself a soft purr, aware that outside the wind was blowing the fallen snow against the windows and somewhere nearby there was a mouse, but that didn't matter, that didn't matter at all. His erection was pressing against her, she could feel it against her hips, and she grasped it in the dark beneath their quilt. Stroked it gently, felt the moistness at the tip.

"I'm beside you," he whispered, a slight pant in his voice because, she could tell, of the way she was massaging his penis. "How could I be anything but happy?" And then he kissed her again, this time on her forehead, her eyes, her nose. But he surprised her by scooting over her mouth. An image crossed her mind: Her hand was replicating her vagina, and it made her want to lick her palm for him. But he raised himself up once again and pulled away so she could no longer fondle his cock. Already he was retreating under the tent of their quilt, slipping down toward her waist and her knees so that she could no longer see him. She knew what he was going to do because they had done this before, and at first she had been shocked. She had been shocked that he would even have such an idea. But then she realized this was just one more way that he had experiences far beyond her ken, and she had given herself over to him and to what he was doing and, yes, to the sensations. He had used his tongue on her in much the same way that she would touch herself when she was alone, only this felt so much better: the orgasms so intense, especially that first time when the feelings had coiled inside her, building until she had come so powerfully that she had feared she was going to pee on the rug at the edge of the ballroom.

Now his hands were massaging her thighs and his head was between her legs, his mouth moist and warm and insistent. In a moment, she knew, he would gently part her pubic hair and stiffen his tongue, and he would be brushing it against her so rapidly that the sensations would swell till she came, and then, when her legs might still be shaking, almost abruptly he would be holding his body up on his arms and sliding inside her—which, now, gave her a pang of apprehension. They had always used the condoms she had found in Werner's bedroom, and she wondered if they had one left. She had given him the box soon after she had discovered it, because she didn't think it was right that such things should reside in her bedroom. What if Mutti discovered them there? But she didn't know if they had any remaining. Still, it seemed impossible at first to open her mouth and ask him. To stop him. She couldn't get pregnant, however, she simply couldn't—not by him, not now. Perhaps not ever. And so she found the resolve within her to reach down for his head, to get his attention. At first he thought she was merely urging him on, massaging his scalp as he lapped at her vagina. But then she asked him, put the question out there. He stopped what he was doing and rose up from beneath her, and he smiled. "Oh, I wish we'd had the time to be such bunnies that we'd gone through Werner's whole stash."

"We've one left?"

"Actually, I believe we have two," he reassured her, and then he disappeared once more between her thighs, and she gave herself over to the feelings there, closing her eyes to the ice and the snow and the death: to the reality that somewhere, not very far away, their army was trying desperately to slow a juggernaut of Russian barbarians. For the moment, all that mattered was that she was with Callum, her Callum, and their bodies were warm and electric and very much alive.

IT WAS STILL DARK when Helmut awoke, and even in the midst of the spring planting or the autumn harvest no one would have been up for another hour and a half. Even today, the morning of their departure, he knew his mother and father wouldn't be rising for a short while. They'd done most of their packing yesterday, and the house was now without power and there was only so much more they could do in the cold and the dark. And so he considered going back to sleep, but once more he saw in his mind the fear in the eyes of his cousin Jutta. The oblivious, happy smile on her son. His uncle's irresponsible complacency in the face of the Bolsheviks.

But mostly he saw Jutta's eyes.

He knew his father was right: Karl and his family had to evacuate, and they had to leave now. If Karl refused, then at the very least he should allow his daughter, his daughter-in-law, and his grandson to join the exodus working its way west. And so Helmut rose and dressed as quickly as he could by the light of a candle, climbing into his new winter uniform and his snow boots, and wrapping his wide belt around him with its weighty, holstered Luger. Then he scribbled a short note for his parents. He didn't believe the roads would be crowded at this hour of the night—it couldn't possibly be as bad as it was yesterday morning—and so he guessed he would be at his uncle's by sunrise. And either he would convince his uncle to gather his family and join him, or he would simply take the two women and the boy.

He grabbed an apple as he passed through the kitchen and found himself glowering at the door to the maid's room. He wasn't sure what he thought of his parents' decision to bring the Scot with them when they went west. He liked the idea of another man on the trek—especially a man as large and physically intimidating as Callum. But, in truth, how helpful would this particular fellow be? Half the time he'd probably be hidden beneath bags of grain and apples and sugar. And when he wasn't? He was a soldier who'd never even fired his gun at the enemy before surrendering. Besides, the last thing his family should do was encourage whatever inappropriate feelings already existed between the prisoner and his twin sister. His parents already gave the man far too many liberties and extended to him far too many kindnesses.

When he reached the barn, he saw there was just enough petrol in the BMW to reach his uncle's estate; he would refill the tank there to get home. His family wouldn't approve of this excursion, but if he brought Mutti's brother and the rest of the clan back, he would be a hero. And right now the Reich needed heroes. It needed them desperately. He had yet to see any fighting—he'd only finished his training last week—and a part of him longed for the respect that his older brother received when he was on leave. To accomplish the things his brother had on the battlefield. To be taken seriously as a soldier.

He didn't expect he would actually see any Russians, and that gave him confidence; at the same time, it diminished in his opinion the scope of the task before him. How heroic was he really if the most difficult parts of his endeavor were battling a river of refugees moving in the opposite direction, and then cajoling his fat, stubborn uncle to come with him?

Then, however, he remembered the shells that were already falling on his uncle's estate, and he stood a little straighter. Yes, the Reich needed heroes, even if they were only eighteen and their mission was to rescue their families.

URI DROVE THE two women and the three children as far as the Vistula, and then he gave them the Russian jeep. They'd spoken little as they had driven through the night, partly because the women were so shaken and partly because the children actually slept in the back of the vehicle. But he learned the women were sisters, and the three children all belonged to the older of the siblings. The younger sister hadn't married yet. They both insisted they had never joined the party, though these days, Uri knew, anyone who bragged about being a party member was either an idiot or a fanatic. Still, he found it revealing how many people were so quick to tell strangers they'd never been Nazis.

"I wasn't in the party either," he informed them, appreciating the irony. "I don't think they would have had a lot of use for a person like me."

The pair implored him to stay with them when they reached the frozen river, to continue to protect them as they went west. But he told them that wasn't possible. He said that he needed to return to his unit. The truth was, of course, that he didn't have a unit, and among the critical lessons he had learned in his different guises in the Wehrmacht was that no one was going to question him so long as he was near the front. It was only when he was in the theoretic safety of the rear that he was in danger of being found out or—and this would have been a bizarre turn of events—shot as a deserter. Yes, he would get west: He had to. But he would have to move judiciously.

In the headlights from another vehicle parked now along the bank of the river, he saw a couple of green Volkssturm teens and a captain with one arm attempting to manage the horde trying to cross this stretch of ice. He climbed from the jeep and started toward them. As he walked a little closer, he recognized that the fellow was, much to his surprise, Captain Hanke—his commanding officer as recently as October. Then the man had gone home to Dortmund on leave and there, Uri had heard, been wounded in an air raid. Apparently he had lost an arm.

Uri had liked Hanke, and Hanke had seemed to like him. The Hanke men had been soldiers for generations—long before there had been a Nazi regime and a world war to compel them into the service.

Already Uri saw that an old couple with a wheelbarrow were descending upon the Russian jeep, begging to put their bags of clothing in the back with the children. Begging to somehow squeeze onto the vehicle themselves. One of the young women looked back at Uri, pleading with him with her eyes to try to solve this problem, too. Rescue them as he had at the castle. He raised his eyebrows and shook his head, shrugging his shoulders. There wasn't anything he could do. There wasn't anything anyone could do. There really wasn't room for the old couple and the meager remnants of their lives, but you really couldn't leave them behind either. Still, this man was persistent and loud, and he beseeched them that if nothing else the family had to find room in the vehicle for his wife. They had to. He said she had a bad heart and she desperately needed to sit. And so, finally, Uri strolled back to them, rested his hand on the warm hood of the jeep, and suggested to the woman in the front passenger seat that she climb into the back and allow the old lady into the vehicle. He reminded her that this was where she had been when he had been driving.

Then he turned away and called out to Captain Hanke, jogging over to the man. Suddenly he had to be away from these refugees. From all refugees. From this whole whining and scared and despairingly sad parade. The officer recognized him instantly, and Uri was pleased. Hanke even had a small smile for him.

"You need some help here?" he asked the captain. "It looks like it's going to get ugly."

"Oh, it's actually been very civilized so far," he told Uri. "It won't get ugly till later."

"When the sun comes up and the real crowds arrive?"

He craned his neck and looked to the south. "When the engineers get here. Then we're going to blow up this ice bridge to slow the Russians. That's when things will get nasty—and that's when I will indeed need your help."

THE MOON WAS mostly obscured by clouds and there were absolutely no stars. Yet the snow was oddly luminescent, as if it had its own source of light—like, Helmut thought, those fish that supposedly lived in the sunless depths of the ocean—and the birch trees were eerily skeletal. Helmut found the cold air more bracing than uncomfortable. There were few families on the road, but he did pass some. And they all told him the same thing: He was going the wrong way. A fellow soldier, his head bandaged beneath a wool cap, warned him that the Russians had pierced their lines everywhere—that, in fact, there was no line left. An old couple pulling two small, sleeping grandchildren on a sled said they had seen a Russian tank on the outskirts of the village.

When he reached the final stretch of road before his uncle's, the sky was lightening to the east, though it was clear there was going to be no sun again today. He was almost out of petrol, but he was so close it really wouldn't have mattered if the car had come to a dead stop right here. He knew from his visit yesterday with his father that he would be unable to drive all the way to the manor house anyway. Still, he coasted whenever he could.

He was just stepping down from the BMW when he heard the metallic rumble approaching. He climbed back on to the vehicle's running board to see, hoping to God it was German tanks or, perhaps, some long antitank guns on trailers. It wasn't. There, no more than half a kilometer distant, were three massive Russian tanks lumbering across one of the fields where his uncle grew rutabagas and carrots. They were moving parallel to the road and clearly didn't give a damn about him or his family's BMW. Because clearly they saw him. If the commander inside any one of the tanks wanted, he needed only to spin his tank's turret and obliterate the car with a single shell.

He jumped back into the driver's seat and raced as far up the driveway as he could, stopping only when he reached the fallen oak where he and his father had parked yesterday. Then he ran to the house, aware even as he churned his legs in the snow that something was different. Something had changed. He couldn't have said precisely how he knew this, and he told himself that his foreboding had been triggered, naturally enough, by the sight of three Russian tanks cavalierly driving westward behind him. Soon, however, he understood his premonition was well founded: He saw that the estate's high and wide front doors had been shattered, the wood slivered and the hinges bent like old playing cards. He stepped over what now were little more than sharp pieces of kindling and called for his uncle. He called for Jutta. A crow flew past him, swooping toward him down the stairs and then darting outside through the hole where the front doors once had stood. The heavy tapestries of hunters and herds of elk that usually adorned the eastern wall of the entrance hall had been slashed with bayonets, and each bulb on the great chandelier—all of them encased in globes with the faces of wood nymphs—had been exploded.

He tried to convince himself that Karl had come to his senses and left with his family, but he didn't believe this. He walked gingerly across the broken glass from the light fixture, saw that the kitchen and the pantry had been ransacked—the doors ripped from the cupboards, the jars of pickles and cabbage and jam smashed onto the floor—and then across the shattered remnants of the mahogany dining room table into his uncle's study. Which was where he saw them. All four of them. The boy with the beautiful, cherubic smile had been hung as if he were a small pig by his ankles from one of the acorn finials atop the high cherry bookcases, his throat slashed so deeply that his head was dangling by twinelike shreds of muscle and skin. The women, including poor, frightened Jutta, had been tied facedown to Uncle Karl's broad desk, their legs naked, their dresses pulled up over their hips. There was dried blood caked like icing along the insides of their legs, and—almost hypnotized—he stared for a moment at the eggplant-colored bruises that marked their buttocks. After they had been violated (or before, for all Helmut knew), each woman had been shot once in the back of the head.

And on the floor nearby, still in his dressing gown, was Uncle Karl. Even in death the man's eyes were wide. The body was on its side, almost curled into a fetal position, and there was something causing the back of the dressing gown to tent. He knelt, pulled the silk aside, and saw that someone had taken the man's crystal decanter full of schnapps and thrust the bottleneck as far into the man's anus as it would fit.

HELMUT WANDERED STUNNED, almost somnambulant, to his uncle's garage, where he found a can of petrol that the Russians must not have noticed. There he filled the BMW. Then he left and joined the throng traveling west. Although he was moving in the same direction as the stream, the trip home still took him nearly two and a half hours. When he passed a woman with five children and all of their suitcases and cartons trudging along on foot, he packed them into the car with him and brought them as far as the entrance to Kaminheim. The only traffic he encountered moving east was two trucks pulling antitank guns, the weapons' long barrels painted white for the winter.

His parents were furious when he got home. His mother, he saw, had actually cleaned the kitchen with the cook in his absence and was draping the furniture in the ballroom with white sheets when he arrived. Their anger dissipated quickly, however, when he told them what he had seen at Uncle Karl's. He didn't share with them all the details, especially after Mutti lowered her head and grew silent. He could tell that it was the death of the boy that first had shocked and then dispirited her. For a long moment she simply allowed herself to be rocked in her husband's arms, her face buried in his chest. She said nothing, though occasionally her body shuddered as she tried to suppress her sobs. She was struggling to maintain a semblance of composure, to prevent her grief and her panic from overwhelming her, but he knew her well enough to know that she would succeed. Then she would resume packing with her usual efficiency and organizing his sister and brother for their departure.

Finally he heard his father murmuring—his voice soft but firm—that it was important they were on the road well before lunchtime. And, sure enough, Mutti stood up a little straighter, pulled away from her husband, and wiped at her eyes.

"Helmut," she said, just the smallest quaver in her voice. "Please check on your brother. See if he needs any help."

ANNA WENT OUTSIDE into the chill morning air when she heard what had happened to Uncle Karl and Jutta and the others, and listened to the firing to the east. She had known people who had died—mostly men, of course, including her cousin at Stalingrad, but some women, too—and she had even known people who had died in their apartments or town houses when RAF and American bombers had incinerated whole city blocks. A girl from a BDM camp in one case, friends of her parents in another. But this was a first: the deaths of people she was related to who had been violated—tortured—before they had been slaughtered. She wasn't completely sure why Helmut had insisted on telling her so much more than he had told their parents, but she sensed by the way his forehead was furrowed and his eyes were glassy that he felt a powerful need to unburden himself to someone.

Callum appeared beside her now and dropped at his feet the trunk he was carrying. She recognized it as Theo's, though she knew that most of what had been wedged into it was either provisions for the trek or valuables that her parents thought they might barter as they made their way west. She and her mother had sewn small, secret pockets into some of their dresses and skirts in which they would hide jewelry, since it was possible that diamonds and gold might be the only currency with any value someday soon. Like her, Theo was taking a single suitcase.

"I'm sorry," Callum said to her simply. "The people who did that to your family . . . well, they weren't soldiers, you know. They were just criminals."

She thought about this, but the idea offered little comfort. What difference did it make? "I'm scared," she said simply. She realized that she really hadn't been before. She had been agitated and apprehensive, she had felt a deep and nagging unease. But until now she hadn't been frightened.

"I can't say I blame you."

"I tell myself it was all my uncle's fault. You know, he did this to himself. To his family. Because he wouldn't listen, he wouldn't leave. If he had, they'd all be alive today. All of them. You realize that, don't you?"

"I do, yes."

"Still: I'm scared."

"Because of the Russians . . ."

"And because it's all over! Everything!" she said, raising her voice more than she'd meant to. "I've never lived anyplace but Kaminheim. Now I don't even know where I'll be sleeping tonight!"

Though her father or mother or Helmut might appear at any moment, he put his arms around her and pulled her against him. She was wearing only a sweater and so she was shivering. He stroked her hair, careful not to disturb the long braid that ran down her back. She murmured something into his chest, but he couldn't make it out and so he gently lifted her chin with his thumb.

"They . . ." she began again. Her eyes were moist, but she wasn't crying and it might have been the cold alone that was causing them to water.

"Your uncle's family?" he asked.

"The Russians," she said, her voice almost bewildered. "They must have been very mad."

A gust of wind whipped the snow on the walkway into a series of small, tornado-like swirls, and the noise momentarily drowned out the cannonade.

"Apparently. But that sort of behavior is always inexcusable," he said, wishing he had found a word that suggested the gravity of the Russians' atrocities. He was parroting, he suspected, something his own priggish uncle once must have said. "Even in the worst moments of a war, it's intolerable. No British soldier would have done such a thing. You know that, don't you?"

"I know you believe that."

"It's a fact," he said, instantly regretting how curt he had sounded.

"I wouldn't have thought German soldiers would, either. But from what you've told me—from what your radio people claim—they did, and that's probably why the Bolsheviks are so barbaric now."

He considered this and wondered, as he did often, what sort of soldier he would have been if he hadn't fallen from the sky into a bog and been taken prisoner so quickly. He didn't fear he would ever have done anything cowardly: He was twenty and still had the remorseless confidence of late adolescence. And he knew that he had handled himself well enough when he was helping his fellow paratroopers survive their first moments in the marsh after that disastrous drop. Rather, what made him curious was how capricious his captors had been before he was sent here to Kaminheim to help with the harvest. The guards, he had observed, might dispense a completely unwarranted kindness upon one POW because there was something they liked about the particular Brit's or American's attitude. He was quiet, perhaps. Or he would smile once in a while. Meanwhile, they would beat another prisoner senseless with their rifle butts because they were annoyed with the fellow's sluggishness or the way he wore his overcoat, or they simply didn't like the shape of his jaw or the color of his eyes.

And, Callum presumed, it was a thousand times worse on the battlefield. Those Germans who captured him: Sure, they wanted prisoners they could interrogate. But had they had a less seasoned commander, they probably would have just opened fire and machine-gunned the paratroopers as they struggled from the swamp. And that would have been absolutely fair and reasonable. Hell, if he'd seen a group of German paratroopers in some bog near Elgin in the midst of an invasion, he wouldn't have asked a whole lot of questions before opening fire.

Still, he would never have killed a civilian. Never. Nor would he have raped some poor girl because she was in the wrong place at the wrong time. He was certain that none of his mates would have, either.

Likewise, he couldn't see Helmut doing such things.

Yet Helmut's peers very well might. And Werner's probably had. For all he knew, they had done far worse, if that was possible. And if they hadn't actually raped the girls they had come across in

Russia, it was only because they didn't rape dogs and pigs, either. It was beneath them.

What the Russians were doing wasn't forgivable. But it was, he feared, understandable. In their minds, they were just taking an eye for an eye.

And so he had to admit that he was a little relieved, too, that he was going west with the Emmerichs and not staying behind to greet the Russian army. It wasn't just that he wanted to protect Anna. It wasn't just that he wanted to be with her. It was, he thought, his best shot at surviving this nightmare.

THEY LEFT WELL before lunchtime, just as Father had insisted. They left on foot, six more people and four more horses, joining the river of refugees planning, if necessary, to walk the width of Germany in the winter. They left as the snow flurries once more began to coat the road and the roof of the manor house, as behind them the chimneys grew cold. They were a solemn, largely silent procession, their thoughts punctuated always by the sound of the cannons, because by this point there was nothing to say. Anna glanced once at Theo and saw the poor boy had a face that was resolute: He was striving to be as grown-up as his older brothers, soldiers both, as sure and as steadfast as Callum. He was also, she imagined, simply too scared to cry now. Didn't dare. She guessed they all felt that way on some level.

As they passed between the imposing stone columns that marked the entrance to Kaminheim, she noticed that neither of her parents ever looked back.

PART II

Winter 1945

Chapter Nine

THE REFUGEES IN THE COLUMNS MOVED AT DIF-
ferent speeds once they were west of the Vistula, not unlike the
runners in the middle stages of a marathon. The Emmerichs on
occasion were passed and on occasion passed others. During their
first afternoon without Helmut or Rolf, they spoke to almost no
one, and when they bedded down for the night at the estate of a
family they knew in Klinger—abandoned, too, they found when
they arrived, and already occupied by a half-dozen other families
trekking west—they were so exhausted that they barely opened
their mouths. Even Callum was largely silent as he and Anna fed
the horses and watched the animals sniff at the strange stalls.
Mutti opened some of the canned meats they had brought, and
selflessly shared the food—as well as some apples and beets—
with the families there, since all of them were traveling on foot
and hadn't been able to bring anywhere near the provisions that
the Emmerichs had. She had, by her own rough calculations,
given away about a day and a half's worth of their food. But it
would have been indecent not to share what they had.

Anna had presumed that they would all sleep in bedrooms, on
clean, crisp sheets that her parents' friends or servants would
place on the guest beds, but other groups who, it was clear, hadn't

even known the people who had once lived at this house had already commandeered those quarters. There were elderly married couples who seemed far too frail to be out on their own in the cold, and women (like Mutti) with children, and three female auxiliaries from the navy who were perhaps a year or two older than Anna. The auxiliaries claimed to have been on their way to Konitz on official business when their jeep was destroyed in an air attack, but there was an air of vagueness about their story and a decided restiveness in their eyes. Both Mutti and Anna had the sense they were lying, and hoped for the girls' sake that they would not be spotted by some doctrinaire Nazi who thought the war could be saved if he turned in these possible deserters. The girls had seized the couches and the divan in the den, but insisted on turning them over to the Emmerichs and slept instead on the thick carpet on the floor. Meanwhile, Callum slept beneath their comforters in the barn with the horses, because Mutti decided that there were too many refugees in the house to risk bringing him indoors. The next morning, he said the barn hadn't been too bad because of the amount of heat that was given off by the horses.

On the second night, the Emmerichs were forced to join Callum in a barn, because there was absolutely no more room in either of the two farmhouses where they stopped. At the first home, Anna peered through the windows while Mutti tried to negotiate their way inside, and she saw people packed so tightly in the living room that it looked like the young mothers were sleeping on their feet with their infants in their arms, while old women were asleep both on the dining room table and beneath it. The second house, four kilometers farther, was just as crowded, and Theo—despite his best efforts to transcend his age—was starting to grow a little hysterical with fatigue. And so Mutti had them camp that evening in the barn with, by the time the moon had risen, two other families of trekkers. They were still weeks from Stettin, and as they spread out their blankets and quilts on the hay, Anna guessed that if this trend continued they would be sleeping in the snow by the time they arrived there.

Nevertheless, she didn't complain. Even Theo didn't complain once he was off his feet and buffered by barn board from the chill winds, and they had all eaten apples and beets and the last of the bread they had brought. As they had the day before, they shared their bounty with the families with whom, suddenly, they were sleeping in unexpectedly close quarters.

But it was clear there was no alternative to spending the night with strangers. Besides, Anna reminded herself, how could she even consider whining when her father and Helmut were off fighting at the Kulm bridgehead and Werner was God alone knew where? At least, she reminded herself, they all had their winter boots and their parkas and their furs, and for the moment it had stopped snowing. And the presence of the moon high above had given everyone in the line trekking west the hope that tomorrow there might even be sun.

INDEED, THERE WAS SUN, a great lemon-colored haze brightening the eastern edge of the horizon in the first moments of the morning, and outside the village of Śliwice Cecile closed her eyes and looked up at the sky. She felt the warmth on the very cheekbones that stood out now like a razor ridge on a cliff. Their guards were stopping to rest for a moment, which meant they were allowed to rest, too. They weren't allowed to sit, but at least she and Jeanne could lean against each other, and not have to endure the pain of their shoes grating against the open sores and festering blisters on their feet. They knew they were among the fortunate ones, because Cecile still had her fiancé's old boots and Jeanne still had Cecile's crocodile dress flats—comfortable, though not warm. Some of the other women had actually chosen to march with rags wrapped around their feet instead of the clogs they had been given at the camp, because the snow got into the clogs anyway, and the rags didn't aggravate the cuts on their insteps the way the clogs did. Others decided to forgo shoes and rags completely, believing—mistakenly, Cecile thought—that their frostbite would not become gangrenous if the limbs remained iced. Then, of course, there were those women who already had gangrene, and there were many; many of them went barefoot, too, both because they found the numbness less uncomfortable than the spikes of cold pain they had been suffering and because they hoped they might die more quickly if they trudged ahead barefoot.

Everyone was envious of Cecile's boots and Jeanne's shoes, and some prisoners would express their jealousy with disarmingly angry glances.

Cecile sighed now, her shoulders and back rolling against Jeanne's. "While we can, we should eat some snow," she said, though she wasn't honestly sure she would be able to stand upright again if she bent over. She thought she might simply fall over if she stooped, and then she risked being shot. Yesterday the guards had executed four women because they had been marching too slowly, lagging behind, or—in one case—because the prisoner had accepted the bread that had been offered by a teen girl as they had marched through a village. The guards had told them they were to speak to no one as they passed through the town, and this prisoner had simultaneously fallen out of line when she had reached for the rye and said something to the girl. The guard who shot her was Pusch, an older man who was known for his thick, white hair, his walruslike mustache, and for the way he refused to beat the prisoners the way most of the guards—especially the female ones—did. He said it was too much work to raise your rod to a Jew: It was much easier to simply shoot them instead.

Cecile guessed there were about three hundred prisoners in their feeble parade and perhaps two dozen guards. Half the guards were women, and sometimes Cecile tried to imagine who was sleeping with whom. Because, clearly, there were romances among the guards. The men tended to be fifteen to twenty years older than the women, and they were the only ones who had rifles. The women had truncheons and clubs. When a male guard wanted to beat you, either he would borrow one of the female guard's rods or he would use the butt of his rifle.

Finally Cecile could bear it no longer, and when none of the nearby guards seemed to be looking—and Pusch was nowhere in sight—she bent over and grabbed a handful of snow in her hand. She licked it slowly, because she had learned yesterday that if she bit into it quickly the cold would send daggerlike barbs of pain against her rotting gums and the holes where her teeth had recently fallen out. Then she passed the snowball back to Jeanne. Instead Jeanne swatted it out of her hand.

"Oh, please," she said simply. "Spare me more snow."

"It helps."

"Not me. It only makes my stomachache worse."

It was approaching noon, and Cecile was hoping that when they finally entered Sliwice they would be given some soup. That was when they had been fed yesterday: around lunchtime. There had been nothing at breakfast and nothing at dinner, but in the middle of the day they had been given a lukewarm cup of a watery soup made from turnips. Since they hadn't been fed yet today, Cecile was telling herself that they were falling into a routine and in a few moments they would be marched into the town and given their lunch. A tepid and largely flavorless soup. But food nonetheless.

Cecile looked ahead of her and saw the prisoner named Vera was saying something. Speaking to her. Vera was taller than most of the women, and so she tended to stoop so she wouldn't stand out. That had been a key to surviving the camp: be invisible. She didn't say much, but Cecile knew she was from Hungary and that prior to the war she had been a schoolteacher. For two years she had avoided deportation because she had had a Wallenberg passport, one of the documents issued by the Swedish diplomat in

Budapest that said the bearer was a Swedish subject awaiting repatriation. Eventually the Nazis and the Arrow Cross fascists simply ignored the passports and deported the Jews anyway.

Now Cecile asked Vera to repeat herself. Sometimes she wondered if her hearing was falling apart along with the rest of her body—as if eardrums, too, could succumb to malnutrition.

"Have you heard where we're going?" Vera was asking.

"I haven't," she answered.

"I hear it's Germany. They're going to put us to work in a munitions factory there. And we're going to be sleeping indoors again in a barracks right beside it."

Jeanne turned to her. Her eyes were running in the cold. "You taught very small children, didn't you?"

The woman nodded.

"I thought so. Only a person who told fairy tales for a living could believe that sort of nonsense."

Cecile felt Jeanne's shivering body against her back; if she hadn't, she feared, she might have slapped her. How many times had she saved Jeanne's life? How many times had she kept the woman going when Jeanne had all but given up? And still Jeanne hurled these malicious, cutting barbs at the other prisoners. At her. It was one thing for the guards to be cruel to them. But it was unconscionable for them to be cruel to one another. If indeed their husbands and their children and their parents were gone, then they were all that they had. When this war was over—and it did seem to be ending, didn't it?—they would all help one another to rebuild their lives. Wouldn't they? Isn't that what families did? What survivors did?

And didn't family members also discipline one another? Keep them in line? She felt like a mother now whose adolescent daughter had grown snappish, and she was about to snap back. To reprimand Jeanne. Before she had opened her mouth, however, the woman on the far side of Vera, another Hungarian whom Cecile barely knew, told Jeanne, "You think you're so clever. Well, you're just mean. How do you know the Germans aren't so desperate for workers they'll use us?"

"Because then they'd feed us!" Jeanne hissed. "If they wanted us to work, they'd give us something to eat!"

"Then you tell me," the Hungarian said, wrapping her bony arm around Vera's shoulders. "Where are we going?"

"To our graves," Jeanne said, narrowing her runny eyes. And then she collapsed, sobbing, into the snow.

ONCE MORE CECILE got Jeanne to her feet, and once more she joined the other women as they started to walk. They lumbered along, some stumbling, all concentrating on the normally prosaic task of placing one foot in front of the other while trying not to think about the pain that came with each step, or the hunger that made their stomachs throb, or the way their work pants or shifts invariably were stained with urine and striped with frozen swaths of liquid feces, because most of them had long since lost the slightest ability to control their bowels.

As they exited the far side of Śliwice, Cecile pushed from her mind her disappointment that the guards hadn't fed them. She tried to think instead about the sunshine and the blue sky, about the way the days were growing longer now. She tried to listen to the birdsong from the beech trees, and she considered reminding Jeanne that, yes, there still were birds in the world. She considered pointing out to her the reasonableness of Vera's supposition that they were going to be put to work in a munitions factory and thus soon would be fed. And she wondered about the carts. There were two of them, long, empty wagons, each one being pulled by a powerful draft horse. The guards had commandeered the animals and the carts from the sugar refinery in the town, and Cecile told herself it was because they were going to fill the wagons somewhere up ahead with provisions. With food and water for the prisoners. With bread and potatoes and milk.

She was considering all of these things, imagining the way cool milk would feel on her throat and her tongue, trying to remain hopeful, when ahead of her she saw an Austrian woman named Dorothea stagger and fall face-first into the road. One of the female guards, a woman perhaps her age with eyes the green of the Mediterranean at sunset and hair the color of freshly cut wheat, yelled at her to stand up. When the Austrian didn't, the guard began kicking at her, driving her boot so hard into Dorothea that the guard was spinning the body with her foot, rolling the woman off the road and into the dirty snow just beside it. Dorothea whimpered, but she made no effort to rise, and Cecile prepared herself for the poor woman's execution. Any moment now, Pusch or one of the other male guards would fall back in the column, turn the Austrian onto her stomach, and shoot her in the back of the head. And, sure enough, here came Pusch, as well as the guard named Trammler, annoyed, it seemed, because yet again one of the prisoners had faltered and slowed down the march.

Then, however, they surprised Cecile. Rather than shooting Dorothea, they actually lifted her up off the ground and brought her to one of the two carts they had taken in Śliwice. Pusch himself carried Dorothea in his arms as if she were his daughter and he were bringing her up to her room at the end of a long day, and then laid the emaciated woman gently in the cart.

"See," Vera murmured to Jeanne. "They do want us alive. They need us and they'll feed us. Soon. You just watch."

For another hour and a half they marched without incident, walking quietly west with the sun at their back. A little past three, however, another woman slipped on a patch of ice on the road and was unable to rise to her feet. She, too, was placed in the cart beside Dorothea. Cecile took comfort in this: Clearly something had changed. Perhaps it was exactly as Vera had said: The Germans needed them alive. Or, even if Vera was mistaken and their eventual destination was not a munitions factory and a warm barracks, perhaps the Russians were closer than they realized and the guards wanted to show their conquerors that they were treating their prisoners humanely.

More humanely, anyway.

In any case, it was possible, wasn't it, that the worst of the march was behind them?

By the time the sun had set they were somewhere between Śliwice and Czersk, and both carts were filled with prisoners. Easily a dozen women had allowed themselves to slip to the ground in the course of the afternoon when they realized they wouldn't be shot but would, instead, be allowed to ride in the carts. The women were sitting or lying down, some on top of each other and some sound asleep, their wheezing and snores filling the dusk like frogs in the swamps in the spring.

The guards stopped for the night when they saw a barn on a small hillside. It wasn't a large structure—it may have been built for horses, not cattle or livestock—and she feared that only the guards would be sleeping inside it tonight. They, the prisoners, would have to sleep outside in the snow. But perhaps there was a farmhouse just beyond the barn, and the guards—most of them, anyway—would sleep there, and the prisoners would thus get the barn. She had to hope that, because the temperature was falling quickly now that the sun had set and she wasn't sure even she could survive a night in this cold in the snow. And so she told herself that any moment now the guards would give them bowls of hot soup, and then herd them all into the barn for the night. Yes, it would be a tight fit, but all that body heat would help keep them warm.

And, sure enough, she saw that three of the guards were pulling down the wooden fence at a corner of one of the fields and using it to construct a fire. Two fires, in fact. Perhaps these would be the flames over which they would prepare them all a warm meal. Perhaps, in the meantime, they would permit them to sit before the fires and warm their skeletal frames.

But the blazes grew high quickly, despite the cold and the still air. They were by no means out of control, but the guards continued to toss thick wooden posts and long strips of fencing into them, until the tips of the flames were dancing high above them, the nearby snow was melting in nearly perfect, concentric circles, and the crackling fires were much too big to cook pots of soup on. Some of the prisoners rushed as close to the twin infernos as they could, rubbing their hands so near the flames that Cecile was surprised they weren't singeing the backs of their fingers. The guards didn't seem to mind. Pusch even smiled and shook his head, murmuring something she couldn't hear to Trammler and the female guard named Inga. In response Trammler smirked, but Inga looked slightly uncomfortable, and it crossed Cecile's mind that whatever Pusch had said had been filthy. A dirty joke of some sort that only men would appreciate. No doubt a joke at the expense of the prisoners.

Then, however, she saw two teamsters leading the draft horses with their carts full of prostrate women as close to the flames as the animals would venture, and then unhitching the horses from the wagons and walking them away from the fires. If Jeanne had been nearby Cecile guessed she would have reassured her friend that the heat must have felt wonderful to those women, and then abruptly her breath caught in her throat and she had the sense that she would have regretted every word. Because suddenly she knew what was going to happen, and she was starting to tremble. To shake in a way that she hadn't all day, despite the cold. Guards, five assigned to one wagon and six to the other, the men and the women working together, braced their gloved hands and their shoulders on the rear and sidewalls of the wagons and started pushing them forward, the wooden wheels turning slowly at first in the melting snow and softening earth, but then gaining speed so they had a momentum of their own, and then with a final push—she heard the guards exhale as one, a loud grunt that sounded uncomfortably like a cheer—they sent the two wagons into the flames, where these great infusions of fuel (flesh and fabric and wood) sent the tendrils of fire and the spirals of smoke spiking ever higher into the night sky, obliterating the stars and masking the moon. Around her the surviving women cried out and gasped, but the screams—if there were any—of the prisoners being cremated alive in the carts were smothered completely by the roar of the flames.

Not far from her was a heavyset female guard with mannish legs and shoulders as broad as a wardrobe. She shook her head and waggled her finger at Cecile and the women beside her. "Let that be a lesson to you," she said. "Shirkers and stragglers will be punished."

Chapter Ten

URI LEANED AGAINST A WOODEN FENCE, EATING
A piece of rye bread slathered with lard, and watched the parade
of German refugees pass by. It was endless. Absolutely endless.
Old people, young people, families. Crippled soldiers. Many had
sleds or carts that they were pulling themselves. The most pathetic were the children, especially in those first kilometers west
of the villages. Invariably, the road heading west from every town
was littered with dolls and stuffed animals and toy soldiers. With
picture books. As the families had packed, the parents had weakened and allowed their little ones to take some toys or books.
Then, however, as they began their trek west, they had discovered just how difficult it was to pull a heavy sled or push an over-
loaded cart, and one by one their children's precious objects had
been tossed aside and left to molder in the ratty snow. He actually
found himself feeling sorry for these people.

Though not that sorry. Just last night he had shot a pair of
Waffen SS troopers on motorcycles as they had sped past him.
Two quick shots. He had no compunction whatsoever when it
came to executing anyone he could in an SS or an SA uniform.
Wehrmacht? Sometimes he spared them, even when the opportu-
nities presented themselves for a clean shot.

He noticed that long strips of the fencing around him had recently been pulled down and used for bonfires in the field perhaps seventy-five meters distant. The snow was melted in two nearly perfect circles, and there were still impressive piles of smoldering black ash. He wondered if the Wehrmacht had had a field kitchen here yesterday or last night. Perhaps some of these refugees had actually been given a hot meal.

Many of the people who passed him were absolutely terrified. When there was sun they expected Russian planes would strafe or bomb them; when there were clouds, they wondered aloud if Ivan would start showering them with artillery shells filled with poison gas. Still, in their minds, being strafed or poisoned was an infinitely preferable fate to being overrun by the Russian army and captured alive: Even some of the children talked with great animation of their families' suicide plans in the event the Russians suddenly appeared before them. Some had stories of schoolmasters and party members who already had done themselves in.

Now Uri was just about to rejoin the procession himself. If anyone asked, he had orders in his pockets to join an assault group forming in Czersk. The army was going to try, yet again, to open a corridor into Danzig. That attack would fail within hours. Uri had absolutely no doubts. But he also didn't seriously plan to be anywhere near it. Czersk was west, however, and these orders—taken off the body of a corporal whose skull had been crushed just west of the Vistula when an artillery shell had sent a sizable chunk of the road into the back of his head—would get him there if any-one asked.

Finally he pushed himself off the fence and started to walk. It had stopped spitting snow a little while ago and the skies were starting to clear. He walked for close to two hours, striding far more quickly than anyone else in the procession and passing everyone he saw. He felt pretty good and thought he might make Czersk by midday—in which case, he would have to make a decision. From there should he proceed northwest along what looked on the map like some garbage road to Brusy? Or should he stay with this crowd and push on to the southwest to Konitz? That was where much of this sorry spectacle was headed next. The road to Konitz was good, there might be food, and there were deserted houses and barns along the way where they might rest in the evening. But on the path to Brusy he would be less likely to encounter German soldiers. And since his orders were to be in Czersk, they did him no good once he was west of that town. He decided he would figure out what to do when he arrived in Czersk. It was likely the village would offer all the chaos he needed to find new orders or a new uniform.

He was within two or three kilometers of the town, noting the way the usually black telephone wires had grown white with snow in the course of the morning, when he noticed something that caused him to pause: He saw a broad-shouldered man a few years younger than him who wasn't in uniform and didn't seem to be either crippled or wounded. He was wearing wool trousers that weren't quite long enough for his legs, and what looked like an aristocrat's winter jacket that was straining desperately at the seams to contain his back and his arms. He was working with an attractive young woman with two blond braids to replace a wooden wheel on a cart, while a younger boy and, he presumed, their mother were looking on. The pair who weren't working had a dusting of snow on their hair and their shoulders—the woman was wearing a fur, the boy an excellent winter jacket—as did the bags of oats and apples the group had unloaded so they could repair the wagon. The young woman was trying to slip a new wheel onto the hub while the man held it off the ground, but it was proving difficult for even this very large fellow to lift the cart up on his own: For every sack or suitcase they had taken off the wagon, at least one remained.

Clearly this family had money: In addition to the cart with the broken wheel, they had a second one parked off to the side. And they had horses. Four magnificent horses. The animals were big, well-muscled stallions, their winter coats lustrous and long.

Curious, he stopped and knelt beside the couple trying to replace the wheel. He motioned at the cart. "You need some help?" he asked.

Beneath that cap the fellow had a thick mane of nearly carrot-colored hair. He barely looked up at Uri from the front axle. Averted his eyes, didn't say a word. Nobody did. A deserter, Uri decided, which meant that he was probably scaring the shit out of him—out of this whole family—and he had to restrain a small smile.

Finally the younger woman with the braids said, "No. But thank you. We expect to be back on the road in a few minutes." He eyed her carefully now. She had a lovely, delicate nose and the sort of full, rich lips that seem always to be slightly parted on very beautiful women. And her hair was exactly that flaxen blond so coveted by Nazi propagandists in search of models. She looked a bit like the boy and a bit, he guessed, like their mother. But those three—the girl and the boy and their mother—looked absolutely nothing like this hulk replacing the wheel. Which meant that he probably wasn't related to them. He was probably this younger woman's fiancé or husband.

"You speak?" Uri asked the fellow.

Now he turned to Uri and nodded.

"With more than your chin?" Uri continued. There was a part of him that couldn't imagine him challenging a man this physically imposing as recently as two years ago. In the first months of his masquerade, he had been more likely either to flatter everyone he met or try to be largely invisible—a nonentity; but he had learned quickly that he was much better off among these people if he was brazen. They were far less likely to question a bully. And now, after nearly two years of fighting, it seemed impossible to Uri not to view every encounter as a confrontation.

The fellow mumbled that he did speak, but he didn't look up from the strut and he spoke in a tone that was striving for annoyance but had just a hint of unease. And there was something in the few syllables that sounded foreign to Uri. American, maybe. Or British. But certainly not Prussian. And certainly not the German Uri had heard growing up in Bavaria. And so another, more interesting possibility occurred to Uri: POW. Not a deserter, a prisoner. He knew that the Germans had been sending British and American POWs to the farms to work the fields the previous summer and fall. Not the Russians, of course. After all, the field work was downright cushy. Instead, the Russian POWs were expected to detonate or remove the unexploded bombs from the urban rubble of places like Hamburg and Berlin. Most of them hadn't the slightest idea what they were doing, and it was just a game of, well, Russian roulette. But they did know that if they were still alive by the time their own army arrived, they'd be killed anyway for surrendering. Or, if they were lucky, sent to some work camp in Siberia.

Uri gazed from this redhead—this Yankee or Brit—to the two siblings and their mother. Like those women he had come across in the castle the other day, one of them might very well have a handgun concealed in a cape or a fur. The pretty blond might have a pistol trained on him right now. Still, he didn't guess they would be crazy enough to shoot a Wehrmacht soldier in broad daylight while harboring a POW.

He wondered what it meant that they were bringing their POW with them. Was he just brawn, like their horses? A pet? Or was he something more? He had heard about romances between Allied POWs and the farm girls. The German men all gone, the girls bored to tears on their estates. Was this one right here before his very eyes?

Finally Uri motioned for the man to move over so he could help him lift the wagon, and the woman would be able to slip the wheel into place. He considered introducing himself, but he didn't want to put the POW in the awkward position of having to speak once again. "Here," he said simply, "let me help. You can't sit here all day with a broken wheel." Then he and the prisoner hoisted the axle just far enough off the ground that the woman was able to place the spare wheel onto the bar and secure it to the wagon. It took about half a minute.

Up ahead, coming from the west, Uri heard the metallic rattle that he instantly recognized as tanks. At least two, and maybe more. Given that the line was moving sluggishly to one side of the road—rather than fleeing like frightened kittens into the brush—he presumed the tanks were German. And, within seconds, he saw them: three Panthers motoring toward them, half on and half off the road so they didn't mow down the refugees. They each had infantry soldiers riding atop them, and they were moving with such purpose that he didn't fear anyone was going to try to recruit him into the assault group.

As they passed he saluted, the sort of lackadaisical wave he offered in lieu of a full-fledged *Heil Hitler*. He watched to see what the redhead would do, and he did, essentially, the same thing. Unlike Uri, however, he was actually sweating, despite the cold.

When the tanks' earth-flattening clanking was beyond them, he glanced at the piles of oats and provisions they had to load back into the wagon. Without asking, he went to one and lifted it onto the cart.

"Oh, we can do that," the young woman said.

"I figured. But you can do it faster if you let me help. And fast is good now that the Russians have broken out of Kulm."

The woman's mother gasped. "Kulm has fallen? Completely fallen?" she asked. She made it sound like Berlin had surrendered.

"Yes, of course," said Uri. He couldn't imagine at first why she might care that such an irrelevant little place had been overrun. As far as he could tell, it was an obscure hamlet that served the aristocratic beet farmers who lived just outside it. But then he glanced at the horses and the quality of the clothes these people were wearing. No doubt they were part of that Kulm gentry. Had probably been on the road only a few days. "Are you from Kulm?" he asked, trying to soften his tone.

"We live there," the young woman said. "My father and my brother were counterattacking the Russians there just the other day!"

Well, they're not anymore, Uri thought, but he kept that response to himself. In all likelihood, the pair was lying dead in a snowbank somewhere. The counterattack had been launched by old men and young boys, and—like everything the Wehrmacht did these days—it had been absolutely fearless and completely ill-advised, and virtually all those old men and young boys had been slaughtered.

The younger brother looked up at the sky now, and he gazed with such curious intensity that the adults around him all stopped what they were doing.

"What is it, Theo?" his mother asked.

"I hear buzzing," he said simply.

Uri had been around enough artillery that he knew his hearing had gone to hell. He couldn't hear yet what this boy—and then, clearly, his older sister—could hear. But he knew what it meant when you heard a buzzing in the sky. The odds were good they were hearing planes. Lots of planes. Far more planes than the Luftwaffe could put into the air at one time these days. And then, before he could warn them, tell them his suspicions, they all heard the sound. In seconds it was transmogrified from insects to engines, dozens and dozens of them, and they saw the great, growling formation, one side actually luminescent as the long swaths of metal fuselage reflected the sun as they emerged from the clouds. The aircraft were British, and suddenly three of the planes were diving toward the column—he wondered if they had seen the German tanks that had just passed—and they all needed to get off the road.

Reflexively he grabbed the mother by her arm and pulled her with him into the fields, sprinting with her past those large, circular piles of ash and toward the barn beyond them. The POW and the two siblings were beside him, racing too, and he was aware that the formerly long and straight caravan had spread like spilled milk into the snow and the fields along both sides of the road. They were nearing the barn when the boy abruptly shrieked, "Waldau! I won't lose Waldau, too!" He let go of his older sister's hand and ran back toward the road, apparently worried about one of those horses.

"Theo!" the prisoner yelled, and then both he and the POW were dashing after the boy.

Up the road they all heard the sound of the screams and the missiles and the diving airplanes, a simultaneous, deafening cacophony, part machine and part animal, and watched as three Spitfires swooped down in a perfect line, one behind the other, their cannons ablaze, splintering the carts and slaughtering the stragglers who remained on the road. One wagon was flying through the air in two massive pieces, its rear wheels still spinning, as were the bodies of three old women who had been traveling together, one of whom had lost her legs in the blast. The air was alive with sheets of newspapers and the stuffing from pillows, and rags of clothing that were either drenched with blood or housing now-unattached arms and legs and feet. Beyond them they saw great plumes of black smoke swirling into the sky like tornadoes, fueled, Uri guessed, by the ammunition and petrol from those Panthers that recently had passed.

And still Theo ran hysterically for the horses.

High above them now the fighters were starting to circle back, preparing for a second pass over the remnants of the column before rejoining their massive, glistening flock. Uri and the prisoner caught up to Theo just as the boy was reaching the two horses that were still attached to the wagon. The animals' eyes were wild and their nostrils were flaring, and they were craning their powerful necks in all directions. But at least they weren't rearing up on their hind legs and attempting to break free. As for the other two? They were nowhere in sight, and Uri hoped for this boy's sake that they had simply run off, and hadn't been blown high into the sky in small pieces like so much else that had been standing on or beside this road just a moment earlier.

With the POW he tried to unhitch one of the animals, while the boy worked on his own to free the other. This was complete madness in Uri's mind, utter lunacy. Had he really lived through so much over the last two years only to get himself killed helping some Nazi boy save his damn horse? He and this prisoner weren't nearly as proficient with the clasps and the buckles as the child, but together they were able to remove the harness and grab the leather reins, and join the boy as he scurried with his horse from the road into the fields.

Behind them they heard more cries and more blasts, and they felt the ground shaking beneath them as they ran, but Uri had the horse now, and the last thing he wanted to do was waste even a second looking back.

FOR A LONG MOMENT after the planes were gone the five of them leaned against an outside wall of the barn. Uri and the POW stood with their hands on their knees, swallowing great gulps of cold air. The boy? He and his sister were each calming one of the horses, stroking them softly along their long, graceful noses. Their mother was standing under the eave, clearly a little numbed. She was, however, the first one to speak. In a tone that surprised Uri with its firmness and control, she said, "That was unwise, Theo. You know that, don't you?"

The child nodded, but said, "I've already lost Bogdana. I shouldn't have to lose Waldau, too." His voice had just a touch of defiance to it.

"Bogdana was his pony," the boy's older sister said, as if that explained everything. Then: "Thank you for helping us. That was completely unnecessary. But very brave."

He looked up. He saw the little boy had cut his cheek at some point, just below his eye, and the blood was trickling like raindrops on glass past his ear and along the side of his jaw. Uri motioned toward it with his finger, and the child's sister reached somewhere inside her cape and found the sort of dainty handkerchief his grandmother used to use—he saw blue flowers, edelweiss perhaps, embroidered into one of the corners—and pressed it gently against the wound. "You hurt yourself, sweetie," she murmured. The boy barely shrugged.

On the road before them the lucky refugees were already starting to restack their bags and their boxes and their suitcases onto their carts and resume their trek west. Others were sobbing over dead children, dead mothers, dead fathers. Some of the dead looked as peaceful as any Uri had seen, while others had died with their arms raised in either anger or despair at the sky. Some were lying perfectly still as their clothing continued to smolder.

Uri turned to this family around him. "What are your names? I know you're Theo. But I don't know the rest of you."

"I'm Anna. And this is our mother."

"And you?" This time Uri spoke directly to the POW.

"He's . . . Otto," said Anna, answering before the man could even begin to open his mouth.

"Like hell he is," said Uri.

"He's—"

Uri waved her off. "He's Otto. I understand." He extended his hand to the POW. "I'm Manfred." The fellow took his hand and smiled at him, his eyes as grateful as a spared fawn's.

"Thank you, Manfred," the mother was saying to him. "Thank you for helping us save the horses."

"We should find the others," Anna said, meaning, Uri assumed, their other animals. She was still pressing her handkerchief against her little brother's cheek. "We have so much loaded on each of the wagons."

"You're supposing your wagons are still in one piece. And your other horses are alive," he said.

"That is hoping for a lot, isn't it?"

"It is," he said. "But let's go see."

URI STOOD WITH this POW over the carcass of what had once been a magisterial stallion. It looked like it had probably run fifty or sixty meters after the Spitfire's cannons had punched great holes in its side and caused the animal's steaming entrails to fall from its abdomen like the contents of a piñata.

"This was Labiau," the POW said, kneeling. He took off his glove and ran his bare fingers along the horse's powerfully muscled shoulders. The fellow's German sounded vaguely Scottish to Uri. "I think they named most of their horses after castles."

"You think," said Uri. "They're not your horses, too?"

The POW realized his mistake and stood. "Yes, I think. I'm not a part of their family. So: Are you going to shoot me?"

The two men hadn't planned on separating from Anna and Theo and their mother, and Uri had the sense that wherever Anna was at the moment, she wasn't happy about the fact that the family's POW was alone with him.

"No," he told the prisoner. "No more than you're going to shoot me."

"Then what?"

He shrugged. "I'm going on to Czersk to rejoin my unit." In the distance, beside an overturned wicker basket that had been blown far from someone's wagon or cart, they saw a horse browsing its contents. "Is that one of theirs, too?"

The POW nodded. "It is. Ragnit."

"And your real name?"

The POW reached into his jacket pocket and pulled out some cigarettes. He handed one to Uri and kept one for himself. "Callum," he said.

"English?"

"Scottish."

"Where were you captured?"

"France. I'm a paratrooper."

"And you wound up this far east . . . how?" Uri asked, lighting the cigarette and savoring the warmth of the smoke in his mouth and his lungs. He realized that he hadn't had a cigarette in at least three or four days.

"I was sent from the stalag to their farm to help with the harvest."

"Alone?"

"No. Originally there were seven of us."

"What happened to the others?"

"They were returned to the stalag."

"But not you."

"No. Their father knew someone. Pulled some strings. He realized he was going to be recruited into the army, and he wanted a man to help manage the estate when he was gone. Do the heavy lifting."

"You know how much trouble you're in now, don't you?"

"How so?"

"Well, I'm not going to kill you. But many other soldiers would. And if the Russians catch you, well, that wouldn't be pretty, either. In their eyes, you'd be either a collaborator or a spy."

"The plan—" Abruptly the POW stopped talking, alarmed that he was saying too much. But it was apparent now to Uri that there was a plan, or at least a vague hope, and it became clear in an instant to Uri what it was: This family, like so many others in this endless and tawdry procession, was going to cross the whole bloody Reich, if necessary, to reach the British or the American lines. And, when they made it, this Scottish para-trooper was going to be their goodwill ambassador. Their cur-rency. Their proof that they weren't your run-of-the-mill Nazis.

There was little doubt in Uri's mind that this Callum and Anna were lovers, and the reason the girl's parents were tolerating their relationship was because this paratrooper was going to be their daughter and son's ticket into whatever post-Hitler world awaited them. For all he knew, the girl's mother was actually hoping the two would marry someday, and they'd all live happily ever after on some Scottish moor. Or, perhaps, she was living under some delusion that in a few weeks' time this man's army would be joining hers to beat back the barbarians from the east. He'd heard people saying such things for a while now. Believing such things. It was, along with their pathetic faith in some wonder weapon that Nazi scientists were supposedly cooking up in underground tunnels somewhere, what kept them going.

Still, this girl's parents might be on to something. Not about the Brits and the Yankees ever aligning themselves with the Germans. And not about the wonder weapons. But he realized if he was still stuck in this German uniform when the end finally came, it would benefit him, too, to have a friend like Callum. He didn't honestly believe that would happen. That it could happen. But he had been a chameleon for so long, what if people didn't believe him when he insisted he was actually Uri Singer from Schweinfurt? What if he awoke one morning and the war was over, and he learned that all the Jews but him had been killed? What if he was actually unable to convince anyone who he was?

"Are you going to Czersk now, too?" he asked the paratrooper.

"Only because it's the next stop on the road."

"And then?"

"Stettin, eventually."

"I've never been to Stettin."

"Me neither."

"Well, why don't I go round up that Ragnit," he said. Gently he touched the toe of his boot to the dead horse at his feet. "And you can tell the family what happened to this one."

The Scot snuffed out his cigarette in the snow and nodded. He put back on his gloves and lumbered off, his shoulders slightly stooped by the weight of the news he was toting.

Chapter Eleven

CALLUM WALKED BESIDE ANNA ALONG THE PATH THAT linked a farmer's field to the road. There was hardpacked snow in the middle, but the innumerable wagon wheels that had preceded them had carved the two ruts on which they were leading the horses. They were down to three animals now, and so they had left behind a few bags of feed and one of the trunks. They had consolidated three trunks into two, with Mutti sacrificing most of her spare clothes. When they reached Stettin, she had said, her cousin would have plenty of coats and dresses to lend her.

It fascinated Callum. It fascinated them all. They were leaving a trunk by the side of the road packed with silks and linens and nightgowns, and no one was bothering to ransack it. No one cared. People could barely struggle forward with the few things they had: They couldn't have cared less about adding more. And so the trunk was just one more suitcase or bag or chest that would sit moldering in the snow until, perhaps, a Russian soldier finally got around to looting it.

On the surface, the Emmerichs seemed fine to Callum, even young Theo. But he knew they weren't. They were stunned by what they had seen and saddened by the loss of Labiau. Still, they were soldiering on, just as they had after Rolf and Helmut had left them at the Vistula. They were continuing now with neither hysteria nor histrionics, because, after all, they hadn't a choice. Nevertheless, he wanted to reach out and embrace them. Especially Anna. Since they had left the estate, it had been difficult to find moments when the two of them could be alone. They had found them, but the kisses and the embraces had been furtive. They certainly hadn't had either the opportunity or the inclination to make love. As a result, it had been the smallest of contacts that had mattered: One time Anna had removed her glove and taken his hand when he had still been riding inside the cart, smothered by all those bags of oats, and the connection—the rediscovery of her skin—had been electric. Another time, one of those nights in one of those barns, when it seemed as if everyone in the world was asleep but them, she had sat beside him and then curled against him, burrowing deep inside his jacket. For close to three hours they had whispered and dozed in their corner of the barn and imagined what their lives would be like when the war was behind them. And they had usually found brief moments to kiss: chaste kisses good night when no one was looking, as well as kisses that were wanton and moist and in other circumstances—simply being warm, perhaps, or being alone—would have left them aroused and desirous of more.

He considered the other girls he had known. He had had girlfriends before, but neither he nor they had ever thought that their relationships might have longevity, and he had made love with only one woman before Anna. The closest thing he had had to a serious relationship had been with the widow nearly twice his age with whom he'd been sleeping—clandestinely—until she had found a more suitable partner and remarried. Her name was Camellia, and her husband had been a friend of his uncle's. That was how they had met. She was tiny: small breasts and boyish hips and dark hair she kept bobbed in a manner that he understood was no longer fashionable. But she was ravenous in bed in a way that, until he was with her, he hadn't realized women could be. She had taught him an awful lot. But he had also understood that their relationship—perhaps even that was too strong a word, perhaps even in his mind he should use the term that she always had, which was *dalliance*—had never had any sort of future. Which, given the fact he was eighteen and nineteen years old at the time and he was being trained to hurl himself from an airplane above blokes who wanted to shoot him like quail, had seemed to make sense. She had actually remarried three weeks before he jumped over France, and he and his mother and his uncle had of course been at the wedding. Her new husband was a few years her senior and worked for the chancellor of the exchequer. The last time he saw her was as he was leaving the reception, and he had kissed her once on each cheek before returning to his barracks. It hadn't felt all that odd. She didn't even wink slyly at him, and he had murmured nothing to her about their past. Already she was back to being a friend of his uncle's. A woman from a different generation.

He thought now about how good it felt to be walking. To be on his feet. With this Wehrmacht corporal accompanying them, he hadn't even considered climbing back under the sacks of feed or the few bags of apples and beets that remained. Before they had set off again he had wanted to tell Anna or Mutti that this soldier knew he was a British POW, but there hadn't been the chance— and the corporal seemed in no hurry to confront anyone. Besides, with only three horses remaining it was clear that the Emmerichs wanted to burden their animals with his weight only when they absolutely had to. With any luck, he told himself, the German soldier's presence would actually prevent anyone from challenging his identity.

When they reached the end of the path through the field, they turned onto a paved road with a sign for Czersk. A teenage boy in a Hitler Youth uniform—no coat, Callum guessed, because he wanted to show off his dagger and his black scarf and his starched white shirt—was barking orders, but no one was listening. He was telling people to keep moving and to continue on to the northwest, but it wasn't as if anybody was going to stop, or anyone in his right mind would even consider turning left and traveling toward the southeast. Still, Callum was careful not to meet his eyes as they passed near him.

"I don't know what we would have done if you and that soldier hadn't rescued the horses," Anna said to him suddenly. Mutti and the corporal were leading the wagon ahead of them, well out of earshot.

"Wasn't all that much. Theo was already up and at them."

"Still . . ."

"It was all reflex," he went on. "Besides, my sense is those that lived were going to be fine, regardless of what we did. Really. There is, it would seem, a good measure of luck involved when you survive something like this."

She nodded. "Imagine if you'd been killed by one of your own planes."

"It wouldn't be the first time someone was. And it wouldn't be the last."

"Mutti was right. What you did—what you and Manfred did—was very brave."

"He knows I'm no one named Otto," he told her. He spoke suddenly, surprising even himself.

She turned toward him, alarmed, her eyebrows collapsing down around her eyes. "How do you know that?"

"He told me when we were rounding up Ragnit."

"What did he say?"

He recounted for her the conversation he had had with the soldier over the remains of poor Labiau, occasionally pausing to listen, almost curiously, to the way the Hitler Youth lad was continuing to scream at no one in particular. The boy was behind them now, and as they had passed him it had grown clear to Callum how very much he was reveling in this role he had been given. He wondered why the boy was having so much fun. Did he really not understand that the end was near? Good Lord, he shouldn't be wearing that ridiculous uniform, Callum thought, he should be burying the damn thing.

"What do you think the corporal's going to do?" Anna asked him, her voice buoyed by little eddies of worry, when he had finished telling her about Manfred. She looked beautiful to him, despite the small, dark bags that had grown beneath her eyes. There were wisps of her lovely yellow hair emerging from underneath her scarf near her ears, and the cold had given her cheeks a rosy flush.

"I don't think he's going to do anything."

"He doesn't care?" She sounded more incredulous than comforted.

"What? Does that seem irresponsible to you?" he asked her, smiling. "Do you want him to shoot me? Turn me in?"

"I'm just surprised. I'm relieved. But I'm also surprised."

"I think he has perspective."

She seemed to consider this. He knew how hard it was even for her to contemplate the end. Then: "Can we trust him? Can we trust him completely?"

"Well, I don't think we have a choice. And, as you observed, his helping me rescue the horses was a rather thankless task. It would certainly suggest he's a good egg."

"Sometimes . . ."

"Yes?"

"Sometimes I wish you were German. Or I were English."

"I know."

"Everything would be easier."

He thought of the first time they had kissed by one of her family's apple trees. And then of the time they had kissed beside a horse chestnut. And, once, near a beech. Always the air had been crisp because they had fallen in love in the autumn. "In weeks or months," he said, "it won't matter."

"But it will."

"No. It's—"

"It's the truth," she corrected him. "Where could we even live, if . . ."

"Go on."

"If we even live through this?"

He saw Mutti and the soldier were engrossed in a conversation of their own and Theo was quietly singing one of his folk songs to himself. And so he took the liberty of actually reaching out his free hand and taking Anna's fingers in his as they walked. Instantly Anna glanced at Theo, saw her brother was oblivious of them, and allowed him to hold on to her.

"We'll live in Elgin," he reassured her. "I've told you, we've plenty of castles in Scotland. You'll think you've never left home." He had thought often about what would happen to them when the war ended. He had even imagined introducing Anna to his mother—his chic, stylish, well-traveled mother who, these days, didn't have a particular fondness for Germans. Nevertheless, he continued to believe that eventually they would all do well together: Although Anna viewed herself as a country girl, the reality was that by any standards but her own she was a bloody aristocrat. A horsewoman par excellence. Even her gloved fingers seemed elegant to him right now.

Still, he understood her fears. He knew she still didn't want to believe the rumors that were spreading fast now about what the Germans had done—for all he knew, were still doing—to the Jews. But he also knew she was beginning to realize there might be some truth to even the most horrifying stories. And so, like many of her neighbors, she had begun to wonder about what sort of retribution might be awaiting her. Not just from the Russians. But, perhaps, from the Yankees, the Brits, and the French, too. He could almost hear in his head his uncle's quiet but intense interrogation of this young German girl he had brought home from the war like a souvenir. *Well, then, tell me, Anna: Precisely where did you think the Jews were going? Oh? What about the Poles, then—you know, your help? And what's this about your mother and the führer? She really seems to have been quite enamored of the old boy.*

And yet Anna really didn't know much, did she? Insinuation. Hearsay. Stories. It was he who had first told her that the Jews were being sent to the camps. And what in the name of heaven was she supposed to do about it—about any of it? She had only just turned eighteen. She had led a life that was at once sheltered and isolated. It wasn't as if she had grown up in a city where she could see the discrimination that was occurring on a daily basis: watch the SA smash the glass windows of the Jewish businesses, round up whole families and send them away. Make them wear those bloody stars. It was more like naïveté, wasn't it? He almost stopped where he was and shook his head, as if he were trying to shed the idea from his mind like chill rain from his hair. Naïveté, indifference. What did that really mean?

He felt her fingers massaging his and exhaled. He told himself that right now he should be focusing on nothing but survival: his survival, and this family's.

Behind them, his hoarse voice finally disappearing into the clamor of the wagons and the animals and the general murmur of the refugees, the Hitler Youth squad leader continued his shouting, despite the fact that no one was listening.

MUTTI COULDN'T RECALL when she had ever been more tired. Her legs felt like giant blocks of granite she was trying to lift with her thighs, and her back was aching in a way it hadn't since she had been thrown from a horse when she was a child and been laid up in bed for six weeks. She remembered the slicing pain well. Then, however, she hadn't had to trudge westward all day long, leading the remnants of her family through the cold, the wind always pricking at their faces and wanting to freeze any exposed flesh.

She half-heard the horse behind her snort in the chill winter air and was vaguely aware of the animal as he shook his long winter mane. Mostly, however, she was focused on this handsome corporal who, like a guardian angel, had appeared out of nowhere and helped to salvage three of their horses and was now leading Ragnit so she could rest her arms. She had been telling him stories of her own sons, of Werner and young Helmut, to pass the time, and he had been telling her about some of his own experiences in the war. She was aware that he was consciously shying away from whatever he had endured in battle, and she surmised this was both because he was such a modest young man and because he wanted to spare her any images that might cause her to worry even more about her husband and her boys. Besides, as Rolf had said on more than one occasion, real soldiers didn't talk about war. It was only the cowards who felt the need to tell people stories about what they had done. And clearly this Manfred was a real hero of the Reich.

Now he was helping to buoy her spirits with his conversation, and to ensure that the Emmerichs kept their place in the stream. There had been rumors that Cossacks—not merely Russians, but Cossacks!—had been sighted nearby.

"Where are your parents?" she asked him. "Are they still in Schweinfurt?"

"They are."

"Have they lost much in the bombing? Until recently, we've been spared this far east. But I know that the western cities are a frightful mess."

"I haven't been home in a while. But my sense is I wouldn't recognize my old neighborhood."

"My cousin said Stettin is largely unscathed."

"Good. You and your family should be safe there for a while."

She thought about this. *For a while.* He hadn't emphasized those words, but they had seemed a meaningful coda.

"Where do you think we'll stop the Russians?" she asked, longing for the sort of reassurance she had once gotten from her husband and her oldest son.

He continued to stare straight ahead, but she saw a small, ironic smile forming at the edges of his—she noticed now—painfully chapped lips. "Oh, I'm just a soldier," he said modestly. "I don't know anything. I just go where I'm told and do what I can. You probably know more about what's going on than I do."

"I know this," she said. "I never thought I'd be running for my life from the Russians. How did this happen? Is it just that their country is so big? Do they just have so many young men they can afford to lose?"

He seemed to contemplate this. "I've asked myself that, too: How did this happen? And it seems to me it has less to do with the Russians—the Russians or the western armies, even—and much more to do with us. I think when this is all over, the Germans will have only themselves to blame."

She recalled how her husband and her brother had talked on occasion about the foolhardiness of attacking Russia—how the Reich had plenty of land and didn't need to take on Joe Stalin. She assumed this was what Manfred was referring to now: the difficulty of waging a war on two fronts. They, the Germans, should have been satisfied with the state of things in 1941 and made peace with Britain. After all, no one had any gripes with the British. Look at Callum. Or the other POWs they had had working for them on the farm through the autumn. Good boys, fine young men. It didn't make any sense at all to be at war with Great Britain.

"Yes, we just don't have the manpower," she murmured, hoping she sounded both agreeable and wise.

"Well, we don't. But that isn't what I meant. I meant we haven't exactly been a civilized empire ourselves. The answer to your question, 'How did this happen?' It's actually pretty simple. We asked for it."

She thought of how long and thin his face was, and how much he had probably suffered. It was as if he had emerged whole from an El Greco canvas, just walked into the world from the frame.

"I've heard that our armies behaved badly sometimes," she said simply. "But then I think of soldiers like you or Werner. Or Werner's friends. We had naval officers at our home in the fall, and they were nothing but gentlemanly. We played music together, they danced with my daughter and her friends. All completely civilized. And so I have to ask: Who? Who then are these German soldiers who have done the things people whisper about? Where are they?"

"I've met some. And it's not just the soldiers. It's the whole German people."

"Who have you met?" she asked. "What have you seen?" She realized that she sounded like a devastated child: a girl who has just learned there are no such things as fairies. Instantly she regretted the tone and tried to reclaim a semblance of dignity. "Tell me, please. I want to know."

He shrugged. "The eastern front is more barbaric than the west, I'll admit that. But there have been atrocities everywhere. And the worst has had nothing to do with the front lines. It's what we have done behind the lines. Behind the barbed wire."

"The work camps? Yes, I've heard stories about them. But I'm sure they're exaggerations, aren't you?"

"I'm not sure of that at all."

"Have you been inside one?"

"No. But once . . ."

"Please. I can bear it," she told him. "I seem to have lost my home and virtually everything I've ever owned. I'm a strong woman, I assure you."

"Once," he said, "I was on a train." His voice had taken on an uncharacteristically somber cast. "It was filled with Jews being sent east."

"You were a guard?"

"No, I wasn't a guard. I was simply a courier. I was bringing some papers to a general in the east. The jeep I was in was strafed and the driver was killed. But I heard a train coming and it was going in the right direction, and so I hitched a ride. There I saw firsthand how we were treating the Jews. It was disgusting. Shameful. Old people, children—everyone—were just jammed into cattle cars. No water, no food, no bathrooms. Inside there they were dying. Literally: They were expiring."

"No."

"Yes."

"Maybe they were criminals."

"The children? The old people? You know that's not true."

"But why would we do that? That's what I don't understand. What could possibly be gained from killing the Jews? It doesn't make sense."

He stopped walking, halting the horse, and stared at her. His eyes seemed sympathetic and kind, and she couldn't decide if he felt guilty for sharing with her what he had seen, or whether he was baffled by how little she knew. Perhaps it was a little of both.

Behind them, on the other side of their wagon, she heard Anna calling out, asking if she was all right.

"We're fine," Manfred shouted back, but Mutti felt his gaze holding her in place. Then, his voice much softer, he said only to her, "No. It doesn't make sense. It makes absolutely no sense at all."

IN THE MIDDLE of the night, Uri awoke and told Callum—who heard him rise—that he was going outside to have a cigarette. They were camped on the floor inside a village gymnasium with perhaps two dozen other refugees, all of whom were asleep at the moment. Callum had said he would join him, but Uri had insisted that he remain here with the women and Theo. You just never knew. And then he walked as quietly as he could in his boots over the sleeping women and children, offering a hearty *Heil Hitler* as he exited the gym to the ancient policeman with a Volkssturm armband who was nervously patrolling the streets.

They were near a train station, and Uri had learned that one of the ways he could slow the ovens was to slow the trains. And so he lit his cigarette and strolled casually there: The village was largely deserted this far east, but he knew there were still trains passing through here going north and south. He'd heard one of those vexing whistles only an hour ago.

When he arrived, he saluted the two guards. They chatted briefly about the state of the war—the pair were noncommittal, unsure who he was and whether he might be the sort who would turn them in if they said something defeatist—and how, at the very least, the trains were still running. Yes, they were slowed by air strikes, but they were still on the tracks and that was testimony to how much fight the nation still had left. He agreed and offered each of them one of the precious cigarettes he had gotten from Callum. They accepted. And then, as they were lighting them, he shot them both. Two quick shots, into the base of the skull of the first and into the face of the second, because that second soldier had turned, stunned, at the sound of the blast. Then Uri had gone inside and shot the fellow who was, apparently, in charge of marshaling the trains onto the proper tracks: It was possible, he saw, to switch and cross the cars onto parallel tracks at this particular station.

He wouldn't have blown up the tracks here, even if he'd had any explosives—which, other than a pair of potato-masher grenades, he didn't. That sound, far louder than three quick shots from his Luger, would have alerted any troops that happened to be nearby. Besides, he didn't have to tear up the tracks to sow a little chaos. Not here. He could stall the trains for hours while the engineers tried to figure out which tracks their cars were supposed to be on; with any luck, one might derail. Now *that* would gum up the works.

Outside he heard voices and the sound of heavy boots on the cobblestones on the street. Already soldiers were coming. And so quickly he ducked out the back door and disappeared into the dark behind the station. Then he started toward the gymnasium, moving—as he did often in the night—with a speed and a silence that once he wouldn't have thought possible.

AT DAWN, Anna traded one of her gold earrings to an elderly woman in the village who rumor had it had potatoes and sausage and bread for sale. They still had apples and sugar, but they had boiled the last of their beets the night before and finished off their remaining tins of canned meat: Their small party had eaten some and given the rest to a young mother and her children who said they hadn't eaten all day. Mutti had been surprised by how quickly their food was disappearing, but they had been generous both with strangers and with themselves. Now Anna bartered with this crone as she stood on the stone steps before the woman's front door. She still had a necklace and bracelets, and she knew that her mother had jewelry as well. Nevertheless, this gold earring was half of a pair that had belonged to her grandmother, and it was the last piece she owned that once had been worn by Kaminheim's original matriarch. The earring was the shape of an oak leaf.

"You have horses?" the woman asked, her voice affectless and cold, when she handed over a half-dozen potatoes that were sprouting eyes the color of dried paste and starting to soften and shrivel with age. Her face was hard-bitten and lined, and her silver hair was hanging lank and unwashed. Anna had heard that she had a husband who couldn't walk, but supervised the transactions from a room near the entrance to the house with a loaded gun in his lap. She had told Mutti none of this.

"We do."

"I have apples."

"We have apples, too. A few anyway. We have apples and oats," she said, smiling in a way that she hoped appeared friendly. "We used to have an orchard."

"I'll save my apples for someone else then."

"What about the sausages and the bread?"

"Sausages?"

"I gave you the earring. You were supposed to give me some sausages and a little bread. Isn't that what we agreed?"

The woman seemed to think about this. Then: "Very well," she said, and she shut the front door and disappeared back into the house. Anna waited a moment and then knocked. No one answered and so she rapped her fingers against the door once again. This time when no one came back she felt a swell of umbrage and offense rise up inside her: She realized that she had parted with her grandmother's earring, and all she had to show for it were a half-dozen mealy potatoes. A part of her comprehended perfectly well that adding a few sausages to the transaction would have made it no less demeaning and exploitive in the long run, but her resentment was tangible: As real as the ice and the snow, as concrete as the soreness in her back from sleeping last night on a gymnasium floor. As painful as the blisters on the sides of her feet. And so she banged her fist hard on the door twice and swore. Used words she had never before spoken aloud. She might have made a scene right there on the street, staying and swearing at the couple through the heavy wooden door that separated them from her, but her family was waiting. They were supposed to keep moving. And so she turned and started back, not completely sure why this small injustice was so affecting, but unable to stop shaking as she walked.

THEO TOOK ONE of their last apples and was feeding it now in slices to Waldau, his favorite, as Anna and Callum started harnessing the other two animals to the wagons. Waldau would be next. Theo liked the feel of the horse's coarse tongue on his open palm as the stallion pulled the fruit into his mouth.

In the last few months, even soap had become scarce and they had had to bathe with a putrescent-smelling cleaner that was made from animal bones and lye, and its stench reminded Theo of the swamp. He knew if one of their horses ever got ill and died, the family would have eaten its meat and made soap from its bones. The whole idea had made him a little queasy. Making soap out of Waldau? Eating meat that had once been Bogdana? He would sooner starve. He would live without soap.

One day in school, Fraulein Grolsch had demanded that all of the students try on a gas mask, because there were rumors that the Allies were going to start gassing them: either the Russians with long-range artillery shells or the Yankees and Brits with bombs they would drop from their airplanes. There were only two masks for the entire class, however, and so the children had taken turns pulling the devices over their faces and hoisting the thick rubber bands behind their heads. Invariably, the bands had pulled at their hair and some of the girls had shrieked for attention, and no one had found it easy at first to breathe through the filter. Theo re-called now how he had asked—yet another stupid, un-thinking thing he had said that had further diminished him in the eyes of his classmates—if the government would be giving them masks for their animals. The students had all gotten a real belly laugh out of that one. He hadn't honestly expected that anyone had bothered with such a thing, and he was really just thinking aloud. Imagining. But it hadn't struck him as a completely non-sensical idea, because this was farm country and the horses were critical to the farms. And he knew that in the First World War they had made gas masks for horses. After all, if you could convince a horse to wear a bridle and a bit, was it really such a stretch to expect the animal to don a mask, too? Apparently not. And if there were going to be masks for animals, Theo would have been sure to tell his parents so that they could get ones for all of their horses.

"Theo?"

He looked up; it was Anna.

"We should hurry."

He nodded and led Waldau to the second wagon. No one had told him why they must hurry, but he had overheard Anna and Mutti talking and so he knew. It wasn't just the Russians. Last night someone had assassinated two Wehrmacht soldiers near the train station and then murdered the stationmaster. As a result, two trains that had been traveling in the night had taken the wrong tracks and collided. They had all heard the noise and presumed at the time it was an Allied bomb. One of the trains, the one moving northwest, was filled with refugees; the other, traveling southeast, had been filled with soldiers. The trains had been approaching the station so neither had been moving quickly. Nonetheless, there were injuries, a few as serious as concussions and broken bones. And for the time being the saboteurs had succeeded in clogging this stretch of track.

As he stood high on his feet to lift the bridle over Waldau's head he felt an unexpected twinge in a toe and grimaced. Still, he whispered into the great horse's ear, "You will never be eaten and you will never be gassed. I promise."

"SO, YOU'VE ALWAYS been here on the eastern front," Callum asked Manfred as they walked along a quiet stretch of road. There were other refugees, but for the moment they seemed to be bobbing almost leisurely between the waves and once more Callum was grateful to be on his feet.

"I have."

"Is it as frightful as everyone says?"

"I think so. But this is my first war, so I don't have a lot to compare it to," Manfred answered, and he smiled.

"Everyone presumes the eastern front is much more horrific than either France or Italy. I take that implication as a compliment."

"Because it suggests you and your American allies are so civilized?"

"Precisely," he replied. It was true, they were civilized. He was sure of that. He and his mates had a much higher regard for human life than either the Russians or the Germans. The western Allies were, he imagined, every bit as brave as these other people. But they were also less likely to kill—or be killed—senselessly.

"Well, we're all nastier on this side of Europe," Manfred told him. "Trust me: If your parachute had landed over here, we wouldn't have taken you prisoner."

Callum thought about this and listened to the sound of the horses' hooves behind them. Their metronomic clopping made him think of a clock, and he tried to place in his mind precisely where he was a year ago now. Then two. Then three. He saw himself once again as a student and recalled the face of Camellia. "You married?" he asked the corporal.

"I am not."

"Girlfriend? Fiancée?"

"Neither."

Anna was on the driver's box on the wagon behind them. She must have heard what they were saying, because she called out to them now, "Manfred is just a warrior." She was teasing him, a small swell of sarcasm in her voice. "He is one of those German men who have too much knight in their blood. I know the type well."

The corporal turned back to her and said, "Now for all you know, I was a mild-mannered young lawyer before joining the army. Or a docile schoolteacher. For all you know, I am actually an extremely peaceful person."

"All right then," Callum said, and he clapped the man on the shoulder good-naturedly. "What did you do before the war? We're all ears."

"Do you know what you remind me of?" Manfred asked him instead of answering the question.

"Absolutely no idea. Haven't a clue."

"A Saint Bernard. That's what you are. A very big dog. The

sort of creature that hasn't figured out yet that he has ham hocks for paws. Wants to jump on the couch, even though he's the size of a pony."

"Quite through?"

"All done."

"Well, I was expecting much worse," he said. And he was. "I rather like big dogs with favorable dispositions."

"You didn't tell us what you were doing before the war," Anna pressed the soldier.

"I say he was a lawyer," Callum told her. "It was the first profession that popped into his head a moment ago." He turned to Manfred: "Am I right?"

"No."

"A schoolteacher then? Really? I wouldn't have guessed it."

"You will be disappointed."

"Dear God, you weren't a student were you?" he continued. "Have you been in the army that bloody long?"

"I worked in a ball-bearing factory."

"Well, that's honest work. Why would I be disappointed?"

He seemed to Callum to be pondering this for a moment. Then: "Perhaps because I was. It wasn't quite what I expected I would be doing with my life when I was fifteen or sixteen years old."

Overhead the clouds parted just enough that they all felt great shafts of sun on their faces, and as one they reflexively stared up into the sky. "I don't think any of us wound up doing quite what we expected," Callum said. His stomach growled loudly and he thought of how hungry he was. For a moment he envisioned himself as a Saint Bernard, and he wished they hadn't finished off all of their meat and their bread and their beets.

THAT DAY THEY passed through a village and had lunch by a warm stove in the kitchen of a carpenter and his wife who seemed oddly prosperous. They were having meat for lunch, some sort of stew made with pork and root vegetables, and they offered the trekkers real coffee. The couple was packing to leave, too, when the Emmerichs passed by and they noticed Manfred. Because Manfred was in uniform, they insisted on inviting them indoors to eat and rest. They wanted to finish off the food they had left that they couldn't bring with them, so the Russians wouldn't get it.

As they ate, the carpenter shared with Manfred and Callum— who said not a word—the secret behind his success: He always got wood because he had joined the party. And, since 1942, he made nothing but coffins. "These days, I can't make too many coffins," he said, his voice at once oddly satisfied and rueful. The pair had two sons, both of whom were missing in action. Their daughters, both married, had gone to Prague where, supposedly, they would be safe from Allied air attacks.

Theo thought Manfred seemed to pay the man special attention when the carpenter told him how recently there had been columns of prisoners passing by, and one of the groups had been nothing but women. Rows and rows of them, he had said.

"And they were marching west?" Manfred asked.

"They were. Starving things. Jews. Belinda here managed to give some of them food. Bread and the last of our sausages. She snuck it to them as they passed. Some of them didn't even have shoes. Can you imagine? I mean, they're just Jews. But still. I'd heard about such things, but never seen them with my own eyes."

"Where were they from?"

"Well, the east."

"No," Manfred continued, his voice a little testy now. "I meant what countries were they from?"

"I heard some of the girls speaking French. I heard others speaking Polish. Even, I think, a little Russian."

"Any German?"

"A few, maybe."

"How old were they?"

"At first I thought they were older than me, and I am sixty-two. It was only when Belinda got close to them that we could tell. They were in their twenties and thirties. They'd have to be. Any older and they would have perished by now in this weather."

Theo watched Manfred seem to take this in. He thought the soldier was seething inside and working hard to maintain an even facade. And his sister? He could see anger on her face as well, but something else, too, and when he understood what it was he grew scared: It was guilt. Shame, as if she were responsible. He felt a small chill in the room, despite the heat from the stove, and for the first time he began to wonder: Was this—*those prisoners*—why the whole world seemed so mad at his country? Was this what those British POWs and Callum on occasion had whispered about? He had a sense that was just beyond perfect articulation in his mind but nonetheless absolutely apparent to him: When this war was over, he and his family—all Germans—were going to have to live with the black mark of this (whatever *this* was) for a long, long time.

Chapter Twelve

ANNA WAS VAGUELY AWARE THAT SHE WAS FAR FROM the comforts of her own bed in Kaminheim. She was wrapped tightly inside a pair of quilts, half-buried in the hay in a barn. Another barn. Not even a gymnasium, albeit an unheated one, such as the one where they had spent the night before last. This barn was far from the main road, perhaps a kilometer distant. They had come here for privacy and quiet. To escape the throngs. She wasn't freezing, but her feet—despite the reality that she had slept yet again in her boots—and her fingers were chilled. Her nose was running from the cold, and when she removed her hands from beneath the quilts she was stunned to discover how warm her face was. Was it possible she had a fever? Was this why she was shivering? Slowly she began to focus, but still she kept trying to push full wakefulness away, as if it were a suitor at a dance she was trying to avoid. She recalled how they had stopped here last night. Her family and Callum and Manfred and the three horses had all taken refuge in one corner, while another family had taken the side nearest the entrance, and the humans had all been grateful to have the heat generated by the Emmerichs' animals. For dinner, Manfred had shown them how to bake the potatoes in the wild: He had buried them in a shallow hole, and then built a fire on the patch of ground directly above them.

Now Anna could tell by the hazy light that was coming in through the cupola and a pair of eastern-facing dormers that day had broken. She heard the low rumble of voices, men's voices, but she couldn't make out what they were saying. It didn't sound like Manfred and Callum, and so she guessed it was that other family. But then, when she visualized those other refugees—their name, she thought, was Sanders—she could see in her somnambulant fog only one male. A grandfather. There were the grandparents, a married daughter and a daughter-in-law, and two small girls. And neither of the voices, as she tried to concentrate, sounded much like the girls' elderly grandfather.

Nevertheless, for another moment she allowed herself to drowse and to wonder, almost as if she were witnessing this happen to somebody else, at the idea that she was sleeping in a barn and she might be coming down with a fever. Might? No, not might. It all came back to her now. Yesterday she had started to grow ill and had nearly passed out. They had stopped here because she simply had to rest. And now it was just so much easier to remain curled in a ball under these quilts, to allow her fever—if, indeed, she had one—to run its course, than to rise from the hay and begin the hard work of continuing west. Melting the snow so she could wash. Feeding the horses. Rummaging for a piece of bread they had scavenged or a small handful of the muesli they had bought with a bracelet. When she'd been younger, there had actually been a servant girl who had laid out her clothes for her in the morning and then had her breakfast waiting. A Polish girl. Jadwiga. She guessed the servant had been with them through 1941. Then? Deported somewhere. The girl's parents were taken, too. Mutti had been devastated. Her father had made phone calls. Sent telegrams. But there had been nothing that either of her parents had been able to do. It seemed that Jadwiga's father had been involved with the Communists. Perhaps even the resistance.

Anna was just beginning to wonder where the rest of her family was—Mutti and Theo—when she was pulled abruptly from her torpor by the distinctive, full-throated whinny of her horse. Balga was, it sounded, just outside the barn. And he sounded furious. She sat up now, imagining that Manfred or Callum was mishandling the animal in some fashion, antagonizing him inadvertently. Instead, however, she saw Balga silhouetted in the massive barn doors, rearing up on his hind legs while two men she didn't recognize were trying (and failing) to convince the horse to remain still so they could place a saddle upon him. These, she realized, had been the voices she had heard.

She rose, pushing her quilts off her, and stormed toward the pair. The cold struck her like a slap, but she didn't care, because these fellows were trying to steal her horse—and she wasn't going to stand for that. Her family had already lost Labiau; they couldn't afford to lose Balga, too. They simply couldn't. She didn't know where the rest of her family was, but she didn't hesitate. She would simply insist that these other refugees leave her horse alone. Steal someone else's. When she was halfway across the barn, however, she stopped, realizing in an instant how ill-advised it was for her to have even considered confronting these men. Because they weren't mere horse thieves; they weren't pathetic refugees like her and her family. They were Russian soldiers—perhaps even Cossacks—working in fur hats and long uniform coats, with bandoliers of bullets draped over their shoulders like scarves. She started to crouch, but it was too late: They had seen her. And they started to laugh, despite the reality that one was straining desperately to hold Balga in place by the reins, and the other was holding on to a heavy-looking saddle with both hands.

The soldier nearer to her dropped the saddle into the snow, said something to the other soldier, and started toward her. He had a long, drooping mustache and perhaps two days' growth of beard, and he had an exasperated smile on his face as he sauntered across the barn: *First the horse*, she imagined him thinking, *now this*. Meanwhile his partner let go of Balga's reins and then fell against an exterior wall of the barn so he wouldn't be kicked by the animal's wildly flailing front hooves as the creature scurried a dozen meters away before stopping. From there the horse eyed them warily, snorting, and raised his nose high into the air. She started to call for him, but the words caught in her throat. She realized the only place she could run was further into the barn, and that would do her as little good as standing her ground. Perhaps she could try to dash past the Russians and jump atop Balga, but the horse was probably far too riled to allow her to climb upon him with neither a saddle nor stirrups. Besides, it seemed unlikely that she would get past the two soldiers. They'd simply grab her like a small chicken. And so she remained where she was, in a half-crouch beside head-high bales of hay, telling herself that she was unmoving now because she was feverish and there was nothing she could do. Suddenly she felt so sick and fatigued that she almost didn't care if they raped and killed her right here. In this barn outside of some village she'd never heard of. Fine. Let it all end this morning. And then, in little more than a heartbeat, the soldiers were surrounding her. She realized that neither was especially tall, and she could look them both in the eye.

"Do you speak Polish?" the one with the mustache asked her, his own Polish marked by an eastern-sounding accent she didn't recognize.

She nodded. She smelled, she thought, chocolate—delicious, real chocolate—on his breath. She wondered if she was a little delirious, or whether they really had eaten chocolate for breakfast.

"She speaks Polish," he said to his comrade, as if this were a great revelation. Then to her he continued, "Your horse—and I'm presuming that is your horse—is a demon." He looked back over his shoulder toward the open barn doors. Balga had inched a few meters closer and was peering inside.

She glanced down at her boots, wrapped her arms around her

chest. She wasn't sure what she should say—if she should even say anything. She realized her teeth were chattering.

"I am Lieutenant Vassily Kuptchenko. This is Corporal Rostropovich. And you are?"

"Anna," she said, the word elongated by the clacking of her teeth.

They both bowed slightly, gallantly, as if they were noblemen. The lieutenant pointed at the piles of quilts and her cape in the mound of straw behind her. "Go get your coat. Or at least one of those quilts. You're trembling." She took a fleeting peek behind her, but she couldn't bring herself to turn her back on the men. When she remained riveted in place, the lieutenant said something to the corporal in a language she didn't understand, and the soldier went and brought her cape to her. Gently he draped it over her shoulders.

"Where . . . where . . . is my family?" she said, the short sentence again punctuated by her shivers.

"We saw the wagons and the horses. But no one else."

"They're gone?"

"They didn't leave you, I'm sure. Your army set up a field kitchen a few kilometers from here, back toward the road. They're probably getting breakfast," he told her.

The corporal rolled his eyes and murmured something under his breath that caused the lieutenant to smile.

"Forgive me. There *was* a field kitchen. Now there's just a field. Your army left rather quickly."

"We've been overrun?"

He brushed the idea away. "Not yet. But you will be. It's all chaos right now. But you should go. Not everyone is as tolerant of nice German girls as I am. I assume that demon of a horse will let you climb upon him?"

"But my family? What about my family?"

"Child—"

"I'm not a child!" she said, blurting the words out. She feared the moment she had spoken that she had made an egregious mistake. She should have just gotten on Balga and ridden off to find Mutti and Theo. Tracked down Callum and Manfred. Given the two of them—the two of them and her mother and brother—a piece of her mind for leaving her here all alone. What in the name of God were they thinking? But the Russian lieutenant didn't seem to have been angered by her remark.

"Fine, you're not a child. More the reason to run," he said, and he held up his hands as if he were balancing a plate on each palm. The corporal was nodding his head earnestly. "Maybe if you're with us, that monster will let us get a saddle on him for you."

"That doesn't look like his saddle."

"It isn't."

"There's a saddle he knows in one of the wagons."

"The one with all that feed?"

"The other one."

"Fine. You take the saddle, if that's the only one he'll allow on his back. But we'll keep the rest. You really are getting a bargain, you know."

She was still shaking, and she wasn't even sure she was capable of riding Balga right now. But she guessed she hadn't a choice. These two soldiers were gentlemen. Or, at least, decent human beings. It was unlikely the next Russians would be as well. And so she started past them toward the entrance to the barn, walking with her head held high—but she hoped, not haughtily—experiencing at once fury over the way she had been abandoned by her family and gratitude toward these two Bolsheviks for sparing her life.

As she passed through the open doors, squinting slightly against the daylight, she saw poised on either side were Callum and Manfred, their backs flat against the barn board. Callum was to her right and Manfred was to her left, and they were both holding guns: The paratrooper was grasping the antique pistol her mother usually concealed under her cape—it had been her husband's during the First World War—and the Wehrmacht corporal had his rifle in his hands. She realized they knew the Russians were a couple of steps behind her and were going to ambush them, and the thought was just beginning to formulate in her head that she should tell Callum and Manfred that these soldiers were kind—that they hadn't harmed her, that they were actually sending her on her way. But the notion was still germinating, finding a warm spot in her mind to put down roots, when the two men spun and were firing. She spun with them, heard a voice—was it her own?—actually screaming *No! Don't shoot!*, the words running together, but she was an instant too late. As she turned, she saw from the corners of her eyes that one of the Russians was being lifted up and off the ground by the force of the bullet—*was this the one named Vassily?*—and the other, the corporal, was simply buckling at the knees and collapsing silently into the straw as if he were one of the elk that were shot each year in the park behind Kaminheim.

For a long moment her ears were ringing the way they had on that first day of their trek, when the Russian shell had exploded beside them as they had approached the Vistula, and so she was only dimly aware of the echoes from the two gunshots. Or of the cries of the birds that had disappeared abruptly from the nearby trees. Initially, she didn't even realize that with careful, tentative steps, Balga had inched closer to her. Mutti, too. And Theo. All she was cognizant of was the smell from the gunshots and the way these Russian soldiers had been only steps behind her just a few seconds ago, and now they were dead in the straw at her feet. They each looked as if their last thought had been only surprise. Not terror, not fear. Not even anger. They had both been shot in the chest, though the almost point-blank wound inflicted by the rifle had created a black, bowl-like chasm in Vassily's coat, and long wisps of steam were rising up from it into the barn. The hole in the corporal's coat was smaller, but no less fatal.

She felt Callum beside her, and she could tell that he wanted to hold her. To comfort her. But she didn't care. She was angry at him. She was angry at Manfred, too. Furious.

"They didn't hurt me!" she said finally, and she could hear the harshness in her voice. "They didn't mean any harm!"

Callum knelt before the corporal he had killed, staring almost aimlessly at the body before him. He seemed numb.

"Do you hear me!" she said, shrieking. "You didn't have to kill them!"

Manfred squatted beside Callum and pulled the bandolier of bullets up and over the corpse's head. He laid it out flat on the ground beside him. Then he removed the man's holster and pistol and started emptying the pockets in the fellow's pants and coat, extracting papers and maps and tobacco. A photograph in an envelope. Yet more bullets. Dried meat in wax paper. A little cheese. Chocolate. Stubs of pencils. A pair of field glasses. A knife in a leather sheath. A canteen. A small bottle of vodka.

"This is good," Manfred said to no one in particular. "All helpful." He took a bite of the cheese and seemed far more interested in the weapons and the food than he was in the papers. He handed the meat to Callum, but the Scot shook his head no. Literally turned away.

"Aren't you listening to me?" Anna shouted at them both. "You killed them and you didn't have to!"

Callum seemed to hear her for the first time. He sat down in the hay and tossed the pistol onto the ground. "I've never killed anyone," he said simply. He looked a little woozy.

"I still find that almost inconceivable," Manfred said, putting the tobacco in a pouch in his own overcoat.

"I told you, the drop was a complete boondoggle. We were captured almost instantly."

"Well, you've killed someone now," he said, rising to his feet and clapping Callum on the shoulder. "It's not so hard, is it?"

"It wasn't. But it is now."

"Of course, you did shoot a pair of your allies," Manfred added, slinging his rifle back over his shoulder. "That can't be good."

"That's not funny."

"Perhaps not. But it is ironic. *Prost!*"

"Are you completely insane? Do you feel nothing?"

"I did the first time I killed someone. I actually sobbed."

"Well, then. Leave me be."

"Oh, I'm sorry. Was *prost* the wrong toast for a Scotsman? Should I have said *cheerio*? *Slàinte*, perhaps? What are the proper remarks? You tell me."

"*L'chaim,*" Callum muttered.

"Come again?"

"I said *l'chaim*. But that would be absurd, wouldn't it? Even if I were Jewish, I would never say *l'chaim* around here. Oh, no. You'd pin a star on my coat and ship me off to God alone knows where."

For a brief moment Anna thought Manfred was going to hit Callum, despite the reality that the POW must have had forty or fifty pounds on him. His eyes widened ominously and his breathing seemed to stop. But then he inhaled deeply and blew the hot air in a stream into his hands. She looked back and forth between the two men. She felt invisible, despite the way she had yelled at them, because they were so absorbed in each other. And so she reached out for Manfred's arm and spun him toward her, since clearly he was the one who had initiated this needless slaughter. "Don't you understand?" she hissed at him. "You didn't have to kill them! They were leading me back to Balga!"

He seemed to think about this. Then: "Very nice. They were letting you keep your horse. And the two wagons? And the other horses? What were their plans for them?"

"They—"

He waved her off. "They were Russian soldiers. The people trying to kill us, remember? Look, I know what they were doing, I heard them. I was just outside the barn. Fine, they didn't rape you. You were lucky—"

"I was lucky?" she asked, her voice an uncharacteristic snarl. "Lucky? Where were you?" She turned to face her mother and her brother. "Where were all of you? How could you have left me alone like this? I'm sick, I'm tired. I have a fever!"

Mutti tried to enfold her inside her arms, but she pushed her mother away.

"Yes, you might have a fever, sweetie, I know," her mother murmured, and then her eyes welled up and she stood there helplessly. "We were just getting some breakfast. Getting you some breakfast. We thought we might even find a doctor among the other trekkers. We were only gone a few minutes, and we thought you would be fine for a moment. We wanted you to rest. We didn't know there were Russians so close. We just didn't know . . ."

Anna noticed that Theo was holding a wicker basket with a couple of biscuits in it and a porcelain mug filled with soup. It looked like it was beans with a little fatty meat floating on top. Theo started to hand it to her, but she brushed her brother aside.

"These two were probably scouts. Or artillery spotters," Manfred said, motioning at the bodies in the straw. "Doesn't matter. We should join everybody else and get moving. Ivan isn't far behind." He looked down at Callum. "You should take the rifle—and one of those bandoliers. And . . ."

"Yes?"

"And I'm sorry if I seemed a little callous just now. I've seen a lot and sometimes I forget myself."

The Scot nodded, grabbed the firearm, and pushed himself to his feet. Manfred took Balga's reins in his hands and started to lead the animal back toward the wagons.

"How do you feel?" her mother asked her. "Can you travel?"

"Of course I can travel. I don't have a choice now, do I?"

"Would you eat something then? Please?"

She shook her head. "Later, maybe."

"And you really must drink something."

"Oh, no, none of you need to help me," Manfred was saying.

"I'll get the feed bags on the horses, I'll get them harnessed to the wagons. I'll throw the blankets and quilts in the back. You all: Just keep chatting and dawdling."

"I'm coming," Callum yelled out to him, and then he went to assist the German soldier, passing by her without saying a word.

"What should we do with those men?" Mutti asked, and with just a small twitch of her head she motioned down at the ground. "We can't just leave them here." Theo was staring at the bodies, too. A small, thin rivulet of blood had begun to trickle across the frozen ground beneath the corporal; a stain the color of rotting cherries—more black than red—was waxing imperceptibly into a moon around the crater in the lieutenant's chest.

"What, you want to bury them, Mutti? Like your Luftwaffe pilot?"

"Is there time? You said they weren't going to harm you."

She was still shivering, and she honestly didn't know anymore whether it was because of the cold or because she was sick or because she had been surprised as she woke by these two enemy soldiers. But she didn't care. She knew only that she was miserable. Still, she reminded herself that her mother was miserable, too. Her mother was losing, in essence, a lifetime's worth of work— her home, the farm, and everything there. Meanwhile, two of her three sons and her husband were off fighting the Russians somewhere.

She glanced over at Callum and Manfred and saw that it was going to take them a few minutes to attach the animals to the wagons. She was more proficient than either man with the horses and so she went to them. She told them that she and Theo could finish harnessing the horses if they could dig a grave for the Russians. She reminded them that they had brought a shovel from Kaminheim.

"I know I would want my husband and my sons to have decent burials if they were killed somewhere far from home," Mutti added.

Manfred dropped the reins to his sides and folded his arms across his chest. "You would?" he asked.

"Yes, absolutely."

"No, I don't think so. Forgive me. But if we bury those two, their wives and mothers—whoever—will never have any idea what happened to them. At least not for a very, very long time. But if we leave them where they are, someone will find them."

"Besides, do you know how bloody hard the ground is?" Callum said. "Burying them would be no picnic, I promise you. It might not even be possible."

From the road they heard an explosion, then another. Anna glanced reflexively in that direction—all the humans did—but the horses were already growing accustomed to the sound and barely looked up. She guessed the bodies would grow cold and then freeze before night. Or wolves might drag them away. Or crows might peck at the exposed flesh until it was gone.

"We could put markers where we've buried them," Mutti said, and Anna wondered if her mother was envisioning precisely the same things that she was.

Manfred looked at Callum and then shook his head. He seemed beyond annoyed to Anna: He seemed downright disgusted. Nevertheless, he went to the back of the wagon and grabbed both the shovel and the pitchfork.

"Fine," he mumbled, tossing the pitchfork like a baton to the POW. "We'll try to bury the damn Ivans. And then we are getting the hell out of here. Okay?"

"Thank you," she said. "I know it must seem ridiculous."

"The ground will be softer inside the barn," he said to Anna. "We'll bury them there. As your mother suggested, we'll put their IDs on the marker," he added, his tone softening slightly, his face losing its severe cast. "You're . . ."

"Yes?"

He clasped his hands behind his back as if, she thought, he were a boy pretending to be a man. Or, maybe, because otherwise he would have reached out to touch her when he spoke. "It is ridiculous. But you and your mother are kind to want to do this. And kindness is in short supply these days."

Then he walked into the barn, muttering something to Callum, and she heard only the very tail end. It didn't make sense to her, at least not completely. It was something about her and her family as Germans. As *those people*. As something other than him, as if he weren't a German himself—or, possibly, as if he no longer wanted to define himself as one. She kept thinking about this as she wrestled the horses into their harnesses, wondering what he had meant. She made a mental note to ask him about it at some point, perhaps when they had once again put some distance between themselves and the Russians.

Chapter Thirteen

THE SKY WAS AS RED AS HOT COALS, AN UNDULATING
river of crimson, and Cecile was confused. For a brief moment
she thought it was the end of the day and the sun merely was setting. But as she staggered half-awake through the front doors of
the train station she realized it was still dark to the west and it
was the eastern sky that was alight. Yet clearly it wasn't morning, either. And, besides, when had she seen a sky like this at day-
break?

"That must be Berent. The whole village must be on fire,"
Jeanne was murmuring, and she sounded more awed than frightened. Berent was no more than eight kilometers behind them.
Around Jeanne the female prisoners were starting to form into
lines.

Cecile vaguely recalled encouraging her friend to curl against
her for warmth when they had gone to sleep a few hours earlier
on the cement floor of the train station. When the guard had
kicked her awake just now, it had taken her a moment to realize
that Jeanne already was gone. Up and about. Apparently they
were not going to wait any longer for the train to arrive that—
the guards had told them—was going to take them to their new
destination. And so the prisoners were being assembled outside in

the cold, and once more they would resume their trek west on foot.

"I wonder if there was an ammunition dump in Berent, or an arsenal, maybe," Jeanne was continuing. "So many of the buildings there were stone. Otherwise, I don't think the town would go up like that."

Cecile nodded and took her place in line with the other women in the road before the train station. There were two streetlights and she was surprised they were on. Usually in the night the Germans dimmed everything to protect themselves from air attacks. She saw that one of their male guards, that bastard walrus named Pusch, was speaking to a pair of young German soldiers she'd never seen before who were sitting atop motorcycles. The three of them were using a flashlight to study a map, evidently deciding which roads were safest.

"There was an SS company back there," Jeanne said. "In Berent. I just heard. I wouldn't be surprised if they set the whole town on fire themselves. You know, leave nothing for the Russians? Or maybe they're just going to fight to the death." She spat on the ground and then rubbed her hands vigorously over her arms. "Well, good riddance to them. Good riddance to them all."

"You're feisty tonight," Cecile told her.

"Well . . ."

"You can tell me."

"When you were asleep, Vera found mess kits under one of the benches. Three of them. Soldiers must have forgotten they were there. And when the lights were out, we feasted."

She felt a pang in her stomach, part hunger and part hurt. "And you didn't wake me?"

"You sleep so little. We didn't think you would want to be disturbed."

She realized she was experiencing more than hurt: This was outright betrayal. Jeanne and Vera hadn't wanted to share this unexpected bounty. And after all she had done for Jeanne. For all of them. She was absolutely positive that if it weren't for her, Jeanne would be dead now.

"What was in them?" she asked, unsure why she was tormenting herself this way by inquiring. Did she really need to know? But in the same way one can't resist picking at a scab, she was unable to prevent herself from asking.

Already, however, Jeanne understood her mistake. "Really, not that much," she said sheepishly.

"Not that much?" This was Vera. Incredulous. "We gorged! There were tins of meat and tomatoes and canned milk! There was *knäckebrot*, and the crackers were still crisp—which meant that mostly we broke them into pieces and sucked on them," she said, offering them all an ironic, toothless grin. "There was even hard candy!"

Jeanne was gazing down at the ground, her guilt a dark halo behind the prickly hair on her head. Cecile imagined them silently unwrapping the crackers and opening the tins with one of those small can openers that came with the kits. In her mind she saw them using their fingers like spoons to extract the meat, then licking the lids from the cans to get the last drops of tomatoes and milk. And then she willed those images away. She reminded herself that all she had left was her attitude. Her mind. They could take everything else from her: In the end, they might even take her life. But they couldn't take away what she thought. They couldn't take away hope. Perhaps Jeanne and Vera simply needed that food more than she did. Fine. Perhaps the two of them wouldn't get through this without that unexpected discovery. Well, that was fine, too. She would.

She reached over to Jeanne with her hand and tenderly lifted her face by her chin. "It's okay," she whispered. "I want you this spirited. I *need* you this spirited. It's how we'll survive."

Her friend looked into her eyes and Cecile wasn't sure how she was going to respond. What she was going to say. Then, like the wind that precedes a thunderstorm, the air between them grew charged and Jeanne was shaking her head and her bony shoulders and starting to sob. She gave in to long, eaglelike ululations of despair—loud, heaving wails of remorse that merged with self-recrimination and self-loathing. Cecile and Vera together tried to embrace her, Cecile cooing softly into her ear that it was all right, to let go of the guilt, but Jeanne continued to cry, her eyes shut tight like a child's, as the tears streamed down the wrinkles in her gaunt, emaciated face. "No, I am horrible," she howled suddenly. "I am as bad as they are!"

She was shrieking in French, but it didn't matter. Pusch had heard her—everyone at the train station had heard her, the prisoners were glancing at them from their places in line—and he was marching over to them now. The last thing he was going to endure in the middle of the night was a scene from a hysterical Jew. One of the female guards was joining him, an unattractive woman with a broad forehead and elflike eyes. The two young soldiers on their motorcycles looked at them idly, not nearly as interested at the moment as the other prisoners or the guards, and then one of them started to fold up the map.

"Shhhh," Cecile was whispering, "you must settle down. It's all right." But already it was too late. She felt Pusch's hands on her shoulders; he was pulling her away from Jeanne. The female guard—was her name Sigi?—was trying to wrench Vera away. But Vera was holding on tightly to Jeanne, her dirty, gnarled fingers grasping the front of poor Jeanne's striped prison shirt and ragged jacket, begging Jeanne so desperately to calm down that she, too, was sounding half-crazed. Suddenly Pusch took his rifle off his shoulder and slammed the butt into Vera's back, holding the gun as if it were a battering ram. Vera let go of Jeanne's clothing and collapsed onto the road, one hand reaching instinctively back for her kidney.

"And you," he hissed at Jeanne, his eyes half-closed in anger. "And you," he repeated. Sigi pushed Jeanne to the ground so she was on her hands and knees like a cow, still shaking her head and bawling. Pusch turned his rifle around in his arms and aimed it at the back of her head. So this, Cecile thought, is how it will end for my Jeanne—and, she realized, she really did view Jeanne as hers, a possession and a pet and a totem of sorts, a good-luck charm that she had to keep alive to assure herself that she, too, was still breathing—shot on a road outside a train station in the middle of the night. Now she was sniveling as well, but her cries were almost silent, certainly not loud enough to be heard over Jeanne's frenzied wailing or Vera's elongated moans.

And yet when Pusch pulled the trigger and the blast was still reverberating in her ears, Cecile realized that he hadn't shot Jeanne. He'd killed Vera. He had meant to execute her friend, but in the second that he was aiming his rifle down at the back of Jeanne's skull, Vera had rolled into Jeanne and taken the bullet instead. In, it appeared, her neck. Now she was flat on her back, still alive but clearly dying fast, choking on the blood that was seeming to run from spigots in her mouth and the gaping hole by her larynx. Cecile wondered: Had Vera rolled into Jeanne on purpose? Or had she been spasming from the blow to her kidney and simply had the misfortune of twisting her body in that direction? The wrong direction?

To their right she heard the two soldiers starting up their motorcycles. One seemed to be shaking his head in annoyance, exasperated either by the wailing Jew or by the way Pusch had shot one of the prisoners. She couldn't decide. And then they sped off, their motorcycles leaving behind trails of blue smoke in the frigid night air.

"You," Sigi was saying, "you Jew pig," and Cecile choked back her tears and stood at attention because she realized that Sigi was speaking to her. "Get that body out of here. I don't want to soil my gloves with Jew blood."

She averted her eyes and bowed her head, a slight, obedient nod. Jeanne was only whimpering now; her cries had grown soft.

Pusch murmured something to Sigi that she couldn't quite

hear and then he was shouting to the women behind them, commanding them to get back in line, telling them there was nothing that interesting to see. They were going to set off once again within minutes. He and Sigi glanced over at the spot where the two regular soldiers on motorcycles had been; they seemed surprised the two men were gone.

"Pigs, too," Pusch mumbled, spitting on the road and narrowly missing Vera.

"Do you know which roads are still open?" Sigi asked him. There was just a trace of nervousness in her voice. "Did they tell you?"

"They did," Pusch said. "The commandant and I know which way to go. We'll be fine." Then he looked down at Vera, whose desperate, labored breathing was starting to slow. "At least we'll be fine if we hurry up and get out of here. You heard us," he barked at Cecile. "Get this pig shit off the road!"

Instantly she bent over Vera, whispering into her ear—lying into her ear—that she would be fine, and lifting her shoulders off the ground and cradling the back of her injured neck in her hands. The bullet, she realized, must have passed right through, because she felt her palm growing moist with the woman's blood. She wasn't sure how to move her without causing her yet more pain, but she didn't have to worry long. Vera's eyes rolled up toward her forehead, there was one last convulsion somewhere deep inside her chest, and then she was gone. Jeanne crawled over to them, still sniffing back tears, and said, "I can help."

Cecile wasn't sure Jeanne really could, at least all that much, but she nodded. They each took one of Vera's arms at the shoulder and together were able to drag her off into the snow on the side of the road.

"We can't bury her," Cecile said, kneeling beside the body. "I wish we could. But we can't."

Jeanne looked at her, wide-eyed, and Cecile was afraid that Jeanne, despite her despair, was going to snap at her for saying something so obvious and dull. But mostly she had just been talking to herself. She did wish they could bury Vera. But they hadn't the time, the ground was rock solid, and even if Pusch had given them shovels she doubted they had the strength left to dig.

She was wrong about Jeanne, however; the woman's eyes, she understood, had grown wide because she was about to be sick. Her friend turned away from Vera's body and, suddenly, she was spewing into the grimy snow the meat and tomatoes and the *knäckebrot* she had consumed, the vomit tinged with white from the canned milk. When she was done, when all that was left was a long tendril of spit linking her lips to the icy ground, she murmured, "I had forgotten what it was like to be full. I had completely forgotten."

Behind them Pusch was screaming, "Move, move!" And so Cecile bent over and pulled down Vera's eyelids and kissed the woman good-bye on her sore-ridden scalp. Then she and Jeanne stood, and with the little energy they could muster they rejoined the other prisoners as they trudged their way west in the night.

Chapter Fourteen

THEO WALKED WITH HIS FAMILY THROUGH A LARGELY deserted village in which the road was almost impassable because of the rubble—at one point he had helped Callum and Manfred move a pile of bricks from a fallen chimney from the road so the wagons could proceed, and twice he had gotten to assist them as they had lifted great slabs of wall that had slid onto the street—and he listened as Manfred wondered why in the name of God there wasn't some otherwise useless Hitler Youth lad to direct everyone onto the road that circled outside of the town. Even the stone church had collapsed upon itself, the buttresses for the walls supporting nothing but sky, and the once-imposing pipes for the organ reshaped by heat and flame into giant copper-colored mushrooms. It was a small village, no more than six square blocks, and none of the structures were taller than three stories high. And yet it had been bombed so severely that almost without exception they were passing buildings in which whole exterior walls were gone and Theo realized that he was looking up into people's bedrooms and bathrooms and kitchens. The buildings were, in a way, like giant dollhouses, with the sides removed so you could peer inside and move the furniture wherever you liked. The fires were long extinguished by the cold and fresh snow, but he could smell the soot and even see deep patches of black where an awning or a ceiling had somehow survived and shielded the burn marks from the latest storm. In one of the dollhouses he saw an old woman sitting before a precarious, three-legged table on the second floor, picking with a fork at some food in a bowl with yellow flowers adorning the side. The stairwell had caved in, and he wondered how the woman would ever get down from her perch. In another skeletal structure he saw three girls, sisters he guessed, standing at the lip of the floor on the third story, staring down at them glumly. The oldest one was probably his age, Theo decided, and she was wearing what had to be her uncle's or her father's Luftwaffe dress uniform coat. The younger girls were wrapped in blankets. He waved at them, but they didn't wave back.

Whenever he saw a rat scuttle across the surface of the snow and into the debris, he feared there were bodies moldering there. When he expressed this concern to the grown-ups, Callum reassured him: The Scotsman told him he was quite positive that a town this small would have been sure to care for its own. Theo thought of that old woman and those three girls, and he wasn't convinced.

"You know, Theo," Manfred was saying to him, "I have never ridden a horse in my life."

"Really? Well, that's only because you're a city person. It's no big deal that I have," he said, because it didn't seem to him that it was. Country people often rode horses. City people didn't. Besides, he could tell that Manfred was only talking about horses now to change the subject from the bodies that might be under the rubble. "If I'd grown up in Schweinfurt, I probably wouldn't ride, either."

"Theo is a wonderful rider," Anna said, and he wasn't sure if it was pride that he heard in her voice or something else. Worry, perhaps.

"Not really," he said, feeling the need to assert the truth. "I only ride ponies."

"Outside of the ring, yes. But in the ring? I don't know any boys your age who ride half so well."

"It's true," Callum agreed. "You're an excellent horseman."

"Frankly, your animals scare me to death," said Manfred. "They're monsters."

"Are you serious?" he asked the soldier.

"Absolutely. Your Balga? A terror."

"He's a horse!"

"He's a giant. They're all giants."

"They're very sweet, actually. And very smart. Sometimes they can be stubborn—even my pony. He's always snitching grass when he's not supposed to. But terrors? They're more like"—and he paused for a brief moment as he tried to find the appropriate analogy—"big stubborn babies. Or, maybe, big stubborn toddlers. That's what they really are, sometimes."

Callum and his mother laughed aloud, and his sister nodded in recognition.

"You think you could teach me to ride?" Manfred asked him. "It might make the animals seem less like monsters to me—and more like babies."

"My sister could probably teach you better than I could."

"Perhaps you could both teach me. My sense is I wouldn't be an especially quick study. I'd need all the help I could get."

"You mean after the war?"

"Yes," he said thoughtfully. "After the war."

"I could do that," he said. He turned to Callum. "And you, too? Do you want some lessons?"

"Definitely."

The notion made Theo smile. It wasn't, he guessed, the idea that he might have some knowledge or talent that he could impart to these grown men—though he did like that idea; rather, it was the realization that he might actually get to see them again when this long journey was over.

PERHAPS TWO HOURS beyond the village, when the sky was growing dark and everyone knew that soon they would have to try to find a barn or a shelter in which to spend the night, Mutti announced that she had an idea of where they should go. "Let's turn here," she said, and she directed Manfred and Anna to lead the horses off the main road and down a path that didn't seem to have been plowed in weeks. With each step Theo was sinking up to his knees, and the men were actually shoveling a path for the carriage wheels as they trudged forward. But Mutti assured them the path wasn't long and it would be worth the effort. She refused, however, to tell them what awaited them at the end, and Theo was surprised by Manfred's patience with his mother. He had expected that the soldier would demand to know what they were doing, and why. But, it seemed, he had faith in Mutti, too.

Nevertheless, it was completely dark when they saw a dim glow before them, and then, in a brief moment when the moon peered out from the clouds and illuminated the earth, they saw a house at least the size of Kaminheim. The glow was from windows along the first floor, and Theo imagined there must have been dozens of candles burning inside since there couldn't possibly be electricity left here.

"Whose house is this?" Manfred was asking Mutti.

"Friends of Rolf's and mine since, well, forever. Eckhard and Klara. We lost touch with them once the war started. But it looks like they're still here."

"Or someone is," Callum muttered.

"Well, it's a roof," Manfred said. "And beds."

"When I realized where we were this afternoon, I thought instantly of my old friends. Then, when I recognized the road, I decided to bring us in the back entrance," she continued, her voice almost gleeful—a little girl who has pulled off a great surprise. "I didn't want to bring a thousand people with us."

They found that a path had been carved between the horse barn and the manor house, and Theo saw that Balga was sniffing the air with interest, tensing and then rolling his massive head nervously.

"Balga must smell the barn," Mutti told them, and tenderly she stroked the animal along his forehead and cheek. "They used to have as many animals as we had."

Callum handed the reins to Anna and turned toward Mutti. "I'll see who's there. What do these people look like? How big is the family?"

"They have a daughter and two sons. But I wouldn't expect the boys to be here. Surely they're in the army. Probably only Gabi will be there."

"And how old is Gabi?"

"Twenty or twenty-one. Just a little older than Anna."

"Okay. I'll go peer in one of those windows. See who's inside."

"What, you don't think it will just be my friends? Looters, maybe?"

He shrugged. "Or Russians."

"I'll go with you," Manfred said, and Theo watched as the two men shuffled through the snow up to the windows with the softly flickering lights.

THERE WEREN'T LOOTERS and there weren't Russians. There weren't even other refugees. When Anna had heard Manfred and Callum conjecturing that the house might have been commandeered by criminals or Bolsheviks, her heart had sunk. Now, however, as her mother's friend Klara was heating tea for her in a kettle over the fireplace in the living room and their wet cloaks and capes and quilts were drying on wooden racks before the hearth, she was almost giddy. She was exhausted and she knew she was ill. But she was clean. She had soaked in an elegant porcelain tub for nearly an hour, savoring the hot water and rose-scented bubble bath, allowing herself to doze in solitude amid the steam and the aroma of the flowers. After her, Mutti and Theo— her brother normally no fan of baths—had bathed, too, and their spirits had risen accordingly as well.

They rejoined Anna downstairs now. She smiled at them and then burrowed even deeper into a thickly cushioned love seat, warm and content, while her eyes wandered aimlessly over the heads of the dead animals with antlers that adorned some of the walls, resting occasionally on the tapestries of unicorns and crusaders from the Middle Ages that hung on the others. There was also a line of stuffed wolfhounds—six of them in various poses, their mouths and marble eyes always open, in one case a tongue thrust out like a snake—serving as an honor guard into the room. At first Anna had found them a little disturbing. They also smelled of something unrecognizable but distasteful, and she feared that the taxidermist had been sloppy. But they were on the other side of the love seat from her and she had, for now, put them out of her mind. She was putting almost everything out of her mind. She was only half-listening as Mutti shared the story of their ordeal with Klara, while her old acquaintance's daughter, Gabi, and a friend of hers seemed to be hanging on every word. Gabi's friend was named Sonje, and like Gabi she was pathetically homely. They were fairy-tale stepsisters, Anna imagined, and she felt bad for them. Sonje was tall and gangly with a skeletal stalk linking her collarbone with a chin as sharp as a goatee and eyes that bulged out like a bug's. Gabi, the privations they had endured notwithstanding, was plump beyond the help of a corset and had a nose that looked a bit like an acorn with nostrils. Moreover, despite the reality that the Russians might be here in days if the army didn't find a way to stop them, they were insisting that they were going to remain in this house. The servants were long gone, as were the men and the horses, but before setting off to join a Volkssturm unit Eckhard had used his party connections to fill the larder and make sure they had plenty of wood and oil for the lamps. He had taught Klara and Gabi and Sonje how to shoot, and left them each a pistol—which, in Sonje's case, she kept with her in a holster she had decorated with red and black ribbons and wore around her dress like a sash. And, if the very worst occurred and the Russians appeared suddenly down their long driveway, he had shown them how they should slash their wrists, assuring them that this was a largely painless way to go—and infinitely preferable to their fate if they didn't.

Still, they were viewing their home as if it were an island sanctuary. They weren't maintaining the driveways, and Klara, at least, actually believed that no one—neither Russians nor refugees—would even know they were here.

"But I found you," Mutti was saying. "You simply have to come with us. You simply can't stay here."

"But would you have turned down that path if you hadn't known this house was here?" Klara asked. "Of course not. You knew to take it because you're an old friend and you've been here before. And the main entrance is even more deeply buried in snow, and—you might remember—all uphill from there to the house. No one would even think there's anything worth looking for at the other end. You're the first people we've seen in over a week."

"It's a cocoon," said Sonje.

"And in the spring we'll be butterflies," said Gabi.

"Butterflies with guns," Sonje added pleasantly.

Behind them the door opened, and Manfred and Callum returned from bedding down the horses for the night in the barn.

"Or," Klara said, "you girls can be butterflies right now! Why wait till the spring! Come, gentlemen, I'll play the piano and you two can dance with my daughter and Sonje!"

"NOW, I AM NO expert," Gabi was telling Callum a little later, though it was evident from the tone in her voice that she was quite confident that she was, "but we had a wonderful professor come to one of our BDM meetings, and he taught us all about physiognomy. It was fascinating." She was running the tips of her fingers along the top and the sides of Callum's head as he sat in the massive easy chair that was upholstered with a scene from a forest that looked positively primeval. The treatment didn't look precisely like a scalp massage, but Anna thought Callum might have enjoyed the physical sensations if Gabi weren't running her hands along his head for the purpose of a lesson in Aryan physical superiority. As it was, he was fidgeting uncomfortably and looked like a cat that wanted to bolt from a stranger's arms.

"Now, it seems to me that people from England have far more in common with Germans than—for example—the Slavs. Your skull is much more like mine than those of many of my neighbors," she went on.

"That's only because my skull is still here. Most of your neighbors' skulls had the common sense to get out of here and head west."

"I am serious. This is science. You map the brain by the bumps on the skull. It's a known fact, for instance, that the Aryan cranium differs from the Slavic cranium or the Jewish cranium. It is far more regal, and it has fewer bulges and ugly swellings. And compare the line of your jaw to the line of mine," she continued. "Though I will say this: For a large man and a Celtic, your jaw is not especially apelike."

"And the jaws of most Celts are?"

"Don't be insulted. It's simply that the jawlines of all races are more apelike than ours."

With that he lifted her hands off his head and then pushed his way to his feet. "If you'll excuse me," he said, "I'm going to go get some water." He was no longer trying to hide the exasperation in his voice, and it was with great, purposeful strides that he started in toward the kitchen.

MANFRED STOOD ALONE with Sonje in the pantry, mesmerized by the plenty at his fingertips, helping the girl decide what they all would eat for dinner. The two of them hadn't spoken more than a dozen words to each other here when abruptly she turned to him, grabbed at the fabric of his uniform shirt with one hand, awkwardly reached around the back of his neck with the other, and started to pull him toward her. Into her. For a split second he thought this stranger was going to try to kill him and he was about to throw her aside, when he realized that she was, clumsily, trying to bring his lips down to hers. She was about to kiss him. Then she was kissing him. Her tongue was trying to force its way through his own lips and teeth, and she was using her hand to push his skull so hard into hers that he feared she would chip off the top of one of his incisors.

He pulled away and reached behind him to take her hand off the back of his head, but the fingers on her other hand were grasping his shirt with such tenacity—such ferocity—that he allowed them to retain their leechlike hold.

"Take me with you," she begged, speaking so quickly that at first he didn't quite understand what she was saying. "I will be your whore. I will be your army whore and do whatever you want. Anything, anything at all. Better to be an army whore for a German hero than to be left behind here for Ivan."

"Oh, I agree," he told her.

"Gabi's mother has lost her mind. It's gone, completely gone. She's insisting we stay. But we can't; you know we can't. You know we'll be raped and killed if we do."

He rested a hand upon her fingers. He could feel her nails against his chest through the layers of fabric from his shirt and his undershirt.

"Of course you can come with us," he said. "And my sense is, if you put your foot down and say you're coming with us—that's all there is to it—Gabi and her mother will come, too. At least they might. Either way, please, let's have no more talk about army whores. Okay?"

She lowered her gawking eyes in a manner that she must have thought was flirtatious and nodded. But then she took her free hand and—though Gabi's mother and the guests were nearby, either through one door that led to the kitchen or through another that led to the dining room—surprised him by grabbing at his crotch. He presumed she had meant this as a bit of erotic foreplay, a taste of the carnal delights that awaited him, but her fingers and her palm, if they reminded him of anything, struck him as only the mouth of a snake.

CALLUM OFFERED TO help Klara set the table in the formal dining room, but she insisted that he rest with the others. And so he went exploring, wandering aimlessly through the conservatory and the living room and the two small rooms that served as maids' quarters. The house was darker than Kaminheim—and not simply because the electricity was out and it was illuminated entirely by candles and whatever oil lamps they were carrying with them—but he guessed it was at least as big. In the library he ran into Manfred. He was sitting on the arm of a leather easy chair, with a book open on a round table beside him, three candles surrounding it. He was hunched over the text and so his face was in shadow.

"What have you got there?" Callum asked.

"A biography of Richard Wagner."

"Ah, a favorite of your führer."

"Apparently." The corporal flipped it shut. Beside it was a second, thinner volume. "How much German do you read?"

"A little," he said. "Not enough to make much sense of your Wagner biography. But it wouldn't be my choice in bedtime reading, anyway. I don't mind biographies, but he didn't write much for the accordion."

Manfred smiled. "How come you didn't bring the instrument? You brought whole wagonloads of stuff. But not the accordion."

"Wasn't mine to bring. Belonged to Anna's uncle."

"Think it was an oversight?"

"Probably."

He smiled: "Sure they weren't just sick of your playing?"

"No one gets sick of my playing."

He shook his head. "I guess I'm just not a fan of the accordion."

"Well, that's because you've never heard me play."

"You're that good?"

"I am."

"In that case, maybe it's just a problem of association. I always associate the accordion with bullies and beer."

"Oh, it's much more elegant than that. It has its earliest roots in Berlin, but it evolved in Vienna and London, too. A hundred years ago, folks were fiddling with bellows and reeds all across Europe. You play an instrument?"

"No."

"Go on!"

"Really, I don't."

"I'm shocked. A cultured German like you?"

"I worked in a ball-bearing factory, remember?"

"Nevertheless," Callum murmured. He was honestly surprised.

"Here. This will show you how cultured Germans really are," Manfred said, and he opened the second book on the table to a specific page and handed it to him. "Even you should be able to get the gist of this. Small words. Big pictures."

He put his oil lamp down on the desk. "A children's book?"

"Believe it or not, yes."

"Oh, good. Now we're motoring along at my speed," he said happily, but instantly the sense of mirth that had been welling up inside him evaporated. He saw that the illustrations were water-color paintings of noses. The noses were grotesquely large and wart-covered, and said to typify those of the Jew. There were five of them on the two pages. And then there was a separate nose that was elegant and small and presented as typical of the Aryan countenance.

"Clearly you don't believe this rubbish," he said, unable to hide the indignation in his voice.

"Clearly."

"A few minutes ago, Gabi was trying to analyze my head. God . . ."

Down one of the long corridors they heard a bell ringing: It was the sound that Klara had said would signal that dinner was being served. When Callum turned back to Manfred, he saw the other soldier had blown out the candles on the table and his face was lost to the darkness.

MUTTI RECALLED WHAT had happened to her brother and his family when the Russians had reached his estate and decided she would tell Klara what she knew—what Helmut had seen. It might convince the woman to bring Gabi and Sonje and join her group as they trekked west. Yet there was a part of her that wondered if even with that knowledge Klara would reconsider. The woman seemed a little daft now. Certainly Klara had always been eccentric—an artistic temperament without any artistic talent— but this evening her behavior was verging on the peculiar. The girls' behavior, too.

Still, she was astounded at their energy. At everyone's energy. The young people's in particular. Anna was continuing to rest and, hopefully, recover, but after feasting on canned asparagus and spaetzle and pot-roasted boar, the other young folks hadn't stopped dancing. They had even executed with precision an exquisite gavotte. Klara had a lovely, light touch at the piano, and Mutti was reminded of those delightful evenings in the autumn when Anna and her friends had danced with those handsome naval officers who had come to Kaminheim to design the antitank trenches. Moreover, Manfred and Callum were such gentlemen: Not only were they waltzing with Klara's sadly unattractive daughter and her friend, they were also showing Theo how to dance with the girls. Her little boy was indeed growing up. She wished that Anna felt well enough to dance, too, but it was heartening just to see her warm and content and sipping a glass of red wine on the love seat. Her cheeks, once again, had some color.

"I wonder if you'll come back when the war is over," she heard Gabi saying to Callum, while Klara was skimming through the sheet music on the piano in search of another song. Certainly no one here seemed to care that he was Scottish. She watched him glance at Anna, who raised her eyebrows behind Gabi's back and smiled at him. Imagine: Did Anna really think that her own mother was born yesterday? That her own mother didn't know what was going on between her daughter and this foreign paratrooper? She remembered when she and Rolf had been courting; it wasn't all that many years ago that she had first flirted with the man who would eventually become her husband.

"Oh, I think there's a pretty good chance," he said, and it was clear to Mutti that he was speaking more to Anna than to Gabi.

"Good. I will expect you. I will hang a glass ornament in the guest bedroom window here where you will stay," she said, and Mutti wondered if the girl was getting tipsy.

"A glass butterfly," Sonje added. "Because by then we will all be out of our cocoons. So, a butterfly for Callum and a . . ." She paused, looking deeply into Manfred's eyes. "And what would you like, Corporal? What kind of glass ornament should await your return?"

"Oh, I will be flattered by whatever you suggest," he said. He looked away from her and briefly his eyes rested on Anna. Mutti couldn't decide what he was thinking, but when Anna looked up—perhaps sensing the corporal's attention—he quickly turned toward the portrait of Eckhard on the far wall. Her daughter, she thought, seemed slightly troubled by the corporal's gaze. Almost as if she were changing the subject, she reached into the tin on the table beside her for one of the florentines and took a small bite.

"Maybe tonight my mother will allow you to sleep with one of Father's dogs," Gabi suggested to Manfred. "A man should always have a wolfhound by his bed, shouldn't he?"

"Oh, I don't think we need to cart them around the house. But I thank you," he told her, his voice drifting, and Mutti couldn't imagine why anyone would bring one of those stuffed dogs with them to a bedroom. Even in a room this large it took the smell of the fire and the tea and the scented candles to smother their stench.

"The führer always sleeps with a wolfhound, you know. Blondi," Gabi continued. She was speaking almost directly into the corporal's ear.

"Blondi is a German shepherd—not a wolfhound," Sonje corrected her.

"No, she's a wolfhound."

"You're wrong."

"And she was a gift from Goebbels."

"From Bormann," Sonje insisted.

"Goebbels."

"Bormann."

"Oh, please, does it matter?"

"I'm just saying—"

"You're just being a Jew. A know-it-all Jew," Gabi snapped at her.

"I'm just being right," Sonje said.

"Girls," Klara said, raising her voice ever so slightly and drawing the word out. "We have guests. No need to squabble. What always is more important is what we agree upon. And we all agree that the führer has a beautiful animal named Blondi and that sometimes a man wants to sleep with a dog."

At that Gabi tittered slightly, but then Klara's usually kind face turned to a glare. "You know I do not approve of prurient thoughts," she said.

"I'm sorry," Gabi murmured, though it was clear that she

wasn't. Not at all. Then she turned to Sonje, and it was evident to Mutti that the moment—already irreparably curdled—was about to get worse. "But Sonje was acting like a Jew: a selfish, piglike, know-it-all Jew. A Jew who probably opposes our führer. A Jew who lives off the sweat of others. A Jew who seduces—"

"Enough!" This was Manfred, and everyone in the room turned. Mutti was embarrassed for Gabi. She was embarrassed for them all. Living outside of Kulm had meant that she had been spared having to hear firsthand this sort of nonsense about the Jews. Certainly in the early days of the war she had worried about her family's acquaintances who were Jewish—hadn't Rolf written letters and telegrams to everyone he could think of on behalf of some families?—but in the last two years their own situation had become so precarious that she had grown oblivious of their plight. She had Werner to worry about. And she had to learn to make do in a world where everything, it seemed, was suddenly scarce. Nevertheless, she had never believed the sort of claptrap that appeared in *Der Stürmer* or that Gabi was giving voice to now.

"Enough," Manfred continued, a mere echo of the word this time, but his anger clearly unabated. "No Jews are living off the sweat of others. No Jews are seducing your precious Aryan children. No Jews—"

"That's right," Sonje said, oddly adamant, and she was, much to Mutti's discomfort, pressing her body against Manfred's and burrowing her cheek against his chest. "That's absolutely right."

"Tell me, Corporal, are you a Jew lover?" Gabi asked him.

He pushed Sonje down into the love seat almost atop poor Anna and then took Gabi's fleshy upper arms in his hands, clenching his fingers so firmly around them that Mutti could see the fabric of her dress sleeve crinkling and she feared for a moment that he was hurting her.

"I don't care that I am a guest in your family's house. I will not abide your monumental ignorance," he told her, lowering his face into hers, his eyes unblinking.

"I was only—"

"He's right, you know," Callum interrupted. "Say one more word like that and I'll walk out that door and put a bloody arrow at the end of the driveway pointing up here for the Russians. I'll even paint them a sign: Nazis and food, right this way."

Gabi looked nervously toward Klara, but her mother was leaning over the piano, crying soundlessly and running the fingers of one hand abstractedly over the woodwork just above the keys. When she saw her mother was going to offer neither assistance nor comfort, she stiffened her back and stood up a little straighter. "That man is a prisoner. Your enemy. Are all of you going to allow him to talk to me like this?"

Mutti felt she should do something—say something—to deescalate the tension. Comfort Klara, maybe. Chastise Gabi. Calm Manfred. But she realized that she was tired, so very, very tired. Wasn't it only a moment ago that these young people were waltzing together contentedly? Still, she wished she could find the words to calm Manfred and silence this strange, half-insane Gabi.

"Manfred, would you have one more dance in you for a sickly girl from the country?" It was Anna speaking, and she had risen to her feet. Her lips were parted just the tiniest bit in a modest, demure smile, though it was clear from the slight quiver there that she was nervous—or, to be precise, unnerved by both Gabi's erratic behavior and Manfred's anger. She rested her fingers gently atop the corporal's shoulder, a leaf coming to rest on a low branch in the autumn, and Mutti worried that what looked to the rest of the room merely like a bit of practiced, coquettish charm was driven actually by the need for help with her balance. Her daughter, she knew, wasn't tipsy—but she was weak.

Without turning to Anna, Manfred released the other woman and allowed his strong arms to drop to his sides. He exhaled loudly, and Mutti hoped his anger might diminish now to something like a more harmless exasperation. She knew the effect a beautiful young girl like Anna could have on a young man. She had been such a girl herself, once.

"Ah, a little sympathy for a soldier home from the front. I won't say no," he said.

"Thank you," she said, dipping her head slightly, and Mutti thought the storm was going to pass. Had, in fact, passed. But not yet. Sonje was glaring at Anna as if she, a friend of Klara's family, had some proprietary hold on the soldier. Meanwhile, Callum was muttering something in English that she didn't hear well enough to translate in her mind, but she thought was an aspersion upon Manfred's character. It sounded as if he were implying that Manfred actually was *hiding* from the front. Or *running* from the front. But he was most certainly not a soldier *home* from the front. She was surprised by this odd spike of jealousy from him and wondered if she had missed signs of it earlier.

"Do you really feel up to that?" she asked her daughter, but it was only out of obligation—because she thought as the girl's mother she *should* ask. The truth was, the sight of her daughter dancing with this handsome Wehrmacht corporal gave her a pleasant, maternal pride. It allowed her to fantasize what might have been if the war hadn't taken such a nasty turn and sent them all scurrying like scared animals from Kaminheim.

"Yes, Mutti, I think I can dance once," she replied and then, when she saw Callum, she continued, "twice even. I don't think my evening would be complete if I didn't have the honor of dancing with every handsome soldier we have in our presence."

Klara sniffled and looked up from her piano, and abruptly her mouth and eyes opened wide like a fish's. There were long stretches of tears running over the swell of her cheekbones and linking her eyes with the cut of her jaw. "Wonderful!" she exclaimed. "I know just what to play!"

Gabi was biting the insides of her mouth so angrily and obviously that she was sucking in the flesh on the sides of her face. Then, almost as if her head were on a spindle, she turned suddenly to Sonje and ordered her to dance with her. "Come, butterfly. Join me so neither of us has to dance with the enemy."

Callum, Mutti thought, looked relieved.

URI THREW ANOTHER log on the fireplace, pushed the massive screen with the finials of eagles in front of it, and collapsed on his back onto the couch. Suddenly, he was almost too tired to retire to the maid's room in which he was supposed to sleep. Their hostess had placed him in one and Callum in the other. It wasn't that there was a shortage of bedrooms upstairs; rather, it was Klara's sense of propriety: She wanted her daughter and Sonje and Anna to be on one floor, and these two men on another. The only male allowed upstairs? Young Theo. Now Uri closed his eyes, vaguely aware that Callum was extinguishing the oil lamps and blowing out the candles. Everyone else was in bed for the night.

"So," he said, not even trying to suppress a yawn. "When was the last time you ate like we did tonight?"

"Actually, the food was pretty impressive at the Emmerichs' right up to the end. Things were rationed and some things were much harder to come by than others. But, remember: The place was a working farm."

"Oh, great: The POWs are eating better than the soldiers. Very nice."

"There is an irony there."

"I haven't eaten like tonight in years. Since I was a little boy."

"Really? Not even before the war?"

He thought of the privations he and the other Jews had endured in Schweinfurt. The possessions they had bartered for food. "Not even," he said simply. Then: "So, how long have you and Anna been lovers?"

"Pardon me?"

"Don't be coy."

"Is it that obvious?"

"Only if you're breathing and have eyes. The dead? They wouldn't notice," he said.

"Well, it didn't stop you from dancing with her."

"Certainly not. So, tell me: How did you convince an Aryan princess to fall for you?" he asked. "I'm interested."

"Why?"

"I just am," he said. His arms were folded across his chest and he imagined himself as a mummy. Somewhere oddly far away he heard Callum starting to answer. Telling him something about an apple orchard at Kaminheim. The extensive harvest. But he felt another yawn rising up inside him. Gave in to it. And was asleep.

ANNA AWOKE, shivering, from a dream and pulled the quilt and the sheet up and over her head. Curled her knees into her chest. She couldn't quite recall what she had dreamed; it hovered like a coil of mist just outside of her reach. But she thought she had been a child in the dream, and as she trembled a blurred image came to her of herself as a little girl in a pinafore and blue dirndl dress. The pinafore, she thought, had been decorated with cherry red hearts. Perhaps she was carrying a basket of flowers she had picked. Perhaps not. What was clear was that the sun was high and she was warm: She could still feel the heat on her face.

The wind was rattling the windows here—it was still dark outside—and she thought if she had been home at Kaminheim and there hadn't been a war that the sound would actually have reassured her. After all, she would have been safe in her bed in a house that, once, had seemed indestructible to her. Now? Anything—people, horses, whole buildings—could disappear in a moment. For all she knew, Kaminheim was gone. Shelled. Ransacked. Or, perhaps, merely occupied. She saw in her mind Russian officers in her father's office. In the parlor. Russian soldiers pillaging the kitchen and the pantry. She fretted about the horses, but she told herself that the Russians would need them—and, thus, feed them. They wouldn't suffer too terribly. But she did worry about Theo's pony. Would the Russians have any use for such a good-natured little creature? Unlikely. The animal might be nothing more to them than a hot stew, and the image caused her to grimace.

And yet even now, despite all they were enduring and all they had lost, life's smallest, most irrelevant dramas went on. She wasn't sure whether this was an indication of how resilient people were, or how pathetic. But she had danced that night with Manfred, and Callum had briefly grown a little jealous. It was unfounded, of course: The corporal had been charming and gallant once they had started to dance, but it was clear that he didn't have a particular interest in her. And now, her pride slightly wounded, she wondered why. Perhaps, she told herself, it was because he was older: eight years. Not a huge difference. But it was possible this was too much in his eyes. Maybe—and this idea actually caused her a small ripple of annoyance—he thought eighteen was too young to be interesting. Well, she had only danced with him to calm him. To settle the room.

She ran the edge of the sheet over her forehead and cheeks, which were damp and hot. She decided she was flattered by the idea that Callum was jealous of Manfred. There was no cause, of course: Her heart belonged entirely to the Scottish paratrooper. A man like Manfred? He was too much like Werner and Helmut. A Teutonic warrior. A killer.

Still, there was clearly a deep streak of rebellion in him that her brothers almost completely lacked. He was with them now, wasn't he, rather than with his unit? And even if he had no special fondness for her and she wasn't attracted to him—at least, she reassured herself, in a meaningful way—she was nonetheless glad he was with them. Oh, she had been angry with him when he and Callum had shot those Russian soldiers. She had been incensed at both men. At the time, it had seemed senseless. Now, however, in the dark of the night, it struck her as a somewhat more reasonable course of action. Those men were going to steal their provisions. They were a part of the army from which her family was fleeing.

Still, it had been more death, and Manfred's reaction to what they had done had been so very different from Callum's.

A powerful gust shook the window glass in the bedroom and she opened her eyes. Tomorrow they would be out in that cold once again. And so what did any of this matter—Manfred's indifference, Callum's attraction—when it was possible that none of them would even survive the month, much less make it through the winter?

No, it wasn't likely they'd perish. They couldn't. She told herself she was being melodramatic because she was sick and scared and it was the middle of the night. The truth was, there was no reason to believe that any of them would die. She had the sense, suddenly, that Manfred would see to that.

IN THE MORNING, Mutti awoke to the sound of someone knocking on the door to her bedroom and cooing that coffee—*real* coffee—was brewing, and for one brief, lovely moment she thought Rolf was beside her in bed. She could feel his warmth; she could hear his low, steady breathing. The pillows once more were those on which she rested her head in Kaminheim, great soft nests of goose feathers, and the bed was the one in which she had slept with Rolf since the day they were married. It was only when she reached out her fingers to brush his cheek and feel the comforting stubble there that she realized she was alone. She was at Klara's and Rolf was . . .

Rolf was somewhere to the east. She tried not even to speculate where, or in what condition.

Now she called out to whoever was knocking that she was awake.

"Lovely," the voice answered, and she realized it was Klara.

"Thank you. I'll be down presently," she told her friend. Then, as she did every morning—in barns or in beds—she prayed that her husband and her two older sons were safe. That, somehow, they would escape harm. She prayed that she would have the strength and the wisdom to protect her youngest boy and her daughter; that soon they would all be together again as a family; and that someday their only concerns would be the price they were paid for their sugar beets and whether a mare would deliver a foal safely.

AT BREAKFAST, Callum listened as Mutti tried again to convince Klara that she and the two girls simply had to accompany them west to her cousin's in Stettin. He hated to admit it, but he really didn't give a damn if they came with them or not. Already he and the Emmerichs were playing with fire. Their motley group consisted of two females, a boy, a POW—who, he had to admit, was spending way too little time hidden beneath the feed—and an army deserter. Did they really need three half-insane women to slow them down? But then, when he was bringing Anna a cup of hot tea in the living room before joining Manfred to load up the wagons, he decided that none of them, not even that reprehensible Gabi, deserved to be left behind. It wasn't these women, after all, who had been machine-gunning Ukrainian civilians or working Jews till they died in labor camps somewhere. Choosing a village and hanging a hundred Poles—filling their mouths first with plaster of Paris so they couldn't cry out or shout patriotic slogans as they died—because an SS officer had been killed by the underground.

And yet when the Russians arrived here in a couple of days, these women would have to atone for the sins of their kin.

"Your mother thinks she can convince Klara to come with us," he told Anna, dipping the tea ball for her one last time in the cup and then laying it on a separate plate that Mutti had given him.

Anna was dressed in heavy wool trousers that had belonged to one of Gabi's brothers and a sweater so bulky that she seemed to be swimming in it. She had been alone in that large, dark room till he joined her, but she looked refreshed from a night in a bed. Now she sat forward on the ottoman and leaned in toward the fire. She brushed a lock of hair away from her eyes.

"She must," she said simply. "They're insane if they stay here."

"Well, they're insane if they come with us. They might be safer with us. But I think they're mad as hatters wherever they are. Here or on the road or in Berlin. Doesn't matter. They'll always be nuts."

"I hate to admit this, but I don't especially like them."

"How could you? How could anyone? They're lunatics. One of them, Sonje? She practically raped Manfred in the bloody larder. I nearly walked in on her as she was going on and on about being his . . . never mind."

"Tell me."

"Oh, no. All I meant is she's desperate. Knows she has to get out of here."

"Well, that's actually an indication that she's perfectly sane."

"It's Gabi who is particularly reprehensible," he said. "Despicable in every imaginable way."

"I agree."

He watched her gaze down into her tea, nodding. He could see her eyelashes, long and lovely and so fair that they almost disappeared against her skin. Then he looked up into the mirror on the wall behind her, a piece of glass the size of a door that was framed in ornate gold-painted wood, and there in the reflection he saw them. Gabi and Klara—the daughter with her mother. He didn't know how long they had been standing there—well into the room, no more than eight or nine feet behind them—but it was clear from the sour expressions on both of their faces that they had gotten the gist of the conversation. When their eyes met his in the mirror, Klara retreated from the room, disappeared, but Gabi exploded toward them, stomping across the thin expanse of carpet that separated them. He stood to greet her—to, he thought in the brief second before she had reached him, *shield* Anna from her. Before he had said a single word, however, Gabi slapped him violently across the cheek, so hard that he felt his head snapping to the right at the moment that the sting had begun to register.

"How dare you?" she hissed, the chalk of her eyes now white-hot, their anger fueled by a blast furnace raging behind a pair of ever-widening black pupils. "We took you in, we fed you, we gave you beds! And now . . . now this betrayal!"

Anna stood beside him and tried to reach out to her. But Gabi sliced at her elbow, using her own arm as a scythe. "We will turn you in. We will turn you *all* in," she said, and she stared at Anna as she spoke.

"I'm sorry, Gabi," Anna said, her voice a quivering, guilt-ridden echo of its usual self. "I don't know what to say."

"You can get out—just get out. We won't be joining you. We would never join you," she said. Then she turned to Callum and added, "I am quite sure that Sonje would never have given herself to your Jew-loving friend. That was all just . . . just talk."

"Please, Gabi, I'm sorry," Anna was saying. "We're tired and we were saying things we didn't really mean. We were just being catty. We—"

"We don't need you," Gabi said. "We don't need anybody. Unlike you, I still have faith in our führer and in our armies. The Russians? Little more than apes. We will stop them well before they get anywhere near this house."

"They are pretty near here right now," he reminded her.

It looked to him as if she were about to respond, to say

something more. Perhaps accuse him of cowardice. Perhaps accuse Anna of defeatism. But she did neither. She glowered for a brief moment and then turned on her heels and stalked off.

IN THE END, only Sonje accompanied them when they left. Mutti had pleaded with Klara to join them, but Gabi wouldn't leave and Klara wouldn't leave without her daughter. The angry young woman refused to even emerge from her bedroom. And so it was only Sonje who threw a few items into a suitcase and joined the group as they started back down the path Mutti had shown them the day before. Anna had the distinct sense that Gabi was gazing down at them scornfully from her window and she felt a deep twinge of guilt. Arguably, it was her and Callum's fault that Gabi, and thus Klara, were remaining behind. But she had apologized, she had apologized profusely; she had all but begged Gabi to forgive her and come with them. But the woman was obstinate beyond all reason. Her mother was, too. Prattled on about her faith in the once-vaunted army. Still, Anna couldn't help but imagine the two of them slashing their wrists in an upstairs bathroom or the parlor, as the Bolsheviks arrived at the gates of their estate.

Once the horses and wagons were back on the road, Manfred and Callum shoveled snow on their tracks and flattened it down as best they could. They threw tree limbs onto the ground where the path to the estate would have been visible to passersby. Then they were back amid the long line of refugees, and although they heard no cannon fire to the east, one young mother reported that Russian tanks had been seen as close as Bütow, and by all means they had to keep moving.

Chapter Fifteen

FOR A WEEK NOW THEY HAD WALKED WITH SONJE as part of their group, the woman a largely silent, stoic, and sepulchral presence. But she kept up and her crying in the night was soundless. That seemed to be about all that mattered to anyone.

Little by little they learned more of her history: Her father was a chemist who worked with the Luftwaffe, and when she had seen him last—months and months earlier, just days after Paris had been liberated—he had said he had been working on nonflammable aviation paints. She said she had believed him, but the mere fact that she felt the need to footnote her recollection this way led Manfred and Callum and the Emmerichs to conclude that she hadn't. Was the Luftwaffe actually producing shells that were filled with poisons or chemical gases? Certainly Manfred and Callum thought it was possible, especially when they learned that Sonje's father's project had been moved around so frequently to avoid Allied air attacks that she no longer had any idea where he was. And her mother? She had died when Sonje had been fifteen, in the very first days of the war. Consequently, Sonje and her younger brother had spent much of the conflict being shuttled between well-meaning family and friends. As far as Sonje knew, her brother was still alive. He had been a soldier since June and missing in action since

October, but that, in her opinion, did not definitively mean he was dead. Didn't missing soldiers turn up alive and well every day? No one saw any reason to correct her.

THEO OVERHEARD THE grown-ups saying that they would reach Mutti's cousin's home within days, and certainly by the end of the week. He hoped so. The days were noticeably longer now than when they had left Kaminheim, but that only meant they were spending more time exposed in the cold and the snow, and he wasn't sure which he hated more. The other day he had heard another refugee, a gaunt and glum-looking old man in a fedora who was traveling alone and trudging along with a cardboard suitcase, sarcastically muttering aloud a part of the Fifty-first Psalm. "Wash me, and I shall be whiter than snow," he kept mumbling, and when the man saw Theo was watching him and listening, he went on, "Ridiculous, isn't it? I am tired of all this whiteness. Really, what's so pure about snow? Would somebody tell me? Besides, that writer lived in the desert. He knew nothing about snow. Nothing!"

Theo wasn't sure he could walk much farther, or—when he was allowed to ride on one of the wagons—even endure many more days outside in the chill February air. That was the thing: If you walked you grew tired, but at least the exertion helped keep you warm; if you rested atop one of the wagons, you slowly froze. It was unpleasant either way. Still, he decided he preferred riding because something was happening to the toes on his left foot. There was a hole in the bottom of the boot and snow had begun to seep in. Three days ago the toes had started to itch and tingle; two days ago they had started to burn; now the skin was swelling and turning yellow, and the toes were as solid as miniature icicles—especially his two smallest ones. Even when he would bundle them up at night they didn't seem to improve. Of course, he wasn't exactly getting to warm them indoors around a fireplace most evenings. Many of the nights since they had left Kaminheim he had slept inside barns—barns for horses and carriages and livestock—or burrowed beneath quilts and sacks of grain in the wagons with only the winter stars for a roof. And one of the few nights they had slept in beds had been their bizarre stay at Klara's. Another of their shelters was a crowded schoolroom with mattresses packed onto the floor like tiles, which by the time they had arrived had been colonized by red insects that swarmed upon them the moment the Volkssturm guards extinguished the lights. The creatures seemed to rise up from the filthy mattresses and burrow under their clothes and nip at their skin. He wanted to sleep with a sack tied around his head so they wouldn't attack his eyes, but Mutti was afraid he would choke and wouldn't let him.

He decided the best night had occurred four days ago now. That evening an elderly farmer just outside a village had taken them in and he had slept alone in a twin bed while Mutti and Anna had slept in the second bed beside him. Sonje had another room to herself and Manfred and Callum had slept in the living room by the fire. The farmer's wife had fed them all a hot soup, and they had eaten sausages and warm bread slathered with butter. That night—and all that food—had done wonders for his sister.

Still, Theo guessed that the reason the farmer had been so kind to them had had much more to do with Manfred than with Anna. Sick and dying refugees were everywhere. But Manfred? He was a soldier who had defended the Reich up and down the eastern front, and there was nothing this farmer and his wife wouldn't have done to thank him. They had practically cleaned out their cupboards when he had introduced himself.

He hadn't told his mother about his toes, because Mutti already had so much to fret about. His sister had improved, but she was still too weak to walk for more than an hour or two at a time, and she was spending most of the trek convalescing in whichever wagon two of their remaining three horses were pulling. And then there were the rumors of military disasters everywhere. The worst story? A ship had left Gotenhafen, a port beside Danzig, at the end of January and been sunk in the night by a Russian submarine. Nearly ten thousand refugees had been on it, and almost all of them, he had heard, had drowned in the half-frozen waters of the Baltic. The vessel was a cruise ship named the *Wilhelm Gustloff*, and his parents had once spent a romantic holiday on the boat in 1938, when he had been little more than a toddler. He remembered—or conjured images from stories and photographs— that he and Anna and their brothers had stayed with Uncle Karl and Aunt Uschi while their parents had been away.

He was pleased that Manfred and Callum seemed to be abiding by the rules of some unwritten truce. When Manfred had first joined them, he had simply been grateful that they weren't killing each other. After all, Callum was the enemy. Well, had once been the enemy. He wasn't quite sure what Callum was these days.

"Where will you go once we reach Stettin?" the fellow was asking the German corporal now. The two men were walking behind him and Mutti and Sonje, each of them leading one of the wagons. The sun had been up for almost three hours, but it was overcast again, and the air felt as cold now as it had when Mutti had gently woken him. It had been one of those nights in which he had slept in the wagon beside Mutti because the nearest barn already was overflowing with refugees when they arrived, and when he opened his eyes and emerged from under the blankets and quilts, he saw around him a field filled virtually to the horizon with people. Hundreds of them, and dozens and dozens of wagons. There were also the remnants of the fires that had been built in the night, all started by the men and women only after they had shoveled out holes in the snow and managed somehow to ignite the green—sometimes sodden—wood they had found in the nearby forest. Callum had built such a fire for them. What Theo found most interesting was how many families had arrived while he had been sleeping. Evidently, he had been in a much deeper slumber than he had realized.

Manfred didn't answer Callum's question, and so he turned around, curious. The corporal smiled at him and winked good-naturedly.

"You can't keep this up forever, you know," Callum continued. "Don't you have to be someplace? Isn't your company missing you?"

"I would think you'd be happy I'm here," Manfred said, clearly avoiding a more revealing response.

"I would think you'd be worried about being shot as a deserter."

"Deserter? POW? Maybe they should just hang us both. You watch: When we get to Stettin, there will be a scaffold in the center of town. For all we know, there will already be bodies swinging in the wind."

"You're frightening Theo."

He turned away, but only briefly, a little annoyed that Callum would presume he was so easily scared. "I've seen worse," he said petulantly, and in his mind once more he saw the refugees on the Vistula being thrown into the roiling, frigid river, and the bodies of the Russian soldiers after Manfred and Callum had ambushed them.

Manfred nodded approvingly at him. "See?" he said to Callum. "It takes more than a few hanging corpses to scare Theo."

He had the sense that Manfred was trying to rile Callum. Needle him a bit. They were all getting a little testy. And while he had indeed seen worse than hanged corpses, he also knew this sort of talk was going to disturb Mutti. Already she was shouldering an awful lot.

"Sometimes you people are such . . ." Callum began.

"Such what?" Manfred asked.

"You're such barbarians."

"Oh, you don't know a thing about my people. Or, for that matter, about me." Suddenly, he sounded morose. The irreverence was gone from his voice.

"I know you're not with your company. That's pretty clear. I know you haven't been since you joined us."

"Well, you tell me: What are *you* going to do in Stettin? Hide in this strange woman's attic? Or just wait on her front lawn for the Russians?"

For the first time Mutti turned back toward the men, and they halted the horses and came to a stop where they were. "You don't really believe the Russians will reach Stettin, do you?" she asked Manfred.

"I don't believe it. I know it. It's only a matter of time."

Theo saw his mother was working hard to remain in control. "Obviously I've been hearing people talk like that for days," she said. "Weeks even. But not you."

He sighed. "Only because you haven't asked."

"Then what will happen? Where will it end, tell me? The Oder? Berlin?"

"Well, my sense is—"

But before he could finish, Mutti was cutting him off. "And why? Why are they doing this to us? Will you tell me that?"

"They?"

"The Russians!" She turned to Callum, her hands upraised to the sky in bewilderment. "And where are your armies? Why aren't they joining us? Don't they understand what's at stake? Where are they? Tell me, in the name of God, where are they?" She was raising her voice in a manner that Theo almost didn't recognize.

"Mutti." The voice was weak but firm, and everyone looked toward it. It was Anna, sitting up in the back of the wagon. "Mutti," she said again.

Their mother shook her head and looked away in disgust. A woman perhaps Mutti's age wrapped in quilts and clutching a silver cage with a dead frozen parakeet inside it passed them; next came a pair of girls in their BDM uniforms with a lady who, Theo guessed, was their grandmother.

"That's enough," Anna went on. "None of this is Callum's fault and none of it is Manfred's. Things will look better in Stettin, I'm sure."

Behind them they heard a man's voice yelling for them to either get moving or pull their wagons off the road. They were stalling the whole column, he barked. And so almost without thinking Theo took Mutti's hand as if his mother were a toddler, and started walking her forward. Moving her and the wagons down the road. Her mother allowed herself to be led and Sonje obediently followed, and once more they were proceeding toward Stettin. He was relieved, though he hoped Mutti couldn't detect the way he was favoring one foot. Perhaps if his toes didn't look better by Stettin; perhaps if Anna continued to mend; perhaps if his mother regained her usually calm demeanor, he might tell her that something was wrong with his foot. But then again he might not. Everyone had so much to worry about, he wasn't sure he should add anything more.

THAT AFTERNOON, Anna and Mutti and Sonje returned from what was supposed to be a brief foray into the woods to relieve themselves. They had been gone so long that Callum had grown worried and was about to start in after them. But then he saw them, and he noticed that Anna and Sonje were stomping through the snow with sacks dangling from each of their perfectly straight arms. The bags were so stuffed that they were the shape of giant pears, and when the women reached them Callum saw they were filled with carrots and turnips and beets. One even had a loaf of black bread. Apparently there was a farmhouse just beyond this copse of pine— they would all see it soon from the road—and Mutti had traded the last of her jewelry for the provisions. A gold necklace that Rolf had given her on their honeymoon, and her wedding band. It seemed like an awfully steep price to Callum, but they were all very hungry and ate ravenously before continuing on to the west.

URI SAW THE SS troops at the crossroads, a four-way inter-section with a cemetery stretching toward them from the south-east corner, before either Callum or the Emmerichs did, and he knew instantly that he was going to be leaving this family. At least for the foreseeable future. He would have to disappear, and then rejoin them at the home of this Emmerich woman's cousin in a few days or weeks—depending upon the speed with which the front continued to disintegrate. There were four soldiers, Waffen SS in their camouflage uniforms, and two of them were brandish-ing Bergman sub-machine guns, smoking cigarettes, and watch-ing the procession. The other two were talking to a middle-aged couple, reviewing their identification papers. The man, whose hair was graying and thin, was at least fifty, and yet he was nonetheless about to be drafted. There was an open truck behind the soldiers with a dozen pathetic-looking fellows—feeble and frail and some quite old—sitting or standing nervously behind the rails in the rear.

Without saying a word Uri put his hand up and signaled for Callum and Mutti to halt the horses. Instantly the Emmerichs saw the soldiers, too.

"Get in the cart, Callum," he murmured. "Trade places with Anna." Anna, as far as they knew, had fallen back to sleep among the bags of oats, a snug warren beneath the quilts. They still had a sizable amount of feed left for the horses, because whenever they could they had fed the animals with the hay they found in the abandoned barns where they slept.

"You don't think they'll search the wagon?" he asked.

"No. Mutti, Theo, and two young women traveling west? Seems pretty natural to me. They'll be fine."

"What will happen to them if I'm discovered?"

"After they shoot you? They'll shoot them."

"That's comforting," Callum said, nodding, and he climbed over the side of the wagon and gently woke Anna. Her hair once more was wild with sleep, and for a moment she didn't seem to realize where she was. There was a trace of the cross-hatching from the burlap on her cheek. She stretched her arms over her head, and Uri imagined her waking in her warm bed, the sun bursting through curtains in the window, on a peaceful spring morning on that estate of hers. The image—the entitlement—briefly rankled him. Made him wonder where his own sister was. How she had died. All she had endured before she had finally been killed or succumbed to starvation or disease. He had the sense that Anna had come to like him more than she should given her supposed affection for this paratrooper, though he thought it was also possible this was mere arrogance on his part. Still, there was a part of him that wanted to put his arm around Callum's shoulders and tell him, *So, my young friend. Anna's people? They're trying to exterminate mine. Trust me: There's no danger I am going to fall for her.* He wouldn't say such a thing, of course. But the idea crossed his mind.

"She looks better, doesn't she?" her mother was saying to him. He feared he'd been staring and quickly glanced back toward the cemetery. There he noticed that the angel on one of the nearest tombstones had lost a wing and the marble at the break was almost albino white. The rest of the statue was ash-colored with age. He looked more closely now at the gravestones and saw other angels—as well as granite women and men, their robes and sandals seemingly inadequate even for stone in winters this brutal—that had lost their arms and their heads as well as their wings. There were decapitated rock cherubs and sheep. He presumed at some point there had been shell fire here, and under the rolling mantle of snow the ground had been chewed up by the explosions, the caskets splintered, and whatever was left of the bodies scattered like dust along the earth. There probably were other tombstones that had been obliterated completely, the remnants—pebbles and slabs and chunks—buried as well beneath the fresh snow.

"How long was I sleeping?" Anna was saying. Suddenly she was beside him, wrapping her head in a shawl as she spoke.

"Two hours. Maybe three," Callum said from the wagon. "We didn't realize you were in such a deep slumber."

"I was dreaming."

"What of?" This was Theo.

She sniffed at the air, wrinkling her nose in a way that made Uri think of a rabbit. "Werner and Helmut," she told her brother. "But you were in the dream, too."

"What were we doing?"

She smiled at the boy. "We were all at the sea. At that beach you love east of Danzig, and we were all on a holiday. There was a boat in the distance. A big one. Helmut and Werner were dunking you in the waves."

"I'm too old for that," Theo said, clearly disappointed that even in Anna's dreams he was deemed a small child. Meanwhile, Uri was left wondering at the way his big sister had taken the nightmarish story they had all heard about the sinking of the *Wilhelm Gustloff* and somehow in her sleep generated images that left her content.

"You are indeed, my little love. You are indeed."

"Where were you? It doesn't sound like you were in the water with us."

She paused. "I was sitting on a blanket on the beach. Watching. And the sun? Glorious. Hotter than it ever is in reality, I think. Scorching. The sand was almost too hot for my toes. But I was very happy."

"You weren't alone, were you?"

Anna rolled her eyes at her brother, but Uri could tell that the boy had hit a nerve. "Tell me who!" the child insisted. "Who was on the blanket with you!"

"No one. I was alone."

"You're lying, I can tell."

Uri saw her glance at him briefly, almost against her will. Then she squeezed her brother's shoulders through his coat, pulling him against her. "Big sisters are allowed their secrets," she said into Theo's ear, and—though Uri knew it was exactly the wrong thing to do—he glanced up at Callum in the wagon. The paratrooper's gaze was darting back and forth between Anna and him, and the fact that Anna had looked fleetingly in his direction—rather than in Callum's—hadn't been lost on the Scot. Uri could see the hurt in his eyes. And now, he realized, by glimpsing up at Callum he had made it clear to this other soldier that he, too, was aware of who had been on the blanket beside Anna in her dream.

The moment was broken abruptly when somewhere in the woods in the distance, somewhere behind the SS soldiers, they heard a single shot. "Russians?" Mutti asked him.

"No," he told her. "Most likely a deserter. The SS simply taking care of someone without the proper papers." He sensed Callum was continuing to stare at him as he said this, and when he turned, he saw he was correct. Only when they heard the SS soldiers signaling for the line to move along did the paratrooper finally disappear beneath the feed. Uri decided that when he rejoined this crowd in Stettin, he would have to be careful not to antagonize this Scotsman. He would have to watch what he said, and he would have to stay the hell out of this Anna girl's dreams. Besides, he liked Callum. But he couldn't focus on any of that right now. He handed Anna his pistol and told her that she should not be afraid to use it. Then he asked Mutti for the address of her cousin in Stettin and, once he had it, started to march with authority back down the road. Against the current, against this boundless stream of refugees. Their good-byes had been brief and, in his mind, completely unsatisfactory. But he had to move fast and he had to move as if he had a purpose, at least until he was far, far from those SS goons.

Then, when he had some distance on the checkpoint, he would figure out how, once again, to reinvent himself.

DESPITE THE COLD, the ground was spongy and soft at the checkpoint, a mix of mud and motor oil and horse manure. Off to one side of the road, opposite the SS soldiers' truck, Anna saw four strong horses tied to the wrought-iron fence that surrounded this edge of the cemetery. Two had their mouths and noses hidden by army feed bags, and two were looking on testily. On the other side of the intersection there was a large mound of debris, clothes and toys and suitcases that families were discarding here. She guessed the suitcases belonged to the men in the truck. But that hairless doll in the torn smock? Or the chipped wooden sword and its matching scabbard? There were certainly no coats or capes, but she saw linens and spring bonnets and picture frames—large ones for paintings and small ones for photographs—with the images removed. Someone had left behind a box that must once have held fine silver, and while the utensils were long gone, the container was still here, the felt lining filling now with snow and clods of mud churned up by people's boots as they passed.

Anna thought the SS soldiers actually looked more tired than menacing, perhaps even a little bored. Still, two of them were coldly pulling almost every male they found from the line and herding them into the back of the vehicle, where the recruits were listening to the music and propaganda—offered at the moment in equal parts—on the Volksempfänger radio that was resting on the truck's cab. The other soldiers, the pair who had been smoking cigarettes, had taken a half-dozen of the men with them to the edge of the forest, and briefly Anna feared they were going to execute the group right here and now. Much to her relief, however, she understood after a moment that instead the soldiers were about to give them an impromptu lesson on how to fire a *panzerfaust*. One of the soldiers was leaning a ratty piece of barn board with a hand-drawn Russian star against a dead chestnut tree at the edge of the cemetery, while the other was showing them how to rest the small cannon on their shoulders. He was warning them to avoid the flame that would exit the rear of the weapon and spurt easily two meters behind them.

Some of those men, she thought, didn't look fit to work on her family's farm, much less try to stop Russian tanks. They were more likely to kill themselves than slow Ivan's advance. She wondered: Weeks ago had one of those men been her father? An aging veteran of the First World War expected now to do what men half his age—with better weapons and better training—had been incapable of accomplishing? It was pathetic, just pathetic, and she was at once mortified and embarrassed and angry.

One of the soldiers who was reviewing her family's papers looked up at her. "Something bothering you?" he asked.

She focused on him, at the shadowy stubble and the deep bags under his disturbingly boyish green eyes, at the pencil-point-thin scar that ran along his jaw from his earlobe to his chin, and tried to erase the frown from her face. Still, the absurdity of his question astonished her. *Was something bothering her?* She was a refugee. She had been sleeping in the homes of strangers or in barns or outside in the snow for weeks. She was hungry; she was cold. *Of course* something was bothering her. But she held her tongue and said—trying to sound pleasant—"I've been sick."

"With what?"

"I don't know. Not typhus. I'm getting better."

He nodded. "I'm glad," he said, and his relief sounded oddly genuine. "It seems you have two brothers in the army, yes?"

For a moment she was curious why he was asking her this and not Mutti—the head of their household. But then she got it. He simply wanted to talk to her. A young woman.

"Yes. My older brother is fighting outside of Budapest. That's Werner. I'm not sure where Helmut is. He's my twin. But he's east of here, with our father. The last we heard, they were part of the counterattack on the Kulm bridgehead."

"That was weeks ago," he said.

"I know."

"No word since then?"

She shook her head and quickly he looked down from her to the papers in his gloved hands. "And your father is Rolf," he said, trying to fill in the silence before it grew awkward. "My father is named Rolf, too. I haven't seen him in months, either."

"I'm sorry," she murmured, assuming she had to say something.

"He's fine. He trains teenagers to fire antiaircraft guns in the west. They're boys practically—not much older than this young fellow," the soldier continued, motioning toward Theo. "He travels between the factories and sets up the batteries. I'm sure your father is fine, too."

Her first thought was to tell him, *You don't believe that.* Once more, however, she restrained herself and said simply, "I hope so. We all do."

"Where are you going?"

"Stettin."

"Do you have family there? Or friends who are expecting you?"

"My mother's cousin lives there."

"It's just the four of you?"

"Yes," she said, wondering why he would even ask such a thing. She thought instantly of Callum, buried beneath the feed, and Manfred, behind them now somewhere amid the long columns of refugees.

"It's awfully dangerous for women and children to travel alone," he said.

She felt a small eddy of resentment: If they actually had a man with them right now, he would be taken away from them and asked to stop a tank with a slingshot. She considered telling him the story of the pair of Russian scouts in the barn, perhaps omitting the small detail that they really did have two males traveling with them at the time and each of those men had shot one of the enemy soldiers. She was awed at the rage that was festering inside her and wondered if it stemmed from the fact that Manfred was gone. Did she actually feel more vulnerable now that he had left them? "I know," she said evenly.

"Do you have anything you can use to defend yourself?"

She reached under her cape and revealed the pistol Manfred had given her. She wanted to give him no reason to search her or the wagons. In addition to Callum, she recalled that the rifles they had taken from the Russian soldiers were in the cart, too.

He looked at it, and despite the fact she had shared the gun with him willingly, his tone changed from one of vague solicitude to suspicion. "Where did you get this?"

"It was Werner's," she said quickly, reflexively.

"Werner is your brother in Budapest?"

"That's right."

"And why doesn't Werner-your-brother-in-Budapest have it?"

She shrugged, hoping her breathing sounded normal, her voice natural. "When he was home on leave, he gave it to me. He knew we were going to have to evacuate soon."

"Rather defeatist of him, don't you think?"

"No."

"When did your brother return to his company?"

"I don't recall the exact date. But it was early January," she lied.

He turned his attention toward Mutti for the first time.

"Do you love your son? This Werner in Budapest?" he asked.

Sonje was huddling against Mutti, and Theo was standing beside them. The boy, for reasons Anna couldn't fathom, was standing on a single foot like a stork, and she wanted to ask her brother what in heaven's name he was doing, if only to divert this SS soldier's attention away from their mother. Already, however, her mother was releasing Sonje and rising up to her full height. "Yes, of course I do," she replied.

"Do you worry about him in Budapest?"

"I don't know what you're implying, young man, and I don't believe I want to know. But, obviously, I worry about my son in Budapest. I'm a mother and I'm a wife. That means I also worry about my son and my husband who are fighting somewhere to the east. And, if you are desirous of a complete litany, I will also tell you that I worry about my brother-in-law who is defending our country on the western front," she continued, as if she were speaking with an inattentive and slightly annoying schoolboy. "And while my older son wanted his sister to have a way to protect herself and her family, his attitude is anything but defeatist. If you had a sister, wouldn't you want her to have a way to protect herself? For goodness' sake, you just said yourself that it's dangerous out here."

The soldier actually smiled at her and seemed slightly and appropriately abashed. *For goodness' sake.* Anna chastised herself inwardly for fretting for even a moment about what her mother might say.

"As a matter of fact, I do have sisters. Two," he said. "And, yes, if they weren't safely at home right now painting plates, I expect I would want them to carry handguns, too."

Nearby there was a small explosion, and almost as one she and Theo winced and turned toward the sound, her brother finally dropping that other foot for balance. One of the older men had just fired the *panzerfaust*. The red star was completely untouched, but she thought one of the tombstones—easily twenty meters to the right of the target—had been obliterated. When she looked back at the SS soldier before her, he was rolling his eyes in disgust.

"And that's what's going to save the Fatherland. Please.

Heaven protect us all," he said, and he placed Manfred's pistol back in her palm and returned to her both the Emmerichs' and Sonje's papers. Then he looked at their wagons, his hands on his hips, and paused.

"May we continue?" she asked him.

He ignored her as if he had a sudden, more pressing thought, and marched over to Waldau. Waldau and Ragnit were leading one cart—the one in which Callum was hidden—and Balga the other. He ran his fingers along the animal's velvetine cannon of a shoulder. "I see you have two wagons and three horses. I hate to do this to you, but I don't have a choice: I'm going to have to confiscate one of your animals. But they look like good, strong pullers: You'll still have a horse for each wagon," he said, and then he motioned for the soldier beside him—a studious-looking fellow with round eyeglasses who was no older than Werner, Anna guessed, but with an oddly weathered face for a man so young— to remove the harness linking the horse nearest him from the wagon. Instantly her mother and Sonje glanced at her, and she could see the alarm in their faces. It wasn't, she sensed, merely the reality that they were about to lose a second horse that was troubling them. Certainly Mutti had to know that Ragnit was capable of pulling the wagon away from this checkpoint on his own, even with the added weight of the paratrooper buried beneath the bags of oats. She looked back at them, trying to understand what, suddenly, had them so unnerved.

"That's Waldau," Theo was saying to the men. "He's named for a castle." Her brother's voice had a quiver to it that Anna recognized. This was his favorite horse, other than that pony of his they had left behind at Kaminheim, and he was trying hard to keep from crying.

"I know the castle," the soldier with the spectacles was saying patiently, and something about the tenderness in his tone made her wonder if it was possible that he was old enough to have children of his own. He pulled off his gloves so he could more easily manage the buckles on the bridle and the reins and the leather suspenders that fell across the animal's neck and chest. "I know precisely where it is in Prussia."

"We've already lost Labiau," Theo continued, as he watched the soldier begin to unhitch the horse.

"Ah, another castle," he remarked.

"He was killed by a plane that strafed our column," the boy added, and Anna found herself mesmerized by her brother's resilience, by the way he was holding back his tears even now. And so before she knew quite what she was going to say or do, she was pointing at Balga and suggesting to the soldier, "Would you please take this animal instead?"

The soldier paused and shrugged. His partner, the one who had examined their papers, went over to Balga and eyed him more closely. "You realize, don't you, that I could take all three of your horses," he said, a statement, not a question.

"I do know, yes."

"Well, then: Why this one?" he asked. "Is there a problem with him I'm missing? If he's dragging this wagon on his own, he must be quite some animal."

"He's my horse," she said simply. "That's why. The first one you picked is a favorite of my little brother. He's already had to leave his pony behind. If possible, I'd like him to keep this animal in his life. He's lost so much else."

He eyed her deliberatively and once more studied the horse, his gaze resting a long moment on the coronet above each of the animal's hooves and then up and down Balga's legs. He looked at the animal's mouth and finally shrugged. "I really have no idea what I'm supposed to look for in a horse's mouth. Do you? Teeth, gums? I've just no idea at all. I've never owned horses; I grew up around streetcars in the city. All I know is I'm supposed to round some more up. This one seems as good as the others," he mused, pushing an unruly forelock of dark hair off his forehead and instructing the other soldier to take Balga instead.

"You don't have to do that," Theo told her.

"I do, sweetie. I do," she said to her brother. Then, with a sickening flutter in her chest, she noticed the boots. Callum's boots. Both of them. Clearly this was what her mother and Sonje had seen a moment ago, this was what had caused their eyes to widen in fear. She could see the thick rubber soles, and as high on one leg as his ankle. His feet were actually sticking out. The SS soldiers were so focused on the horses, however, that they hadn't looked back yet. But, eventually, they would. They would. How could they not? Eventually their eyes would roam casually in that direction, and there would be the two shoes. They stood out against the canvas bags like lit candles on a Christmas tree.

"Here, let me do that," she offered quickly, struggling to make the words sound normal when she felt as if she were trying to speak with a giant popover in her mouth. She realized that she needed an excuse to stand between the soldier and the incriminating side of the wagon. Once there, perhaps she might be able to drape something atop Callum's feet. Her cape, maybe. But why? Why in this cold would she do such a thing? Still, as she began to work the complicated series of straps and buckles that linked the animal with the wagon she wondered if it would seem suspicious to either of these SS troopers if she were to go and rearrange the bags of feed behind her. She decided, however, that she hadn't a choice, and she was just starting in that direction when the soldier without the eyeglasses, the one in charge, suddenly ordered her to halt, to stop whatever it was she was doing. He snapped at the old men in the truck behind him to be silent. To shut their mouths. He commanded his partner to cease work on the harness. His face grew into an elongated mask with a rictus of rage in the middle, but otherwise he, too, stood perfectly still. She didn't dare venture a glimpse back at the boots, those awful, incriminating boots that were about to get them all—even her poor, young, innocent little brother—killed, and instead kept her eyes fixed upon this suddenly furious soldier. And then she understood that his anger had nothing to do with the boots, nothing at all. It had nothing to do with anything he had seen. It was what he had heard. Was hearing. Abruptly he jumped up onto the hood of the truck and reached with both hands for the Volks-empfänger radio on the cab. She had been so focused on his questions about her brother and Manfred's pistol and where they were going that she hadn't been listening to the broadcast. She had been aware that some particularly somber music had been playing, nothing more. Now she realized that the music had been replaced by an announcer, and in tones even more solemn than whatever song had been on the radio he was describing an air raid on Dresden. For a brief moment she felt only relief: This wasn't about the paratrooper in their wagon. It was only about an air raid. And air raids were, unfortunately, common these days. But then she understood this was a raid of a very different sort, a very different magnitude. Apparently Dresden was gone, all but burned off the map in the night, the once lovely city bombed in mere hours into ruins. The British, the announcer was saying, may have used a new, more deadly sort of explosive: The firestorm that engulfed the city seemed to have melted even the stone buildings that were two and three hundred years old, and there were reports that the Elbe itself was ablaze. He said the casualties were well into the tens—perhaps even hundreds—of thousands, and this attack represented an escalation in the RAF's medieval brutality: After all, Dresden was known for porcelain, not munitions. It was almost completely undefended. Even the Art Academy and the Belvedere, with all of their paintings and pottery and sculpture, had been bombed, an indication that the western Allies were as shameless and savage as the Russians. Still, he vowed that the führer's new wonder rockets would exact revenge on the United Kingdom from London to Glasgow, and this sort of viciousness would only stiffen the German resistance. It would never, he insisted, encourage capitulation. Then, after a drumroll, the grave music resumed.

The SS soldier was still holding the radio before his face, and Anna wondered if he might raise it aloft and hurl it from the roof of the truck like a boulder. But he didn't. He had merely been trying to hear every detail the announcer was offering. Now that no more news was forthcoming, he put the Volksempfänger down on the cab and jumped to the ground from his perch atop the vehicle. "Wonder rockets. That's horseshit," he said, a little calmer now, his rage having been subsumed by disgust.

His partner murmured a pair of female names to him, and Anna presumed the fellow was referring to the soldier's two sisters—the ones who were home somewhere painting plates. She watched him place his hands on the man's shoulders, squeezing them firmly and saying something more that she couldn't hear. But she understood: Those poor girls lived in Dresden. That's where the family was from. The two men were both envisioning those sisters in the firestorm.

Then the soldier with the eyeglasses returned to them, but only to take Balga away. He was going to lead the stallion to the wrought-iron fence with the other horses at the edge of the cemetery. Briefly the animal looked at Anna, those big, dark eyes uncomprehending and curious. A little wary. He snorted once at the stranger, and it was clear that he was being led away under duress. But it looked to Anna as if he was going to be stubborn only, not vicious. She saw Theo already was walking Waldau to the second wagon.

"Don't bring him too close to those other animals," Anna called out to the soldier, just in case, and Balga's ears twitched at the sound of her voice.

"He might kick them?" he asked.

"Or you."

"And you said he was your horse?" the soldier asked.

She nodded.

"Come then," the soldier said. "Say good-bye to him. And then you had better get on your way." Quickly she went to the animal.

For a moment she ran her hand along his mane and heavy winter coat, pressing and warming her palm against him. Then she brought her fingers to her lips, inhaling one last time his scent, and pressed them against his cheek. When she pulled them away he brought his nose almost to hers, and exhaled from those great, gaping nostrils a puff of steam that smelled perfectly sweet and struck her as the gust from a fairy-tale dragon. He didn't take his eyes off her, and she decided that what she had initially supposed was wariness in her animal's intense countenance was actually more akin to despair.

WHEN THE SS CHECKPOINT was well behind them, Sonje grew animated: She unleashed a frenzied, fist-pounding assault on the sacks of feed underneath which Callum was hiding. Mutti realized that the girl's sudden, violent anger at the paratrooper was unreasonable: It wasn't he, after all, who had bombed Dresden. He wasn't a pilot. He'd never even fired a bullet at a German before surrendering. Besides, it was growing increasingly evident to Mutti that her people had asked for this. She, with her blind eye, had asked for this. Hitler, that man whom she had once viewed as the führer—as *her* führer—had tried to bomb most of Europe into submission. He and that pompous fop Göring. She recalled Manfred's story of that train full of Jews, and she shuddered. What else had they done? What else?

Nevertheless, she was so worried about Sonje's precarious mental health that she didn't defend Callum as the girl lashed into him. When the young man climbed from the wagon, it only got worse. Sonje's grim face grew red as she ranted, and it looked as if she might physically attack him. But Mutti concluded that Sonje needed to vent—they all did, she guessed, for different reasons— and she would give her that opportunity, as unfair as that might be for poor Callum. Even Anna seemed to have realized that everyone would be better off if they allowed Sonje her say.

"I can't even bear to walk beside you right now!" she was telling the paratrooper when he climbed from the wagon, her voice strident and shrill. Callum seemed largely unperturbed, as if it were easier to allow this wave of anger to wash over him than it was to rise up and risk it cutting his columnar legs out from under him. Occasionally he would glance at Anna, and he seemed more bemused than defensive, but he was listening and nodding, as if he were receiving nothing more from Sonje than a shopping list for the village. "Are you really the people we are supposed to surrender to? You are no better than the Russians! No better at all! You are a horrible, violent people and you are brutes! When will you have had enough? When? When you've killed every last woman and child in Germany? Destroyed every single home and museum?"

Mutti presumed that part of Sonje's anger stemmed from fear: from the reality that Manfred had left them. She knew that she herself felt a little bereft, a little more anxious, and so why wouldn't Sonje—or, for that matter, her own daughter? Why shouldn't all their tempers be a little short? It was a small miracle they weren't constantly snapping at one another now that their Wehrmacht corporal was gone. It wasn't that Manfred was braver than Callum—though Mutti had to admit to herself, he probably was. Unlike their young Scot, Manfred would not have allowed himself to be captured without firing a shot. Rather, it was that he was resourceful and focused and just a little bit fierce. Moreover, he was a man in a uniform: His presence gave them a clout the other refugees lacked. The result? When they'd had this handsome Wehrmacht corporal as a part of their group, they couldn't help but feel a little bit safer, a little more secure.

"Barbarians!" Sonje was insisting, shaking her head. "Barbarians!" she repeated.

Yes, it was clear that Manfred had spent more time away from his unit than he probably should have; but she couldn't begrudge the man that, not after all he had endured in his years in the army and all, undoubtedly, he had seen. Besides, he might have saved Anna's life in that barn. Who knew what those Russians might have done to her in the end?

"And now Dresden!" Sonje hissed, her voice eerily reminiscent of Klara's when she said the name of the city, but Mutti had the sense that the girl's tirade might finally be winding down. "Why would you bomb Dresden? What could possibly be gained from bombing Dresden?"

She shook her head and wiped at her eyes and her cheeks with her gloved fingers, and Mutti reached out and rubbed her back in long, slow circles. Russians, British, Americans, she thought. Perhaps Sonje was right. Perhaps it didn't make a difference in which direction they walked. It really did seem as if the whole world was against them.

"What, Mutti?"

She looked over at Anna. She hadn't realized that she had spoken aloud just now.

"What were you saying?" her daughter was asking her, the girl's eyes shining and a little wide with concern. Callum, too, was watching her.

"Oh," she said to them both, noting an especially forlorn-looking birch by the side of the road. "I was just being an old woman. Talking to myself, I guess."

"You are hardly an old woman," said Anna.

"I wasn't three or four months ago. I think I am now. I seem to be easily distracted." She heard the despair in her voice and felt ashamed. Had she ever before sounded so gloomy?

"Well," her daughter was saying kindly, "the mind's bound to roam when all we do is walk out here in the cold. Half the time, I find myself nodding off on my feet. Just listen to the horses' hooves: It's like a metronome. Of course we get distracted!"

We. Anna was kind enough to say *we*, Mutti noticed, and so she stood up a little straighter. Stopped rubbing Sonje's back. She forced herself to take strides that were longer, more vigorous, and reminded herself that she still had a part of her family with her. Her lovely daughter. Her brave little boy. This was a great blessing. And it meant, as their mother, that she had to remain steadfast and resolute, and do all that she could to protect them. Under no circumstances could she allow herself to break down and become an additional burden.

"Come," she said to no one in particular, "we should keep moving. It won't be dark for another few hours."

ANNA UNDERSTOOD ON a level that was more intellectual than visceral that aging represented a steady winnowing of life's possibilities. She grasped death from bullets and bombs and bayonets far better than she did death from old age and cancer. But she was not uncomprehending of the reality that the infinite steadily contracted, the options narrowed, and eventually one's future would be as shallow as a spoon. As predictable—and enervating—as the mud that followed the first thaws in March. And so as they walked on toward Stettin, three more days beneath a dreary, ever-lowering sky, in her mind she recited a litany of names. Yes, they did get distracted. All of them. They were distracted as much by their memories of what—of whom—they had lost as they were by what loomed before them. Gone, she thought, at least for the moment, was Werner. And disappeared behind him into that great fog of battle were her father and Helmut. Her twin. Then there was her mother's brother, dead, as well as the obdurate man's daughter and daughter-in-law and grandson. There were Klara and Gabi, not certainly dead but most likely dead. Russians, two killed in a barn in the midst of an act of inexplicable kindness. No, that wasn't right: It wasn't an act of kindness at all. They were stealing everything her family had: They had simply chosen not to rape and murder her in the process. Funny how a war altered one's definition of mercy.

And then, of course, there were the animals, some profoundly beloved. There were the animals they had left behind at Kaminheim and the ones they had lost since starting west: Labiau, senselessly butchered, and Balga—her favorite—commandeered. Already she could see the physical strain on the two horses that remained. Callum was walking beside the wagons most of the time, but at least once or twice each day he had been forced to crawl beneath the remaining bags of oats and one of the horses had had to struggle extra hard to proceed. She had sacrificed her suitcase soon after they had left that first SS checkpoint, telling no one when she did it, though in hindsight it hadn't been very heavy and she had regretted her sacrifice as soon as they had stopped at the end of that day. Still, when she had looked into the eyes of Waldau and Ragnit, when she had watched the white foam ooze from their mouths, she had been almost unable to bear it.

Yet as they trudged west, the loss she found herself ruing with a frequency and a depth that surprised her was neither her father nor her brothers nor even her precious horse. It was Manfred. It wasn't that she cared for him more than anyone else. She was quite sure of that. (She was, wasn't she?) But she nonetheless found herself thinking of him even when she tried not to. She thought of him when Callum was trying to cheer her up with his stories of the Scottish coast and what a life might be like for them in Elgin. His accent pained her now, because while his German vocabulary was extensive—he was, more or less, fluent—his pronunciation was still slightly off, and every conversation reminded her of how different they were. She thought of him when Theo was asking her if she thought there was a chance they might come across new boots for him soon, because his, he said, were getting a little tight. Manfred was capable and ingenious: He would have found her brother some boots. And she thought of him when she traded two bags of feed for a small sack of muesli and a little milk, and when Mutti would talk reverentially about her husband and her two distant sons. Mutti was, essentially, whistling in the dark, talking aloud about how resilient the Emmerich men were, and how they would get through this. They would, she was certain. They'd find a way.

Anna was considerably less confident, but she wasn't going to disagree with her mother. You believed whatever was necessary to keep putting one foot in front of the other in this cold and gray and ice.

Almost imperceptibly, however, over those three days the fields and the forests were slowly transformed into lawns and garden plots, still white with snow or silvery pearl with ice, but the houses were growing closer together and eventually they grew even into rows. Behind them, to the east, the front had apparently stabilized. The Russians were no longer licking at the rear wheels of their wagons.

And then, as if Mutti were discussing a common bird she had seen at a feeder at Kaminheim, one morning her mother casually remarked that they were on the Altdamm road and Altdamm was an eastern suburb of Stettin. Any moment, she said, they might hear the sound of ships in the great harbor. She reminded them that her cousin lived at the edge of the city—on a cliff overlooking the lake—and she guessed they would be there by midafternoon.

Anna turned to her brother, who at the moment was riding on the driver's box of the wagon Waldau was pulling.

"We did it," she said, and she found herself smiling more broadly than she had in a very long while. "We made it."

Theo tried to smile back, but she was surprised to see there were tears running down his cheeks and his eyes were red. Theo, crying? The child struggled so hard to be brave that she wasn't sure if he had cried once since they had left Kaminheim.

"Sweetie, don't cry," she said to the boy. "Don't you see? We're here. Tonight you'll have warm food and a warm bed."

The boy sniffed back a small sob and said in a voice that was barely above a whisper—it was hushed and scared, as if he didn't want Mutti to hear him—"Anna? I think . . ."

"Tell me, sweetie."

"I think something bad has happened to my foot."

PART III

The First Days of Spring 1945

Chapter Sixteen

CECILE HADN'T REALLY BELIEVED THEY WERE DES-
tined for work, even though she had said such things to Jeanne
and to Vera and to anyone else who would listen. As often as not
as they had walked west in the winter, she had begun to conclude
that either there was no purpose to their marching other than to
march them to death or they were being marched to a camp that
was beyond the reach of the Soviets. Perhaps one with a gas
chamber to asphyxiate the prisoners and a crematorium. She'd
heard stories about such camps. And yet here they were, working
by day at a factory that made a small part for airplane engines
and sleeping by night in a barracks. During the last part of their
trip, and the part that had covered the most ground by far, they
had been locked inside windowless vans—not gas vans, as they
had all briefly presumed, some grateful that their misery was finally going to be ended. Actual transportation vans. Eleven of
them. They were driven inside the vans for two days and then
deposited at barracks that smelled of alcohol. Each of the prisoners had a thin bunk to herself, a pillow filled with straw, and a
blanket. Russian women had worked here before them and the
blankets still were infested with body lice, but they were no
longer sleeping outside or in barns, and they were given the

clothing the Russians had left behind before they had—the Jewish women supposed—been executed themselves. And so while some of the prisoners concluded that eventually they would be machine-gunned or gassed as well, for the moment they had warmer clothes and their rations of soup and bread were more substantial. Not generous, not even remotely satisfying, but larger. Moreover, they were grateful for that soup, even on those days when it was watery and thin, because if nothing else it had been boiled and that meant they could drink it and slake their thirst without fear of typhus. And though the barracks weren't heated, the walls kept out the worst of the wind. Besides, it was March now and the sun was higher during the day and the most brutal weather was behind them.

And soon the Russians would get here. They had to. Or perhaps, Cecile and Jeanne had conjectured, they were so far west that the British or the Americans would rescue them first.

The barracks were about two kilometers from the factory, and they walked along the edge of a small village to reach it. Cecile still wore her hiking boots and Jeanne still had the crocodile dress flats that Cecile had given her. And always, whether it was dawn or dusk, they saw townspeople. Sometimes the townspeople would avert their eyes when they saw the women trudging back and forth, and sometimes they would go about their business as if the prisoners were invisible. They would pass them on their bicycles. They would continue to prepare the loosening soil for their gardens. If they were children, they would walk to their school. The prisoners knew they didn't dare say a word to the Germans, and the Germans, it seemed, had neither interest nor curiosity in this group that had replaced the Russians at the factory.

The work wasn't hard. Some days they assembled pistons, using four long bolts to attach the fire plates to the piston's crown; other days they screwed the parts of the nozzle together for the fuel injection system for a particular Junkers fighter. Always there was a Dutch foreman, a prisoner, too, who inspected their work. He wasn't especially rigorous, and the women grew to understand that his lackadaisical attitude was his own personal form of resistance. Could a badly fitted piston or imperfect fuel nozzle bring down a German fighter plane on its own? They didn't know for sure, but they could hope.

Cecile knew she wasn't actually recovering her health with her new diet, her threadbare jacket with lice, or the reality that she was no longer sleeping in the worst of the cold like a wild animal. But she understood, as did all of the other women, that it was going to take a lot longer to die in this fashion. They might expire walking to and from the gates of the factory. But they were no longer actively being killed.

THERE WAS ROUGHLY ONE guard for every ten or twelve women escorting them between the barracks and the factory. Usually, Cecile scoffed at the idea that any prisoner was even capable of trying to escape. All of the girls were disappointed that so many of the guards from their original camp—the real sadists, it seemed, women like Sigi and men like Pusch—had accompanied them when the vans had picked them up and were brutalizing them here, too, whenever the opportunity arose. The guards were supplemented by older men who seemed to live in the town with the factory. Most of them weren't SS, and many of them seemed a little frail-looking themselves. Still, they carried their guns and they walked the prisoners back and forth between the barracks and the factory, and the only time they spoke to the women was to yell at them to keep up or move faster. They didn't seem to see any reason to be kind to the prisoners.

Consequently, Cecile was surprised one morning when a guard, as he walked beside the column of women, unwrapped a piece of butcher's paper to reveal a plump, cooked chicken breast and offered it to her. The guard was one of the older men from the town.

At first she was afraid to touch it, and so she said nothing. She didn't think this was a trick precisely, but she wondered whether accepting it might be suggesting that she felt the camp wasn't feeding her sufficiently and lead to an additional punishment. Moreover, she was completely unprepared for this—or any—act of mercy. Finally, when she hadn't taken it from him, he shrugged and handed it to Jeanne, who promptly tore the meat off in pieces, giving some to Cecile and some to the woman on her right, and keeping some for herself. The three women ate their chicken ravenously, almost swallowing their chunks of meat whole. The guard was, Cecile guessed, close to sixty years old, and his uniform didn't match the outfits the other men were wearing. She wouldn't have been surprised if it was the uniform he had worn in the First World War.

On the way back to the barracks that evening she realized that once more she was marching near that guard, and so she went to him to thank him. To explain why she hadn't seemed more grateful in the morning. He looked at her as if he didn't have the slightest idea what she was talking about and ordered her to shut up, stare straight ahead, and keep moving.

Two mornings later she found herself walking beside the older man a third time. Once more he reached into his uniform coat pocket and, as if he were a magician unveiling a bouquet of flowers he had somehow concealed up his sleeve, pulled out an object draped loosely in butcher's paper. He unwrapped it and this time revealed for Cecile a cooked pork chop. He motioned for her to take it.

"Why me?" she asked him, a reflex, still a little afraid to reach for it.

From the corner of her eye she saw Jeanne eyeing the meat and then glancing at her as if she were a complete lunatic—which, perhaps, she was. There was a part of her that knew she should just grab it and eat it. Suck every small scrap of flesh from the bone. Before she had moved her fingers toward it, however,

she heard another guard, a younger man named Blumer, screaming furiously at—she supposed—her. She curled her arms
against her body and ducked, preparing for the blow. But Blumer,
who had probably been a real soldier until he had lost an eye and
a part of his ear, wasn't furious with her; she was, at the moment,
all but invisible to him. Instead he was yanking hard at the older
man with the pork chop, pulling at his sleeve so suddenly that he
dropped the meat and it fell to the muddy street, where Blumer
used his boot to smash the bone and grind the pieces into the
ground. Then he whisked the fellow away from the column, or-
dering the other nearby guards to keep a close watch on the
swine, while the rest of the group plodded on to the factory.

"When did they start hating us?" a woman named Eve asked
her aimlessly.

"They've always hated us," said Leah, a seamstress from
Budapest who had only arrived at their original camp the previous autumn. "Even when I was a little girl, my friends all called
me the Dirty Jew. My friends! Hitler simply made it acceptable to
kill us."

Behind them they heard the sound of a hard, vicious slap and
reflexively turned. There they saw the old man who had tried to
give them the pork chop on his hands and knees in the mud by the
side of the road. Standing over him, shaking his head in disgust,
was the one-eyed guard named Blumer.

IT WAS AN ALMOST idyllic existence compared to the other
camp, and so most of the women knew it couldn't last—even Cecile. They had spent not quite six weeks here. Now the Soviets
once again were approaching, and when the wind was right they
could hear the periodic cannonade. As they walked to and from
the factory, they saw the locals in the village either packing up
wagons and carts to leave themselves or lining up in a park with a
gazebo to drill with a group of Waffen SS. There the new recruits

seemed to be learning to fire small arms and throw grenades, and sometimes Cecile guessed the explosions the women heard when they were inside the factory were merely a part of the training.

Still, they knew they were going to leave here soon, and they did. Usually they were awakened by a piercing, trainlike whistle at five thirty, but one morning the whistle went off closer to four thirty and they were roused from their beds and informed they were leaving that very moment for a different factory. They might stop for breakfast in a few hours, but only if they made sufficient progress.

And so once again they were walking, marching that morning in a direction that she thought was actually more northern than western. She was grateful she had her hiking boots and she presumed Jeanne was appreciative of the dress shoes she had given her. Yes, their shoes were falling apart—both pairs—but they were still better than those wooden clogs so many of the other prisoners were forced to wear. And while the sun hadn't risen and the air was brisk, it was infinitely more endurable than the march on which the group had been taken in late January and early February. No one knew for sure, but Cecile guessed at least a third of the group had died in those weeks, expiring in the cold by the sides of train tracks or roads, shot by the guards, or immolated one particularly awful night in great bonfires on wagons.

URI LOOKED UP into the woods, the first buds on the branches creating a small but perceptible green haze around the silver birch trees. The morning sun felt good on his face, and the last of the mist had almost burned off. Today he was wearing the uniform of a Russian rifleman named Barsukov, minus his cap, because the fellow had been shot through the head. Uri hadn't killed him, but he guessed he might have if he had come across the soldier first. He needed a Russian uniform badly.

The problem, of course, was that he spoke far too little Russian to pass for more than a few minutes if he tried to join the Bolsheviks. Moreover, their army was not nearly the shambles that the Wehrmacht had become; they would expect him to be with the right company at the right time. Unfortunately, yesterday the Germans—desperate old men and teen boys, and a few SS with mortars and antitank guns—had counterattacked and successfully retaken the nearby village. There was a factory there that made important airplane parts, and the Nazis wanted it back. When he had left an hour ago, there was still a pair of destroyed Russian tanks smoldering in a small park with an idyllic white gazebo, which, inexplicably, was completely undamaged.

Somewhere in these woods, however, he had heard a rumor that there was a group of armed Jewish resisters. Or there had been. They were living in a couple of caves and an underground bunker, and there were men and women among the group. Supposedly, the Russians had originally taken that village with their help. Somehow Ivan had contacted them ahead of time, and the Jews had blown up the bridge north of the town over which the Wehrmacht initially planned to send in reinforcements, and then cut the railroad tracks that linked the village with an officers' training school to the west. The town's mayor was a maniac, however, and there were just enough Nazi diehards in the area—and, unknown to the Russians, the remnants of a company of Waffen SS—to launch an assault on the Soviets before they could solidify their position.

In the chaos of the battle, he had melted from one side to the other.

Now, supposedly, the Jews had disappeared once more into the woods, into their hidden grottoes and fissures and dugouts. At least that's what he thought he had been told by another rifleman—a boy, really, from some icy village near Murmansk, who didn't seem to care that he spoke about seventeen words of Russian. Seemed to assume he was simply an Armenian or Azerbaijani from the Caucasus.

As he stood now at the edge of the woods, he considered his options. He could try to find those Jews, shed his uniform, and finally become Uri Singer from Schweinfurt once again. Or he could make one last attempt to reach Stettin and rejoin the Emmerichs. Just head straight north. That had certainly been his intention in the weeks since he had left the family, but it seemed there had always been a checkpoint, an artillery barrage, or a couple of extremist (and, at this stage, completely delusional) Nazis in the way. Like the mayor of this village and his entourage who had pressed him into service for their counterattack.

It surprised him how frequently he had thought of the Emmerichs this spring. Originally, of course, they had been nothing more to him than his ticket to the west. Or, to be precise, Callum had been his ticket to the west. But then something had changed, and he was left wondering: Was he so hungry for kinship and camaraderie that he had grown to like them? Was he that lonely and desperate to replace his own forever lost family? Apparently. Now, here was an irony: The people he felt closest to were the remnants of some clan of Nazi beet farmers from Prussia. A boy, his older sister, their mother. A paratrooper from Scotland who was captured almost the moment he hit the ground. He didn't honestly believe he had any sort of future with this family, but he also found himself thinking about them often. About where they were, whether they were safe. He would recall the impressive way that Anna and her mother and young Theo had managed those massive horses. The way they had endured no small litany of indignities and privations. He would hear in his head Mutti's determination to protect her children—a determination, he knew, that resembled his own mother's. Even that hulking paratrooper seemed more interesting to him now that he had some distance from the fellow, and he recalled instead their long conversations as they walked and the unexpected moments when they would laugh. Certainly Anna saw something in him. Cared for him. Besides, for all of the fellow's size, he was barely more than a boy.

How old was he? Twenty? He shouldn't be so hard on the young man.

Likewise, had he become so unhinged that he thought Anna might be a worthy substitute for his courageous sister, Rebekah? Perhaps. He would see in his mind once again Anna's lovely yellow hair and the elegant curve of her cheekbones. Her face when it was flushed from another day in the cold. The way the smallest things could make her eyes sparkle. He knew the guilt that he felt for jumping from the train that his sister might have been on was never going to leave him.

Interesting that he felt remorse for that, but not for the innumerable Germans and Russians he had killed over the last two years. He had lost no sleep over their deaths—and had, in fact, felt only satisfaction each time he had assassinated some Brownshirt or SS thug. They deserved it. The whole German people, it seemed, deserved it. But then he would find the personal and the anecdotal in the cauldron. People like the Emmerichs. A child like Theo. A young woman like Anna. The other night he had gunned down two older German soldiers standing guard outside a jail in the village. But what if one of them had been Mutti's husband, Rolf?

He really had no idea who he was anymore. He had been so many people lately that he simply hadn't a clue. Which, he guessed, was a part of the reason why he was here at the edge of the woods, looking up into a hill in which there were still small piles of snow in the shade beneath some of the trees. Perhaps here was his destiny. Not Stettin, not the Emmerichs.

Still, how in the world was he going to find these partisan Jews if the Nazis back in that village hadn't even known they were out here somewhere? Perhaps that young Russian rifleman—rifle *boy*, if he was going to be precise—had been mistaken, and someone else had blown up the bridge and torn up those railroad tracks. They were right on the border that had separated Germany and Poland five and a half years ago, and in the area there might be

Polish as well as Jewish resistance. There were also all of those Russian units eager to be among the first to reach Berlin. Perhaps the boy hadn't realized that his own artillery had taken out the bridge or the railroad.

He had his German uniform in his knapsack and wasn't sure now if he should dispose of it here. If he did find the Jews—or, perhaps, the Poles—it wouldn't look good if he was traveling around with a Wehrmacht corporal's outfit in his backpack. On the other hand, with the front this fluid it might not be advisable to be Rifleman Barsukov either. At least not for very long. If some fanatic Nazi didn't shoot him, the Russians would as soon as he opened his mouth. How could he possibly explain his bizarre picaresque these past two years to Stalin's NKVD without incriminating himself? He'd killed a lot of Nazis, but he'd killed a good number of Russians, too.

Besides, did he really want to wind up a Soviet citizen? His plan certainly wasn't to survive this nightmare only to wind up in a labor camp or a farm collective somewhere. Somehow, he had to get west. Which brought him right back to the Emmerichs and to Callum Finella. He would remind himself that the paratrooper might ease his entry into the British or the American lines. And then his internal compass once again would long for the north. For Stettin, where the Emmerichs might still be. If they had any sense, of course, they would have left by now and continued their own journey west. He hadn't heard if the Russians had reached that city yet, but if they hadn't already he guessed they would within days—unless they simply decided to bypass the town in their rush to Berlin.

Still, would he have lost anything if he ventured north to Stettin and discovered that the Emmerichs were gone?

Well, yes. Time.

In the distance he heard airplanes, and initially he presumed they were Russian. But they were coming from the west and so he changed his mind. Probably RAF or American. It wasn't likely they were German. These days the Luftwaffe still had planes, but their airfields were cratered, fuel was almost nonexistent, and it was nearly impossible to find any pilots left who had the slightest idea what they were doing. And so he lit a cigarette and leaned against a tree, waiting, wondering what the RAF's or the Americans' target would be. He thought it was possible it was that factory in the village he had just left. Of course, it was slave labor working inside there. Girls, he had heard, just like his sister. At this stage in the war, were those nozzles or pistons or whatever they made there so important that it was worth torching the Jewish prisoners assembling them? Of course not. He hoped those girls had left. Been moved somewhere else. He hoped the target was that officers' training school further up the tracks.

He couldn't see the planes because of the angle of the hill and the trees, but he guessed there were probably a half-dozen. Not a massive bombing onslaught, but not a single fighter or two planning to strafe a couple of horse-drawn Wehrmacht wagons, either.

After a moment, he decided the target most likely was the town. The engines were growing louder. And just as the bizarre idea was starting to form in his mind that he was the target, a lone man with a cigarette standing beside a birch, behind him he heard an explosion, then another, and the sounds of branches being shattered and trees upended, and he felt himself being lifted off the ground—his rifle, which had been slung over his shoulder, was suddenly twirling ahead of him like a baton and he was aware that he was no longer holding his cigarette—and he was flying as he never had before. Then he landed and the feeling was reminiscent of the experience of diving headlong from that train two years earlier; he might even have hit the ground on the same part of his hip. But he didn't have time to consider this more carefully, because the shells were continuing to churn up the ground and the forest, and tree limbs and clods of earth were raining down upon him like hail, and he could smell the fires that were igniting in the woods.

He scampered, rolling and crabwalking as much as he actually rose up on his legs and ran, but then he remembered his rifle and scuttled back for it. His knapsack, too. Somehow that had been blown off his back. Meanwhile, the planes were coming back, diving in at the height, it seemed, of his apartment house back in Schweinfurt. He grabbed his pack and felt around in the debris for his rifle, found it, and dashed as far from the woods as he could, into an open field and then down into a deep gulley beside it, aware that his hip was hurting and his hands were bleeding and there was a long red stain forming on his pants.

Ankle-deep in cold water, runoff from the snow on the nearby hills, he looked back now and saw that the mountain was completely ablaze and the planes were departing as quickly as they had arrived. But against the blue sky he saw the swastika on the tail of one plane and iron crosses on the wings of the others. The aircraft were German. Luftwaffe. He wiped at the blood on his leg and looked at it. Wondered if he was badly hurt. He didn't think so. Mostly, however, he wondered at the lunacy of this Nazi regime, its colossal hate. Here its air force couldn't find the wherewithal to protect Berlin or Hamburg or Dresden. But tell them there were Jewish resisters in the woods near some pathetic town on the border of what used to be Poland, and they could find the runways and the resources to bomb a small forest into ash.

He watched the creosote plumes rise into the air and obscure a wide ribbon of sky, but he knew the ground was still so moist that the fires would burn themselves out within hours. Still, he wasn't going to wait. Did he need a more convincing or obvious sign? No. He didn't. He was getting the hell out of Germany; he wanted nothing more to do with this country. Ever. And that meant he would limp north now to Stettin. With any luck, the Emmerichs and their Scottish POW would still be there.

Chapter Seventeen

THEO OPENED HIS EYES AND FELT THE SUN ON HIS face. Looked up at an ivory ceiling, at unfamiliar walls that were papered with columns of violets. A painting of the seashore, the watercolor lighthouse on the cliff looking strangely like a sea serpent to him. It took him a moment to orient himself in this room, to place the bed and the bureau—both the brilliance of fresh chalk—and the window. Windows, actually, because there were two of them, and they were wide and tall. They faced east and north, and one was open just a crack. He thought he heard a ship, and so he understood instantly that he wasn't home in Kaminheim. And then, slowly, it all started coming back to him. The trip through the winter cold with the wagons, the nights in the frigid barns. Being warmed by the animals. The stay at Klara's, the dead Russians. The loss of the horses, the attacks from the air. The shelling. The rubble. And now, he believed, he was in Stettin. Finally. At the home of Mutti's cousin. At Elfi's. He tried to sit up in this bed on his elbows—the mattress was soft and it was almost as if he were sinking deep into it—but he couldn't. He couldn't. It was strange and then it was scary. For a moment he felt a panic at his immobility rising up from inside him, a desperate fear that suddenly he was paralyzed. But this wasn't paralysis; this was something else. It was as if either he were pinioned to the bed or a massive, invisible weight were atop him. And the panic began to recede as quickly as it had begun to appear. He couldn't say why, except that he was warm and he was aware of the smell—and, after a moment, the sound—of the surf, and he sensed it was spring. And so he began to relax. Or, rather, he felt something relaxing him. Eliminating both that sense of weight on his chest and the desire to fight. He heard himself singing somewhere inside him, his very own voice, and it was that folk song he liked about horses and clouds. He wasn't opening his mouth—he couldn't—but there was clearly the sound of music, and it made him content. Suddenly he had the sense that he was riding atop someone's shoulders as if he were a very little boy, and for a moment he couldn't say whose shoulders they were. But then, though he couldn't see the face, somehow he knew they belonged to Werner. The two of them were on a beach. And there in the morning fog before them was their father, smiling and waving at them as they made their way toward him across a wide expanse of sand.

He wondered what time it was, but then he didn't care. When it was time to rise, someone would get him. And perhaps then he would be able to move. In the meantime, he would stay here and doze, and he closed his eyes once again. Almost instantly he was asleep, his mind submerging itself in memories of the park behind Kaminheim, and the days he would ride his pony along the trails in the woods, or run back and forth between the seemingly endless beet fields and the house, or eat the delicious jam in the kitchen that Anna or Mutti always seemed to be boiling on the stove.

MUTTI WATCHED THE boy sleep. For a brief moment Theo had opened his eyes and Mutti's heart had leapt in her chest. It had been days. The child's gaze had seemed to wander all around the bedroom, taking it in as if for the first time. But, in the end, Theo hadn't seemed to notice she was there. It was as if she had been invisible. Or, perhaps, the boy really hadn't woken at all. His eyes had opened, but he had remained asleep.

Initially, the surgeon had hoped the tissue on his foot and lower leg would respond to treatment—warm water, lotions, elevation—and he would only need to cut off the toes. But it soon became evident that the foot wasn't responding and was in fact becoming gangrenous. Moreover, it was a wet gangrene, and it was spreading quickly up into the leg. And so instead of cutting away his toes or even his foot, in the end the physician had had to saw through the bone at midshin. The surgery had been performed at Elfi's because the small hospital already had been overwhelmed by wounded German soldiers, and there had been reports of patients with typhus. Consequently, the surgeon had recommended cutting off the leg in a bedroom of the house on the cliff. He was an old man, as accustomed to operating in homes as he was in hospitals.

And that, Mutti had presumed, was that. It was a tragic loss, but perhaps it would be the last loss the child would have to suffer. When Theo emerged briefly from the anesthesia, the boy had whispered in a hoarse, soft voice that he hoped he would be able to ride his horses by summer, and he wondered how hard it would be to run with a fake leg. He murmured that those were the things he thought he did best. Ride and run. Then he fell back into the gas-induced torpor.

Over the next few weeks he seemed to mend, fighting his way back from the agony and the shock and the weakness; he was even hobbling around the house on a pair of crutches with so much daring and casualness that Mutti found herself scolding the boy, reminding him to be careful, to take it slow. Mutti's cousin, Elfi, was telling the child the same things, though it was also clear that she thought Theo's behavior was more impressive than alarming. Together the two mothers even chuckled, briefly, at the resiliency of youth and took some much-needed comfort in it. It suggested to them both that their nation had a future after all, and the children would rebuild what their parents had destroyed.

By the second week in March, as the sun was warming the rooms that faced the water, it was possible to believe that the worst really was behind them. Yes, the army was losing and the Russians were nearing. But so were the British and the Americans. After five and a half years, the war was finally going to end. Hope, suddenly, didn't seem such a fanciful proposition.

Then, however, the infection set in. It set in weeks after the amputation, long after they had ceased to worry about Theo's recovery. Oh, they had still worried about his rehabilitation. About finding a good prosthetic limb in a country that could no longer even find coal. Yet even when his temperature started to spike, they didn't begin to fret. It was only when they couldn't bring the temperature back down that they began to grow anxious. When, for three days, they couldn't even get a doctor to come to the house. Finally, they bundled him up and Callum risked everything, carrying the boy inside the hospital from the wagon. But there were no beds available and the staff could do nothing for him. And so Callum carried him back outside and placed him in the wagon beside Anna, and together with Mutti they brought him home.

Over the last week and a half now he had gone from eating an occasional slice of toasted bread to sipping a little broth to, almost all of the time, sleeping. Three times in the last four days they had thought he was dying or had fallen into a coma. Once, for a brief and horrible moment, Mutti was sure that her youngest child was dead. But then the boy had inhaled and, a few hours later, opened his eyes. He hadn't spoken in half a week, however, and the weight had just melted away. They would moisten his lips with water and soup, keep cool compresses upon his forehead, and gently wipe the sweat off his neck. Everyone was a little dazed by his endurance.

When he had opened his eyes once more this morning, Mutti had sat up expectantly, convinced that this was it, this was the moment when her altogether astonishing little boy would turn that corner and begin to recover in earnest. But then the child's lids had sagged shut and his breathing had slowed.

Now Elfi put her head in the door, saw how quiet and still the mother and son were, and then gingerly entered the room. Mutti was sitting in the rocking chair that Elfi usually kept in the sunroom, and so she took the armchair by the window and dragged it next to the bed.

"You look like you're ready to leave," Mutti said.

Elfi nodded. She was wearing her gray flannel traveling skirt, her most comfortable walking shoes, and a heavy cardigan sweater she had knit that winter with the very last of their wool. It was thick enough to keep her warm in the early morning and dusk this time of the year, but she could tie it around her waist during the heat of the day. She was also bringing with her a winter coat, because she knew well how cold it could still get once the sun had gone down. She fully expected more snow, and Mutti and Anna had described for her the ordeal they had survived before they had arrived here in February.

"But, if you want, I will stay. You know that, don't you?" she asked. "Sonje will, too."

Mutti considered her cousin, her square face with the lines furrowing deep along her eyes and around her lips. Her hair was in that odd translucent phase, no longer blond but not yet gray or white, and it was pulled back tightly now into a bun. She had grown only a little wide with age, in part—like Mutti—because of the deprivations they had been enduring for a little more than two years.

"I do," she told Elfi. "I know you'd both stay. But you have the chance to go now, and so you should." People had been leaving Stettin ever since Kolberg had been surrounded, and now that Kolberg had surrendered, they were fleeing in massive, less orderly numbers. This was especially true since the German troops had begun to withdraw from Altdamm, just east of the Oder. Elfi and Sonje were planning to leave on what people were suggesting might be the very last train to depart Stettin. It was supposed to arrive around five o'clock, and so Elfi had said that she wanted to be on the platform no later than noon: Although much of the city had started west days ago, there were still plenty of people left, and it was very likely that a crowd was already forming at the station.

"What will you do?" Elfi asked her.

She had been thinking about this for much of the past couple of days, as Theo's condition had worsened and she had realized that the boy couldn't possibly travel. *What, precisely, would she do?* And the answer was simple. She would stay here. Elfi and Sonje would head west, catching a train that would take the two women to the comparable safety of central or northern Germany. What, in any event, was left of central or northern Germany. But they would go and she would stay. She wished Callum and Anna would leave, too, but—for the moment, anyway—they were refusing. They wouldn't leave her and Theo. She thought this was a decision more foolish than noble. It was far more probable that the Russians would hurt the two of them than her and her son. A middle-aged woman and an ailing little boy.

"Irmgard?"

She looked up. Since Rolf had been gone, she was called that so infrequently that it always gave her a small start. Sometimes she forgot that she was not simply Mutti. Mother. That she had other guises and roles and personalities.

"When will you follow us?" Elfi was asking.

"As soon as we're able," she answered, and the idea crossed her mind that they were just playacting. Going through the motions. They were both pretending to believe that they honestly thought they would be reunited within days. That she and her children and Callum would harness the horses to the wagons and set out any day now, too. Or, perhaps, leave the horses to the Russians and find a train yet. Perhaps there would be another one tomorrow. Or the day after. Then she asked, "Has Sonje packed?"

Elfi nodded. "We won't wait for lunch to leave. We shouldn't."

"No, of course you shouldn't," Mutti agreed, and she reached for her son's hand, and when she did she felt a pang dart across her chest. The skin was cold. The very flesh was cold. She tried to control her breathing, to reassure herself that it might just be that the fever finally had broken and Theo's temperature was starting to fall. But she was the boy's mother, and she knew this was different. This was the cold you felt in the extremities when people were dying. When the heart was growing selfish and cocooning for the chest and the head whatever warmth it could offer, and allowing the fingers and toes, the hands and the feet, to fend for themselves. Quickly she tucked Theo's hand beneath the quilt and rubbed it between both of her palms.

In the hallway she heard Callum and Anna starting down the stairs, chatting about something. A part of her wanted to cry out to them that Theo was dying and to be still. To be silent. To mourn. But another part of her wanted to rise to her feet and order them out of the house. To insist they go west right now with Elfi and Sonje. Because Rolf and Werner and Helmut were gone—she had hoped for weeks that a letter might arrive, but none ever had, not from her husband or either of her sons—and now, before her eyes in this bed by the lake, Theo was leaving, too.

Instead, however, she sat quietly with Theo's cold hand between hers and felt Elfi's dry kiss on her suddenly moist cheek.

"You're crying," Elfi said.

"I know."

"Why don't we bundle Theo up and just bring him with us? We'll wrap him in quilts."

Mutti realized her cousin hadn't any idea why she was tearing, and she hadn't the energy to tell her. Besides, then Elfi would stay behind with her. She would remain here because Theo's death was imminent, and then she would expect her cousin to accompany her and Sonje. After all, there would no longer be any reason for her to stay.

But the opposite was true, too, wasn't it? Once Theo was gone, what reason would there be for her to go? She'd have no reasons left to live but selfish ones. It would mean that everyone else but Anna was, it seemed, dead. And Anna had her paratrooper to care for her now; she no longer needed her *mutti*. No one would. Hers had been a life of service, and now there would be no one left to serve. Soon enough they would all run out of places to run, anyway; there would be no west remaining. Already the Reich was an hourglass, and the enemies were pressing hard against the upper and lower globes.

"You know we can't do that," she murmured simply to Elfi. "But we'll catch up with you as soon as we can. I promise." At breakfast they had created an elaborate list of all the people they knew and all the places they might go in Berlin, Neubrandenburg, and Rostock. All the places where they might seek refuge and where they might find one another.

"All right then," Elfi agreed, and awkwardly—because Mutti would not stand up and risk releasing Theo's cold, cold hand—Elfi embraced her. A moment later Sonje came in to say good-bye, too, and to thank her for letting her come with her from Klara's. Again, Mutti didn't rise from the chair or release Theo's fingers. Then she heard Callum and Anna saying their farewells to the two women downstairs, their voices largely, but not completely, muffled by the stairway and the corridor that separated them.

She presumed that Anna would join her in a moment. Either sit with her, as she did for a large part of each day, or spell her, which she did, too, when Mutti needed to stretch her legs.

Outside the window she watched a pair of seagulls shooting down from the sky toward the rocky shore at the base of the cliff. Then she closed her eyes and rested her head on the pillow beside

Theo, praying in her mind that this one child be spared, though she realized that—for the first time in her life—she didn't believe there was anybody there who might listen.

WHEN THEO DIED, the train with Elfi and Sonje—six cars, each one overflowing with women and children and men who were either wounded or very, very old—was three hours to the west of the city. It was so crowded that many of the passengers had to either hold their suitcases over their heads or balance them on their shoulders because there wasn't room on the floor. It had arrived a little past seven at night and didn't stay long.

In the morning, Callum dug a grave in a patch of softening earth in the backyard that looked out upon the water. Again Mutti noticed the seagulls. As Callum worked, she recalled once more the grave she had dug by herself in September 1939 for the Luftwaffe pilot who had been shot down near Kaminheim and crashed in their park. The sky had been blue that day, too. Mid-morning she had happened to notice two planes in the sky, darting around each other as if they were a part of an aerial barnstorming show, but then abruptly she saw a wide, frothy rope of black smoke trailing behind one. It dipped its wing and then, as the other plane continued to the north, started to plummet like an arrow into the park between the marshes and the beet fields. She'd never witnessed anything like this: A plane was about to crash. She half-expected she would see a parachute emerge and the pilot floating safely through the air, but she didn't, and then she realized that she wasn't merely watching a plane auger into the ground: She was watching a person—a pilot—die. She didn't actually see the aircraft when it smashed into the earth, but she was standing on the terrace and she felt the stones shudder beneath her feet at the impact.

The small dogfight had occurred in the very first days of the war, soon after their Polish field hands had fled, the workers unsure whose side they were supposed to be on. At least that was what Mutti had told herself at the time. When they returned after the Polish surrender, however, it was clear by the combination of contrition and resentment that marked their attitudes that they had been hoping for a Polish victory. They had known very well whose side they were supposed to take, and it wasn't hers.

Earlier in the month, almost immediately after German tanks had crossed the Polish border, the Poles had rounded up Rolf and Werner—along with most of the other German men and male teenagers in the district—and were detaining them in the schoolhouse and one of the churches in Kulm. Helmut was not quite thirteen, just young enough that they hadn't bothered with him. And so after leaving Anna and Helmut and little Theo back at the house, she alone had ventured to the wreckage. There, much to her surprise, she discovered that the fires already were burning themselves out. Right away she spied the German's body, even though the cockpit had collapsed violently around his chest and his legs. He was dead and his head was twisted almost completely around so that the back of his skull was pressed against the glass canopy, but he didn't appear especially disfigured. No scorch marks, no burns. She pulled off his helmet and was surprised by how young he looked. Not much older than Werner. His eyes were closed, as if he merely were sleeping.

Like her Theo now.

His hair was jet black and his bangs had fallen over his forehead.

She couldn't bear to leave him where he was. There wasn't anything she could do about the blackened and twisted metal, but she could, she decided, bury this poor young man. In addition, she could alert his family. Let them know what had happened. And so she dragged him from the remains of the plane, aware by the way his legs sagged like great bags of cornmeal that the bones there had probably been ground to a fine powder and that even most of the bones in his arms and his rib cage had been shattered. She could feel long splinters that once had been scapulae underneath his flight jacket.

Initially she couldn't find his papers, but as she rooted around the pockets inside his vest she discovered them. His name was Hans-Gunther Sprenger, and he was from Leipzig. He was twenty-three. She carefully put the papers aside so she could return them, along with the watch he had in his pocket and the gold ring he was wearing, to his family. Then she prepared the young man for burial. She washed the body with alcohol there in the field and decorated his forehead with oak leaves. She placed a bouquet of wildflowers from the field inside his hands. And all by herself, because she didn't want to frighten poor Helmut who was already alarmed by the sudden way the older boys and men had been taken away, she dug a grave. The soil was dry and rocky here, and it took most of the day. But with only a shovel and her gardening gloves, she dug a rectangle big enough and deep enough for a casket—though, of course, there would be no casket. There would be only a corpse wrapped tightly in sheets. And then in a German flag. She had one hidden among the hay bales in the barn.

When she had laid Sprenger in the dirt, she said the Lord's Prayer and thanked him for his service. She placed beside the body some of the dials and pieces of the cockpit that had been thrown clear of the fuselage. The combination of the corpse swaddled in sheets and the items she had placed beside it gave the burial an unexpectedly Egyptian feel, she decided. Then she covered the body with dirt, flattened the ground with the back of the shovel, and used a honeycomb-shaped piece of debris from the wing as a tombstone.

Days later, when the men were back home and the Germans had taken control of their corner of the country, they dug the pilot back up. Rolf and Werner and the wheelwright crafted for him a decent casket, but then a Luftwaffe administrator appeared and returned Sprenger to Leipzig, where he was buried with full military honors. Mutti remained in touch with the airman's family until 1943, but Sprenger's mother stopped writing after the pilot's father died fighting in Italy. Mutti never heard from her again.

Now, here in Stettin, she placed another makeshift marker atop another makeshift grave. They had discovered in Theo's bag that the child had brought with him the wire currycomb with the wooden handle on which Helmut had meticulously engraved the name *Theo* and his birth date and the words *Kaminheim's von Seydlitz*, a reference to a great Prussian cavalry commander under Friedrich the Second. It had been Helmut's birthday present for his younger brother two years earlier. While Callum was digging the grave, Anna hammered the comb into a piece of timber that was leaning uselessly against the stone foundation in the basement of Elfi's house, and then painted below the comb a line from a Wagner opera the family had particularly liked. The line was sung by a young woman named Senta, but the character sings it before she throws herself into the sea and so it was fitting here on the cliff, and Anna thought Theo would have liked the sentiment more than he would have been troubled by the idea it was a line that belonged to a girl: "Here I stand, faithful to you until death."

Then the three of them buried the boy, standing for a moment in the morning sun beside the flattened earth with the tombstone made of timber, aware of the sound of the surf and the gulls and—somewhere to the east and the south—artillery fire.

When they were done, Anna and Callum went to harness the two horses to one of the wagons. It didn't seem to make sense anymore to bring both wagons. They only had the two horses, Ragnit and Waldau, which meant they didn't need all that feed. Besides, it was Balga who had been the insatiable eater, the warhorse with an appetite that matched his charisma. Moreover, the snow was largely melted now and the pair that remained could graze on the spring grass that was slowly transforming the world from gray to green. And Theo and Sonje were no longer traveling with them: They were down to a party of three. Fewer people, fewer horses. Everything was dwindling. If they ever did reach the British or the Americans, Anna wondered who would be left.

It was as they were finishing the task, as Mutti was draping a sheet over the divan in the bay window that looked out upon the street, that the three of them saw Manfred. A motorcycle roared down the almost preternaturally silent road and skidded to a stop perhaps a dozen meters from the horses, kicking up gravel and dust. At first neither the lone woman inside the house nor the young people with the animals outside recognized him. Instead of the gray and green uniform of a Wehrmacht corporal, he was wearing a rubberized motorcycle coat, with an officer's shoulder boards attached to loops there.

"He's a bloody captain," Callum said, the incredulity apparent in his voice, and together with Anna he started over to him. "The man deserts his company for weeks at a time in the middle of winter—in the midst of an enemy offensive, for God's sake—and he winds up an officer come the spring."

Manfred was wearing a steel helmet with an eagle and a swastika on the side, and when he pulled it off Anna thought his face looked longer and thinner than ever. His cheekbones seemed especially chiseled because he had shaved in the morning. When she went to stand beside him, she smelled soap and was surprised. She understood intellectually that the reality that he had found a place to bathe and shave before coming here didn't belie the privations he had almost certainly endured. But it seemed to suggest to her a level of comfort and ease that she hadn't expected. And, for reasons she did not initially understand, it upset her, and so instead of greeting him warmly—or even politely—she blurted out the first thought that came to her mind, the first news that mattered: "Theo passed away. He died just last night." And then, suddenly, her shoulders collapsed and she was sobbing, and she felt Callum's large hand on her back and she shook it off with a violent shudder as if it were an animal that had leapt there unexpectedly from a branch in the jungle.

"What? How?" Manfred asked, and he reached for her. He started to embrace her, to pull her into him, and she pushed him away, too, just as she had Callum. She was angry and she wasn't sure why. But she knew she was. Yes, Theo would most likely have died even if Manfred hadn't left them—*deserted them*—back in February, but the fact he hadn't been present when her little brother had finally expired infuriated her. And while she could see that she wasn't being reasonable, she didn't care. She just didn't care at all. She had seen too much, she had heard too much, she had lost too much. At the moment, she simply wanted nothing to do with either of these men. With any men. With the men, like her father and her brothers, who were dead somewhere for reasons that made absolutely no sense, and with men like these two—men who were all too willing to fight the first chance they got, who had shot those Russians needlessly in that barn and would probably have shot each other by now if it weren't for her and Mutti and Theo. She turned from them both and stormed up the front walkway, where she saw Mutti standing just inside the heavy wooden door. Her mother saw her tears and the way she was shaking her head in disgust, but before the woman could even try to console her Anna barreled upstairs to the guestroom in which she had been staying and threw herself facedown on the bed. The paper blackout shades were still on the glass, and she was glad. She wanted the room to be dark. She knew they had to leave Stettin soon—they should have left yesterday, or the day before that—but she no longer cared. Let the Russians do what they wanted. Theo was dead, as—she had to presume—were her father and both of her soldier brothers. She simply didn't give a damn whether the Russians raped her or hanged her or crucified her. Let them do to her what they did to those poor girls in Nemmersdorf and Pillau. To her own cousin, Jutta. She found herself envying the German children who had been given small envelopes with poison to carry with them, or—like Gabi—been taught how to slash their wrists. If she were braver, she thought, she would have cut her wrists long ago.

Outside her room she heard the sound of her mother padding up the stairs, but she lacked the energy to push herself off the bed and go lock the door. In a moment she was aware of the mattress sagging just a bit when her mother sat down beside her, and then she felt one of Mutti's strong hands making gentle circles around her shoulders and her spine and massaging the back of her neck. She didn't know how her mother could do it, how her mother could handle so much. She just couldn't imagine how anyone could shoulder a loss this great after so many others.

Mutti said nothing, and soon Anna heard her own cries slowing to mere sniffles. She was relieved that her mother wasn't asking her questions and seemed content at the moment merely to rub her back and ruminate on the cataclysmic losses that she herself had no choice but to endure.

CALLUM SAW THE two rucksacks strapped to the motorcycle and the clothing that was protruding from the loosely buckled opening at the top of one of them. He recognized the color of a Russian uniform, but he didn't say anything. There were myriad explanations, but none in the paratrooper's opinion were going to shed an especially favorable light on Manfred. It was strange, but Callum found himself viewing the corporal—or, perhaps, the captain—as a Machiavellian deserter and thinking less of him for it. But then he would remind himself that someone who deserted the German army was thus his ally and should be viewed as a friend. It was the reality that he had deserted *them.* This was what it was about Manfred that disturbed him now. Moreover, he recalled those moments in February when it had seemed to him that Manfred was trying to catch Anna's eye—or, perhaps, she was trying to catch his. He feared that Anna saw something in Manfred, something he lacked, and the notion made him uncomfortable. Why was it, he wondered, that Anna had only broken down when Manfred had arrived? Was it simply the fact that Manfred was German, too? Had these people become such an insular tribe under Hitler—such a race unto themselves—that they were drawn to each other like seals in April and May? He told himself he was being ridiculous, reminded himself that Anna was his and his alone, but his anxiety continued to linger.

"Did the boy suffer long?" the captain was saying to him now.

"Yes, I think so," he told Manfred. "He was in and out of consciousness, and that might have spared him some pain. But his mother suffered. As did Anna. It wasn't pretty to watch."

"And you think it was an infection from the amputation?"

"Versus?"

"Typhus, maybe."

"No, it wasn't typhus."

"He seemed like a nice kid—"

"He was a wonderful boy. He was smart. Courageous. Plucky. Don't call him a nice kid," Callum snapped. "It sounds like you're dismissing him. It's as if you feel you have to say something, and so you say he's a nice kid. Well, Theo was that. But he was also bright and giving and stronger than any of us realized. Yes, he was quiet. And he was shy. But that child didn't miss a thing. And he endured a hell of a lot this winter before he died. I have a cousin who's fourteen, and I can't imagine him putting up with half of what poor Theo did before he passed away. You told me in February you don't have any brothers or sisters, so I doubt you can even begin to imagine that sense of loss."

"I've lost others."

"Losing your mates in battle is not the same thing. That's hard, too—"

"Not that you'd know."

"All I meant is that Theo was one hell of a good chap. I don't want to see his memory diminished."

"I'm sorry for him. And for his family."

"Thank you."

The German looked at him briefly with his eyebrows raised, clearly a little bemused by the way he had accepted the condolences on behalf of the Emmerichs—as if he himself were a part of the family. Then Manfred seemed to shrug it off and asked, "So, do you think I should bother to put the motorcycle in the carriage barn? Or should I just leave it right here on the street for the Russians?"

"I don't suppose you're actually going to join the defense of this city."

"I'm not sure there is a defense. Everyone is scurrying west as fast as they can."

"Then why in the name of God would you leave the motorcycle behind?" Callum asked him. "You can't possibly prefer walking."

He tapped the gas tank. "No petrol. I coasted the last stretch on fumes. And there isn't a liter of fuel to be found in all of Stettin."

"Not even for a dedicated soldier of the Reich?"

He smirked. "Ah, and none for me, either."

"So you're going with us . . . again?"

"I am."

"Why?"

"I like your company," he said, not even a trace of sarcasm in his response this time.

"Tell me something."

"Yes?"

"How have you not been shot?"

"By the Russians?"

"By your own bloody army. I would think you would have been executed by now, not advanced to an officer."

He seemed to think about this. Then: "I do my share, it seems."

"Where have you been the last four or five weeks? Dare I ask?"

"Well, I haven't been hiding out in a lovely house near the Baltic. Tell me, is this the first time they let you out? Have you been a house pet—an indoor cat—the whole time?"

Callum inhaled slowly through his nose and tried to remain composed. He was a Scot in the middle of Stettin. He was unarmed at the moment and he was talking to a German captain. And, the truth was, he had indeed spent most of his time here either indoors or in the backyard. His greatest, most risky excursion? Carrying Theo to and from the hospital. He was only outside in front of the house now because they were harnessing the horses and loading the wagon, and were about to try to catch up to the long columns of refugees streaming west. And while Mutti must have suspected that he and Anna were now something more than friends, they had not gone out of their way to specify their relationship for the woman. He and Anna had discussed whether they should. But first the fact they were in Elfi's house had precluded them, and then Theo had gotten sick. And so instead of answering Manfred's question he said simply, "You got here just in time. If you'd come half an hour from now, we might have been gone."

"That would have saddened me," he said, and he took a pair of the leather straps that were dangling near the horse's chest and buckled them together.

"Really?"

"Yes."

"I have to ask, then: Why?"

"Why have I come back?"

"Exactly. Is it Anna?"

At the far end of the block, along the cross street, they watched a German staff car speed past and then, a moment later, a pair of half-tracks loaded down with soldiers driving in the oppo-site direction.

"There are staff officers still here in town," Manfred said and he sounded surprised—almost incredulous. "I would have thought they would have left days ago. Most of this ship is under-water. The rats should be long gone."

"You didn't answer my question. Are you in love with Anna?"

Manfred seemed to smirk. "Oh, I don't think I know her well enough to be in love with her."

"But you might be?"

"No, not likely. You can sleep easy. And I promise you, I did-n't come back here because of her. Can we leave it at that?"

"We can," he said. "But I really don't see why you're with us and not with your unit."

Nearby a shell fell and exploded, one of the first to hit the out-skirts of the city itself. Callum guessed it was no more than three or four blocks distant, and along the street a block to the west. A plume of brackish smoke began to curl up into the spring air. Seconds later another shell detonated even closer, this one no more than a block away, and the men watched as both horses sniffed at the air.

URI HADN'T PLANNED on telling Callum his story that mo-ment. There were still plenty of Nazis who would have been all too happy to gas him or shoot him, despite the fact their cause was ir-retrievably lost. And he certainly didn't want to get into the details at the start of an artillery barrage. But, the truth was, a reason why he had come back was this Scotsman standing before him now, and so—almost impulsively—he said, "I don't really have a unit."

"Well, that's a surprise. How come? Dare I ask?"

"Because, my friend, I'm a Jew," he said, the words liberating in a way he hadn't expected, a stupendous, bracing, and unfore-seen release. Abruptly, his story was spilling from him. "You asked if I know loss? Trust me: I know loss. I've spent two years trying to stay alive by hiding out in the German army—and for a few days not precisely in Ivan's army, but with a Russian coat on my back—and my goal now is to get to your army in the west. Get to your people or the Americans. I want out of Germany. I want off this continent. And so if I have come back for anyone, Callum, it is for you."

"Me?"

"Indeed."

In the doorway, driven outside by the proximity of the falling bombs, were Mutti and Anna, each of them wrapped in a shawl and carrying a small bundle with clothing. The larger suitcases were already in the wagon. The air was starting to fill with dust from the building on the next block that had been hit, and somewhere in the distance there was a siren.

"I'm trusting you not to tell them," he added before the two women had reached them.

"Why?" Callum asked. "You know them. You can't possibly think they're anti-Semites."

"You're the first person I've told, and I only told you because I thought it might make our walk together a little more peaceful."

Callum wasn't completely sure he believed him. He thought he did. And he wanted to believe him. But this fellow seemed willing to do whatever it took to survive—impersonating all manner of German or Russian soldiers—and now he was insisting he was Jewish. It was just as likely he was SS. Nevertheless, he had come back here to be with them. And that had to mean something. Moreover, he had made them all feel a little safer when he had been with them, hadn't he? He was a chameleon, but he was also as tough as any soldier Callum had met in either army.

Still, he wasn't going to hide something from the Emmerichs. "If you don't tell them, I will," he said finally.

"Tell us what?" Mutti asked. "Is it about the Russians?" She sounded almost fatalistic.

"Manfred here has a bit of a bombshell."

"Uri, actually. My name isn't Manfred. It's Uri."

Mutti looked a little perplexed to Callum, and then her eyes widened as if she understood. "You're a spy?" she asked.

Anna turned to her mother, took the bundle from her arms, and tossed it unceremoniously into the wagon. "No, Mutti, I don't think that's what he means at all." She looked at him, her eyes still red from her tears, and said, "Is this your way of telling us you're Jewish?"

He realized that he was shifting his feet anxiously. "Yes."

"Fine. It's lovely to have you with us once more as a traveling companion. We missed you. Now, shall we leave?"

A small series of shells landed on the next block, close enough that Waldau snorted nervously and turned his massive neck as far as he could in the direction of the noise.

"I told you they wouldn't care," said Callum.

"Okay, then," he agreed, and he took the two rucksacks off the motorcycle, tossing one over his shoulder and grasping the other by one of its buckles.

"Why don't you put those in the wagon?" Anna suggested. "I think the horses can handle them."

He thought about this, but only for a moment. Then he placed the packs in the long farm cart beside the bags of feed and the luggage and turned back to the women.

"Mrs. Emmerich?"

"Yes."

"I am so sorry about Theo. He was"—and here he paused, glancing briefly at Callum—"a courageous and wonderful young man. I can't tell you how much I liked him. It's a terrible loss."

She looked back at him with a strength that he found a little disarming. "It is," she said. "But I thank you. And I am sure you have had your losses, too."

He nodded. He had, he had. He could feel Anna and Callum watching him, and their gazes made him uncomfortable. He realized he had put them at risk by revealing his identity and began to regret his spontaneity with the Scotsman. "As far as you all know," he told them, "I'm Captain Heinz Bauer."

"Not . . . Manfred?" Mutti asked.

"No. And you've absolutely no idea I'm Jewish."

"Do you really believe anyone cares at this point in the war?" Anna wondered, an eddy of annoyance in her voice.

"Oh, I don't believe it. I know it."

"What? Have you seen something?"

"I see things every day."

"Something specific?"

He rested his fingers on the handlebar of the motorcycle. "Bauer—the fellow whose uniform I'm wearing—had just delivered orders to the commandant of a work camp to march his Jewish prisoners west. Young women, all of them. They could have left them for the Russians to liberate. But they didn't. Even now, the leaders of your Reich are gassing or shooting or walking as many of us to our deaths as they possibly can. Bauer's orders, and the signed receipt from the commandant, were in this coat."

Anna seemed to be absorbing this, contemplating the idea that there were whole camps of female prisoners being marched away from the front. "Where are they now?" she asked finally.

"The women? I don't know. I assume they're on the road somewhere."

"And this Heinz Bauer?"

"He's on the road, too."

"But he's not walking, is he?"

"No," Uri said. "He's not. He's not even breathing."

In the distance they heard planes approaching from the east, which meant in all likelihood they were Russian. Callum looked up, his eyes scanning the flat, gray horizon, and took the lead for one of the horses. Anna took the other. Then, without saying a word, the four of them started their way down the street and out of the city of Stettin.

Chapter Eighteen

WHEN THEY HAD FIRST STARTED TOWARD WHAT THEY
were told would be a new factory in a new town, they had walked
four abreast, taking up roughly half the width of the road so vehicles could wind their way around the procession. Now, however,
it was their third day and the columns had grown ragged. The
length of the parade also had shrunk. Their first night they had
been fed some boiled water with celery slivers and spring grass
floating atop the surface like pond scum, but otherwise they had-
n't eaten since they had left their barracks and begun marching to
the northwest. Some of the prisoners had started to collapse yesterday between midday and dusk, perhaps a dozen of the girls,
whereupon the one-eyed Blumer or a guard named Kogel would
shoot them in the back of the head. Others, as many as six or
seven if she had overheard the guards properly, had escaped by
simply melting into the woods that bordered some of the towns.
Four more had tried to flee and been caught, and the procession
had been shaped into a half-circle in a meadow beside the road so
everyone could watch Blumer and Kogel and a guard whose name
Cecile did not know strip them, whip them, and beat them until
the white and pink of their emaciated flesh looked like the remains
of animal carcasses. Then they, too, were shot. She guessed when

the prisoners had originally left the factory there had been about 150 of them. Now it was closer to 125.

None of them knew where they were going, but Cecile was taking comfort from two realities: The weather was considerably less nightmarish now than it was when they had set off from the camp at the end of January. It was chilly and today they had been forced to march all afternoon in a cold rain so their clothes clung to them, thick and heavy like chain mail made of ice, but the snow was all but gone and only at night did the temperature fall below freezing. It was also clear that they were in a more populated section of the country. There were still stretches in which they would walk through farmland or woods, but those stretches were shorter than they had been in January. She wouldn't use the word *civilized* to describe where they were—no part of Germany was civilized in her mind, not even Berlin, because it was still filled with people who either would do this to her or would allow it to happen—but the towns were much larger and she never felt as if they were walking in an endless, near-arctic wilderness.

And so an idea formed in her mind that night as she lay down among bales of hay in a cow barn between Leah and Jeanne, the three of them pressing their bodies tightly together for warmth. Even though four of the girls who had tried to escape had been rounded up and beaten to death, at least six or seven others had gotten away. As a result, the guards were being more attentive. But escape might nevertheless be possible because the weather was more accommodating and there was a greater chance they might be able to find shelter or someone to help them. There were rumors—treated by the prisoners with the reverence that small children have for fairy tales—traveling among the girls of a priest in one nearby town who had a way to hide Jews, and of a mayor in another hamlet who actually helped Jews get the papers they needed to pass as Aryans with the necessary pedigree. She also recognized the names of some of the towns through which they had marched, and had the sense that here there had to be

Germans—either Germans who were good or Germans who simply could see the end was near and it was in their best interests to help a couple of Jewish girls who were flirting with death—who might feed them. Warm them. Offer them refuge.

There were guards here in the barn with them, as well as guards just outside. And so Cecile had no illusions that it might be possible to merely slip away that moment into the night. The next morning, however, might be a different story. There would be those first minutes when the girls would be herded from the barn into their lines to march—she had no expectations they would be fed—and there was usually chaos as they all maneuvered from wherever they were expected to communally empty their stinging bladders and diarrheic bowels to their spot on the road. Moreover, the sun probably would not yet have risen. Perhaps in those brief moments of bedlam, she—she and Leah and Jeanne—could melt into the woods. And here, on the northern side of this barn, there were woods, a forest of evergreen, oak, and birch. The guards would thus have them stand to the south, but still . . . still . . . there would be that brief frenzy as they exited, the guards themselves sleepy and hungry and anxious.

The key to her plan? Leah, the girl from Budapest who had once been a seamstress. Leah's German was impeccable. If she and Jeanne kept their French mouths shut, Leah might be able to pass as a refugee Christian from the east until they could find a sympathetic household. She could ask the right questions of the right people. Find a kind priest. Or a convent. Anyplace that might provide asylum. It was a long shot, of course, because how did you know whom to ask? But were the odds really any worse than simply continuing on yet another death march? In three days their group had shrunk by a sixth, and no one—at least none of the prisoners—had the slightest idea where they were going or when they would get there. Consequently, she gently tapped the girls on either side of her, poking first Leah and then Jeanne, and whispered to them what she wanted to do.

"This is your plan?" Jeanne grumbled, her soft voice near a whimper. Occasionally her body would spasm against the cold. "We run into the woods and find someone to help us?"

"There are people here. Lots of people. You've heard the rumors about priests and mayors who are hiding Jews."

"And I don't believe them. If we've heard those tales, so have the Nazis. Any priest who helps us is hanging by his neck somewhere or is long dead in the ground."

Outside in the night there were great whistles of wind, but there was no longer the sound of the rain on the roof of the barn. "You're probably right," said Leah, and briefly Cecile's heart sank. Then, however, the seamstress continued, "But the people here have seemed a little more uncomfortable when we've passed them. A little sickened, even. That's a good sign. Maybe we could find someone."

"All we'd have to do is pass long enough to get a name—or an address."

"Why not? We're just going to die if we keep on this way."

Beside her Jeanne snorted. "For months you kept telling me to be strong. Be patient. All fall and all winter, that's all you kept saying. The Russians will get to us, the Russians will save us. Now you've changed your tune. Why?"

"Because I have a sense of where we are in Germany."

"Oh, we're in Germany now, instead of Poland. That makes me feel much better. Much more confident."

"This war is going to be over soon. The Americans and the British have crossed the Rhine. All we need is a place to hide for a little while. Till the summer, maybe."

"Do we stay together tomorrow morning or do we separate?" Leah asked.

"I think we separate. Scatter."

"Ah," Jeanne muttered. "Very good. Then we will use our compasses and our radios to make sure we rendezvous at the same point in the woods."

"We agree to return to this barn tomorrow night. At dusk. How's that? Then we walk back to the town we passed through earlier today. There was a church there. And so there must be a priest."

Cecile felt Leah pressing her chest against her back, trying to spoon ever more tightly against her for warmth. "Do we have a signal?" Leah asked.

"You mean in the morning?"

"Yes. For when we escape."

She contemplated this for a moment. "I don't think we need one. But in that moment when the guards are screaming for us to go to the bathroom and line up, that's when we leave."

"We should go in different directions," Leah offered. "And not at exactly the same second."

"Yes, that makes sense," Cecile said, pleased with all that the woman was contributing to the plan. "And so we'll do this? We'll leave?"

"Absolutely," said Leah.

"Jeanne?"

There was a pause. "Jeanne?" She put her ear against her friend's chest, afraid that the woman had, once and for all, stopped breathing. But the chest rose and then fell, and with her head against her friend's body, she heard Jeanne informing her, "Don't worry, I was only thinking. Not dying. At least not immediately dying. But, yes, I'll go. I've thought I was going to die for six or seven months now, and I'm still here. Still starving. Still cold. At this point, I might as well expedite the process by trying to escape."

THE FEMALE GUARDS were screaming at them to get up and get out, cursing them for either dawdling or moving too slowly, when most of the girls were moving as quickly as they could, and Cecile stood and started to stumble toward the wide barn doors, open now for the first time since they had been herded in here the night before. She could see that the skies were overcast and it was drizzling outside, and the sensation of proceeding toward the great square of light from the dark of the barn was reminiscent of walking through a tunnel. She glanced once at Leah, their eyes met, and she nodded. She tried to capture Jeanne's attention, but she couldn't find her: Already her friend had fallen behind. At least two girls were either incapable of rising or they had died in the night, and the female guard kicked once at each of their bodies and then bellowed for Blumer. He wasn't far away and Cecile passed him as she approached the entrance, shrinking against the door so she would not be in his way, while anticipating the sound of his pistol, two shots, in the coming moment. Then she looked back and saw Jeanne: The woman was plodding with the gait of a sleepwalker toward the entrance, her arms wrapped tightly around her frail frame and her hollow eyes blinking against the daylight. Cecile tried to catch her attention, too, because—and she felt guilty for even thinking such a thing, but it was a reality—the additional chaos that would occur when Blumer shot the women left in the barn might be exactly what she and Leah and Jeanne needed to disappear successfully into the woods.

Already the other prisoners were starting to squat in a line in the field to the south of the great structure, some silently and some straining. Others didn't bother to crouch, but simply stood where they were and allowed their pee to run down their legs. At this point, what did it matter? All of them seemed oblivious of the rain that was continuing to fall.

She saw Leah was moving to the end of the line, fading behind the woman at the very end, and then squatting. Sitting. Then— and here she felt her heart starting to pound—Leah was rolling along the wet grass, away from the prisoners and the guards. Inside the barn she heard the first shot and the birds on the peak of the barn flew high into the air from their perch. Cecile watched everyone reflexively turn toward the sound, and when she looked back toward the end of the line she saw that Leah was rising to her feet and starting to run toward the woods, her legs moving as they hadn't in years.

Quickly Cecile followed her lead. She went to the end of the line, took a spot beside—and then behind—the very last woman, and crouched like a toddler. She closed her mind to the smells all around her and breathed, as she did always at this moment of the day, only through her mouth. She had to pee badly, she felt pressure and pain in her groin, but she didn't dare start because she knew she wouldn't be able to stop. She realized that she had lost Jeanne—hadn't actually seen her emerge from the barn—and so she scanned the lines and the meadow, but she didn't see her friend anywhere. She guessed it was possible that for some reason the woman had remained inside, but it seemed that by now all of the prisoners who were living had been marched outside into the field.

The guards were hollering for them to finish their business and line up so they could be counted, and the woman before Cecile stood and started away, the back of her ragged trousers moist from the grass and brown with her feces. Cecile moved in the opposite direction. A foot, then two, crabwalking toward the woods. Still, however, she kept her eyes open both for Jeanne and for the guards. She honestly wasn't sure that she would be capable of rising to her feet in a moment—and in a moment she would indeed have to—and scurrying toward the woods if she didn't know for sure that Jeanne was escaping, too, because she was convinced that without her Jeanne would die. Her friend would simply give in to the pain and the hunger and the cold. Why not? Many of the prisoners did. Jeanne had given up perhaps a half-dozen times already and it was Cecile's encouragement alone that had kept her going. But any time now she would hear Blumer's second shot, and that would be her chance to run for the woods—and run she would, she told herself, regardless of whether she had seen

Jeanne. She had to hope that her friend was already scuttling through the brush somewhere, scampering far from this motley column with whatever energy she could muster.

"You there! Stop, stop now!" It was one of the female guards roaring, and Cecile stood perfectly still, fearful that they had seen the way she had edged just a bit toward the forest. But it wasn't her they had noticed. Why would they? She was, essentially, still with the group. It was Leah. The guard had seen Leah.

"Now, stop!" the woman screamed again, but it was clear Leah knew she didn't dare. They'd shoot her anyway. Besides, the woods were no more than thirty meters distant. She'd be there in seconds. And so Leah kept running along the wet ground, and even when she heard the gunshot she didn't break stride. She didn't turn around to see that the male guard named Kogel had come up beside the woman who had ordered her to stop. There he was, his arm extended parallel to the ground, his pistol aimed at Leah as she fled. He was about to fire a second time, and Cecile knew he wouldn't miss twice. The idea entered her mind that she would be responsible for her friend's death—directly, clearly, unequivocally responsible—and she experienced a dagger of guilt so pronounced that it caused her to emit a small, choking cry. But then there was Jeanne. Beside the two guards. Or, rather, between them. Her friend wasn't in the woods, she was still back with the other prisoners. And she was pushing Kogel's arm upward toward the sky as he discharged the weapon once more, sending the bullet uselessly into the overcast mist as Leah disappeared into the woods.

Meanwhile, from inside the barn, almost like an echo, came Blumer's second shot as he executed the other prisoner who had failed to rise from her patch of straw. The birds that had returned to the peak flew off. And then, when they were still circling above the fields and the trees in search of a quiet place to land, Kogel shoved Jeanne to the ground, where she had neither the time nor the inclination to beg for mercy, and at point-blank range he discharged his pistol once again, this time into the back of poor Jeanne's skull.

Cecile couldn't hear what the female guard said to Kogel, but it was clear by her countenance and the way she was using one of her gloves like a rag to wipe Jeanne's blood and the gray-white tissue from the prisoner's brain off her skirt that she was annoyed. He had shot the woman at such an angle that the two of them had been sprayed with the gelatinous ooze from the inside of her head.

SHE WALKED BETWEEN women whose faces she knew but whose names were a mystery, and while one of them wanted to talk, Cecile was now all but incapable of speech. It wasn't that she couldn't stop crying—though that was a factor. It was that she no longer gave a damn and there was absolutely nothing she wanted to say. Her oldest friend from the camp was dead and it was her fault and only her fault. Moreover, Jeanne—grumbling, whining, meandering Jeanne—had actually died so that Leah might live. The woman had given herself up. Halfheartedly Kogel had looked for the seamstress in the woods, but he had spent no more than four or five minutes wandering through the soggy underbrush. They needed to get the column moving. And so Leah was on her own now somewhere in this foreign countryside, hopefully speaking her elegant, perfect German to someone who would shield her until the world had come to its senses or the Russians had arrived and it was safe for her to emerge from the shadows. Meanwhile, Cecile was left alone with her incapacitating guilt. She neither deserved to live nor saw any possible future. For the moment she would keep marching, struggling on with the other prisoners, but one of these times when the bastards allowed them to lie down or sit, she simply wouldn't bother to rise. Jeanne had died fast and it couldn't have been very painful. One bullet, she decided, and there would be no more hunger or pain or cold. That's all it would take. A little bit of courage and then forever she could let go of this enervating charade she called hope.

Chapter Nineteen

THERE WERE LARGE ANTITANK GUNS AIMED AT TWO
of the bridges, and the white paint on their barrels had started to
peel. Anna guessed that once she would have found the weapons
frightening—or, at the very least, disturbing. The same with the
shell fire that seemed, their first morning back on the road, to be
falling only blocks behind them. Or the skeletal remains of the
brick buildings, their whole front and rear walls sheared off. Or,
certainly, the corpses of the hanged men, their bodies still dangling from makeshift scaffolds with the handwritten signs tied to
their jackets that said, simply, "Coward." But she didn't. The
litany of the absent in her life had grown so long and the future
was so relentlessly bleak that she had grown numb to it all. She
could see that her mother had, too. It was odd: Anna was continuing on this path now only for the sake of her mother, and she
had the sense that her mother was doing the same only for her.
Mutti, Anna had decided, couldn't possibly believe that she
would ever see her husband or her two older sons again. They
were as dead and gone as poor Theo. And they all knew they
would never return to Kaminheim—assuming Kaminheim even
was standing.

So what was propelling this woman forward, Anna would ask

herself, what was giving her mother the resolve to put one foot in front of the other and, sometimes, take the lead lines of one of the horses? In the end she decided that she herself was the answer: Mutti would not give up completely so long as she had even a single child remaining.

At one point they stopped to rest the horses and allow them to graze on the early spring grass, and a pair of women older than Mutti came up behind them and exhorted them to keep moving. Their skin was whiter than milk, and they were each carrying a single elegant valise. Their skirts—though streaked with mud and fraying along the hems—were stylish. They were both wearing leather riding boots.

"Ivan's back there," one of the women said to Mutti. She had a kerchief around her head that looked as if it had once been a part of a window curtain. "You can't stop."

"We'll just be here a minute," her mother told them.

"Suit yourself," said the woman. She then remarked, so casually that Anna found herself studying the storyteller to see if she was lying, that she had been raped multiple times only two days before and was here now only because the Russians had passed out drunk after assaulting her. A third woman, a friend of theirs, was dead because she had resisted: She had been shot, her corpse violated, and the body was left impaled on the ends of two captured German bayonets. The woman claimed that both she and her traveling partner had been attacked in broad daylight by a half-dozen Soviet riflemen. Then, after the soldiers either had fallen asleep or left them to find other, younger victims, the women had continued on their way west.

And so Anna helped Callum harness the horses so they, too, could resume their trek. Overhead there were seagulls circling the field where the horses had been grazing. She thought how lately when she had looked into the sky, it had usually been because she had heard airplanes approaching. It was surprising—

and reassuring—to notice something as mundane as seagulls looking for food in the fresh grass and loosened soil.

"Would you like to ride for a bit? You've been walking all morning," Callum asked Mutti, but her mother shook her head. She would continue on foot.

"I just don't understand why the Russians are so brutal," her mother said after a moment. "Was war always this horrid? Is this a secret you men always have known, and you just never told the women?"

Uri had been sharing his story with Callum off and on for hours now, and when he heard Mutti's remark he turned to her and asked, "Do you really wonder?"

"I do."

"After all you've heard about what your armies did these past years in Russia—or just last autumn in Warsaw—can it possibly be a mystery? My God, after what some of your people did to my people, do you even have to ask?"

Behind them they heard motorcycles, and then four Wehrmacht engineers sped past them on the vehicles. Anna saw they barely paid any notice to either Uri or Callum. "I can see why you don't want to remain with those boys," Callum said, motioning toward the German soldiers, already disappearing into the distance. "But tell me: Why aren't you just waiting here now for the Russians? Why is it so important to you to get to the west?"

"I didn't go through hell the last two years only to wind up a Communist on some collective farm in the Ukraine," he answered. "Besides, somehow I don't think the NKVD would take kindly to my having impersonated a German soldier since 1943. They probably wouldn't even believe that it was an impersonation."

"You could always drop your drawers," Callum said lightly, and Anna couldn't resist turning to watch her mother's reaction. Mutti was staring straight ahead, pretending not to have heard.

"I could, yes. But I have also spent the last two years peeing only in the dark or when I'm alone. I hate to think of the damage I've done to my bladder."

The idea crossed Anna's mind that she had only the vaguest idea what a circumcised penis might look like. She had seen her twin brother's genitals when they had been children, as well as Theo's. And she had seen Callum's. It seemed, she decided now, an awful lot of work to care about such things. Too much work for an issue that didn't seem that important.

"You're blushing." It was Uri and he was speaking to her.

"Have you absolutely no sense of decorum at all?" Callum chastised him, but his voice was light and good-natured.

"Nope. That's what happens when you live your life on the run. You tend to care less about such niceties. Of course, it was you who just suggested that I drop my drawers for the Russians."

He was grinning. And then, suddenly, Callum was grinning. She loved it when the two men wound up smiling together at precisely the same time.

IT WAS ALMOST as if the town house had been charmed: The structures to its immediate right and left—every house on the block on this street in the village—had been bombed or shelled recently. The buildings either had been reduced to large mounds of fallen timbers, crumbling stone, and dust or were the skeletal cutaways the Emmerichs had witnessed so often as they had trekked west. Unlike in the past, however, there were no refugees camped out in these husks or families who had chosen to remain. There were ornery, skinny dogs wandering the streets, growling at the horses; there was the occasional rat; and there were birds— mostly crows. But otherwise there was no sign of life in the town. Everyone either had died or had fled.

But then there was that one town house. The windows facing the street were broken and the wooden shutters on the second floor were askew, but the brick facade was largely undamaged and the slate roof was mostly intact. The curtains on the second floor and the drapes on the first, all a little shabby now, would occasionally billow out through the frames like a ghost.

It was nearly seven in the evening and the sun had set, and so they decided they would stop here for the night. To savor their good fortune. There wouldn't be running water or electricity, but perhaps there might be beds or couches inside on which they might sleep. In the three days since they had left Stettin, they hadn't dozed for more than a few hours at a time, and always those naps had been inside barns or—one night—on the floor of a bombed-out gymnasium.

But they had, once again, managed to put some distance between themselves and the army that they were trying to elude. It wasn't, however, that they were making such good time: They had simply veered farther away from Berlin, trekking not exactly along the coast but still well north of the capital. Uri believed that by now the Russians almost certainly would have overrun them if the Soviets hadn't been so focused on the prize to the south, and their race to plant the hammer and sickle atop the Reichstag. Moreover, by remaining so far to the north their small group had also managed to separate themselves from the hordes heading west or southwest. There were long intervals when they had had the road to themselves.

Now as they all stared with some measure of disbelief at the brick town house, Uri took his rifle off his shoulder and approached the front door. He said that he was just making sure it was empty.

"You want some help?" Callum asked, and Uri nodded.

But the house was every bit as deserted as it seemed, an odd oasis in the midst of the rubble that once had been a small hamlet. They were all asleep within the hour.

ANNA FELT SOMEONE gently rubbing her arm, long, tender strokes, and she opened her eyes. The room was dark and it took her a moment to orient herself. She recalled that she was in a town house in . . . in that place without a name. In the one town house that remained standing in the whole village. She was in a small bed—a child's bed—in a room by herself, while her mother was resting in the massive bed in the other bedroom on the floor. She was buried deep beneath quilts because the windows had been blown out in the bombing and there was no heat. But she had been warm enough to have fallen into a very deep sleep. Until now. Until someone—Callum—was rubbing her arm. Waking her up. The men had been asleep downstairs on the couches, but now one of them was upstairs.

She looked up at him, and even in the dark saw him bring one finger to his lips. He was wearing his gloves.

"Are the Russians here?" she whispered. She was so weary that the idea didn't fill her with dread. Terror, she realized, was an emotion that demanded energy.

"No," he said, smiling. "Nothing like that. Nothing like that at all."

"Then what?"

"Come with me. There's something I want to show you."

"What time is it?"

"Not quite two thirty."

She nodded. She'd been asleep, she thought, for just about seven hours.

"Come, come," he said again, his tone almost boyish. "Hurry!"

Though she had gone to bed in her clothes, the moment she emerged from beneath the bedding she felt a nip of the frost in the air.

"Do I need my boots?" she asked.

He nodded. He already had them in his hands.

"Are the others awake?"

"No. This is just for you. For us."

When she had her boots on, he helped her slide her arms
through her parka and gave her her gloves. Then he led her down
the stairs, past the living room in which Uri was sleeping, and
outside. He took her hand in his and she looked up at him. His face
was inscrutable: not anxious, not whimsical, not stoic. It was the
face of a man, she thought, who was impassively reading a book.
Over his shoulder he had slung a backpack.

As they started down the street, past the piles of debris, she
heard a wolf howling in the distance, and the sound—so different
from the rumble of artillery—caused her to smile slightly to herself. A wolf in the night. How natural.

"Can I have a clue?" she asked him.

"No. But you'll see it for yourself in a moment."

And indeed she did. They quickly reached the edge of the village, the end of the last block. He pointed, but she would have
been blind not to see it. She was surprised she was only noticing it
now, and decided she must have been looking down at the street
as they walked, either because she was so sleepy or because she
was being careful and watching her step as they navigated their
way along the churned-up cobblestones that once had been road.

"The northern lights," she murmured, and she felt him
squeeze her fingers and then wrap his long arms around her and
pull her into him purposefully. They were standing at the edge of
a lake, and there were three fountains rising up from the horizon,
over the Baltic Sea in the distance, each of the sprays a throbbing
column of gold that flickered like a gargantuan candle. They were
illuminating the sky, causing the tips of the highest evergreens to
stand out in relief, while reflecting off the glassy surface of the
lake. It was almost as if the fountains of light were coming toward
them as well as shooting up into the sky. There were two passing
clouds the rough shapes of ovals, and it looked to Anna as if they
were eyes in the face of the universe—a countenance that tonight
was the color of saffron. "I've never seen them so beautiful," she
said.

"Me either. In Scotland, we call them the merry dancers. Sometimes I've seen them more colorful than this. Some violet, some red. But I've never seen them look quite so much like bloody torches."

She burrowed against his shoulder. "Bloody," she repeated.

"Yes. Bloody torches."

"Would you do something for me?" she asked.

"Anything. You know that."

"Never use that word again. *Bloody.* I know what you mean. But lately there has just been too much real blood."

"I'm sorry, I only—"

"Shhhhh," she said, as the lights shimmered to the north and that wolf she had heard back in the village bayed once again at the sky. "I know what you meant." Then she turned toward him and stood on her toes to kiss him. He tasted like one of the old peppermints they had found in a tin by the fireplace on the first floor of the town house, and she guessed that she probably tasted like sleep. But she didn't care and she had the sense that he didn't either. When they parted she started to nestle back into his coat, pressing her elbows and her arms against her ribs, but he was already pulling his pack off his shoulder and unbuckling it.

"Watch," he said proudly. He removed a blanket that had been rolled into a tube, and as if he were a magician with a cape he whisked it flat like a sail and allowed it to float to the ground. Then he reached inside the bag and removed a bottle of schnapps and a single tall water glass.

"I couldn't fit a second glass in here," he said apologetically. "And there didn't seem to be any crystal in the house."

"Do you really think you're going to take advantage of me in this cold—with the ground as a bed?" she asked him, raising her eyebrows in mock horror, but she knew she was just being coy. It wasn't that cold, not after all they'd endured. And she was, suddenly, hungry for him in a way that she hadn't been in a very long time—perhaps ever—and she felt a warm quiver between her legs.

"True, no bed," he said, but then he motioned up at the golden fires in the sky. "Still, I can't think of a better canopy, can you?"

She tried once more to nuzzle against him, and this time he wasn't preoccupied with his pack and he wrapped his arms around her. Kissed her. The truth was, she thought, beds were overrated: When they had used her bed back at Kaminheim, she had seen around her the accrual of her childhood self—dolls and clothing and books—and she had found the sheer quaintness of the silt to be antithetical to her idea of herself as a woman. As a lover. On other occasions, including their last night at Kaminheim, they had used his bed in the maid's room, and that had been infinitely more fulfilling. She considered herself fortunate that so many of the other times when they had made love, it had been on the oriental rugs in the living room at Kaminheim—thick and sumptuous and romantic—or on the divan in the ballroom, or, yes, outside in the apple orchard. There had been beds in Elfi's house in Stettin, of course, but the quarters were close and Theo was dying and it hadn't crossed their minds to avail themselves of them. At least, she knew, it hadn't crossed her mind.

The thought of her little brother momentarily made her reassess what they were doing, but she felt Callum's hand working its way beneath her coat and her sweater, finding her breasts and stroking and cupping them, and the sensations there became her focus. At some point he had taken off his leather gloves and the palms of his hands were warm and her nipples were growing hard against them. She massaged the back of his head as they kissed, her fingers deep in that red, red hair and along that long and elegant cleft at the base of his skull, and then she allowed her neck to fall back so she could stare up at the lights that were dancing low and high and everywhere in between in the sky. Then she felt him lifting her up and off the ground and laying her softly on the blanket. He knelt beside her and kissed her some more, his tongue—blunt, serpentine, hot—moving down her neck and then jumping over her clothes to the flesh at her waist. He tugged at her skirt, unfastened the two hooks along the side, and started to pull it down. She arched her hips to make it easier for him to slip it off her legs and over her boots, and then she spread wide her thighs. The air was more invigorating than cold and she felt ripples of goose bumps rising up along her flesh. A moment later he was inside her and the sky above them was alive with color, great flaxen plumes of light that were illuminating the horizon as far as she could see. She recalled what the Vikings had named the phenomenon: the reflections of the dead maidens. Typically Nordic, she decided, with its implausible beautification of death. She had seen enough of death to know it was never beautiful. It was delusional to think otherwise. Henceforth, she resolved, she would refer to them in her mind the way Callum had: They would be the merry dancers.

She could feel him gazing down at her, watching her.

"Good?" he asked, a wrinkle of worry creeping into his voice in even that one syllable. Clearly he sensed that her mind was wandering tonight. "Are you warm enough?"

"I'm fine," she reassured him, her voice a purr for his benefit, and she smiled. She hadn't felt this alive since they had left Kaminheim. "I'm just fine," she murmured, and then she gave herself over completely to the swelling rush inside her that would build and build till she came.

THE SUN WAS higher and hotter than it had been on any day since they had started west months ago, and there were rumors that to the south of them the western Allies were nearing the Elbe. They had the sense that they themselves were close to the Americans and the Brits.

Now they rested at the edge of a shallow river that ran parallel to the dirt farm road and allowed the horses to browse upon the moist spring grass. Anna and her mother were in the knee-deep water, bathing, shielded from the two men by the wagon.

Uri sat down on a stone the size of a footstool at the side of the road and stretched his legs out before him. Callum collapsed flat in the grass and for a moment lay on his back with his eyes closed against the sun. Then, when he had caught his breath, he sat up and pulled off his boots and stared at his socks. They were ash gray now, but once they had been white. He had two more pairs in his pack, but he knew they were even worse: They smelled unbearable and were riddled with holes.

"When I'm home," he said, "I am never going to wear boots again."

"Nonsense," Uri told him. "You'll be wearing boots again by November. You'll have forgotten your blisters by then."

"I doubt that."

Uri took the tobacco and two sheets of cigarette paper from his pouch and started to roll a cigarette for the Scot. "You forget pain. We all do. We tell ourselves we remember the specifics, but it's all just a lot of pictures and words in our heads. No sensations. I think we actually remember life's humiliations much better. The degradations. The cruelties. But the pain? We seem to forget what pain actually feels like. It's a cloud after the sky has cleared."

"You are awfully philosophic this morning."

"I can finally see the end."

"Well, I will never forget how much my feet hurt."

In the river behind them they heard Anna shrieking cheerfully because the water was so cold. Uri handed Callum the cigarette and rolled one for himself. "You won't even be thinking about your feet in a couple of months," he continued. "You will be married to that girl back there and you will be home in your beloved Scotland."

"There were times when I didn't think I'd ever hear her laugh again," Callum said, and he motioned his head in the direction of the women. "Her or her mother."

"I know what you mean."

"Tell me: What are you looking forward to most when you get to America? If you get there. What's the one thing?"

"Oh, I'll get there. I've no doubts. The one thing? Mass transportation. The subways and the buses they have in New York City. Like you, I don't ever want to walk again. I am going to ride everywhere."

"And where will everywhere be?"

"I want to go to school."

Callum nodded and seemed to think about this. "I usually see you as so much older than me."

"Six years. Not so much."

"And so I usually think of you as having finished school. I keep forgetting they didn't let you."

"Of all the things they took from me—other, of course, than my family—that's what I want back the most. An education."

"I must confess, I don't think much about that. I guess I will enroll in university. But when I'm done? I honestly don't know. I really don't. After all this . . . after the last year . . . well, I just can't imagine what God has in store for me. I can't conceive of what possibly could come next."

Uri took a long drag on his cigarette and decided his throat was too sore. He really wasn't enjoying it much, and so he licked his thumb and forefinger and squeezed the smoldering tip. When he was sure it was extinguished, he placed it back in his pouch.

"What about you?" Callum was asking. "When you finish school, then what?"

"I've lived my entire adult life just trying to get through the present. Today. I have never for a moment thought much about what I will be doing tomorrow." He stared up into the sky, savoring the warmth against his eyelids. "And I certainly don't think there's a God in heaven who has a plan for me. Or, for that matter, for anyone."

"No?"

"No."

"No plan or no God?"

"Either." *Shema Yisrael, Adonai Eloheinu, Adonai Echad.* Hear, O Israel, the Lord our God, the Lord is one. It always surprised Uri when he recalled a prayer. Was this, he tried to remember now, what he was supposed to say when he was dying? Was this the incantation that would ensure that he didn't die alone—that would link his passing with the passing of all other Jews? He thought so, but it had been so long. Still, he wondered if Rebekah had whispered this prayer when she'd been killed. If she had, he hoped it had given her comfort. In all likelihood, it had given his parents some consolation; perhaps it had helped his sister in some fashion, too.

He heard Callum taking another long drag on the cigarette, but he didn't open his eyes. Then he heard a songbird. The water as it rolled through the channel on the other side of the wagon. Anna and Mutti, giggling once again in that river. One of the horses snorting. A fly. Finally he said to Callum, "If my sister were alive, I might view tomorrow differently. But there's no one now. Just me. And so I don't. I just try to keep myself alive. But even that seems less important than it once did."

"It's plenty important."

"No, not really. I'm not the last Jew left in Germany."

"What?"

"There are others. I know that now. I didn't always. But I swear to you, there were moments when the only thing that kept me going was my determination to live so I could someday tell people what the Germans were doing."

"That was a lot of pressure to put on yourself."

"It seemed to matter."

"You know . . ."

"Yes?"

"You could always come to Scotland."

"Excuse me? I couldn't possibly have heard you correctly,"

Uri said, turning from the sun to the paratrooper and smiling at him.

"Oh, I'm sure America is a terrific place. I liked most of the Yankees I met. Not all. But most. Anyway, it was just a thought."

"Ah, yes. I could just move in with you and Anna. Is that what you had in mind?"

"Well, as a matter of fact, you could. My mother has plenty of room. I'm sure we'll live there when we first arrive."

"And what would I do in Scotland?"

"Same as you'd do in America. Go to school. Meet a nice girl. Fall in love."

"Huh."

"Think about it."

Behind him, Uri could hear Anna and Mutti emerging from the water and starting to get dressed. He didn't precisely view Mutti as anyone's mother but Anna's; likewise, he didn't see Anna as a sister. But his own mother and his own sister were long dead. So, certainly, was his father. His whole family. He didn't know the details—would never know the details—of how they had perished, and on some level he was relieved. But there was still a part of him that craved the specifics: where and when and who was responsible. Who held the angry, barking dogs on their leashes? Who raised high the truncheons, who marched them into the pits? Who fired the machine guns? Or, perhaps, switched on the gas? These were Germans and Poles and Ukrainians with faces and names, men and women who before the war had had families and ran streetcars and bars and butcher shops—people he and his sister and his parents might have seen on any sidewalk and hardly given a second look.

"Uri?"

"Yes?"

"I'm serious."

No, he wanted out of Europe. He wanted away from those streetcars, those bars, those butcher shops.

But then there were these few survivors of what had once been a family named Emmerich. There was this Scot. The reality was, these people were the closest thing he had to a family now. They were all that he had in the world. With this thought—one he found at once oddly and uncharacteristically hopeful—he stood up and hollered good-naturedly at the women. Asked them if they were decent, and whether the men might actually get a chance to bathe, too.

FOR ANOTHER WEEK they walked and they slept and, on occasion, Mutti or Anna rode atop the wagon. Every other day, it seemed, there had also been moments when the men—both of them now—would need to crawl quickly beneath the feed because they were nearing diehard SS troopers who, even though it was clear that not even the führer's wonder weapons or the death of an American president could possibly roll back the tide, were either commandeering deserters or shooting them outright. Whole truckloads of teen boys passed them, the vehicles heading toward the Oder or the outskirts of Berlin, where the young men would be expected either to repulse the final Soviet advance or to die trying. Many looked as if they were Theo's age, their cheeks in some cases rosy and round, in others hollowed out by hunger and dread. One day there were snow flurries and on another it rained, but frequently the sun was so warm that they all tossed their jackets and capes onto the wagon and walked for hours in only their blouses and shirts.

They were no longer a part of a lengthy column. There were still plenty of other refugees on the roads: They passed mothers with children, exhausted old people, and men of all ages who had lost all manner of limbs. But the tragic and interminable parade that had started west from East Prussia and what once had been Poland had all but dissipated. Some elements had simply given up and allowed themselves to fall prey to the Russians, while others had reached whatever destination they had originally had in mind. Still others—many, many thousands, it seemed, based on the bodies and the debris that littered the roads that spring—had died in the cold of January and February and March. One afternoon they learned a pair of Wehrmacht battle groups were counterattacking a Russian spearhead no more than ten or twelve kilometers to the southeast, and that particular Soviet column was now moving away from them toward the southwest. Other days, their footsteps would be energized when they heard how the British and the Americans were moving in great numbers into the heart of the country, encountering only the most token resistance virtually everywhere. The four of them knew that the distance separating them from their western saviors (and that was how all of them viewed the Brits and the Americans that April) was narrowing.

Still, the walking was hard. The ground was often sloshy and soft, and though pilots were less likely to waste time strafing them since they weren't part of a caravan easily seen from the sky, occasionally an aircraft would swoop down from the clouds and fire a missile or two in their direction. A wagon no more than fifty meters ahead of them was blown up one afternoon by a British plane, slaughtering a sweet young mother and her two little boys: The Emmerichs and Callum and Uri had rested with them for thirty minutes in the middle of the day, only hours before the woman and her sons would be killed. Another time, they passed through the smoldering remains of yet one more town that recently had been bombed, and in the rubble of what had been the stone schoolhouse they saw the bodies of students. There were easily a dozen of them, perhaps a few more, all girls, and at first they assumed that the children had been brought there to protect them. Then, however, when Callum and Uri went to pull some of the stones and fallen timbers away to examine the corpses—make sure that none of the girls were still breathing—they realized that the bodies were largely unscathed. Moreover, there was very little bruising or blood, even on the parts of their bodies that had been crushed by debris from the crumbling structure. They understood then that the girls had probably been poisoned, their lives taken from them by adults who feared a far worse death awaited them when the Russians arrived.

No one in the group was precisely sure anymore where they were going. At one point Anna suggested they consider Schweinfurt, since it was far to the west and Uri might know people there. But it was also far to the south—so far that the distance, even after the hundreds of kilometers they had trekked, seemed prohibitive. Moreover, Uri wanted nothing to do with the city: He was quite certain that all of his family and friends were dead, and anyone still there had been all too happy to see the city's Jewish population degraded, deported, and, in the end, exterminated.

Consequently, their plan was simply to continue west, trying to avoid the major cities with their desperate, inevitable congestion—and, at night, the air raids that continued to pulverize the metropolitan areas even now. They would steer clear of Berlin at all costs, given the desperate battle that loomed there. When they heard cannonade to the east, they walked briskly; when they heard only birdsong, they allowed themselves the opportunity to shamble.

IT WAS URI who spotted the woeful column first. Their road was almost converging upon the one the column was on, separated from it at the moment by an expanse of triangular field cratered by shell fire and filled with the remnants of charred and blackened Wehrmacht vehicles—wagons, motorcycles, half-tracks, and what Uri alone recognized as the remains of two or three small, turretless Bushwhacker tanks. The soldiers had probably been encamped there when they had been spotted by an enemy pilot and attacked from the air. It must have been at least a

day or two earlier, however, because there were no signs of soldiers either wounded or deceased, and the dead horses had started
to smell.

Still, it was what was across the field that caused Uri's heart
to race: There, no more than two hundred meters distant, was a
plodding line of the most pathetic, despairing old men he had ever
seen. At least he thought they were old men. Most of them were
clad in shirts and trousers that even from this distance he could
see were little more than threadbare rags, but some seemed to be
wearing sacklike shifts and skirts and kerchiefs on their heads.
There were also a few in striped prison uniforms. He guessed
there were a hundred of them, perhaps more, and without exception the group was haggard and stooped and lumbering along at a
crawl. He counted nine guards, three of whom seemed to be female.

"What do you make of that?" Callum was asking.

"The old men?"

"Old men? Are you blind?" the paratrooper admonished him,
his voice indignant. "They're girls! They're young women!"

Uri squinted and studied the column of prisoners. He decided
that if Callum was right, then those guards deserved to be shot.
Hell, they deserved to be shot regardless of the age or the gender
of the walking skeletons they were prodding along.

"Women," he murmured, when he realized that Callum was
correct.

"Young women!" Callum said again, more loudly this time.
"Girls! Some are probably the same age as Anna here! Some could
be as young as your sister!"

Anna and Mutti had come up beside them, standing so close
that he could feel the warmth of Anna's breath and smell the
damp wool of her sweater. Her parka was in the back of the wagon
at the moment.

"Are they . . ." Mutti began.

"They're Jews," Callum said to her. "No doubt, they're Jews."

He was at once incredulous and disgusted, and it sounded to Uri as if he were chastising the woman. *This,* he was saying in essence, *is what your people are doing. Have done. Here it is in full view: No more hiding it behind barbed wire fences and cement crematoriums, no more burying the corpses in ditches. Here's a whole bloody parade of the walking dead.*

Mutti held her hands before her mouth and a small moan—a cry, almost—escaped. "They're girls, you say?" she murmured finally.

"Yes!" Callum said. "They're Jewish girls! Here's what your ten-thousand-year Reich was really all about!"

Uri watched as the column seemed to drift: It looked to him as if the individuals were bobbing in a river. It made absolutely no sound.

"Those guards: the most abominable bastards on the planet. What kind of person would do that?" Callum was muttering. Uri had never seen him so angry. Didn't know the Scot had it in him.

"Well, then," Uri said, aware of precisely what he wanted to do—what he was going to do—and wholly unconcerned with the ramifications. "Let's take care of them." He pulled his rifle off his shoulder and released the safety. "I'd suggest you get one of the Russian rifles out of the wagon."

"What are you doing?" This was Anna, and he heard a little tremor in her voice.

"I am going to kill that fellow"—and he paused as he squinted through the sight, moving his rifle like a pointer—"right there. The one with that ridiculous white mustache."

"But there are too many of them," Mutti said.

"And, I'd bet, they're all cowards. They're pathetic bullies and cowards."

His angle now was such that he was going to have to shoot the man in the back. So be it. He aimed heart level, just to the left of the guard's spine and below the man's scapula. And then he squeezed the trigger, experienced the recoil in his shoulder as he heard the blast in his ear, and watched as the guard with his preposterous resemblance to a walrus fell like a straw man whose braces have been removed, the fellow's knees buckling, his chin rolling into his neck, his arms flapping once like a dancer's. The idea somehow crossed Uri's mind that he might have been eating something as he walked: He thought he saw a large chunk of bread fly from the man's fingers as he died.

CECILE HEARD THE gunshot and saw the black bread Pusch was gnawing—she knew that his teeth were as bad as most of the prisoners', though in his case it had everything to do with slovenly personal hygiene and not malnutrition—fall to the mud near her feet, and for the briefest of seconds she thought one of the prisoners around her had somehow acquired a gun and shot the guard for the bread. And so she didn't dare pick it up. Consequently, a woman named Luiza darted around her with the speed of a rabbit and scooped it off the ground, in one fluid motion brushing a clod of dirt from the crust and tearing off a piece the size of a ball of milkweed.

Then, however, Cecile watched as the armed male guards fell to their knees and aimed their rifles in the direction of the field they were passing. She was confused: The pasture was filled with dead horses—their carcasses being nibbled by crows—and wagons and destroyed Nazi vehicles. Were there Russians—or, better still, Americans—hiding among all those burned-out tanks and trucks? The idea crossed her mind that this was it, their moment of liberation was at hand, and any second now Allied soldiers were going to rise up from behind the wrecks and demand that their guards surrender. In her mind they were all wearing French army uniforms, because she realized that was the only Allied uniform she knew, and she felt an unfamiliar pang of giddiness. But she was pulled from her brief reverie when that female guard named Inga bellowed furiously, "Down, now! Down, down,

down!" and then, suddenly, swatted her so hard on the back of her head that she fell forward onto her knees on the road beside Pusch. The dead guard was on his stomach and there was a hole in the back of his tunic around which a red stain was already starting to spread.

Across the field, beyond the blackened metal hulks and twisted lattices of steel, she saw a wooden farm wagon and a pair of horses. She thought—but she wasn't completely sure—that she had seen people near them from the corner of her eye, falling abruptly almost flat onto the ground. One moment they had been there, and in the next they had been gone. Clearly, however, the guards thought the gunfire had come from there. Their suspicions were confirmed almost instantly: There was a second crack—a female guard near Cecile shouted once, as much in surprise as in pain—and this shot had very definitely come from somewhere near that wagon. Perhaps a dozen and a half meters to her right, the Hungarian guard—a woman who was about the age of her prisoners and seemed to have the same disdain for the Germans as she did for the Jewish women she was herding west—had been shot. Apparently the guard had been up on her knees. Now, when Cecile turned, she saw the woman flapping on the ground as if she were a live fish on a dock, shrieking in a dialect that was unfamiliar to Cecile, and trying, it seemed, to pull something out of her side—as if she had been shot with an arrow, not a gun. The other guards were flat on their stomachs, eyeing the wagon, trying to see where the shooter was, and ignoring the woman who was writhing and screaming for, Cecile presumed, help.

Then, however, she saw Blumer rising up and darting into the field, diving quickly behind the remains of a half-track before a shot whizzed harmlessly past him. The guard had a potato-masher grenade on his belt and he reached for it, signaling to someone—another guard, she assumed, probably Kogel—to cover him as he scuttled closer still to the horses and the wagon and the faceless shooter.

Beside her there was a prisoner on her hands and knees whose name Cecile thought was Vivienne, but that was little more than a guess based on something she may or may not have overheard, and the fact the girl usually spoke French. Vivienne was younger than she was and had arrived at the factory in February from another camp. "Cecile, I'm leaving!" she whispered urgently. "Come with me—now!"

"Just run away?"

"Yes! Into the woods! Come with me, you've nothing to lose!"

She saw in her mind that awful moment when Kogel had executed Jeanne—there he was again, his arm straight with his pistol at the end, an extension of his hand—shooting her friend in the back of the head as Leah fled into the dark of the forest. She was just starting to wonder where Leah was—an image formed in her mind of the girl in a farmhouse somewhere, perhaps sitting before a fire in a wide brick hearth, a bowl of soup and an actual spoon in her fingers—when there was another gunshot in the field. She turned toward it, reflexively putting one of her hands over her eyes like a visor. There was Blumer, within a stone's throw of the wagon and the horses, shielded from it by the charred remains of a tank.

"Cecile, this is it," Vivienne was saying, "I'm going." And then the girl was gone, crabwalking carefully toward the woods, scuttling on her fingers and feet, her eyes darting back but one time.

Kogel spotted her almost instantly. "You, stop!" he shouted, but instead Vivienne stood up and started to run in her clogs, her legs stretching out one last time, the wind just starting, perhaps, to whistle in her ears, before the guard shot her with his rifle and she collapsed in the brush at the edge of the trees. Then he turned and aimed a second shot at one of the horses across the meadow, firing, apparently, for no other reason than anger and frustration and spite. The animal whinnied, reared up on its rear legs, and then sunk into the ground in its harness. Briefly it tried to reach the hole in its side with its nose, to nuzzle it, examine what had occurred there and would cause it to die, but then the horse's long, great head rolled around as if it were dangling on the head of a stick, and the animal expired. Kogel pulled his rifle down and surveyed the field. He seemed oddly satisfied.

She glanced back and forth between the body of the prisoner at the edge of the forest—a young woman whose forehead may once have been stroked by parents as they softly cooed her name—and the Hungarian guard, who was continuing to wriggle and moan and was now slapping at her side with the open palm of one of her hands. At least Vivienne had been granted a quick death, Cecile thought, and decided that she might as well try to scurry into the woods, too. Probably she would be shot, and that would be fine. There were no liberators here, no army about to rescue them. There was one idiot somewhere across that field with a gun. That was all.

And so she was about to stand when she noticed that Blumer was rising up from his crouch behind the tank to hurl the grenade at the wagon, blow it up and kill anyone behind or beside it— those lumps of clothing she had seen briefly falling to the ground—including the one horse that remained alive. She watched, hypnotized, sad for the horse that was about to die in a way that she wasn't for whatever people were near the wagon. He had pulled the pin and his arm was rearing back, when there were shots—two, maybe three, she wasn't sure, because it happened so fast—and Blumer with his one eye and mutilated ear was doubling over, the grenade beside him, kicking out his leg to try to push it away. But it was too late, far too late, and the grenade was exploding, the flash sending a cloud of dirt and fabric and flesh and metal from the tank high into the air, the plume darkening one vertical swath of sky and instantly making the world smell like sulfur and smoke. She wasn't quite sure what happened next because she had ducked into a ball, her arms across her face and her head, her eyes closed. When she opened them, she saw there was a gaping hole in the ground where a moment earlier Blumer had been kneeling. Kogel was on his back, dead—shot, she assumed, because the grenade couldn't possibly have done him in— and there was a large man with red hair and a smaller one in, of all things, a German uniform running across the meadow toward them and then disappearing behind the metal carcass of a half-track. She looked around and realized that the pair hadn't needed to dive behind the vehicle for cover. Pusch and Blumer and Kogel were dead. The Hungarian was dying. The other guards—three other men and two other women—had seen this skirmish as a reason to flee. To escape themselves before they were held accountable for all they had done. Around her the prisoners were starting to rise, to mill about, and so she did, too. She stumbled over to Vivienne, and much to her surprise she found that the girl was still breathing. Her eyes were small slits in the hollows of her skull and the front of her worn shift was soaked with her blood, but she looked up at Cecile and murmured, "In my pocket, there's a photo. Take it."

She carefully lifted the girl's head and rested it on her own bony thighs. Then she saw the slit in the tattered dress and reached in. She found the picture instantly, an image of five children and two parents. The father was wearing a white V-necked sweater, and his eyes and his cheekbones were striking. He could have been a movie star. The mother was lovely, too, though there was something vacant about her eyes—as if, perhaps, she were blind. The children looked as young as three or four and as old as fifteen or sixteen. The family was on the deck of a cruise ship, and Cecile had the sense that the small, rocky islands in the background were Greece. The children were in tidy shorts or sleeveless summer dresses, their mother in an elegant skirt and a blouse. She was wearing pearls. All of their faces were windblown and their hair in vacation-like disarray.

"On the back," Vivienne sputtered.

She turned it over and saw five names, including, yes, Vivienne, and the words *father* and *mother* in French.

"Where are you from?" Cecile asked.

"Limoges."

She nodded, recalled a visit there once with her parents when she'd been a little girl, and stroked Vivienne's forehead with her fingers. Then gently she dabbed at the spittle that was forming on the prisoner's lips.

"Cecile?"

"I'm here," she murmured.

"Tell them what happened. Please."

"Your family . . ."

"Yes."

"I will."

"I never gave up. That's what I want them to know. My parents. My brothers and sisters. I know they can't all have died."

"No," she answered, "of course not," but she didn't see any reason why it wasn't possible that this whole family had been machine-gunned or gassed or simply worked till they collapsed in a quarry or a brick factory somewhere. Certainly the woman's younger siblings were dead. "Someday," she added, "you'll tell them yourself."

"No." The word was barely the tiniest puff of air, a syllable spoken without even moving her lips.

"What is your name?"

"Viv . . ." she answered, too weak now to link together more than a syllable at a time.

"I know that, silly," she said. "Your whole name. Your surname."

The girl started to nod, to answer. But this time when she tried to breathe she discovered that she couldn't, and she grimaced with the pain of the effort, her eyes and mouth becoming parallel lines below a series of deep creases upon her forehead. Her eyes opened one last time, the panic and fear and desperation apparent, and Cecile willed herself to smile down at this scared dying girl, to keep her own tears from her eyes. And then Vivienne—like the litany of others who had died near Cecile, beside Cecile, or in her very arms—died, too.

She looked up and saw a woman with a mane of yellow hair protruding from beneath her dirty kerchief wandering through the field toward the prisoners. She had worn but elegant leather riding boots on her feet, and Cecile thought she appeared to be a few years younger than she was. Near her an older woman in a coat with a tired-looking fur collar was already starting to kneel before two other prisoners and hand them . . . something. Bread, perhaps. And there was that German soldier offering his canteen to a prisoner, and that tall fellow with terra-cotta red hair literally lifting another prisoner off the road and carrying her to a patch of earth in the field where there was sun and the ground was warm. She noticed that the crows had flown back and resumed their lunch on the entrails of the dead horses.

Some of the other girls started to follow the redheaded man onto the grass. Others looked around nervously, wondering whether even this—this apparent rescue—was a mere trap of some kind. An ambush. A trick. They glanced down the road to the east and to the west; they peered apprehensively at the woods. Some even scanned the sky.

Then one of the girls walked over to Pusch, leaned over his body, and spat. She glanced around to see if anyone had noticed, her eyes mischievous and childlike. And then, with the suddenness of lightning, she kicked the dead guard in the ribs, using her clog like a bludgeon. She kicked him in the face, too, slamming the front of her clog into his nose and mouth with such force that the head seemed almost to lift away from its neck.

Other prisoners watched for a moment—but only for a moment. Within seconds the girls were kicking and stomping on the corpses of all the dead guards, battering them with their feet, and when that wasn't sufficiently satisfying, using the butts of the guards' rifles to smash the bones in their faces and pummel their skulls into the earth. They cheered as they worked and, like that first girl, spat on the bodies. Then they turned on the Hungarian guard—the woman still hadn't died—and they drilled their clogs into her wherever they could and walloped her with the rifles, swinging them like axes in some cases and in others like plungers, until she grew completely silent and her body moved only in response to the way it was kicked or beaten or shoved.

Cecile wasn't sure how long she had been watching when the German soldier came over and squatted on his haunches beside her. She knew enough not to be scared of him, despite the uniform. Hadn't he just killed or driven off their guards? He asked her if she spoke German and she said that she did, though she was French. He asked her if the girl in her arms was a friend.

"I didn't really know her," she answered.

He ran his hand gingerly along the line where the girl's hair was growing back along her forehead. "What was her name?"

"Vivienne. I never got to know her last name."

"And what's your name?"

"Cecile Fournier."

"I'm Uri. Uri Singer."

"That sounds—" she said, but she stopped herself before she could finish the sentence.

"I know what it sounds like," he said. Then he smiled slightly and added, "And, yes, it is."

"Jewish."

He nodded.

"I thought we were all going to die."

"You and the other prisoners?"

"No. The Jews. All of us. I tried to keep my hopes up, but these last weeks . . . it was gone, all gone. I thought they were going to exterminate us all."

"I thought so, too. There were times when I wondered if I was the only one left."

She offered him the smallest of smiles. "Your name should be Adam."

He chuckled, but the sound was rueful and she thought he was just being polite. "No, not me," he said. "I am not the beginning of anything. If anything, I am the end of everything." Then he cradled Vivienne's head in the palms of his hands and laid it gently on the ground so Cecile could stand.

"Tell me . . ." he said.

"Yes?"

"Did you know any Jews from Schweinfurt?"

"Is that where you're from?"

He nodded.

"I may have. I don't know. Were you looking for someone special? Your wife? Your parents?"

"My sister."

"What is her name?"

"*Was* her name, I suppose. It *was* Rebekah."

She had probably known girls named Rebekah; she had probably known German girls named Rebekah. But none came to mind now. She shook her head. "I'm sorry," she said.

"Don't be. It would have been a miracle if you had," he told her. Then he added quickly, "Well, we have to get you some food," and he motioned his arm at the prisoners in the fields and the prisoners still pummeling the Hungarian guard and the prisoners staring wide-eyed into the sun. "We have a little in the wagon, but not nearly enough for all of you. But we'll find some."

"How?"

"There's a village up ahead. We may be able to wait there for the Americans. At the very least, we'll be able to rest for a bit and scare up something to eat."

"Is . . ."

"Go on."

"Is the war over?"

"Not yet," he told her. "But soon. Very soon. And I believe, at the very least, it's over for you."

THE VILLAGE WAS no more than three kilometers distant, but even that seemed too far to expect some of the women to walk. Still, Uri didn't think they could possibly bring back enough food and water—assuming they could even scare up provisions there—for the whole group with a single horse and a single wagon. Waldau was strong, but he was weary. He guessed that the women who felt up to it could come with him to the village, and those who didn't could stay where they were. Callum and Anna and Mutti could wait with them.

When he told Anna his idea, she looked up at him and said, "Bring back a doctor, too. They need a doctor badly. All of them." Her voice sounded very small. She was sitting on the grass, rubbing the blackened and mangled feet of a woman who seemed unconscious.

"I imagine the village will be mostly deserted," he said. "If there's a doctor anywhere near here, I'm sure whatever's left of the army has pressed him into service. But I'll try to find out how close we are to the Americans and the British."

"They must be near," said Mutti.

"One would think so," he agreed. He didn't want to get their hopes up, including his own, but when he looked at the map he guessed the western Allies might be as close as fifteen or twenty kilometers. It could be more. They'd heard that the British and Americans had paused, as if they had reached an agreement with the Soviets to be sure that each side received an equitable share of the remains of the Reich. Nevertheless, their armies were within reach—though, of course, so were the Soviets. It was possible that by remaining with the prisoners, the four of them would be overrun by the Russians. But these women were viewing the Russians as their liberators. And for the prisoners they would be. But for the four of them—especially for Anna and Mutti? The Soviets might be merciless.

And so a different idea began to formulate in Uri's head: He would tell the Emmerichs that they should leave the horse and the wagon behind and proceed ahead without them. The two of them should just walk west as quickly as they could. For all he knew, they might reach the Americans or the British by tomorrow. Meanwhile, he and Callum and the women who could walk would bring back whatever food and water and medicine they could find. But Anna and Mutti should leave now—make one last dash for the west.

He decided he liked this plan; he liked it a lot. He would strip off his German uniform, climb into some of Werner's ragged old clothes they had in the wagon, and allow his circumcised penis to vouch for his identity. And Callum? For God's sake, he was a POW. The two of them would be fine. He didn't completely believe this, but he reiterated the idea in his mind. They'd be fine. He shared his plan with Callum, and then he squatted beside Anna and told her what he thought they should do. And then he climbed atop the charred metal husk of a tank and clapped his hands together and shouted to get the attention of the women around him. He was just starting to speak—just beginning to open his mouth in earnest—when he heard the rifle shot and then, before he could even turn in its general direction, felt himself being punched ferociously hard in the chest. He fell backward off the tank, the wind, it seemed, knocked completely out of him. He was aware that Anna was shrieking—he thought she might have been saying no, but already her voice sounded to him as if he were underwater—and he felt the back of his head hitting the ground. Then he was staring up into the bluest sky he had ever seen. For a split second he felt crushing pain and experienced a pang of frustration at the realization that he had come so far only to die now. He wondered who had shot him, and he wondered at the way the myth he had concocted of his indestructibility was so easily shattered. One bullet: That was all it took. Apparently, his soul was negligible, after all. But this recognition lasted just the briefest of moments, because then he was, much to his surprise, in the dining room of his childhood home in Schweinfurt, once again a teenage boy, and he and little Rebekah were using long, slender spoons to scoop the mascarpone cream from the tops of parfait glasses, and their mother and father were chatting casually about nothing. At least nothing of consequence. Then they were laughing. And the sky was blue there, too, more blue than even this Anna girl's eyes, and the sun was streaming in through the gauzy curtains. He was warm and content and his stomach was comfortably full. And then: Nothing.

CALLUM SAW THE shooter instantly: It was one of those older men who had been guarding the women, and so Callum shot him. He picked the man off as he was pulling his rifle down and starting to retreat into a thicket of pine. His first bullet only wounded him, and so Callum shot him a second time. Then he scanned the field for any other Germans, saw none, and stood there, panting, for a long moment over Anna and Mutti as they crouched above Uri's body. Two of the prisoners were with them, including one whose name he had overheard was Cecile. Uri's eyes were open, but it seemed that he was already dead. His first thought? It had all happened so quickly. One minute Uri was with them, and the next he was gone. Anna was crying gently, shaking her head and shuddering. He knelt beside her, and when she realized he was there she leaned into his arms, as Mutti, once again, used her forefingers to gently shut the eyes of a body emptied abruptly of its soul.

"I know," Callum murmured, his chin against the top of

Anna's head, his chest against her almost violently trembling body, "I know." He wasn't sure what he meant—if, in fact, he meant anything. What it was that he knew, he couldn't say. *I know it's hard? I know it's tragic? I know you'll miss him?* "I know," he whispered softly. "I know." Surrounded by a small sea of starving, tortured women, he thought to himself—and he heard the words in his head in Uri's frequently mordant voice—*Please. I know nothing at all.*

Chapter Twenty

HELMUT EMMERICH PRESSED HIS KNEES AGAINST HIS chest and wrapped his arms tightly around his shins: He was an egg. He couldn't have made his body any smaller. Still, however, he feared that the toes of his boots could be seen from the road if any of the Soviet soldiers happened to glance to their right at the remnants of the stone wall. And the column was endless, absolutely endless. First there had been the trucks and the half-tracks, and then there had been the assault guns and the tanks. And, dear God, in the whole history of the war had there ever before been so many tanks in one place? It just didn't seem possible. It had been an interminable parade of them, a procession so long that for a while it had seemed to Helmut that the ground was never, ever going to stop vibrating beneath him. And now there was the infantry and the horse-drawn wagons. Every living man from Belarus had to be marching past him right now—or, for all he knew, every living man from the Ukraine. And Georgia. He had heard a variety of languages and dialects as the troops walked along. He guessed it was an entire tank corps and a rifle division marching west.

It was not simply terrifying—though that was the principal sensation—it was frustrating. After all, he had been sure that he had, finally, gotten ahead of the Russian army. He wasn't merely far, far to the west of Kaminheim: He was west of the Oder. He was west of Dresden. After nearly four weeks of hiding, of skulking, of lurking . . . of stealing carrots from root cellars and eating nothing but snow for days at a time . . . of using his last bullet a week ago now when he had shot at a hare and missed . . .

Evidently the war was over, or it would be within days, because clearly there was no Reich remaining. There was no Germany left. He knew how far west these soldiers were, and he had heard just enough rumors and stories to know that the western armies were well beyond the Rhine and the Russians were fighting in Berlin. Moreover, these Soviet riflemen were a joyful bunch, and that meant something, too. They were singing and laughing and whooping up a storm as they marched.

He considered, as he had often that winter and spring, simply surrendering. Just giving up. And if he was ever going to surrender, now was as good a time as any. There were plenty of officers marching past and plenty of witnesses: It seemed unlikely that they would shoot him right here by the road. At least he thought it was unlikely. They would, after all, have to do something with him if they didn't shoot him. And so while they might not execute him out here in the open right beside this stone wall, he guessed in the end some lieutenant and a pair of riflemen might escort him seventy or eighty meters into the woods and shoot him there.

He decided he would remain where he was. He stared down at the tears in his pants and the way the skin he could see on his knees had grown as coarse as sandpaper. He reminded himself that eventually the sun would set once again and this army would be gone. He would be able to uncoil his body, to rise up and go . . .

That, of course, was the problem. This morning, just when he thought he had finally gotten west of Ivan, here he was. Again. And so Helmut was beginning to fear there was no place left in the west that could become his eventual destination. Yes, the war was all but over, but he could only dimly imagine what sort of world was going to remain when there was nothing left of the Reich to bomb into rubble. The one thing he was certain of was that there would no longer be the Germany he had known his whole life. He still had vivid memories of Kaminheim when it had been a part of Poland, since he had been a Polish citizen for the first twelve years of his life. But even as a little boy he had viewed himself as a German. And the world that was dawning wanted no part of the Germany he knew. What would remain of the empire that once stretched from the westernmost tip of France to the oil fields in the Caucasus? From the ice of the Arctic Circle in Finland and Norway to the desert heat of North Africa? It would become a compact little vassal state. The victorious armies would divide up the nation the way the Germans and the Russians had carved up Poland into halves.

Well, such was the fate of conquered nations since the beginning of time.

Still, he didn't want to die. He had seen more than his share of death, including his father's in that ludicrous counterattack on the Kulm bridgehead hours after the two of them had said good-bye to Mutti and Theo and Anna, and he wanted to postpone his own as long as he possibly could. Somehow he had survived ill-advised counterattacks on Russian positions for almost two months, until he alone in his battle group was alive, and he couldn't imagine he had any luck left. It wasn't that he was afraid of death—though he could readily admit to himself that he was. It was the fact that his father was dead and he had to presume that Werner was dead, and so it seemed to Helmut that he alone was left to look after the Emmerichs who remained. Consequently, he vowed to stay where he was until this latest procession was past and then—as he had for weeks now—try to work his way west.

IT WAS THE BRITISH who reached the female prisoners in the field first, a long column of Churchill tanks that had pressed to the south and the east of Lübeck. When they saw the women— by no means the first camp survivors they had encountered— they radioed back for medics and set up a hospital inside what was rumored to have been an estate Martin Bormann had commandeered for a mistress. An opera singer. Some of the women had scattered by then, fearful that the Germans would return, but most had been incapable of fleeing. Anna and Callum had already filled the wagon with whatever food they could find in the village, which hadn't been much. They made two trips that first afternoon—on their second excursion, they returned with all the blankets and quilts they could steal—and a third one the next morning. Waldau never faltered. Mostly they brought back moldering root vegetables they discovered in sand barrels in empty basements and loaves of bread that were so hard they were like clubs. Still, they softened the bread in hot water they warmed over a fire and boiled the vegetables into a hot soup. No one was able to eat much, but everyone was able to eat something. They'd been there a little more than a day when the British tanks arrived, a loud, rumbling procession that caused the earth to tremble and caused Anna and Mutti and Callum to hold their breath until they knew for sure that the approaching army wasn't Russian.

In the days that followed, more and more British troops arrived. Canadians, too. And, suddenly, Callum was gone. Interrogated first—at length, apparently—then cleared, and then absorbed back into the army. Anna saw him one more time before he was returned to his division. He had hoped, he said, that she would come with him. There were displaced persons all over Germany, and did it matter whether she was a refugee here or seventy-five kilometers farther south? Probably not. But she and Mutti were assisting the nurses at the makeshift hospital, doing whatever they—or anyone—asked. They cleaned bedpans and washed dirty sheets, they fed soup to the girls. They assisted the translators to find out who the prisoners were and where they were from. They acted as intermediaries with the Germans living nearby.

And so Callum told her that he would come back for her as soon as he could. He didn't know when that would be, but he was confident he would return before long. In the meantime, he urged them to stay where they were so he could find them.

There was, however, no chance that either of them was going to leave. The camp in which they were staying with other refugees was adequate, and Mutti seemed no less discomfited by the slit trench that was their bathroom than she was by the fields and woods she had used so frequently that winter and spring. There were soldiers who hated the German refugees for what their people had done, but there were others who seemed to view them merely with boredom. They gave chewing gum to the children in the camp—often having to explain what it was—and cigarettes to the younger women. They tended to ignore the women Mutti's age, as well as the men who were there—none of whom, it seemed to Anna, could possibly have been younger than fifty-five or sixty.

Every so often, Mutti would bring up her husband or her sons, and her hopes that they would all be reunited before the end of the summer. Anna would say nothing to disabuse her of this possibility. She would carry the dinner trays for the women who were, slowly, starting to mend, and she would read to them from the books that she found in one of the massive house's bedrooms. She became friends with a woman named Cecile, and told her what she could of the man who had rescued them—had, arguably, rescued them both. And she would do whatever they or the British doctors would ask of her, though it seemed the women wanted only to sleep and sip broth and inquire whether the suddenly omnipresent Red Cross had found someone they loved: A husband. A sibling. A father, a mother, a child.

In the first days there was never any news to report. By the end of June there was, and invariably it was bad.

Sometimes, the British wondered if her silence, other than when she was reading aloud to the patients, was sedition. Some conjectured that she might actually be an unrepentant little fascist, and perhaps had secrets she was shielding. Who knew what her father or her family really had done during the war? Others, however, sensed the truth: She rarely opened her mouth unless she was speaking the words of authors long dead because she felt she had lost all moral authority to speak a word of her own. She and her family had prospered under the Nazis; now the Nazis were gone and there was a price. Besides, when she saw these women in their cots and their beds in the estate, she understood that the more she spoke the more likely she was to cry. She didn't precisely hate herself—nor did she hate her mother, though when she would look at Mutti she would experience daggers of frustration that her parents and their whole selfish generation had forgotten the most fundamental of human decencies—but the guilt was nonetheless debilitating. Sometimes, she wanted to rail at Mutti, at all the refugees her mother's age, and ask them what they had been thinking. How they could have done this to their children—to the world.

She began to pray, but it had been a long time and it seemed that praying took a concentration she lacked. Moreover, other than the health of the camp survivors around her and the safe return of her father and brothers, she wasn't quite sure what to pray for. One of the other young women among the refugees, a war widow a few years older than Anna, told her that she personally prayed for forgiveness. The war widow said she hadn't been a party member, but that didn't matter.

And so Anna tried that, too. Unfortunately, with Callum gone—Callum who had loved her despite her naïveté—she wasn't confident that self-loathing wouldn't forever be her companion and cause her to walk with a distracted, disconsolate gaze. She didn't care so much whether the world would ever forgive her people; but she did hope that someday, somehow, she would be able to forgive herself.

EPILOGUE

1948

THE RUINS OF THE SCOTTISH CASTLE LOOKED OUT UPON the North Sea from the edge of a steep cliff, and the waves rolled against the base of the ledge like wild, excited ponies. Parts of two of the original four towers remained, the stones butterscotch in the sun, and the tower nearest the ocean looked as if a giant had taken a tremendous bite out of the top. Across the road and perhaps a hundred meters distant, sheep were grazing and the herd's dog, a brown and white border collie, was running ecstatically in circles around them. Two of the sheep had been dozing half on and half off the thin road.

There had been fog in the morning, but this time of year there was always fog in the morning, and now it had lifted and the sky was cerulean blue. There were wispy, achromatic clouds far out to sea, but they posed no threat to the picnic.

The baby, a moonfaced boy with thin, poppy-colored hair, was just starting to wake up, and Anna put down the letter she had been reading and leaned over to watch him on the blanket. When they had first arrived, she had put two pillows around him to shield him from the breeze off the water. He was making small, birdlike clucking sounds, a signal that he was emerging from his nap. Anna thought she would feed him in a moment. Beside them, on the grass on the hill near the crumbling remains of the castle's east wall—the roof was long gone—sat Callum, his long legs extended well beyond the edge of the blanket. Mutti had been back in Germany a full week now, and though Anna missed her mother's help with the baby, she was relieved that she and Callum had their apartment to themselves once again. It really wasn't big enough for three grown-ups and an infant. Still, Mutti had arrived in time for the birth of her first grandson and stayed almost three months—which was at least a month longer than she had planned to visit, but she had found the role of grandmother irresistible. She shared the position contentedly with Callum's mother, who would appear with sprightly regularity at eight thirty every morning. Mutti was living now in a rooming house in a village a little west of where their trek had ended three years earlier, in the corner of Germany that was occupied by the British. Her room, she assured Anna, was more than sufficiently cheerful: It had a window that faced south and was bright most of the day. She had no plans to try to visit Poland, and no expectation that she would ever see Kaminheim—or whatever remained of Kaminheim—again. Helmut lived near her and had found work as a custodian at one of the British air bases. He hoped eventually they would train him to become a mechanic.

Anna and Callum had named the child Uri. In the months before Uri was born they had vacillated wildly between the names Theodore and Uri, debating passionately the merits of each option, but in the end Helmut had made the decision for them: He told them that someday he would like to name a son after Theo. He said that he hoped eventually he would be able to name boys after both Theo and Werner, their brothers who forever were lost.

And so Anna and Callum had a son with a name that was uncommon in Scotland, but sometimes made Anna smile when she said the full name aloud. On occasion those smiles were wistful because she was contemplating all that was gone from the world, or she was recalling in her mind's eye Uri's grave, well-chiseled face; but other times, especially as days passed and small hints of her baby's own personality began to emerge, those smiles would verge on the ecstatic because she was pondering all that nevertheless remained.

Nearby the dog barked and Uri opened his eyes. Blinked. Rolled his small head slightly toward the sound. Then he closed them again, as he slowly began to reacclimate himself to the waking world. She decided if she was going to finish the letter from Cecile, she had better return to it right now. And so she picked up the paper and started to read, catching up with the Frenchwoman with whom she had been friends since their paths had crossed at the very end of the war. Once Cecile had left the displaced-persons camp outside of Lübeck, she had returned to Lyon. Her fiancé had indeed perished, as had her mother and father, but she remained surprised by the number of friends who had somehow survived. She worked now as a secretary in a small publishing house and had a cat and a boyfriend. Cecile made the future, as always, sound promising.

Anna had almost finished the letter when Uri once again opened his eyes and looked up at her. He shaped his impossibly small mouth into an oval. A greeting, she thought, though she presumed he might simply have been hungry and in a moment would use that mouth to cry out for food. She loved the glimmer of recognition she saw in his eyes when his lids first rolled back after a nap and he recognized her.

Now she lifted the boy up and into her arms, brought his face to hers, and thought of nothing and no one—not Cecile or parents or siblings or in-laws or even her husband—but her baby, and how remarkably warm this small person's skin was against hers.

A GIRL STOOD beside one of the pomegranate trees on a narrow street in Beersheba, savoring the shade she had found and watching the long parade of captured Egyptian trucks passing by.

The trucks were filled with victorious Israeli soldiers now, whooping and hollering and singing. The driver of every second or third truck would press exuberantly on the vehicle's horn. She herself had been on one of those trucks until a few moments ago, when she had hopped off.

She wiped the sweat from her brow with the sleeve of her shirt, made sure that her machine gun's safety was on, and then wandered down the street to the gray-green awning of the restaurant. The ground was so hot that she could feel it through the soles of her boots—a sensation that she knew well, and one that always reminded her of how profoundly different the Middle East was from Europe. She couldn't imagine ever living in Germany again. She knew she was young, but she was confident that she would never again want anything to do with that country—or, for that matter, with the whole European continent.

The café was a joyous mob scene in which every table was taken and the bar was filled with young and old soldiers who were toasting to victory and the Negev and the future of Israel, and everybody was at least as happy as the soldiers who had just ridden by on the trucks. She found a table with three soldiers, including the lanky fellow whom she had agreed to meet here today, God willing. She saw him before he saw her, and so she snuck up behind him and kissed him on the cheek, pressing her lips against the coarse stubble there. He hadn't shaved in two days.

"Ah, my Rebekah," he said, standing and smiling. He took her in his long arms and embraced her. "I knew you would make it."

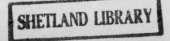

ACKNOWLEDGMENTS

SKELETONS AT THE FEAST HAS ITS ORIGINS IN 1998 when good friends of my family, Gerd and Laura Krahn, first shared with me the diary that Gerd's East Prussian grandmother kept from roughly 1920 through 1945. Eva Henatsch raised her large family on a sugar beet farm in a tract of land that in her lifetime was a part of Germany, then Poland, and then Germany once again. Much of the diary chronicles the day-to-day minutiae of helping to manage a sizable estate in a remote, still rural corner of Europe; but then there are the pages that chronicle 1945, and her family's arduous trek west ahead of the Soviet army—a journey that was always grueling and often terrifying.

When I first read the diary in 1998, translated into English by Eva's daughter, Heidi Krahn, and enhanced with the memories of other family members, I was fascinated. But I certainly didn't anticipate that it would ever inspire me to embark upon a novel.

Eight years later, however, in 2006, I read Max Hastings's remarkable history of the last year of the war in Germany, *Armageddon*, and I was struck by how often the anecdotes in Hastings's nonfiction chronicle mirrored moments in Eva Henatsch's diary. Apparently, the horrors in Henatsch's diary—as well as the more ordinary moments in her life—were not unique. It was thus

almost out of intellectual curiosity that I asked Gerd if I could re-
visit his grandmother's diary. And then, on that second reading, I
began to imagine a novel.

In addition to *Armageddon*, there were a great many books
that were helpful to me while writing *Skeletons at the Feast*. Among
them were *D-Day, June 6, 1944*, by Stephen E. Ambrose, which offered descriptions of paratroop landings that I used to create the
chaos that surrounded Callum Finella's drop; *Neighbors: The De-
struction of the Jewish Community in Jedwabne, Poland*, by Jan T.
Gross; *Hitler's Willing Executioners*, by Daniel Jonah Goldhagen;
On Hitler's Mountain: Overcoming the Legacy of a Nazi Childhood, by
Irmgard A. Hunt; *What We Knew: Terror, Mass Murder, and Every-
day Life in Nazi Germany*, by Eric A. Johnson and Karl-Heinz
Reuband; *Sins of the Innocent: A Memoir*, by Mireille Marokvia; *The
Lost: A Search for Six of Six Million*, by Daniel Mendelsohn; *German Boy: A Child in War*, Wolfgang W. E. Samuel's memoir of his
life in the final days of the Second World War (with, coinciden-
tally, a foreword by Stephen Ambrose); and *The Holocaust: Personal Accounts*, edited by David Scrase and Wolfgang Mieder.

Three novels I read in the past two years also helped guide me
through this period in history: *Wartime Lies*, by Louis Begley;
Crabwalk, by Günter Grass; and *Suite Française*, by Irene Ne-
mirovsky, which is set in France in 1940 and 1941, but includes
some of the most haunting scenes I have ever read of a scared people on the move.

One memoir that I found both informative and inspirational
was Gerda Weissmann Klein's poignant and powerful account of
her adolescence and young adulthood, *All but My Life*. The fictional character Cecile Fournier in this novel owes much to her—
as well as to my neighbor here in Vermont, Gizela Neumann, a
Holocaust survivor whose memories are moving and whose wisdom is extensive. Neumann and Klein attribute their survival to
both the profound and the prosaic: The profound was their faith;
the prosaic was their shoes. Klein wore what she calls ski boots in

her memoir; Neumann, meanwhile, had her hiking boots. On the death marches of early 1945, those shoes made all the difference for both women.

I also want to thank some of my earliest readers, including Dr. Michael Berenbaum, creator of the United States Holocaust Memorial Museum in Washington, D.C., as well as a rabbi, an author, an editor, and an award-winning filmmaker; Larry Wolff, a professor of history at New York University and a scholar on the history of Poland; Johanna Boyce; Stephen Kiernan; Dr. Richard Munson; Adam Turteltaub; my editor, Shaye Areheart; my agent, Jane Gelfman; and my wife, Victoria Blewer. I owe much also to the guidance of Jenny Frost at the Crown Publishing Group and Dean Schramm with the Jim Preminger Agency.

It is important to note that although characters in this novel endure some of the same trials as Eva Henatsch and her remarkable family, Irmgard Emmerich—Mutti—is not Eva. Nor is Anna Emmerich a re-creation of Eva's daughter, Heidi. But I hope the fictional Mutti and Anna have at least a semblance of Eva's and Heidi's monumental courage and resiliency and compassion.

Finally, I must express my deepest gratitude to the entire Krahn family for sharing with me Eva's diary and then reading this manuscript. Heidi Krahn, Gerd Krahn, and Laura Krahn gave me observations about this novel in its earliest drafts that were helpful and wise, and they always shared their thoughts kindly. Their graciousness, their friendship, and their candor have meant the world to me, and I thank them once again for being a part of my family's life over the years—and for their patience with me while I was writing this novel.

CHRIS BOHJALIAN
SKELETONS AT THE FEAST

READING GROUP GUIDE

by Jessica Lickun

A NOTE TO THE READER
In order to provide reading groups with the most informed and thought-provoking questions possible, it is necessary to reveal important aspects of the plot of this book—as well as the ending.

If you have not finished reading Skeletons at the Feast, *we respectfully suggest that you may want to wait before reviewing this guide.*

ABOUT THIS GUIDE

In the chaotic months before the final collapse of the Third Reich, the Germans living in the eastern part of Hitler's empire fled their homes to escape the onslaught of the Soviet Army. If these refugees didn't know the specifics of the atrocities their people had committed on Russian soil—and, in fact, were still committing in concentration camps across Poland and Germany—they nonetheless understood that the Russians were going to be merciless.

It is this world that Chris Bohjalian brings vividly and powerfully to life in *Skeletons at the Feast*. A Prussian aristocrat struggles west with her beautiful daughter, her young son, and a Scottish prisoner of war. Meanwhile, a female Jewish prisoner endures first the horrors of a concentration camp and then a forced march west in the ice and snow of a German winter. And a Jewish man who has leapt from a train bound for a death camp learns to do whatever he must to survive.

This reader's guide is intended as a starting point for your discussion of the novel.

1. Do you know—or are you yourself—a veteran of World War II? Discuss what you know of the war and any reminiscences that veterans may have shared.

2. Both of Anna's parents are members of the Nazi Party—though it is clear that they are not die-hard believers. Living on their farm in rural Prussia, they are largely sheltered from the atrocities perpetrated against the Jews. As Germans, do you think they share responsibility for the Nazis' actions even if they didn't know the full extent of what was happening? Why did they join the party? Did they have a choice? Consider Helmut's teacher who questions the boy about his father's loyalty to Hitler and the consequences of resisting. If failure to join meant death for you, what would you have done?

3. A group of POWs is brought to the Emmerich family's farm to help with the harvest, including a Scot named Callum Finella. He and Anna fall in love. What brings them together? Does the kindness of the Emmerich family, and Callum's love for their only daughter, change his view of the German people as a whole?

4. We meet Uri on the train to Auschwitz. What kind of man is he? How does he behave on the train? Imagine yourself in those deplorable conditions. Do you think you would seize the opportunity for freedom and jump as Uri did, leaving behind your family to an uncertain future?

5. While arguing with Anna about what is really happening to Jews, Callum says, "Suppose my government in England just decided to 'resettle' the Catholics—to take away their homes, their animals, their possessions, and just send them away?" What if this was happening where you live? What actions would you be willing to take

to protect your friends and neighbors? At what point would the risks have been too great?

6. To survive, Uri impersonates German soldiers, stealing papers and uniforms from men he either kills or finds dead. Discuss the events that lead up to his first killing of a Nazi. Discuss his reaction to what he has done (page 59). Do you believe his actions were warranted?

7. Although the world is essentially collapsing around them, Anna and Callum fall in love, Theo cries over leaving his beloved horse behind, and Mutti carefully drapes the furniture in sheets to protect it before they flee their home ahead of the Russians. What do these simple, ordinary actions reveal about them as people? About the human capacity for hope?

8. Theo is only a child but he feels lacking in comparison to his older brothers Werner and Helmut, both off fighting in the war. What kind of child is he? Does he fit in with his peers? Why doesn't Theo tell his mother about his foot? What does this reveal about him? Does Theo change over the course of the novel?

9. Describe Cecile. What kind of woman is she? What keeps her going in spite of the cruelty and degradation she suffers every day? How is she different from her friend Jeanne? Do you think you would act more like Cecile or Jeanne in the same circumstances?

10. In Chapter Eight, Helmut and his father, Rolf, try to convince Uncle Karl to leave his home along with the Emmerichs. He refuses, keeping his daughter, daughter-in-law, and grandson with him in spite of the danger. Why won't he evacuate? Why won't he let the women and the child leave? On page 118 he refers to them and their way of life as "skeletons at the feast." What does he mean by this?

11. Describe the circumstances that bring Uri and the Emmerichs together. Why does he choose to stay with them after running alone

for so long? How does he feel about them initially? How do his feelings for them change?

12. On page 178, Callum is thinking about bringing Anna home with him to Scotland after the war. How does he think she will be received? Why is he troubled?

13. During their long march from the prison camp to the factory, Jeanne and another prisoner find soldiers' rations and eat them. They do not wake Cecile to share them with her. Why? In the same circumstances, what would you have done?

14. Given the odds of success, would you have been brave enough to attempt to escape with Cecile and her friends?

15. Describe Mutti. What was she like at the beginning of the war? At the end? What does she view as her primary responsibility? On pages 291–293, she remembers burying the young German pilot whose plane crashed in her park. Why was burying him—and the enemy Russian soldiers—important to her?

16. How does Anna change as the novel progresses? Why does she feel the need for personal forgiveness at the end? Is she right to feel guilty?

17. Discuss the importance of hope in survival. Which character is the most hopeful? Which character is the most defeated? What moments at the end of the novel symbolize hope most poignantly?

18. Discuss the legacy that Mutti's generation left for Anna's. As a nation, what kind of legacy are we leaving for our children?

POCKET
BOOKS

THE DOUBLE BIND
CHRIS BOHJALIAN

When Laurel Estabrook is attacked while out riding her bike one Sunday afternoon, her life is changed forever. She begins work at a shelter for the homeless and there meets Bobbie Crocker, a man with a history of mental illness and a box full of photos he won't let anyone see.

When Bobbie dies suddenly, Laurel discovers that he was once a successful photographer, and her fascination with his former life begins to merge into obsession, not least because some of the photos are of the very same forest trail where she was attacked and nearly killed.

Laurel becomes convinced that his photos reveal a deeply hidden, dark family secret. Her search for the truth leads her further from her own life and into a cat-and-mouse game with pursuers who claim they want to save her.

978-1-84739-193-3
£7.99

POCKET
BOOKS

MIDWIVES
CHRIS BOHJALIAN

On an icy winter night in an isolated house in rural Vermont, a
seasoned midwife named Sibyl Danforth takes desperate
measures to save a baby's life. She performs an emergency
caesarean section on a mother she believes has died of a stroke.
But what if Sibyl's patient wasn't dead - and Sibyl
inadvertently killed her?

As Sibyl faces the antagonism of the law, the hostility of
traditional doctors, and the accusations of her own conscience,
Midwives engages, moves, and transfixes us as only the very
best novels ever do.

978-1-84739-339-5
£7.99

POCKET
BOOKS

These books and other Simon & Schuster and Pocket Books
titles are available from your bookshop or can be ordered
direct from the publisher.

978-1-84739-193-3	**The Double Bind**	**£7.99**
978-1-84739-339-5	**Midwives**	**£7.99**

Please send cheque or postal order for the value of the book,
free postage and packing within the UK, to
SIMON & SCHUSTER CASH SALES
PO Box 29, Douglas Isle of Man, IM99 1BQ
Tel: 01624 677237, Fax: 01624 670923
Email: bookshop@enterprise.net
www.bookpost.co.uk

Please allow 14 days for delivery. Prices and availability
subject to change without notice